CAPITAL JUSTICE

A LEGAL THRILLER

JAMES CHANDLER

SEVERN RIVER
PUBLISHING

CAPITAL JUSTICE

Severn River Publishing
www.SevernRiverBooks.com

This is a work of fiction. Names, characters, businesses, places, events and incidents are either the products of the author's imagination or used in a fictitious manner. Any resemblance to actual persons, living or dead, or actual events is purely coincidental.

ISBN: 978-1-64875-451-7 (Paperback)

ALSO BY JAMES CHANDLER

Sam Johnstone Legal Thrillers

Misjudged

One and Done

False Evidence

Capital Justice

The Truthful Witness

Conflict of Duty

Never miss a new release!

Sign up to receive exclusive updates from author James Chandler.

severnriverbooks.com/authors/james-chandler

For the justices and judges of the Wyoming judiciary.
Proud to keep your company.

PROLOGUE

Simi Valley, California
One year ago

Maxim "Max" Kovalenko took a deep drag off an imported cigarette and stubbed it out, then hid the ashtray in a desk drawer. He looked at his expensive watch. Fifteen minutes until the kids arrived. They weren't going to be happy to begin with, and he wasn't in the mood for Lana's scolding. She was her mother's daughter. That one had been a good wife, God rest her soul—but not afraid to speak her mind.

He stood and waved a folded newspaper to disperse some of the smoke. He remembered the cheap cigarettes his parents rolled themselves and the acrid smoke befouling the air in the tiny apartment in central Ukraine, thick as a forest fire. The answer then was to open a window, but for convoluted environmental reasons, California commercial building codes didn't allow windows that opened. At this point, other than marijuana, he wasn't quite sure what California *did* allow—which partially accounted for the impending move.

Well, that and taxes and traffic and congestion and energy prices and power outages and droughts and floods and forest fires and, most of all, regulations and the scowling bureaucrats intent on their enforcement. It was a wonder anyone got anything done around here anymore. When a decade prior he had started UkrCX—the acronym for "Ukrainian Cryptocurrency Exchange"—he'd been intent on taking advantage of California's educated workforce to build an empire. And for the most part, he'd been in the right place at the right time. The computer geeks and MBAs churned out by nearby universities provided a steady source of eyeglass-wearing pencil necks and harridans with a basic knowledge of cryptocurrency and blockchain technologies, but the price of that intellect had become increasingly steep: vapid politics and constant whining. As a kid in rural Ukraine behind the then-existing Iron Curtain, he'd known actual hunger, seen real supply shortages, and experienced true tragedy. For these people, hunger was missing a meal, a supply shortage occurred when the ubiquitous health food store ran low on kumquats, and a "tragedy" was some C-list celebrity's calculated and entirely predictable reality show downfall. The constant preening and pretentious talk about "responsible sourcing" and "sustainable supply" was grating. Only when food was plentiful could one worry about how it was sourced—that was a full belly's concern. Now, the ingrates were trying to force him into "responsible management practices," including reduced hours for workers, more "humane" conditions, and who knew what else. Word from insiders was that a movement was afoot to unionize! He'd have none of that—he'd battled unions in New Jersey before relocating to California.

The kids would be unhappy about the relocation, but it was still his company. When and if they took over, they could look at moving back. He removed his glasses and looked around his corner, top-floor office at the photos and memorabilia adorning the walls. There was a certificate marking his commission as a second lieutenant in the Soviet Air Forces. Next to that was a framed set of pilot's wings and a picture of him standing proudly in front of his Su-24 Fencer on the date of his promotion to captain in the fledgling Ukrainian Air Force. Soon after that promotion he immigrated to the United States with a pregnant wife, an infant son, the money in his pocket, a working knowledge of English, and a dream to make it big in a country promising unlimited opportunity.

His most prized possession was on the wall, as well—a framed certificate from his 1994 naturalization ceremony marking his American citizenship. Finally, there were pictures of him at various storefronts—the physical evidence of ever-increasing success in his new homeland.

On his runway-sized desk were four portraits. He examined each in turn, lifting and handling them with care, occasionally tracing the lines of a young face with a thick, gnarled index finger. Three were of his biological children from his first three marriages: his oldest son Danylo, a useless layabout whose name had been anglicized to Danny; his oldest daughter, Svetlana "Lana" Kovalenko-Brown, who was the second coming of her mother: smart, ambitious and beautiful. And last but not least, his favorite, little Anastacia—Stacy, they called her. She wanted to be an actress. And why not? She was prettier than the women he watched on American television. She'd had him wrapped around her finger since the day of her birth, and he funded her fledgling career without hesitation, much to her siblings' chagrin.

Alongside their photos was one of his godson Aleksander "Alex" Melnyk, the son of his best friend Igor, who had remained with the Russian Air Force following the demise of the Soviet Union until he was shot down in 2003 during the Second Chechen War. When Igor's alcoholic wife later took her own life, Max had honored a pact made with his friend and in 2006 pulled some strings to get young Alex relocated and naturalized, taking him under his wing. Four very different young people who were about to come together and who—along with Lana's husband, Mike Brown —would soon be united in their opposition to his plan to relocate UkrCX.

Too damned bad.

His assistant Maria knocked and entered. "Your family is here, sir. Will you see them here, or would you like me to have them escorted to your private conference room?"

He thought about the smoke and decided not to risk it. "In the conference room," Max said. "And hold all calls. No visitors. And I want Paulie here as well." Pavlo Reznikov was Max's former flight line mechanic who now served as his head of personal security.

Max entered the conference room through a private door and awaited the family. Seconds later they entered. Not surprisingly, Lana led the way, followed closely by her husband. What she'd seen in Mike was beyond Max's understanding. He was short, slight, prematurely balding, and not particularly bright. As Max had begun to wind down his day-to-day involvement in business affairs, at Lana's insistence he had given Mike first shot at running the daily operations of UkrCX—a decision he was beginning to regret. Too bad Lana was a woman—she'd have been a fine executive. But business was no job for a woman, even a smart, tough one like Lana.

Alex was next. Igor would have been proud of him. He'd recently graduated from the California Institute of Technology with a degree in microbiology. Smart boy. If, as Max was beginning to suspect, Mike couldn't handle the job, Alex might be the answer. Handsome and outgoing, he was the first to speak to Max as they gathered. "Good morning, Max."

"Good morning, Alex," Max said. His grin morphed into a smile when Stacy followed Alex into the room. Beautiful Stacy. His heart skipped a beat as he eyed the child, the daughter of his third wife, Ursula.

While Stacy seated herself, Max nodded to Paulie. "Sit here," he instructed, indicating a chair to his left. He was overtaken by a coughing fit but waved off any assistance aside from a glass of water proffered by Paulie. The fits were increasing in frequency and Lana had been haranguing him about seeing a doctor, but it was probably just allergies. When the attack subsided, he noted his son was missing. "Where is Danny?" he asked irritably.

"Said he had to use the restroom," Paulie explained.

"Go get him," Max ordered. The big man stood, but before he could leave the room, Danny entered, wiping the back of his hand furiously at his nose. "Sorry, Dad, I had to take care of something."

All eyes turned to Max, anticipating his rebuke. "Have a seat," Max directed, disappointing all but Danny. He stifled yet another cough, then looked at each family member in turn. "I've made a decision," he began. "We're moving operations—all of them—to Wyoming." Despite having emigrated three decades ago, he pronounced it "Wyomink." As he awaited the family's reaction, he reached down to pet Laika, his constant companion, a Doberman Pinscher named after the first dog put into space by the USSR. The silence was lengthy. He owned all of the shares in the company; he could do whatever he wanted. He knew it; they knew it.

Lana spoke first. "Dad, are you serious? We've been here more than ten years now. We—you—have built UkrCX from an idea to one of the world's leading cryptocurrency exchanges—"

"*The* leading cryptocurrency exchange," Max interposed.

"All the more reason to continue building on success," Mike interjected, then—fearing Max's ire—shrank in his chair. Max enjoyed his son-in-law's discomfort and simply stared at him until Lana tired of her father's intimidation tactics and came to her husband's rescue.

"Dad," she began. "We have connections here. Our workforce is stable —we have a pipeline into the local universities for our technical force; we've got a ready source of cheap labor for janitorial, maintenance, and groundskeeping staff; the physical plant is new; our lines of supply are established . . . Is this because of your disagreement with the state energy management commission?"

Max smiled. "The bastards want to tell me, a private citizen who provides hundreds of jobs, a guy who brings billions of dollars into the state's economy, how much energy I can use to produce all that?" he asked. "It's socialist. I could have stayed in Eastern Europe for that." He was getting worked up thinking about it and wiped at his broad forehead with a silk handkerchief extracted from his sport coat. "I'm not going to put up with it!" He put the handkerchief away, then looked at each of the children in turn. "What?" he asked Danny, who was shaking his head.

"You're kidding, right?" his son asked. "You're going to leave all this for a state full of cows and rednecks?"

"You know nothing!" Max roared. "Have you ever been there? Of course not, yet you sit here and run your mouth. I have been there. I went out there last month with Mike and Paulie. Wyoming has recently passed legislation allowing for the chartering of cryptocurrency banks. Yes! The first in the nation to do so. They have no corporate or personal income tax—that alone will save us millions. It's a right-to-work state, meaning our ability to hire and fire a trained workforce—"

"In Wyoming?" Danny mocked.

Max's eyes narrowed. "Yes, in Wyoming. They actually have schools and paved streets and colleges. Just like here. But in Wyoming they have something else we lack here: power. Billions and trillions of megawatts of predictable, dependable power. No blackouts. No brownouts. I want to expand our Bitcoin mining operations. Right now, even if I could get the state regulators off our backs, we are paying too much for power. I have already purchased an existing, underproducing coal-fired plant and—oh, why am I trying to explain this to you? You couldn't begin to understand," he concluded in disgust. Then he turned to Stacy. "What do you think, princess?"

"Where is Wyoming, Daddy?" she asked, picking at a manicured nail. It didn't matter; she had no intention of leaving California. But it would keep Daddy happy if she acted interested.

"Well, it's . . . Do you remember when you were little, and your mother and I took you to Vail to ski?"

"Kind of . . ." Stacy lied.

"Well, it's kind of out there, honey," Max explained. Then he turned his attention to Lana and Mike. "I think I've got this nailed down. There's a coal plant near the town of Custer. The owners declared bankruptcy some time back and the plant cut workers' pension funds, reduced production to one shift per day, forbid overtime, the whole bit. Several potential buyers have come and gone without doing a deal."

"If they are walking away, what makes you think you—we—could make this work?" Danny asked, wiping his nose with his palm.

"The complication for traditional coal producers is getting railroad contracts and port permission from west coast states so they can ship coal through the northwest and then overseas to users," Max explained. "But we'll use the coal on-site to power mainframe computers to run our Bitcoin mining operation. We will sell the excess capacity to the locals at a deep discount—that will cut the city's and county's energy costs and likely elimi-nate any doubts they might have."

Mike had known generally of Max's plan and informed Lana, hoping she could talk the old man out of it. Now he asked questions Lana had fed him. "Max, I've been wondering. Are we going to have to take on the seller's debt? And what about the Environmental Protection Agency? Any pending action there?"

Max was pleasantly surprised by the insight the questions revealed. Maybe Mike was smarter than he thought. "I think we can step in and re-start operations without assuming the debt, and as part of the deal we'll get the seller to agree to either post a bond or conclude any reclamation ongoing or pending. That should satisfy the feds. The workforce to run the plant is there; the county commissioners and city council will welcome the relief—sales and property taxes have been on the decline for a while now. We can drive some deals and get real estate taxes reduced substantially if not eliminated entirely. These people are desperate for an economic shot in the arm."

Lana shook her head. "But Dad, the relocation costs will be—"

"Substantially subsumed by tax savings and not having to answer to regulators day and night," Max explained. "There will, of course, be some upfront expenditures. But Wyoming government is funded in large part by taxes on minerals, oil, and gas. The downturn in the energy sector is killing them."

"What about the greenies?" Mike asked, referring to environmentalist groups sure to oppose any increased operations at the plant.

"I've looked at the numbers. I'll promise to maintain current production schedules—that's barely keeping the local economy afloat. If the environmentalists oppose that, they'll get carried out with their heads on sticks. We'll adhere to that level for a while, and then we'll gradually up it. At that point we'll have the townies dependent on us and we can do what we want."

Mike clucked his opposition. "You're going to bait and switch them?"

Max stared at his son-in-law for a long time. "No, I'm going to adjust to economic conditions as they arise—how does that sound?" Seeing no response, he continued. "Again, we'll use most of the power produced on-site. I figure that, along with a substantial contribution I'll make under the table to the nonprofit of the environmentalists' choice, will encourage them to look elsewhere," he concluded. "What else?" He looked around the room.

"Wyoming," Danny snickered.

Lana side-eyed Danny and looked to Max. "Dad, what about infrastructure? What's the price of real estate? Can their schools handle it?"

"Working on it. I've hired a consultant—a retired judge named Daniels —who has been there for decades. We spoke by phone; he knows the law and just about everyone who is anyone in the state. He assures me everything can be worked out. Some concerns about the airstrip and the work-ers' housing, but he is confident we can swing the locals our way with the infusion of jobs and cash. The politicians will follow. It's local government —people still vote with their wallets, and therefore elections still work."

Danny wiped feverishly at his nose and then stood unsteadily. "So, because you are pissed off at state and federal regulators doing their jobs here in California, you're going to move a successful, billion-dollar opera-tion to a one-horse town in Wyoming based in part on the advice of some old judge? Are you serious?"

Max looked steadily at his son. His mother had been a gorgeous, green-eyed blonde with a head as empty as a Monday morning altar. Following their arrival in the US, she had almost immediately left him for a miniscule stipend and musclebound Newark dockworker. Out of the corner of his eye, he could see the others watching closely. Such a waste, this boy. "I am," he replied evenly. "And frankly, it is none of your concern, really, as I do not see a role for you in all of this. You are more than welcome to stay here and make your own way in life."

"Fine!" Danny barked. "Just fine! Move the company to some hellhole—"

"Paulie," Max said calmly. "Would you accompany Danny to the waiting area? I think the boy needs a break."

"Yes, sir." As the family watched, Paulie gently herded a protesting Danny out of the room, closing the door behind them. When they had departed, Max looked around the room at each of the remaining family members. "Anyone have anything to add?" When no one replied, he contin-ued, "Thank you. I will get back to each of you soon enough."

Moments later, everyone but Max gathered in a conference room down the hall from his office. "We can't allow him to do this!" Danny protested.

"There's not a lot we can do," Mike observed. "UkrCX is a close corpora-tion, and he owns one hundred percent of the stock."

"But we've got to do something!" Danny extended his arms to stave off Stacy as she approached with a proffered tissue. "What?" he asked as she wiped at his face.

"You've got a little coke on your nose," Lana said. "He's not going to take you seriously until—"

"He doesn't take any of us seriously!" Danny responded.

"It's his company." Mike shrugged.

"And that's what needs to change," Danny said, and stomped out of the room.

Stacy looked to Lana. "What are you going to do?" she asked her older half-sister when Danny had left.

"Get ready to move to Wyoming, I guess," a resigned Lana said. She looked to Mike, who nodded, then turned her attention to Alex. "What is your plan?"

Alex grinned, showing a row of immaculate teeth. "I guess I'll have to learn to ride a horse."

Stacy wasn't smiling. "Lana, he respects you. Can't you talk him out of it? I don't want to go. I have an audition next week; I think this one might turn out."

Lana looked lovingly at her little sister. Stacy had auditioned repeatedly, but to date her performances—many of which Lana suspected were conducted on a casting room couch—hadn't resulted in a job. "I think you are going to have to make a decision, Sissy. You can stay here and try and get parts, or you can move with us to Wyoming and . . . well, I don't know." She stood and looked to Paulie. "You'll keep us up to date?"

"Of course, Ms. Lana."

She nodded. "Great. I could use a drink. There's a new bistro downtown —Magnifico's. I'm buying."

When the family had left, Paulie walked back down the hall and knocked on Max's door. When commanded to enter, he reported, "They're all gone, boss."

"Good," Max replied. "Now . . . who said what?"

1

"It's nice to put a face to a voice," Max said. According to his sources, Preston C. Daniels was a retired Wyoming judge. Apparently, he'd been a pretty good one, but had retired when a defendant whom he had released on a reduced bond used the newfound freedom to kill his wife and then himself. As Max understood it, Daniels now spent his time puttering about in his yard, traveling, and doing some legal consulting on the side. Max had sought this face-to-face meeting to ensure Daniels would meet his needs. "Welcome to the new headquarters of UkrCX." He gestured around the room. "It's small, but we've got plans. Can I offer you a drink?" When Daniels looked at his watch, Max added encouragingly, "I'm going to have one."

"Why not?" Daniels said. He could think of several reasons, foremost among them that he would need to get Marci's lunch ready. She wasn't feeling well again today. Probably the damned chemo. "Maybe just a couple fingers."

"Paulie?" Max nodded to the large, brooding man sitting to his left. "Would you be so kind?" The men sat quietly while Paulie made the drinks. "Budmo!" Max said when both men had their tumblers.

Daniels raised his glass to the toast he didn't understand and then sipped. "That's good," he observed.

"Private stock." Max licked his lips and put the tumbler down. "Now, Judge Daniels—"

"Press will be fine. I'm retired."

"As you wish," Max agreed. "I asked you here because I need some advice. You see, Press, as we have previously discussed, I am in the process of relocating my company's operations here to Custer, and—"

Daniels had been watching Paulie, who sat next to Max. A third person who was not a party caused complications should an attorney-client relationship develop.

"Mr. Kovalenko—"

"Please call me Max."

"Max, the presence of a third person can mean that the attorney-client privilege—if one was to develop—is not fully formed. That means—"

"I know what it means," Max interrupted. "Perhaps I have not made myself clear. I am seeking your counsel not as an attorney but as someone who knows this community and its people. I have plenty of attorneys, although I would welcome your recommendation for a local man when the time comes."

"I see," Daniels said. He did not.

"Shall I explain?"

"Please do." Daniels sipped the vodka. It was extraordinary.

Max sat forward, warming to the task. "What do you know about cryptocurrency?" he began.

"Not a lot," Daniels admitted. "Just what I read in the newspaper."

"Sadly, so much of that is wrong." Max shook his head. "People are afraid of what they do not understand. You see, Press, a cryptocurrency is a kind of virtual currency—a digital representation of value, if you will. Do you understand?"

"I'm with you so far," Daniels said.

"Right. The cryptocurrency is found on a decentralized network of computers utilizing blockchain technology." Max was looking at Daniels for signs of understanding. Daniels was watching him steadily, saying nothing and sipping from the tumbler. "A blockchain is a database. The database contains every transaction made. The idea is that all users retain collective control of the ledger. No central authority—like a bank or a government—has control. Instead, the individual users exercise a sort of decentralized, collective control. All transactions are transparent and public so that once a transaction—say, a purchase or sale—is entered, it is permanently recorded on the chronological ledger and available for all to see."

Daniels drank more vodka. This stuff was great. Smooth. "I hear you."

"The most famous of the virtual currencies, of course, is Bitcoin—you've heard of that, surely?" When Daniels nodded, he continued. "For Bitcoin, each investor using a computer to engage in transactions has at his disposal the entire transactional history of Bitcoin. Because all the computers can see everything, it is theoretically tamper-proof. If anyone tried to adjust the history, all the other nodes would see it was suddenly different and automatically correct the incorrect entry—does that make sense?"

Daniels was wondering how much this booze cost per bottle. Probably a wad. "It does."

"Security is inherent because everyone knows what is going on," Max explained. "For example, if your computer got hacked and someone stole your Bitcoin, they could be traced because everyone knows what Bitcoin you had—without knowing exactly who you are, of course."

"Of course," Daniels echoed. His head was buzzing. He'd had an eye-opener earlier in the day.

"What you have is a virtual currency system, with no trusted third party, that is truly peer-to-peer," Max concluded. "Now, I should say that the IRS treats cryptocurrencies as property or financial assets rather than as cash or currency—they want to tax capital gains."

"Now you're starting to lose me."

"That's okay," Max assured Daniels. "We're just about there. So, what UkrCX does is to act as an exchange—to assist investors in buying, selling, or trading cryptocurrencies, to include Bitcoin. In return for the use of my platform, we take a small but fair fee."

"So, a guy wants to buy some Bitcoin or whatever, he calls you—"

"And for a fee, UkrCX accepts his fiat—that means traditional—cash or whatever asset he wants to use and exchanges it for Bitcoin or whatever cryptocurrency he wants."

"I see," Daniels said. He didn't, really. "So why here?"

"Two reasons. First, Wyoming banking laws changed a couple of years ago. The state's banks are now able to serve as custodians of digital assets, which may be retained by institutional investors in a bank operating under a special banking charter called a 'special purpose depository institution.'"

"Now you lost me."

"Let's say it this way. Let's say you buy some cryptocurrency. We'll call it 'Danielcoin.' In most states, you've got nowhere to put it—it simply exists on the network or whatever. Wyoming, however, allows you to 'deposit' your Danielcoin in these specially chartered banks so that you can store or transfer cryptocurrencies traded on an exchange like mine."

"Sounds good."

"It is, and with the cryptocurrencies, Wyoming allows the banks to hold the codes that allow owners and investors to access their cryptocurrencies."

"Okay," Daniels said. "Now you lost me again."

"Think of it like you would putting the keys to a cash safe in a safe deposit box—see? One more thing—in regard to Bitcoin specifically. Unlike fiat currencies, where the government decides when to add to the currency in circulation, Bitcoin increases the number of Bitcoins in circulation by a process called 'Bitcoin mining' whereby computer systems compete to solve almost irrationally complex math problems that validate the entire system. The first computer to solve the equation is awarded a Bitcoin token, which is worth big money. The problem is that the computational power necessary to do this is enormous. By way of example, UkrCX Bitcoin mining will use enough electricity to power a town like Gillette or Rock Springs."

"Holy cow!"

"Indeed. That's why UkrCX purchased the Elk Flats power plant just north of town. We're going to continue operations, only this time instead of shipping coal off to China or electricity to LA or wherever, we're going to use the power right here in Custer to power our own Bitcoin mining operation."

"So, you'll be mining Bitcoin, at which point you—"

"Find it and place it on my exchange, ready for investors to buy or sell—"

"At which point you skip the middleman and get another piece of the action."

"*All* of it," Max corrected. "You want another drink?" He doubted it. Most Americans couldn't hold their liquor.

"No thanks." Daniels looked at his watch. "Where do I come in?"

"I need an influencer." Max handed his tumbler to Paulie for a refill. "I'm going to need some zoning variances."

"Where?"

"Right here, for one. As I understand it, you have some sort of historical society that has put limitations on building design. I want to demo this building—"

"This is one of the oldest buildings on Yellowstone Avenue," Daniels observed.

"I heard," Max said, accepting the glass from Paulie. "I need at least four floors for office space. I'll comply with the design limitations and use wood and brick—hell, I'll put some decorative bison horns out there if they want—but I need at least four floors. You sure?" Max asked, raising his glass.

Why not? "Okay." Daniels handed Paulie his glass. "Just a little. What else?"

"Well, right now we're living in a smaller place on the edge of town—I think the old college president owned it?"

"I'm familiar with it." Daniels knew the place well. Formerly occupied by Vincent and Lucy Beretta, the place was a ten-thousand-square-foot mansion.

"Well, it's a little small for my needs, so I bought a couple of smaller ranches—the Barber and Detloff places, I think they were, a little further out. I want to start building on my ranch headquarters soon. I've got the permits to build my living quarters out there, but I'm told there are going to be complications regarding the airstrip. What I need is too long, or something. Anyway, need you to look into that and see what you can do so I don't need to sue."

"Anything else?" Daniels asked, licking his lips.

"Well, there's some hang-up getting UkrCX chartered—but I've got some guys in Cheyenne for that."

"Nice. What else?"

"I bought several square blocks down near Reno Street. I guess they are zoned for multi-family up to a certain number, but I want to see to it that I can house about two hundred families there."

"Two hundred families?" Daniels was incredulous. That would increase the population significantly, thereby impacting schools and services. Custer had been through this before with the booms and busts of the energy industry.

"Yeah. And keep this between us, but I'm willing to cough up some money to help offset increased costs for schools until your legislature can appropriate the money. I just need some help getting this done. I'd like to break ground in January."

Daniels snorted. "January? You aren't gonna get a builder in here in January—"

Max's eyes narrowed. "I've already got them lined up. I just need the red tape cut. That's where you come in." The men looked to the door when they heard the knocking. "It's probably Alex," Max informed Daniels. "My godson. Enter!" he commanded.

Daniels observed the young man enter, then stop short. "I'm sorry, Max. I didn't know you had—"

"That's fine, Alex," Max said. "I wanted you to meet Judge Daniels. He's doing some consulting for us."

"Press," Daniels said, standing somewhat unsteadily and extending his hand. "I'm retired."

"Nice to meet you," Alex said.

"Sit down, Alex," Max instructed. "Mr. Daniels and I were just going through how he can help us." He turned his attention to Daniels. "Alex's father Igor was my best friend. Another pilot in my squadron back in the USSR. We had a bit of a pact—an agreement to take care of each other's children if necessary. Igor got shot down years later and . . . well, it became necessary. In any event, he is here and learning the ropes—aren't you, Alex?"

"I am, sir." Alex beamed.

Max nodded approvingly, then returned to the subject at hand. "Press, one more thing regarding the Detloff and Barber places. We've got all kinds of people crossing my land to get to public property—how do you say it, a 'school section?'"

"Yes," Daniels said. A school section was a section of public land owned by the state of Wyoming from which any income—grazing leases, mining, or the like—was funneled to the state's schools. As public lands, everyone had a notional right to use and enjoy them, but accessing the sections from private lands without permission was a no-no and source of legal controversy.

"Well," Max said. "I don't want that. Get a lawyer to get them off. Whatever agreement they had with Barber or Detloff is over."

"I'm not sure we can do that," Daniels hedged. Max almost assuredly had the right, but it wasn't *right*. "I'll have to take a look at it."

"I don't care how you do it, just do it," Max insisted. "Hell, pay 'em off, if you need to. Same with those damned environmentalists. Do what you gotta do. You'll be the face of progress."

Daniels was quiet for a moment, considering. "These people are my friends and neighbors," he explained. "I've known them for decades. They have a job to do. The politicians, the environmentalists, the townspeople . . . I can't guarantee anything. And there are rules and ordinances and laws and—"

"I know all that. That's why I need you."

Daniels thought about it. Maybe this wasn't such a good idea. The time away from Marci—she needed him. Trying to twist arms, gain influence—not really his style. "I don't know, Max—"

"I'll pay you a thousand dollars per hour," Max said. When Daniels didn't respond, he continued. "Cash under the table, to your LLC, to a third party, to your church, to a favorite charity—whatever. You want it in Bitcoin or a different currency? I'll do that. And I'll pay your expenses," he added. He held up a hand and rubbed his thumb against his index and middle fingers. "Whatever you need."

Daniels was in a quandary. He had developed an almost immediate dislike for this man. On the other hand, he hadn't been asked to do anything illegal, Marci's medical bills were beginning to pile up, and Medicare wasn't going to pay for that experimental treatment he'd read about. "I'll think about it," he said noncommittally, figuring he might reject the offer later. He stood.

"Think fast," Max said, studying Daniels. "Oh, hell—you know what? I'll make it fifteen hundred per hour, plus expenses. But you don't have a lot of time. I'll find someone else if you don't want in. Paulie, show the judge out, would you please?"

As he followed Paulie out the door, Daniels remembered he needed to stop by the pharmacy and pick up Marci's medications. Coincidentally, the co-pay this week was fifteen hundred dollars.

After Daniels had departed, Alex looked to Max. "Will he help?"

"Oh yeah," Max said. "No doubt. His wife is on her deathbed." He coughed into his hand until Paulie handed him a bottle of water and a couple of pills.

2

Sam Johnstone was stringing fly-fishing line on an ancient bamboo flyrod, anticipating a quiet late-summer day on stream when he thought he heard someone outside. The cabin was well inside the property line; there shouldn't have been anyone close to the structure. Placing the rod on the old kitchen table, he drew a pistol from the shoulder holster he habitually carried, then carefully opened the cabin door. He looked around and saw only the tall Engelmann spruce that lined the small creek swaying in the morning breeze and heard only the water pushing against rock. He closed the door, satisfied that he was alone.

To be certain, he checked each room in his friends' cabin. Tucked away in a draw on the southwest side of the Bighorn Mountains, it was accessible only by a small, deeply rutted private road. The owners allowed him to use the place in return for legal work consisting primarily of occasional changes to their estate plans.

Sam took a deep breath and his eyes rested on the well-stocked bar in the corner of the kitchen. Not today. His counseling with the VA was helping. Slowly, the goosebumps on his arms subsided, and the hair on the back of his neck relaxed. Must have been imagining things. Nightmares, anxiety, paranoia—they all still occurred on occasion, but the VA was helping with them, too. Satisfied he was safe, he turned his attention to finishing stringing and dressing the fly line, then affixed a furled leader to the line, and finally attached a tippet (a small piece of monofilament fishing line) to the leader.

With a steady hand, he sat and sipped a cup of coffee, pleased with himself. He hadn't had a drink in eleven months. Not coincidentally, he also hadn't said or done something for which he'd felt guilty or ashamed in eleven months. He had successfully coped with the shaky hands and "drop-sies" associated with post-acute withdrawal syndrome brought on by years of chronic alcohol abuse and now enjoyed the return of his once-excellent manual dexterity.

He sipped and smiled to himself and repeated the mantra he'd once heard from a now-sober judge in northeast Wyoming: "The world is an ugly place for a sober man." Indeed, but he knew he was a better man sober. His newfound sobriety, combined with the cognitive processing training he was undergoing through Bob Martinez, his counselor at the VA, was helping and he was feeling less guilt, less shame, and—because he wasn't drinking—he was spending a lot less time looking for his car keys (or his car) upon waking. He'd sometimes go days now without nightmares or regretful memories of the five men he'd lost in Afghanistan or driving Veronica Simmons away. For decades, booze had substituted for the devel-opment of coping skills and had precluded his feeling real emotion. He was only now getting to know himself.

Scanning the fly-box, he looked over the dozens of flies contained therein, all affixed neatly in rows by type and size. There were several hundred dollars' worth, he knew. But he could afford it; business was good and he wasn't pouring several ounces of premium vodka and craft beers down his gullet every evening. Despite the variety, he selected an old favorite—a Blue-Winged Olive tied in a parachute pattern (meaning the calf tail wings were tied vertically). Whether that attracted fish or not, Sam was unsure. Fish at this elevation were not selective—they had only a few brief months to feed before the snow returned. What he was certain of was that *he* could see the fly on the gin-clear water, making the fly one of his favorites.

He locked the door behind him and sat in an old wooden chair on the deck, struggling to don the waders and boots. The VA had provided him with a custom orthotic made to replace the lower half of his left leg that he had left overseas. It worked fine for day-to-day wear, but not so well when he tried to get it into a pair of fishing waders. At last, he stood and shouldered the vest. Lots of fishermen now wore sling or hip packs to carry their gear, but Sam preferred the old-fashioned fishing vest. He was comfortable with weight on his shoulders. It reminded him—in a good way—of his time as a light infantryman, humping a rucksack. Back when he was young and healthy. Before he got blown up in Afghanistan. When he still had two legs. Before he'd lost five men. Before all the trouble.

He drew a flask from his vest, then poured and drank the tepid coffee he had brewed earlier that morning from a plastic cup. For years, the same flask had held whiskey or vodka, and his coffee bore the faint aroma of the booze. Sporting goods stores were stuffed with better options for holding and dispensing coffee, but he was content to leave things as they were. There was enough change ongoing. Pouring the dregs out, he stood. "I'm good," he said aloud, and began the hike downstream.

~

Daniels slowly opened Marci's door. She was resting, but her eyes fluttered when he entered with the cup of chicken broth and a couple of crackers. She smiled wanly, then winced at the pain from dry, cracked lips. He placed the tray with what passed for her lunch on an end table, sat on the bed, then reached out and smoothed her hair.

"I know," she said. "I'm a mess."

"You're beautiful," he said, meaning every word. He applied some balm to her lips with a shaking index finger. "Just as you were forty-five years ago."

"And you're just as big a liar now as you were then," she scoffed. "But I love it." Had a sparkle appeared in her eyes? She took a deep breath, held it, and then released it. "I was going to go in and comb my hair and put on some makeup, but I just don't seem to have any energy."

"It's the chemo. And the medication."

"I know, but still," she said. "You'd think I'd be able to get out of bed long enough to care for myself and maybe do some chores. But I'm so . . . tired."

He looked determinedly at the wall, the ceiling, anywhere but at her. Standing, he turned his back and tried to surreptitiously wipe the tears away using his upper arms before faking a smile and turning to her. "Ready for some lunch?" he said, indicating the tray.

"Darling, try not to worry," she said. "And no, not right now. I'm just not real hungry. I'll be fine. I'm just a little . . . tired, I think. Maybe a quick nap will help?"

According to the doctors, it would not. In fact, there was nothing that would, if you listened to them. But what the hell did they know? The bastards still hadn't gotten back to him on the feasibility of alternative treatments. No sense of urgency. It wasn't their wife. Not their cancer, not their problem. "Okay. I just . . . you know," he said. He set the alarm to remind him to administer her next round of medication, then lay down next to her and—as she held him—quietly cried himself to sleep.

3

On the first day of September, Max stood and looked desultorily at the lukewarm, untouched breakfast on his desk. Between a lack of appetite and the omnipresent pain in his abdomen, he couldn't bring himself to eat much. Before he left California, he'd stopped in to see his doctor, who had said little but ordered a bunch of tests and blood draws. It's what American doctors did. In Ukraine when he was a kid, you saw a doctor who examined you, made a diagnosis, and instituted some sort of treatment. But here, it was test, test, test.

He'd sent Paulie to get Mike, who didn't go anywhere without Lana, and —because sitting made the constant pain in his guts worse—he remained standing as they took their places around the large conference table. "Thank you, Paulie."

Paulie nodded and left, closing the door behind him. Mike and Lana sat quietly, awaiting Max's wrath. He'd been in a mood of late, and they had a pretty good idea this wouldn't go well.

"Dad, are you sure you're okay?" Lana asked. "You look, I don't know . . . yellow, I guess."

"Well, I'd be a helluva lot better if I had a little help around here!" he snapped, then tugged viciously at the lid on a medicine bottle until it opened. Extracting a small handful of pills, he shoved them in his mouth and chewed, then made a sour face and reached for a tumbler filled with amber liquid.

"Dad!" Lana began, rising from her seat.

"Shut up and sit down, Lana!" Max ordered. "You're turning out just like your mother."

"You can't mix pain pills and alcohol!"

"I'll do what I please. Damned doctors—what do they know? Test and bill my ass off. *That's* what they know. Back in Ukraine, we had guys who knew how to make people well. Of course, we didn't have American lawyers running around handing out business cards—"

"Dad, you're getting yourself all worked up!"

"Lana, I swear if you keep nagging at me, I'm going to run you out of here."

Lana looked to Mike for support. None was forthcoming—Mike was afraid of raising Max's ire. She returned her gaze to her father. "Dad, you *do* understand that if you keep quaffing pills and drinking and being angry, you're not going to be around long enough to see these projects to completion—you'll be dead, right?"

"Then I'll join your mother in hell," Max said. "An eternity of her mouth should be sufficient penance, I would think."

"Max, please!" Mike said, at last attempting to intervene as a red-faced Lana folded her arms and sat back in her chair. "She's just trying to—"

"Quiet! I run this company and this family! And while I do, you're going to sit there and listen. And if that doesn't work for you, then don't let the door hit you in the ass," Max concluded, looking to each, knowing full well neither would leave. They couldn't afford to. He focused on Mike. "Now, where are we on the plant?"

Mike looked at Lana uncertainly. "Well, Max, so far we've completed the purchase and sale agreement, and I've had our attorneys in Cheyenne alert the Wyoming Utilities Commission that we're going to be doing business as—"

"That's it? You've had months. Months!" Max yelled, and slapped the top of his desk, startling them. Laika moved from near Max's feet and walked to a corner, turned a circle, and sat warily. "And you're still working transactional documents and alerting bureaucrats? That's it?"

"Max, these things take time," Mike explained. "We've met with the regulators and county commissions and the planning and zoning commission. They'll take some time to look at things and make their decisions, then get with the city—they have a dog in this fight. People just need some wiggle room. I mean, we've got to spread a little love around—you know what I'm saying?"

"There is no time!" Max exploded. "I told you I want ground broken and construction started by January 1! What part of that don't you understand?"

"Max." Mike wiped at his forehead with a hand. "This is a small town with unsophisticated people—hicks, really—running things. Grocery store owners, bankers, retired small business owners. They aren't in a hurry, especially where it involves change. They're perfectly happy here in their little world."

Max stared hard at Mike. "Then it's your job to get with them and explain to them that if they won't get off their asses and get this done, I'll either put my own people in office or find somewhere else to take my money and jobs."

"I'm not sure that's the threat you think it is," Lana interjected. "Dad, these people thought they were just fine before we got here. They think they'll be fine long after we leave."

"And I suppose that's true, Lana—if you're talking about the local real estate broker or school principal or bank vice president," Max said. "They're secure. They got theirs. But what about that gal working double shifts at the box store on the edge of town, or that guy putting hot dogs on the rollers at five a.m.? What do they think? Do you know?" Max looked around the room. "Have you talked with the townspeople? The little guys? Sat on a bar stool and bought a round?" When they wouldn't meet his gaze, he focused on Mike. "Oh, crap on a cracker, Mike—why not?"

"Max, I've been busy . . . I mean, it's hard. . . I—I just—" Mike looked to Lana for help. "Max, look. Instead of going through all of this, why don't we just leverage your name and history and commission our own currency? I've spoken with some people, and I think we could leverage existing equity in other holdings. We could stop being the middleman and—"

"Because that's not what I want!" Max slapped the table again. "There are a million reasons not to do that, but I don't have time to explain them to you. You need to execute the plan as I've given it to you, or I'll find someone who will!" Max began coughing, and quickly accepted a bottle of water from Lana. "I've made my decision," he said when he could speak again. "Get your ass out of whatever office you've been hiding in and convince the man on the ground that we are the best thing that's happened to Custer lately."

"But—" Mike began.

"No buts, damn it!" Max interrupted. He unwrapped a cough drop, popped it in his mouth, and bit down on it viciously. "Go! Get off your ass and make these mouth-breathers understand there is a sense of urgency in all of this!" As he broke into another coughing fit, Mike scurried out of the room, leaving Lana alone with her father, who shook his head in regret. "I don't know, honey. I think I've given him every opportunity. I don't know if he's got it in him."

"I think you're being too hard on him, Dad," she said. "There are a lot of moving parts to this and a lot of variables we don't control. I think he just needs time. Dad, I—"

Max looked at her kindly, anticipating where this would go. "No, dear. I've told you before: no daughter of mine will run my business."

"Dad, that is such an antiquated, paternalistic view of—"

"But it's my view! Mine! Now go and rescue your husband. Give him a good kick in the ass."

"Dad—"

"Go help your husband, dear," Max said, softening. "But make sure to tell him I am expecting results, and I don't want to hear or see anything else."

With a last look at her father, Lana left.

"I will never understand her," Max lamented to Paulie after the big man returned. He put down the water, replaced it with the tumbler, and drank deeply, then coughed and—to Paulie's disgust and horror—picked up a small wastebasket and vomited in it. Wiping his mouth with the back of his hand, he continued. "She could have any man—why that one? What do you think, Paulie?"

"I think you need to get well, boss," Paulie said carefully. "I'm not sure any of them have what it takes."

~

Lana traced a path in the perspiration on Mike's chest with a brilliantly manicured index finger. To her unending surprise, she had found a nice nail salon in town. Mike was lying on his back with his hands interlocked behind his head, brow furrowed. "Don't worry, baby," she said. "It happens. You are distracted. You just need to not worry so much."

"Your dad hates me. He always has," Mike said. "He promised me control of the company, said this was my opportunity. But he's done nothing but undermine me the entire time! He just did it so he can say I screwed the pooch, then he can justify handing everything over to Alex the ass-kisser."

Lana smiled wryly. It was true, of course—Max had no use for Mike and would never have given him a chance had it not been for her urging. "Honey, if it makes a difference, Max thinks everyone is incompetent except himself. It's who he is. And I don't think that's what's going on," she added, referring to Mike's fear of being replaced by Alex. "I don't think there's a plan. He's sick, I think. Did you see his color?"

"I did. But that doesn't give him the right to abuse me!"

Lana looked at her husband of seven years. He was rapidly balding, getting paunchy, and drinking too much of late. He'd never been much to look at, but until recently he'd at least kept himself in good physical condition. "I think it does," she began, halting when Mike turned to look at her. "I mean, it's his company."

"Lana, would he really hand this over to Alex? He's not even family, for Christ's sake!"

"I have told you, that won't happen. Things start looking that way and I'll ensure some of Alex's—what do we call them?"

"'Questionable transactions.'"

"Right," she said. "I'll make sure those *questionable transactions* come to light." She reached for a glass on the bedstand that appeared to have water in it.

"It's fraud!"

"It is, but no reason to get all upset," she said soothingly.

"Max thinks Alex is the golden boy. How do we know he'll do anything about it even if Alex's fraud comes to light?"

"Because it's Max's money. Here, drink this," Lana urged. "It will make you feel better. Chug it."

Mike obliged, then immediately looked around for somewhere to spit.

"Here." Lana produced a cup.

After Mike had regurgitated the contents of his mouth into the cup, he looked at her. "What the hell was that?"

"Just some water with a little flavored vodka," she said. "I thought it might help relax you."

"Some kind of rot-gut," he said, shaking his head.

She put the cup on the end table. "Back to Daddy. He can think what he wants—for now," she said, stroking Mike's arm with her hand. "I'll make sure he knows what I want him to know."

Mike was unpersuaded. "Will that be enough?"

"Are you kidding?" She straightened a long, well-tanned leg and examined it. "Max finds out Alex stole a penny and Alex is toast."

"If—If he'd just listen to me and let me run this company my way, I could get it done!" Mike complained. "But between the micromanaging and the constant changes of direction . . . no one could meet his expectations."

Lana watched in disgust as a tear rolled down Mike's cheek. He was even weaker than she'd thought he was—she'd somehow missed that. "It'll be okay, honey." She patted his arm.

When he was asleep, she took the cup and poured the contents into a jar, then capped it and put it into her purse—just as Alex had coached. That boy's college degree was coming in handy.

4

Kenneth "Punch" Polson was an investigator with the Wyoming Division of Criminal Investigation. Formerly a member of the Custer Police Department, he knew his way around the courthouse and was familiar with most of its occupants. He was waiting to see Cathy Schmidt, one of the deputy county and prosecuting attorneys. She'd called him and asked him to stop in when he had a minute. While he waited, he thumbed through four-year-old magazines, then checked the late season box scores on his phone. He'd been on the road for weeks and it was good to be back in Custer; last night he'd had dinner with his wife and kids, and he was hoping to watch football practice later today.

Right on time, Cathy's secretary retrieved him, and he was soon in her office. "Good to see you, counselor," he said. He'd forgotten how tall she was, especially in heels.

"Punch, same to you. We miss you around here. I mean, Miller is doing a good job, but she doesn't have kids whose sports lives I can follow." Cathy was referring to Ashley Miller, the detective who had back-filled Punch when he'd been detailed to DCI.

Punch smiled. "And how is Kayla doing? Dominating yet?" Kayla was Cathy's athletic daughter.

"Well, she made the travel team," Cathy admitted almost shyly.

"How many?" Punch asked.

"Well, sixteen points per game—but in her defense most of the kids are two years older," she said, warming to her subject. Punch laughed. Same old Cathy. She had played point guard for the University of Wyoming in her time and remained ultra-competitive.

She handed him a cup of coffee. "It's black."

"Thank you," he said. "Now, how can I help my favorite prosecutor?"

"You can tell me what you know about Maxim Kovalenko," Cathy said, looking at him over her cup.

"What makes you think I know anything?"

"The fact that I spoke with an assistant attorney general from Cheyenne yesterday," she said. "Don't be coy with me, Punch."

He smiled, as well. "I've got a little background—what's going on?"

"He and his company—UkrCX—have got all kinds of requests for variances going on around the city and the county. Demolishing and rebuilding requests in the historic district, wanting to build a compound and an airstrip out in the county, looking to build housing for two hundred employees. One of my extra duties is to advise the county commissioners on civil matters—"

"On top of prosecuting felonies? Wow, that's a lot!"

"Maybe I need you to talk with Rebecca," Cathy said, referring to Rebecca Nice, the elected county attorney. "Budget cuts are killing us and we're down two attorneys, but the show must go on—right?"

"Yikes!" Punch sympathized. "Well, here's what I know." Punch gave her a quick run-down of Max's emigration and early activities. "He settled initially in New Jersey and got a job in a technology outfit—literally as an office boy. Somehow, he caught the right people's attention and leveraged his technical knowledge from being a pilot into getting a low-level security clearance and got read-in on some weapons development projects. At the same time, he started his own business, dabbling in computers on the side."

"Ahead of his time," she said.

"Right. Anyway, within a couple of years, he founded some sort of digital start-up there in Jersey and ended up moving the outfit to California —Silicon Valley, I think. From there, he was in early on cryptocurrencies, founded UkrCX, then moved to Simi Valley to escape high real estate prices and made a shit-ton of money by facilitating the initial public offering for several cryptocurrency outfits. Most went out of business, but he apparently took a bite out of every offering and chose wisely when keeping or dumping his stock. Made a killing, is what they say."

"Nice," she observed. She drank coffee from a basketball-shaped cup and thought wryly about her decision to go to law school, the seventy-hour weeks she was working and the five-figure salary she was earning.

"Not the all-American story we'd like it to be, though. The feds suspect him of laundering money. Theory is Max and his people are washing fiat currency using cryptocurrency, and he's taking a piece of every transaction. Word is he's the sole shareholder of UkrCX, and—get this—he is rumored to be one of the biggest holders of Bitcoin out there. Dude has big-time moolah."

"Fiat currency?"

"Uh, yeah," Punch said. "Regular money. As opposed to cryptocurrency."

She smiled. "I'm surprised—dinosaur like you using words like that."

"Yeah. I'm almost ashamed of myself." He laughed. "But back to Max. The feds give us bits and pieces and very specific things to look at, but I've no idea what the big picture looks like. I'm not real comfortable making any sort of guess regarding what you might find."

Cathy bit her lip in thought. "Is it fair to say that as of right now he has a clean record and UkrCX is a legit . . . uh. . ."

"Cryptocurrency exchange? As far as we know, yeah," Punch concluded, helping her out. "We've seen nothing to indicate he is anything other than what he says he is—a wealthy businessman with a big idea. The feds might have something, but like I said, they aren't particularly forthcoming. And his money's good. There's nothing to indicate he can't or won't post whatever sort of surety bond you might need posted or follow through with any kind of promise the commissioners extract in return for whatever he wants."

"Don't know if you heard," she began. "The last commissioners' meeting was insane. On one side of the room, we had contractors and small businessmen who desperately want the commission to push this stuff through. Can't say I blame them. With COVID and economic downturns, they need the work. On the other side, we had a bizarre coalition of obnoxious conspiracy nuts and concerned environmentalists who for their own reasons see Max's arrival as the death knell for the area. Complicating it all are labyrinthine procedures to be followed, studies that have to be done—"

"And the environmentalists will be sure those happen."

"Right?" she laughed. "Kovalenko's wanting to build housing for two hundred workers right on the boundary of the city and county, and he wants to subdivide a piece of property to build a compound for himself and his family this side of that airstrip. Max sent his son-in-law and he basically said, 'We're bringing this money and these jobs to your community, so you need to genuflect or we'll go elsewhere.'"

"I'm sure the old-timers didn't appreciate that."

"Oh, no. It was loud. And you know the old Custer National Bank down on Yellowstone? Go look for yourself. He is in the process of demolishing the inside as we speak. Took years to get the city council to approve building codes to make downtown look nice, and now comes Max and a wad of cash, seeking variances."

"They'll get approved," Punch predicted.

"Money talks," she agreed. "I was kind of hoping that maybe you had some information I could pass on that might torpedo this whole thing."

"Nothing on paper."

She raised her eyebrows. "Meaning?" When he hesitated, she pressed. "You know you can count on me to keep my mouth shut."

"Look, the word is, he is one dirty, underhanded bastard," he said. "He's left a string of broken business partners, associates, and the like a mile long behind him. He's busted unions, worn out federal and state regulators . . . Max is ruthless—I hear he's kicked his own kid out. Read every contract carefully, hold his feet to the fire, and make sure you've got your asses covered—because he sure as hell will."

"Got it," she said. "I'll be on my best transactional behavior."

They looked to the door when they heard the knock. "Come in," Cathy instructed. She smiled at the tall man who entered. "Grant, good to see you. I'd like you to meet Detective—well, Investigator—Kenneth Polson. He's one of ours, but currently detailed to DCI. This is Grant Lee."

Punch had stood during the introduction and extended his hand. "Call me Punch," he said, and withdrew his hand quickly when the gesture was not returned.

"Nice to meet you," Lee said perfunctorily.

"Same," Punch said.

An uncomfortable silence ensued, until broken by Lee. "Cathy, I need to talk with you. Should I come back?"

The desired response was manifest, so Punch excused himself. "I'll keep you posted, counsel. Tell Kayla to keep shooting," he said, closing the door behind himself.

5

Daniels had been on hold for ten minutes and was furious by the time the oncologist picked up the line.

"Is this Mr. Daniels?"

"It's *Judge* Daniels," he said. He rarely used or allowed his title to be used anymore, but by God this doctor needed to know he was someone to be reckoned with. He could hear keystrokes.

"All right, just let me make sure we have a signed release of information here—" she began.

"Doctor Goings, I've been caring for her for months. I'm the one who brings her in to chemo. I'm giving her the prescriptions. I'm changing—"

"I'm sorry, sir, but—"

"But nothing! You've seen me and spoken with me and—"

"You cannot expect that I would remember every patient and family member—can you?" she said tightly. He'd struck a nerve.

"Well, perhaps I should do something that will cause you to remember me?"

As a human being, she understood his frustration. As a doctor, she was relieved to find what she was looking for. "Judge Daniels, I see that we do in fact have a release of information on file," she said. "Now, how may I help you?"

"I'm calling to see what the results of Marci's tests were, and where we are on getting her into that study."

He heard more keyboard tapping. At last, he heard the doctor move closer to the phone. "It looks like we don't have a final decision on that yet. As I mentioned, a lot of this will be dependent on your wife's insurance company."

"She doesn't have insurance! She has Medicare. She's got the socialized medicine everyone dreams about!"

"Please don't be sarcastic."

"She can't be the first cancer patient you've treated who is on Medicare," he replied. "Surely you know what they will fund and what they won't. And if they won't fund it, I'll do it out of pocket. Put that into your computer."

"Mr. Daniels, the records indicate we do not have a decision yet," the doctor said, biting off every word. "And you should know this treatment is prohibitively expensive."

"This is my wife," he explained. "There's no such thing as *prohibitively expensive*. I'll pay whatever it costs. You can have our savings, our investments; I'll sell the house, the cars, whatever. I'll borrow the money . . . This . . . it's my wife. I can't. . ." He faltered as he ran out of breath.

The keyboarding had stopped. "Mr. Daniels," she began. "I am so very sorry. I will personally do everything I can to speed the process along. I'll call you as soon as I find something out," she promised.

"What happens in the meantime?" he asked. "I'm giving her medication and she sleeps twenty hours per day."

"Let's just renew the prescription and try and keep her comfortable until we get a decision—"

Marci was getting worse by the day—he didn't have to be a doctor to see that. "What if she's not accepted?"

"We'll discuss that when and if that happens. To me, she is a viable candidate—"

"Then what are we waiting for? I told you—I'll pay the tab." He felt a pounding in his forehead. "Call someone! Do something!"

"Mr. Daniels, please lower your voice. I promise you I will do whatever I can."

"This is my wife! She is all I have!" Daniels said. "This is my wife!"

"Sir, the process is in place," the doctor began, "but—"

Daniels heard nothing else, because he had hung up when he heard Marci in the next room.

"Press?"

He entered in a rush. "What? What do you need, honey?"

"Nothing," she said. "I'm—I'm fine. But I thought . . . I just thought I heard you yelling at someone and . . ." She drifted off, and in seconds was snoring softly. He was certain it was the medication, although Dr. Goings wasn't sure and wanted to order another test. Screw that. He'd slept next to the woman for forty-five years and all of a sudden she starts snoring? Bullshit. All Dr. Goings had done was order tests. Test after test after test. Maybe if she had begun treating Marci earlier, instead of running all the damned tests . . . He pulled the sheet up over Marci's shoulder. Despite himself, he smiled, thinking about her cold feet under the covers. How many times had he asked her, "How in the hell can you complain about being hot when your feet are like a couple of ice blocks?" Inevitably, she'd laugh and wrap her legs around his lower half while he groused. Her color was bad today. He closed his eyes.

God, I promise I will never complain again. Just let her live and I swear to you I will love her and hold her and treat her like I should have all these years. Just let her live and I'll—

"What are you doing, dear?" Marci had awakened.

Do not cry. "I'm just getting your medicine, darling," he said, turning quickly from her. "It's that time."

"Already? I feel like all I do is take pills and sleep and see doctors and get tests."

"Dr. Goings says we have to stay on top of the pain, or it'll get to be too much." He offered the pills to her. That was probably the only good advice he'd gotten to date. The couple of times Marci had tried to hold out had ended badly. She accepted the painkillers with an unsteady hand. "Just hold these," he instructed. "I'm gonna prop you up with a pillow here."

"Yes, Dr. Daniels," she teased, placing a hand on his forearm. "I remember when you rarely told me what to do in the bedroom."

He leaned down and kissed her forehead. "There was no need," he said, feeling his stomach tighten. Do not cry. "Take your pills," he croaked, smoothing her hair.

"Be easier with a little water." She smiled briefly.

"I'm sorry," he said, opening and handing her a small bottle.

"It's okay, dear," she said. "You're doing a great job. Maybe in a little bit you can get me up and we can go to the store? I'd like that."

There was no way in hell. "Maybe," he said, adjusting the pillows behind her, allowing her to lie back. "Let's see how you are feeling." Somehow, she had kicked off the covers by her feet. He moved to that end of the bed to adjust them for her. "I don't know how you do that," he said. "I've never seen anything like it." When he had her all tucked in, he turned to face her. "I—" he began, but closed his mouth when he saw she was again fast asleep. He turned off the television and left the door open just a crack behind him. He needed to get his credit card out and call in that refill on her prescriptions. He'd pick them up tomorrow after he stopped in to see Sam.

6

Max was lying in bed watching a movie featuring George Peppard as a WWI fighter pilot. He'd always like Peppard, and as an old fighter pilot himself, he had an interest in the seat-of-the-pants flying depicted in the movie. Also, it just so happened that Ursula Andress—who bore a more than passing resemblance to Lana's mother—portrayed Peppard's love interest. He was reflecting on a comparison between the two when his phone rang.

"This is Max."

"Max, this is Michael Shapiro, from Atlantic City."

Max had kept his New Jersey accountants through the years. Shapiro & Associates had gotten him through more than one scrape with the IRS, as well as Jersey toughs, union bosses, crooked cops, and other assorted troublemakers. He could almost see Michael sweating. He was always sweating. Sweating and pushing his glasses back up on his nose. "What do you have for me?"

"You asked me to look into some questionable transactions—"

Max had gotten an anonymous tip telling him he had a problem. "I remember."

"Well, we did. You were right. Somehow, that young man was able to set up a fake cryptocurrency wallet and sort of mimic the transactions made by an actual, authentic currency holder."

"How?"

"Well, he must have gotten ahold of the physical hardware wallet and then obtained the key. He then set up accounts using the electronic key and the information he had about the account holder, including legacy banking information. Then he had the new account, the ledger, as well as the cryptocurrency registration account information sent to him at electronic and physical addresses he provided. Basically, he was running a shadow account using the real account holder's information and credit."

Max felt his pulse increase. "Not very original."

"No, sir," Shapiro agreed. "This is along the lines of traditional fraud. It was actually pretty easy to detect."

Max smiled despite himself. "Not the actions of a crypto expert."

"Not at all. This is an unsophisticated, rather common thief delving into areas he doesn't understand," Shapiro said. "It didn't take us long to figure out."

"What's the damage?"

"A couple of hundred thousand."

"Who is the perp?"

"We're showing the fraudster as a guy named . . . Aleksander Melnyk—know him?"

That little bastard. "I do," Max said. He stood and made his way unsteadily to the credenza in his office where he kept a bottle in reserve, out of Lana's sight.

"Oh. Sorry, Mr. Kovalenko."

"No problem," Max said, selecting a glass. "I needed to know. I have another question."

"I figured. You're not going to be happy."

Max breathed deeply and felt a burning in his guts. "It's me, right?"

"He had your key," Shapiro said. "You're the victim."

Max was silent for a long time, thinking. "Okay, Michael," he said at last. "I want you to do something for me. Who knows about this?"

"Right now? Just me, my associate, you—oh, and whoever tipped you off. But we are required to report—"

"I want you to keep this under your hat for a bit, you understand?"

"Well, I understand—but I do have a reporting requirement."

"I need a little time. Will you wait, or do I need to talk to Abe?" Abraham Shapiro was the firm's founder and Michael's father. He would understand the need for restraint.

"Oh, uh . . . no need for that, Max," Michael said quickly. "We can sit on this for a while."

"Thank you," Max said. "And tell Abe I said hello and that he needs to get out of the smog and out here sometime. The fresh air would do him good."

He was disappointed, but not surprised. The vodka burned wonderfully.

7

Sam and Daniels were in Sam's small conference room. Daniels had asked to see him and had given Sam a quick overview of what Max and UkrCX needed done. Sam was skeptical, but aware this was important to Daniels. He looked at the retired judge, who was looking a little peaked this morning.

"Press, are you okay?" Sam asked. "You look like half a mile of bad road."

"Just a little tired. The chemo is making Marci sick. She was up half the night puking. I was on the line with the on-call nurse a couple of times, but we finally got it under control. Called the doc this morning and . . . sorry. Not your problem."

"Aw, crap," Sam said. "I'm sorry. You know what? If you're not up to this—"

"Sam, I need to do this. I'm going crazy playing nurse. I mean, she sleeps and eats and is sick and . . . I need something else to occupy my mind. And the money, Sam. I need the money."

"Press, I can spare—"

Daniels was still formidable when angry. "Don't you try and patronize me, Sam! We'll pay our own damned way! I just—just need your backing. I can knock out most of this stuff part-time, but I've got no secretary or staff."

Sam sat back in his chair. "Not trying to offend you, Press. Just thinking that maybe your time would be better spent with Marci, is all."

"I got a new gal—her name is Julie—set up to watch Marci a couple of hours a day. She's good people. I sentenced her years ago for theft and shoplifting—she had a meth problem but got treatment and she's been sober for eight years. A real leader in the sobriety community. Marci will be in good hands," Daniels said, as if trying to convince Sam as well as himself. Seeming to realize it, he softened. "But thanks, Sam. Look, I'm—I'm a little worn out, is all."

"Okay. Let's make a list of projects you told me about last week," Sam said, writing on a whiteboard quickly. "That about it?" he asked, indicating the list.

"No. We've got another deal going. Just north, I think, of the property that Max bought, where he wants to build his compound—you know that?"

"I think so," Sam said, writing the fourth item. "The property that used to be owned by the Barbers and Detloffs, right?"

"Yeah. It's actually adjacent to the compound and airstrip property. The problem is way north. A couple of the neighboring property owners—you know Casey Sprague?—have been accessing a school section for decades. They've been hunting, guiding hunters, looking for arrowheads, grazing cows, and the like. I think the Barbers and Detloffs were cool with it. Well, Max has said he won't allow anyone to access that school section."

"That's going to piss some people off. They've been crossing forever, right?"

"Right," Daniels agreed. "Sprague and his little band of minions are especially tight-jawed."

"What about adverse possession?" Adverse possession was a legal concept holding that if an individual used property not belonging to him without permission for a statutory period, the individual could be deemed to have rights to the property.

"I don't think so. From what I recall, the Barber and Detloff families had given Sprague and them permission to cross," Daniels explained. "Max is withdrawing that permission. I think it is straightforward and I think the law will support him. But just so you know, I'm trying to talk him out of doing it."

"Good, because that's gonna be unpopular as hell," Sam observed. "Is there another way in for those folks?"

"Yeah, but roundabout," Daniels advised. "I don't know what Judge Bridger might decide." Bridger was the judge who had taken the bench following Daniels' retirement. "He could order Max to provide the access, or he might order another property owner to provide access. Hell, he's so political he might recuse himself and make another judge hear it."

Sam looked at Daniels for a long minute. "Press, do we really want to get involved in this? I mean, for decades Sprague and his people—"

"I know, Sam. I've been here for decades," Daniels said. "People know I'll do the right thing!" He wiped at his brow with a handkerchief.

"True," Sam allowed. "But I thought you and I had discussed that you were going to do the work behind the scene, and that *I* was going to be the face of this effort?" He observed Daniels closely. "*I* don't have that kind of credibility with the community. I'm still considered an outsider around these parts. I'm not opposed to running some of this other stuff up the flagpole, but on this one—"

"I think it's all or nothing, Sam," Daniels said. "Max has made that pretty clear."

"Can you talk to his people and explain the situation?"

"Doubt it," Daniels said, then, seeing Sam's misgiving, he continued. "Sam, I understand your concerns, but I seriously think the incoming jobs and money already present—as well as what's promised—will alleviate many of the townies' concerns. Money talks." Seeing Sam's continued reluctance, he pressed on. "Sam, can you trust me on this one? I think I've got a pretty good feel for the people of this town, and I think most are sophisticated enough to understand that you are merely representing a client. They understand that you doing the job doesn't mean that you necessarily adopt the position. You're just the face of the effort."

"I understand," Sam said. "*Being* the face isn't my issue; getting my face *slapped* is."

8

In his home office, Max took a couple of pills with a glass of water offered by Paulie while Mike looked on, concerned. The day prior, as Paulie told it, he and Max had been riding Max's property and observed trespassers led by Casey Sprague, a well-known local troublemaker who insisted he had a right to cross the property. Max had confronted Sprague and his companions. During the ensuing argument, Max had taken ill and Paulie had to remove him from the scene. Max had been both ill and irascible ever since.

Max looked scornfully at the younger men. "I'm fine, dammit. Just a cough. Allergies, I bet."

Mike looked to Paulie, who nodded his approval. "Max, Paulie said yesterday you were so sick—"

"You're both exaggerating." Max coughed into his hand, then lifted the trash can and—while the other men winced—spit into it.

"You need to take it easy," Mike counseled.

Max glared at Mike. "I'm going to do whatever I need to do to see this project through. I don't have the time to take it easy. That's how business gets done."

The knock at the door was unexpected. Paulie looked at Max. "Go ahead," Max instructed him.

Paulie stood and opened the door, then stepped aside to allow Danny and Stacy to enter. With Max's sixty-fifth birthday just days away, the younger children had shown up to show their respect (in Stacy's case) and to party (in Danny's).

"Stacy, sweetheart!" Max said. "How are you?" He spread his arms wide, anticipating a hug.

"I'm good, Daddy." She walked around the desk, hugged him as expected, then straightened and placed the back of a hand to his forehead. He was warm and she had counted his ribs during the brief embrace. "How are you feeling, Daddy? I've heard it hasn't been so good."

"I don't know who is telling you that. I'm doing fine . . . Just fine." He looked at Paulie and Mike meaningfully. "Right?"

"Uh, right," Mike said, glancing at Paulie for support. He said nothing.

Stacy ran her fingers through her father's thinning hair until he reached up and removed her hand. "Have a seat, honey."

Max looked to Danny, who was watching it all and alternately scratching each arm. "Well? What do you have to say for yourself?"

Danny rubbed at his nose with the back of his hand. "What do you mean, Dad?"

"I gave you a job before I left California. Did you get those buildings listed?" Max looked at Danny intently. "Have you got someone lined up to either auction off the hardware, or are we going to truck it out here? I asked you to get that done for me. Where are you on all of that?"

Danny's face turned red. "I'm—I'm working on it. I met with some guys and—"

"Working on it?" Max exploded. "What the hell have you been doing? I gave you a simple task and . . ." Max's rant was interrupted as he began to cough.

Paulie approached while pouring water into a glass from a plastic bottle. "Here, boss. Try this," he said, carefully eyeing Laika, who was emitting a low growl.

"I don't need any water." Max pushed the proffered glass away with the back of his hand. He then began a sustained coughing fit that lasted some time.

"Oh, Daddy," Stacy said. "We've got to get you to a doctor."

"I agree, Max," Mike offered.

"Dad, I think they are right—" Danny began.

"I don't give a damn what any of you—especially *you*—think," Max sputtered, pointing to Danny. "The last thing I need from you, Danny, is advice. You're too damned stupid, or too damned lazy, or too busy snorting cocaine, to accomplish a simple task." Seeing Danny's look of surprise, he added, "I'm not stupid. And because of that, I'm done with you—do you hear me? Done!"

Danny's face was pale. He wiped at his nose. "What?" he asked, looking around the room for support. "What are you talking about, Dad?"

"You think I'm blind and stupid, but I'm not," Max replied. "This is still my company. And you've shown me over and over you don't have what it takes to be a part of it! You're getting no part of this company, do you understand? In fact, next time I see my lawyer you are out of all of it. You'll get nothing!"

Stacy had made her way back around the desk next to Max. She put a hand on his shoulder. "Daddy, please calm down. You're getting yourself all worked up—"

Max shrugged her off. "Of course I am! I have an alcoholic cokehead for a son! My own flesh and blood and he's not worth a damn. I give him simple tasks and he can't even. . ." As another coughing fit overtook him, Max held his stomach with both hands until, at last, he collapsed in his chair. "Out, all of you," he said in a voice just above a whisper. "When I need something, I'll let you know."

Paulie stood and ushered the family out the door, then closed it behind them. Before she left, Stacy said to Paulie, "He just thinks I'm dumb. Everyone thinks I'm dumb."

Paulie waved her out and turned to Max. "You want me to call the doctor, boss?"

"No, no," Max said. "I've got a call in; just waiting for a call back." At that moment, Max's personal phone rang. It was Dr. Esteban, who had been calling Max for a couple of days, but Max had been too busy to get back to him. "There, see? It's the doc. Probably wants to order more tests. I'll take this, Paulie. Wait outside for a minute, huh?" When the door closed behind Paulie, Max answered. "Doc, it's Max. I'm out here in Wyoming. I'm puking blood."

There was a brief silence before the doctor replied. "I'm not surprised, Max. I've been trying to get ahold of you—why haven't you answered my calls?" When Max didn't respond, the doctor continued. "You are a very sick man."

"I know," Max said. "I just told you, I'm puking blood. Don't have to be a doctor to figure that out. Can you give me something—"

"Max, you have a very serious condition, one I would really rather not talk about on the phone," Esteban said. "Can you come to my office tomorrow? I've got a full slate of patients, but I can set aside some time—"

"I told you, I'm in Wyoming," Max said irritably. "I'm hosting a party tonight. Tomorrow I've got meetings lined up all day. I don't have the time to fly out and back. What's going on?"

"Is—is anyone there with you? The news I have is . . . well, it's bad, Max."

Max looked at the ceiling, weighing his options. He could ask Paulie to come in. Or maybe Lana would be better. But Lana and Mike were probably getting ready for the party. Paulie had things to do. "Just tell me, Doc."

"Max, you've got cancer."

Max wasn't surprised. He hadn't been feeling particularly great, people had commented on his color, and the doctor himself had avoided eye contact before ordering all the tests. "And?"

"And it's . . . well . . . not good."

"Stomach, I bet."

"Well, yeah—but that's not the bad part."

"Oh, for Christ's sake, Doc! What's the bad part?"

"It's pancreatic cancer. Advanced. I've shown your results to a couple of oncologists already. There's nothing we can do," Esteban said. "Well, I mean to cure it. We can, of course, work to manage pain and try to keep you comfortable."

Max sat quietly. He'd led the kind of life that others dreamed about. Fighter pilot. Successful businessman. He had loved beautiful women—a lot of them. Three kids. He'd done a lot of things right. Made some mistakes, as well. Picked wives poorly, for one thing. "So, what next?"

"Well, there are a number of things we could do," Esteban began. "The oncologists suggested we try some chemo—that might help extend your life by a few months. There are some experimental drugs available—no guarantees, of course, but the initial testing looks promising and—"

"I'm not going to do any of that," Max said. "I've been around long enough to see people try and squeeze out another year or two. They usually end up sick the whole time, wearing out their family while they circle the drain. What else?"

"There aren't a lot of solutions at present. I—I can prescribe some painkillers, some stuff for the nausea—what other symptoms are you having? Who's your pharmacy?"

Max smiled wryly. "I've got no idea about a pharmacy," he said, and listed his symptoms. "I puke when I drink, I'm tired and cranky . . . Oh hell, not much is working right, come to think of it." Esteban was quiet on the line. Max thought he heard the faint tapping on a keyboard—probably the doc cranking out some prescriptions. "How long do I have?"

The tapping stopped. "The oncologists I spoke with informed me the five-year survival rate is five percent. Your cancer is advanced, so maybe six months? I still think you ought to consult with one, by the way."

"Why?"

"Well, just to get a better understanding of the disease and its progression."

"I'll think about it," Max lied. "For now, I'm going to take care of business. I've got deals to close here."

"Well, you need to get your affairs in order," Esteban advised. "Meantime, I'll find a pharmacy in town and send your stuff there."

"Got it, Doc. Anything else?"

"I'm sorry, Max," Esteban said. "I wish there was something else I could do or say."

"Nothing to be sorry about, Doc. Who's had a better run than me?" He said his goodbyes, hung up, and went to the small bar in the room and poured himself a tall one. He finished that in a long draw and was pouring another and thinking about telling the family when he heard a knock on the door. "Yes?"

"Boss, I just got a text from Aiden," Paulie said through the door. "They're gonna be calling you."

"That'll be fine," Max said. Might as well compound the bad news. He knew what was coming. Seconds later, his phone rang. "Aiden, my boy. What's happening?" Aiden Moore had been a twenty-three-year-old computer prodigy when he and Max had started UkrCX. It had been tough getting things going initially, but with Aiden's technical know-how UkrCX quickly outpaced competitors in the development of software facilitating the exchange of cryptocurrency, and they had managed to stay afloat. As the business expanded, they transitioned from a limited liability partnership to a close corporation—at which point Max had forced Aiden out, albeit with a million-dollar severance package. When UkrCX had subsequently become a leading force in the industry, Aiden had come to regret his decision to take what had seemed like a lot of money at the time. Now, suffering seller's remorse, he would occasionally get drunk and threaten Max.

"You freaking ripped me off is what's happening, you sorry—"

"Now Aiden, is that any way to talk to your friend? Your mentor? Your boss?" Max asked levelly. "I taught you everything you know about investing in cryptocurrency. I—"

"You ripped me off! You manipulated the books, paid me bupkis for my shares, then released your hold on a bunch of assets and made millions. You sorry bas—"

"Now hold on, Aiden. I'm afraid I don't have to listen to that. You and I reached an arm's-length agreement for the purchase and sale of your shares."

"That's because you cooked the books. You had assets on hand you didn't tell me about and didn't disclose. You intentionally drove the company's value into the ground, until I couldn't afford to hang on any longer!"

"That's not how I remember it," Max countered. "As I recall, we agreed to reinvest any proceeds and to eschew taking salaries or distributions. And you'll remember you were struggling to make payments on some purchases you made. I think you had a Porsche 911, a house in the valley, and a long-legged, high-maintenance blonde. And I think my accountants will testify that I paid you twice what the shares were worth at the time."

"Because you were manipulating the stock price! I simply didn't know it at the time! As soon as you had my shares you dumped millions into the market, artificially inflating the price per share. I didn't realize it at the time, but you were cornering the market before we even spoke."

Max began coughing and pushed a button, summoning Paulie. "Aiden, what you're saying isn't true, and even if it was, you can't prove any of it," Max said. "I'll simply open my books and show that I made a number of fortuitous transactions—including the one where I bought your shares."

"You bastard! I—"

"Aiden, I'm growing weary of your allegations," Max replied. "And I would caution you to be very careful to whom you air your complaints, because depending on the method of communication you could very easily be sued for libel, slander, or both—do you understand?"

"I understand you are a crook! I understand you are a jackass," Aiden countered. "Now you understand this: I'm going to get my money back."

When Paulie entered, Max indicated with his head where he should sit, and placed the phone in speaker mode. "Aiden, if you are in need of funds, I'll gladly—"

"I don't want *your* money. I want *my* money! All of it! Every penny, at what it is worth now!"

"Now Aiden, don't be silly."

"Silly? You call me silly? Well, how about this? You're a dead man!"

"Oh, Aiden, I'm not going to hear that from you," Max said, suddenly feeling faint. He beckoned silently to Paulie.

"You are!" Aiden ranted. "You'll hear it when I stick a gun in your ear—"

Paulie was now at Max's side, his face darkening as Max hung up on Aiden. "Paulie," Max gasped. "Can you help me get upstairs? I'm feeling a little under the weather today." As Paulie helped him up, Max commented, "Don't worry, he's full of shit."

"Maybe, maybe not," Paulie replied. "Boss, you want me to talk with some of my people back in the valley? You want me to shut him down?"

"No, I don't think so. He'll cool off."

"Are you sure?"

"I am," Max said. "Aiden doesn't have the balls to do anything but talk. That's exactly why I had to get his shares. No balls. Wake me in two hours."

9

While Max napped, Mike and Alex drove a new truck Mike had bought down to the local shooting range. Mike had gone to the local dealer and paid cash for the vehicle, then paid extra to have it lifted and get a winch and light bar installed on the front end and large off-road tires affixed. "If we're going to be here, we're going to look like everyone else," he'd said when Alex had inquired as to the reason for the modifications.

"This is such bullshit," Alex said. "No one is going to come after us in this country, for Christ's sake." He was referring to Max's directive that all the men in the family—save Danny—learn to shoot guns. "You see what happened in Ukraine with the Russians? It could happen right here!" the old man had said.

"Yeah, well, he asked me yesterday when the last time was that we'd been out," Mike said. "I lied and told him last week, so we need to get on the books here before he checks on us."

"I suppose," Alex agreed.

"Besides, the property Max bought is apparently large enough that it qualifies for us to get two landowner tags."

"Two what?" Alex asked.

"Landowner tags," Mike said. "Apparently, there are elks on the property. They—"

"Elk," Alex corrected. "The plural of elk is elk."

"Whatever." Mike shrugged. "We get two tags from the state of Wyoming, allowing us to shoot two elk."

"You know how to hunt elk?"

"How hard could it be?" Mike shrugged again. "Big, dumb animal walking around eating grass. Hell, these people can figure it out, we can figure it out." He parked, and as the men exited the truck, Alex reached into the rear door on the driver's side, retrieved two identical rifles, and handed one to Mike.

"I got us an instructor so we can get certified to hunt," Mike observed as a large, rumpled man approached. "I think this is our guy."

"I'm Bob Davison," the man said. "Could you point those weapons downrange, please?"

Alex looked to Davison blankly. "Downrange?"

Davison looked at both men. "That way," he said, indicating the direction behind himself. "And keep pointing them downrange," he instructed. "Follow me." He turned and walked toward a large, one-story building with windows on one side. "Let's get you registered."

Having arrived in the sparsely furnished building, Alex walked around looking at framed pictures of smiling gun owners lining the walls while Mike filled out paperwork. "You've been here for a while," Alex observed.

"Oh yeah," Davison agreed. "The club was started right after World War II by a couple of returning vets. Grew from there. At one point, we had more than two hundred members. That was back in the late 1960s, but we've hung at around one hundred members since then."

"What accounted for that?"

"Oh, I'm not sure. Not as many veterans, maybe," Davison guessed. "But then we started to pick back up after the Gulf War, and now—given what's going on overseas—we're going gangbusters. You were lucky to get time, being short notice and all."

"Nice," Mike said.

"Okay," Davison said. "We'll be here in the classroom for a while. Once you pass the written test, I'll take you outside and we'll put a few rounds downrange." Davison then gave a quick overview of Wyoming gun laws and gun safety in general, complete with photos of accident and suicide victims. "It always helps to bring the point home," he said in conclusion.

"Great," Alex observed. He was feeling a little queasy and was ready to get outside. Both men passed the simple written test, and they took a break before meeting outside on the firing line. They followed Davison when he indicated the range was ready.

As Alex strolled up to the line, Davison barked at him, "Get your barrel pointed downrange, damn it!"

Alex was clearly offended, but Davison was unconcerned. "You've got to understand that firearms are dangerous weapons! There is no room for mistakes!" Alex's apology seemed to calm Davison some. "All right. What are you fellas shooting?"

"Not sure." Mike handed his weapon to Davison, who looked at it quickly and handed it right back.

".270 Winchester. Good rifle. You?" He lifted a chin toward Alex.

"Same," he said.

Mike saw Davison was surprised. "My father-in-law bought 'em from the same place and had them shipped out here. He's afraid of an *invasion*," Mike said derisively.

"Could happen," Davison said, then indicated the rifles. "Did you try one, feel it, weigh it in your hands or anything?"

"No," Mike said. "He talked with a guy, and he said they'd work for most anything."

"You?" he asked Alex.

"No."

"So you have never shot—or even held—these guns?" Davison smirked. Rich people. "Well, boys, let's put some rounds downrange. You did bring some ammo, right?"

Alex pulled two boxes of cartridges from a pocket. Davison looked at the rounds and rolled his eyes. "Seriously? Who was he talking with when he bought this ammunition?"

"I dunno. Some guy—"

"Yeah, well, these are frangibles—bullets designed to break into small pieces when they hit something harder than themselves. You use these in tight quarters, like self-defense, so if you shoot a guy it explodes in him and doesn't go through him and hit someone you don't want to hit. Make sense?" He held the boxes up for their view.

"I suppose," Mike said.

"We're going to be shooting at some distance, so I'm gonna get a box of hollow points I have, and we'll shoot those. On me, okay?"

Alex shrugged. "Okay."

"Everyone has .270 Winchesters," Davison explained. "Hang tight. Be right back."

Moments later, he returned, and shortly thereafter the men began the shooting lessons. Davison got each man zeroed in fewer than ten rounds; thereafter Mike struggled while Alex seemed to be more naturally inclined.

"Squeeze it, Mike! Don't jerk it! Good, Alex. Good. Now remember, you've got to control your breathing," Davison coached. "Know where you are in your breathing!" Davison had hoped to get through two boxes of fifty rounds, but both men began to flinch from the recoil after having fired approximately twenty rounds following their successful zeroing.

"Let's take a break," he said, eyeing the men carefully. "I think we've done enough. Let's call it a day. You've passed your tests. But I'm gonna need you guys to come back and practice. You aren't ready to hit an elk."

"Why not?" Alex asked. "They are huge, right?"

"Well, they are," Davison said. "But to kill one humanely—and that's the only killing I approve of—you gotta hit 'em in the right spot. And that is surprisingly small. It takes practice. Come on, I'll get your paperwork. And keep them barrels pointed downrange!"

Back inside the clubhouse, the men racked their weapons while Davison retrieved the paperwork. When he was done, he retrieved the rifles and brought them to the table where Alex and Mike were waiting. "Whose is whose?" Davison brandished the two rifles. When neither man claimed a rifle, he said, "You know your serial number?"

"Dunno," Alex replied. "Aren't they the same?"

"No," Davison said. "Each of your zeroes is different. Has to do with your eyes, the placement of your face, and things like that. Tell you what: when you come next time, we'll mark the weapons and confirm zero before we get started. That way you'll never get 'em mixed up."

10

Days later, Max and Daniels were awaiting Sam in his small conference room when he entered. Daniels was already pouring clear liquid into two coffee cups. Max stood as Sam entered, and Sam extended a hand in greeting. "Mr. Kovalenko, I'm Sam Johnstone."

The handshake was firm and dry. "Call me Max. I am pleased to meet you," he said. "This is Paulie."

A large man sitting on a chair he had dragged to a corner merely nodded. Sam returned the bare acknowledgement.

"I see Press here has got the bar open," Sam observed, sipping coffee from a cup depicting a brook trout.

"Would you care for a drink?" Max asked. "Direct from Ukraine. I have a . . . how do you say it? A source."

Sam smiled. "Not me," he said. "On the wagon."

"Too bad. This is good stuff, as Americans like to say." Sam smiled, and Max continued. "You've spoken with Press here?"

"I have."

"So you understand what I am trying to do?"

"I think so, yes." Sam looked steadily at Max, then gestured at the whiteboard. "That's what we're looking at right now, is it not?"

Max looked at the whiteboard for a moment. "Yes, that's it. The important thing is that we get this done, and get it done quickly. Wyoming's law is
fortuitous, but we must take advantage of it. Surely other cryptocurrency
exchange entrepreneurs will follow. As far as I know, we were among the
first. We must press the advantage."

"I understand the need for some of these projects," Sam said. "On the
other hand, some of them—like the exclusion of long-time residents from
your property—do not seem to make a lot of sense in the big picture."

"What do you mean?" Max asked. He glanced at Daniels, then focused
on Sam.

"It seems to me that the easier way to do this would be to focus on the
projects that are the least controversial, and then take on the more controversial projects later," Sam observed. "That would facilitate getting the job
done while not infuriating the locals."

Max drank from a cup Daniels had given him, swirled the liquid around
in his mouth, and then swallowed. This one was strong, which was a nice
change. Too many men this one's age were weak. "You are bold," he said.

"My license says counselor and attorney at law," Sam countered. "I'm
not doing my job if I do not advise you."

"I don't need advice," Max said. "I need people to do what I tell them."

"Then you don't need me," Sam said.

"Sam, hold on a second—" Daniels began, but quieted when Max
raised his hand.

Max looked steadily at the younger man. "My sources tell me you are a
hero."

"Your sources are wrong."

"They tell me you were blown up in Afghanistan," Max said, awaiting a
reaction. When none came, he continued. "That country is—how do you
say?—a shithole. I flew a Fencer over there and dropped bombs on the
Afghan people. I would do it again tomorrow."

"I've got no issue with the people," Sam said.

"Then you weren't serious," Max observed, exchanging a look with
Paulie.

Sam reflected on American dead, the broken men and women he'd seen in VA hospitals, and the disgraceful American withdrawal. "Perhaps not," he concluded. "Now, why don't you and Press just—"

"Hear me out, Mr. Johnstone," Max began. "I came to this country to make money and raise a family. I've done that. But now, I want to give back to my adopted country. And I want to help this community."

Sam sat back in his chair. "I'm listening."

Max then gave Sam a primer on cryptocurrency and Wyoming law. "It really is a unique situation—one I think we can all benefit from." He drank deeply from his glass and stifled a cough. "Being here first will give me an advantage over everyone else. But I need dependable power and low start-up costs. I need Custer. And I need you and Press to help me."

Sam stood and walked to his window, moved a shade with his hand, and then turned back to face Max. "I don't know if I want to get involved in this," he said. "Look, I came here a couple of years ago to get a fresh start."

"I want that same thing," Max said.

"The difference is, I was willing to accept the new community as it was. As it is. You are trying to change everything."

"I am only trying to provide opportunity—"

"As a side benefit to getting rich."

"I might point out to you, young man, that I am already rich."

"I'm not. But I am in the position to take only the clients I want," Sam said. "Press, can you see him out?" He looked to Daniels, and then to Paulie, who was sitting rigidly in the corner. "I'll be available if you want to talk . . . later," he said to Daniels as the three men left the room.

Outside, Daniels spoke to Max while Paulie helped him into the car. "He is a proud man, but a damaged one."

"A hero," Max said.

"For sure."

"I'm not used to being spoken to like that," Max said.

"Don't take him at his word," Daniels said. "He doesn't mean it."

"He surely does," Max said. "And to be honest with you, that's one of the things I like about him. He's got—how do you say it? *Gumption*, I think. He'll do fine. Tell him I will pay fifteen hundred dollars per hour for his help. If he would like a retainer, all he needs to do is name his number. I want him on my team." Max made a face and looked to Paulie. "Paulie, let's go. I am not feeling so good."

Daniels watched as Paulie drove Max home. He looked at his watch. Time to get medication to Marci.

11

Cavalry Creek ran through downtown Custer. A freestone stream, it was fed primarily by runoff from the snow accumulating in the Bighorn Mountains and augmented by springs on the east slope. The clear waters hosted rainbow trout of moderate size, as well as the occasional brown trout. Since he'd quit drinking, it was not unusual for Sam to spend the last hours of daylight on stream before picking up a burger on his way home. It was just after six p.m. on an unusually warm late September evening and he was casting a nymph into the base of a small falls when he got the feeling he was being watched. He surreptitiously touched the left side of his chest and felt the small revolver in its holster. Taking a deep breath, he tried to side-eye in search of the danger to avoid alerting the enemy to his awareness. He wondered if he was being observed from more than one direction. As he became more attuned to the possible threat, the sound of water gave way to a loud buzzing that blocked out all else. He could feel his breathing rate increase. The riverbank to his left would afford some cover. He risked a look to the right and saw Daniels waving vigorously at him from the bank, accompanied by a man and a woman.

Not the Taliban after all.

Sam picked up his line, cradled it in a hand, and waded to the bank. "What's going on, Press?"

"Sam, this is Lana Kovalenko-Brown—Max's oldest daughter, and her husband Mike. Mike is the CEO of UkrCX. Lana, Mike, Sam Johnstone."

"Hi," Sam acknowledged the couple. "Nice to meet you."

"We've heard a lot about you from Press here," Lana said. She was at least as tall as Cathy Schmidt—had to be a six-footer. Mike was a smaller, balding man. A fleeting image of the two of them in bed passed quickly.

"Max wanted us to touch base with you," Mike began. "See where we're at." Lana watched with what Sam thought was barely concealed disdain while Mike sputtered through all the reasons why they needed to check on Sam's progress. He had a high-pitched, grating voice.

"I'm thinking it over," Sam said, sitting on the bank.

"Max wanted us to remind you that he is willing to pay you good money," Mike said.

"Fifteen hundred per hour." Lana looked pointedly at Sam's dilapidated waders and aging vest. "Honestly, it looks like you could use it," she added.

Sam smiled at the insult. "Looks can be deceiving, for sure." He drank from his flask and replaced it, then wiped his mouth with the back of his hand and squinted into the sun's reflection on the water. "Sometimes, things that appear plain can be deceptively, well, fulfilling. And sometimes, things that are beautiful on the outside can be, well . . . let's just say dry and lifeless."

She flashed a smile that didn't reach her eyes but showed rows of perfectly straight white crowns. The silence endured until Mike coughed loudly and spoke again.

"Sam, can we tell Max you are in?" he asked. "We think having you aboard will help us achieve our goals. You are well-respected and you know the law—"

"Press knows the law," Sam interrupted.

"I can't do it all, Sam," Daniels said. "I've got to take care of Marci."

"Tell Max I'm thinking about it," Sam said. "I have other clients, as well."

"Set them aside briefly," Mike said. "They'll be here long after—"

"You're gone?" Sam finished.

"I was going to say, 'long after our immediate business has been concluded,'" he said, reddening.

"And I'll be here, cleaning up the mess," Sam said. "Having to live with these people."

Mike shrugged and spread his hands, palms up. "That could well be the price of admission, yeah."

Lana looked to Sam. "Do you have a conference room we could use for a brief moment?"

Cassie would be gone by now, so Sam tossed Daniels the keys to his office. "Press, show them the conference room, would you?"

Daniels nodded and the three departed. Sam returned to his fishing, quickly catching and releasing a couple of rainbows. The water was cold, and his good leg began to stiffen. Just before dark, he clambered with some difficulty onto the bank and walked down the street to his office. When he entered, he could hear voices in his conference room. He was sitting on a chair in his office removing his waders when Daniels knocked on his door.

"Sam," he began, closing the door behind him. "What the hell are you doing? You are blowing an opportunity to make a shit-load of money here!"

"I'm not a whore, Press. I'm an attorney. And I've busted my ass to get to the point where I can pick and choose my clients. I don't have to work for anyone I don't want to."

"Oh, bullshit, Sam," Daniels said. He pulled a flask from the inside pocket of his blazer and took a quick swig, then replaced it. "You're no different than any other lawyer. You represent the clients you have—good, bad, or indifferent. I know we all want to think differently, but the fact is a lot of the people we help are jackasses."

"Yeah, but they're my jackasses."

"Real sweethearts, your clients," Daniels said, voice dripping with sarcasm. "Tommy Olsen? Philandering loser. Davonte Blair? Arrogant punk. And don't even get me started on Lucy Beretta." Tommy Olsen had been one of Sam's first clients upon his arrival in Custer. Charged with murder, he'd been convicted by a jury, but only because a then-assistant prosecutor had withheld evidence. Daniels had presided and made some questionable decisions, but ultimately Tommy was absolved of guilt. Blair had been acquitted when the son of Sam's then-business partner had taken the stand and confessed to the crime, a confession Sam still didn't quite believe. Lucy Beretta was a woman Sam—with Daniels' help, following his retirement—had represented on a murder charge. She'd been acquitted on that one, but later was convicted of two other murders in part as the result of false evidence she had offered on the record against Sam's advice in her successful effort to beat the rap on the first charge.

"She was a piece of work," Daniels continued. "And didn't you also represent the gal who stole from the Girl Scout Cookie fund or something, too?"

"I get it—okay?" Sam snapped. While Daniels was speaking, Sam had finished taking off his boots and waders. He now looked across his desk, ready to call it a night.

"I know you don't want to do this, Sam. But I wish you would. For me."

"Press, what's really going on?" Sam asked softly.

"It's Marci." Daniels uncapped the flask and took a deep swig. "She's dying. That breast cancer she had a while back. I don't know if they didn't get it all or what, but apparently it's metastasized or whatever and it's everywhere."

"You're seeing doctors, right?" Sam asked. "Can't they operate or something?"

Daniels' eyes watered and his face reddened. "They thought so. They cut her open last time, then just closed her up and said they can't do that anymore. We're on to drugs and chemo and radiation and all she does is sleep and . . ."

Sam was stunned when Daniels broke down. On the bench, he'd been a stern man—fierce even. Now, he was just another old man broken over the thought of losing a loved one.

"There's some kind of treatment available in Mexico—"

"Mexico? Jesus, Press! Their medical authorities. . . It's—"

"Sam, it's her only chance!" Daniels said. "I know it's probably all a bunch of crap. I know it might not be tested to our standards to make sure it's safe. But what's it going to do? Kill her? Insurance won't touch it. Not tested and approved—that stuff."

"Aren't they trying some new treatments here?"

"I got her enrolled or whatever and they say they are checking her for suitability for admission to a program whereby they would, might, or could try some experimental drugs on her."

"That sounds promising."

Daniels' face reddened in anger. "They've been looking at her for weeks, Sam! Meanwhile, she gets sicker and sicker!" He slapped Sam's desk with a wrinkled hand. "And even if she gets admitted, she could be on the part of the test that is administered a placebo!"

"Oh, for Christ's sake. Surely—"

"It wasn't supposed to be this way," Daniels said. He took a deep breath, held it, then let it out. "We worked hard. We saved our money and I was going to retire, then we were gonna travel and . . . well, like an idiot I kept working as a judge and we got older and now . . . Our savings are gone. The house is paid off, but I've already taken out an equity loan to get her what she needs," he said. "We need what we've got left."

Sam considered an offer of assistance, then recalled the judge's earlier reaction.

"Sam, I can't lose her. I can't. Forty-five years . . ." His eyes welled up again. "It's not supposed to be this way. I—I can't live without her. I know it sounds like some lame country song, but Sam . . . I can't lose her. I can't. I've prayed for God to take me and leave her."

"How would it work?"

"I'd take her down there, pay them cash—almost twenty thousand— then they do some sort of treatment before bringing her back here to recover. Rinse and repeat."

"Holy shit!" Sam said. "That's a lot of money. And wouldn't it be easier to stay down there?"

Daniels offered a wry grin. "She knows how sick she is," he said. "She made me promise she could die in Wyoming. I'm . . . I mean if . . . I'm not going to break that promise."

"I don't know what to say," Sam said.

"There's nothing to say. It's life." Daniels shrugged. "I hope . . . I hope you'll find a woman like Marci, Sam. And I hope to hell you kick off before she does. It's a man's God-given right to die first. We're useless without them."

While Daniels looked at the floor, Sam grabbed a tissue and blew his nose, then wiped his eyes. And he thought he had problems. "All right," he said. "I'm in for whatever it takes."

Moments later, the parties were seated in Sam's office. "Sam, we're prepared to up our offer," Lana said. "Two thousand per hour. I'll put a three-hundred-thousand-dollar retainer in the account of your choice upon our signing an agreement. Are you in or out?"

Sam looked at Lana, Mike, and Daniels in turn. Daniels was leaning forward in his chair, apparently holding his breath. Mike looked at him hopefully. Lana sat back and picked at a cuticle.

"Done," Sam said. "I'm in."

Daniels stood. "I'm sorry, I've got to go and take care of something for my wife," he said with a meaningful look at Sam. "Thank you all. See you soon."

In their new truck moments later, Mike started the engine and then looked sourly at Lana.

"What?" she asked.

"That's an outrageous amount of money for some small-town ambulance chaser," he groused. "It's fiscally irresponsible."

"Yeah?" she asked. "Okay, Mr. Fiscal Responsibility. What's the price on you *not* having to go back and tell Max you couldn't get Sam signed up?" When Mike didn't respond, she pushed the issue. "How much is *that* worth to you?"

Mike shook his head and backed out of the parking spot in front of Sam's office. Lana looked out the window at the storefronts as he drove. "I told you these small-town rednecks are all the same," she said. "Pride and principles all go silent when money talks."

~

Later that evening, Mike was in Max's office for a no-notice meeting called by Max, who wanted an update. Mike led with the information that they had Sam on board.

"Holy buckets! You're paying him *what*?" Max asked.

"We're paying what we had to in order to get him on board, Max," Mike said. He had a roaring headache, the smoke from Max's stinkweed cigarettes was killing him, and all he wanted was to get out of that office.

"Christ," Max lamented, shaking his head slowly and then fixing a stare on Mike. "I'm not happy, you know."

"I know, Max. You make that clear every single day of my life."

"You can always step down."

"No. I'm not going to do that. I'm going to finish what I started."

Occasionally, this failure of a man showed a spark of something. "Then do it! It's almost October!" Max pounded his dusty desk with a frail fist. "I'm going to remind you—"

"All the shares in UkrCX are going to go to one person," Mike said. "I know that. You've threatened to cut me off a hundred times."

"I'm trying to get you moving—to succeed," Max said. "Lana assured me you were up to the task."

"I am, but you're making it impossible," Mike argued.

"No! You are showing yourself to not be up to the challenge. I could change the succession plan right now and remove you. I could replace you with—"

"Alex?" Mike smiled sardonically. "He doesn't know shit."

"It's not knowledge I seek, Mike. It's effort. It's willingness. It's . . . guts."

Mike sat back. "It doesn't matter, does it?"

"What's that?" Max asked, stifling a cough.

"What I do. It doesn't matter. You're going to dump me and replace me with Alex."

"Results count, Mike. If I do not see the results I want, it could happen," Max said. "One phone call to my lawyer is all it will take. In fact, it *will* happen—" He was interrupted by a lengthy coughing fit. When at last he had it under control, he concluded, "It will happen if I don't see progress in the next few days. Every project must be proceeding according to plan, or you are out on your ass. We'll see if Lana keeps you around then, huh?"

12

On the 1st of October, Sam swallowed some coffee, then took a deep breath before dialing. This would not go well. When Casey Sprague picked up, Sam tried to be as upbeat as possible.

"Casey, this is Sam Johnstone."

"I'm getting ready to move some cows," Casey said. "How can I help you?"

"Well, that might be what I'm calling about," Sam began. "I represent Max Kovalenko and—"

"That sonuvabitch," Casey muttered.

"I hear you, but he's my sonuvabitch," Sam said, trying to keep it light. When Casey neither laughed nor responded, Sam continued. "I'm calling about the trouble up on Arrowhead Ridge."

"Wouldn't be no trouble if your client would act right. My family has been crossing that land to get to that school section for generations. Now him and his people come in and think they can keep us off that property. That's not right!"

"Casey, right or wrong, it's my client's land," Sam said. "He has the legal right to limit access."

"But I've got hunters lined up for later this month!"

"And I'll try and get Max to give permission for you to guide a few in there. Just let me work with him and his people and—"

"I don't need permission. Been doing it forever," Casey interrupted. "I've got three parties who've spent a lot of money to have me guide them on that school section. I'm gonna have access; I'm not going to lose that money."

"Well, in all honesty, you might have to refund that money if you don't have Max's permission," Sam said. "Just work with me and—"

"I ain't got it no more!" Casey exclaimed. "I used it to buy an outfitters license and supplies and food and . . . well, stuff. I ain't got it!"

Sam looked at the planner on his desk. Elk hunting would open in a couple of weeks. Time was short. "Look, let me do this: I'll talk with Max and see if he'll make an exception this year, due to the recent purchase and all."

"Sam, this is bullshit! You know that. We've been using that access across the Barber and Detloff places for years. Before that it was all the Ankula place."

"I understand," Sam began. "You had their permission. But Max has decided—"

"Can he do that? I thought we had adversity of possession, or whatever?"

"Well, it's complicated—"

"I ain't stupid!"

"—But the reality is that because you had permission to use the access, the permission can be withdrawn, and you cannot possess the access adversely as a matter of law."

Silence followed as Casey attempted to comprehend. "So he can just come in here and kick us out?"

"Well . . . yeah."

"And you support that?"

"Not really," Sam admitted. "I'm just the lawyer, Casey. I've got a job to do."

"And you don't care. You and him, you're just here to make money off of us."

"I do care, Casey. I've tried to advise Max, but it's his land." That was true—Max had disregarded Sam's advice. "Look, why don't you hire your own attorney and have them look into it if you don't believe me?"

"Oh, I believe you, Sam. I believe I'm getting screwed. I believe this is gonna cost me plenty—maybe put me right outta business!" Casey snarled. "And you better believe this: I ain't gonna take this sitting down, and I'm gonna guide them hunters. You tell that to your buddy Max. And if'n he don't like it, I'll deal with him my way!"

"Casey, please don't make threats. Let's work together to see if we can sort—"

When the line went dead, Sam finished his now-tepid coffee and made notes in his file. He couldn't blame Casey. Around Custer, people on the margins tended to work together to help each other scratch out a living. Sam imagined that Casey had repaired a lot of fence for the Barbers and Detloffs over the years in return for being allowed the access necessary to graze a few cows and guide some hunters on that school section. Max's decision to unilaterally and without warning withdraw access was naturally going to be met with anger. Hopefully, anger was where it would end.

The knock startled him. "Come in, Cassie."

"Have you seen this?" She handed him the *Custer Bugle*.

Above the fold on the front page was a story by Sarah Penrose, head-lined, "WHEN CULTURES COLLIDE." Sam scanned the piece quickly. "Well, that's not going to do my clients any favors," he said. "She paints Max and his people as thinking everyone already here is some kind of bumpkin."

"Well, that *is* what they think—right?"

Sam sat quietly, considering. "I think it's not that so much as it is the idea that improvements could be made. I think most of Max's people truly believe that they can help Custer transition from what it is to a more progressive community."

"What if we don't want that?"

"Yeah, I know," Sam observed while reading. "But the stuff that Casey Sprague says in here: 'These out-of-towners bring in their screwed-up culture and pose a danger to our way of life,' and, 'We intend to defend our way of living at all costs,' isn't particularly helpful."

"No, but they got no right to come in here and upset—"

"Oh, but they do, Cassie," Sam corrected her. "They've got every right—as long as they do so in accordance with the law."

"But it's not right!"

"Now you're talking a different kind of right. And I might agree with you, to a point. But look here: Casey Sprague says, 'Max Kovalenko and his people need to watch their back'—what the hell is that?" he asked. Seeing her redden, he softened. "Excuse my language, Cassie, but that's not helping. Now, I'll be the first to admit that I'd like to see Max and his people come in here with a little different attitude. I'd like to see them be a little more understanding, a little more accommodating."

"But you are helping them, Sam." He could tell she was disappointed.

"I am," he admitted. "But Cassie, make no mistake. I like Custer just the way it is. If I didn't, I'd be gone."

"Then why help them?"

"A couple of reasons. One, someone will—it might as well be me. Maybe I can help them do this right. Two, the judge has asked me to help out—that means something to me."

"Marci's so ill," she said, shaking her head.

"I know. And three—"

"The money."

Sam nodded. "The money. It's ridiculous money. Play money, almost. Cassie, the money they have offered will set us up in this office for a long, long time. Enable me to update our equipment, maybe put some carpet down."

"Money's not everything, Sam," Cassie counseled. "You've got your reputation to think about."

"I've done a lot of thinking. And while I'd much prefer to not work for these people, I know that my ability to stand on principle is limited."

"What do you mean?"

"When poverty knocks on the door, principles jump out the window."

"I don't understand."

"You keep the books," he said. "How long can we continue without a big case coming in?"

She nodded her understanding. "Something will come along. It always does."

"It always has," he agreed. "But I'd be a fool not to take on this work while I can."

She nodded. "I know," she said. The front door chimed, and she turned to head out of his office. "That will be Mrs. Wilson. I think she wants to change her will again."

"Who is she mad at now?"

"Her son Levi. Got divorced."

"Okay. Give me a minute and then show her in," he said. "And Cassie? The longer I'm in this business, the more I find attorneys do a lot of things they don't like, for a lot of people they don't particularly care for."

~

The Longbranch Saloon had been on Yellowstone Avenue for almost one hundred years. A destination watering hole, it offered drinks and moderately priced bar food while serving as a place where business got done. Because most mineral exploration and extraction activities were limited during periods of snow and high moisture, the roads across the surface owners' lands were easily ruined by truck traffic. Accordingly, a lot of men who would otherwise be afield had hit the bar early and were several drinks up by lunchtime.

Gino Smith had been a part-owner and head bartender for more than a decade. During that time, he had seen and experienced a lot of things and —like all good bartenders—he had developed a sixth sense as it related to potential trouble. While filling ice buckets and cutting lemons and limes in preparation for the lunch rush, he eyeballed the men in the room, anticipating drink needs and performing a mental evaluation of the likelihood of each to cause trouble. He quickly determined the most likely source of any problems would be Casey Sprague, who had already downed several eyeopeners. Gino kept up with local developments and knew that Casey was no fan of the new arrivals in town, some of whom were now arriving in pairs for a quick lunch. A couple of loud parties had taken adjoining tables, and Gino was about to suggest a move by one side when he heard raised voices.

"See, I'm thinking these newbies," Sprague began, loud enough for anyone at nearby tables to hear, "what they need to do is pack their shit and go back to where all they came from, 'cause all they bring is trouble and maybe the clap." He smiled as his companions elbowed each other and looked surreptitiously at the adjoining table.

There, a large young man named Ian took the bait. "I'm thinking the fear of these old-timers is that their women are sick of their shit, and it will only be a matter of time before they leave their deadbeat, red-neck baby daddies for real men who make real money."

Gino wasn't sure who threw the first blow, but he had a call in to 9-1-1 within seconds, and then waded into the middle of the brawl. He fought with several men until the law—in the form of Custer Police Department Corporal Mike Jensen—arrived. Jensen knew the townies, of course, and got them under control quickly. The new men backed off under the threat of being tased. As backup arrived, Jensen got everyone separated and began to question men from both sides. Predictably, no one saw anything.

"Gino, what did you see?" Jensen asked.

"I didn't see anything," Gino said, looking at all parties. "I heard guys running their mouths, and then these jackasses started fighting. I need someone to pay for my chairs and that table."

"Are you wanting me to bring charges?"

"Not if my stuff is paid for," Gino said.

Jensen looked at the men gathered around, then to Gino. "Cash okay?"

"That'd be good."

"Well," Jensen said, "I'm gonna step outside and make a call on my radio. No one leaves. Gino, when me and my men come back inside, you can tell me if I'm going to need to write some citations or maybe take some folks down to the station."

"Thanks, Mike," Gino said. "I'm sure you'll be able to get on your way here in a minute."

Jensen walked out the front door. As he was leaving, he snuck a peek and saw several men reaching for their wallets.

13

Grant Lee's office was sparse, decorated only by a stock picture of a Wyoming landscape and—as required—his law degree and license to practice. Beyond that, the office was entirely bereft of any personal memorabilia, giving no insight into Lee as anything other than an attorney. He had called the meeting, and he motioned Cathy to sit as he finished a phone call. While she looked around and opened her portfolio to get a pen, he finished his business, drank from a plain white coffee cup, and then looked directly at her. "Good morning," he said.

"Good morning," she replied.

"How was your weekend?"

"It was fine," she began. "Kayla had a couple of games; I got a good workout in on Sunday morning. All in all, good. You?"

"Fine," he said simply. "So, the reason I wanted to talk with you has to do with what I'm told was some kind of disturbance a couple of days ago at the Longbranch Saloon."

"I don't know anything about it."

"Didn't you look at the police reports this morning? You really should be aware of what's happening."

Had her hair not covered her ears, he'd have seen them turning red.

"No, I didn't," she said tightly. "I'm due in a meeting with the county commissioners here shortly; that's my first priority."

"Understood," he said. "I'm just wondering what you might know. What I'm hearing is that there was a brawl there the other day, but no arrests were made. Wondering if you had any intel on the participants."

"You got their names?"

"Sure," he said. He read off a list of names and saw her nod and make a note at the mention of a couple. "Thoughts?"

"I think a couple of those folks are regular court customers—*local color*, if you will—but I don't see anyone who poses a particular problem. Why? Who filed the report?"

"Corporal Jensen."

"What are you looking for?"

"What I'm told happened was that a number of locals again attacked some employees of UkrCX—jumped them without provocation. I think the cops are still sorting out who did what, but what is clear is that the UkrCX employees were essentially blameless."

"Huh," she said. She hadn't missed the word "again." If the attacks had been unprovoked, she couldn't imagine Jensen not at least writing a citation. "I guess I'm surprised. Jensen is a good cop. A pro."

"Frankly, I'm surprised we haven't had more incidents like this, with some knuckle-dragging red-necks attacking newcomers—"

"Are you sure that's what happened?"

"Well . . . I mean, that's what the report indicates probably happened."

Cathy smiled. "Of course, no affidavit ever contains *facts* later shown to be wrong."

Lee stared hard at her. "Perhaps I am jumping to conclusions," he admitted. "But we need to take allegations of violence—especially political violence—seriously." His eye contact was constant and somewhat unnerving. "I'd like to get a beer sometime—see if we can hash out any possible differences we might have. Are you interested?"

"Absolutely," she said, feeling herself blush. "Sounds good."

"Great. I'm looking forward to hearing your thoughts on this and other issues," he said. "I've been out of town for a while; clearly, things have changed. But more change is necessary."

~

That evening the county commissioners convened and quickly approved the re-zoning changes necessary for Max to build his luxury ranch and runway outside Custer. Max had shown up and between bouts of heavy coughing had answered locals' questions thoroughly and completely. Sheriff's deputies patrolled the aisles, and the commission chair did a good job keeping the frequent interruptions brief. Several demonstrators were told to be quiet and respect the process; when they failed to do so they were summarily removed, some literally kicking and screaming.

Daniels appeared with Max, and—just as hoped—the mere appearance of the well-respected retired judge seemed to assuage some of the anger and won over some of the undecided attendees. Sam watched from the back of the room, careful not to involve himself directly in the proceedings. In addition to addressing citizen-voiced concerns directly, Max took the opportunity to vouch for himself and jobs that he contended would be created once full operations were up and running. He promised to limit inbound and outbound flights, and to limit use of the runway to working hours. He also bragged up the environmental considerations that had been undertaken and implemented in the design and build of his projects, as well as modernization efforts to be built into the coal plant. At the conclusion of Max's presentation, the commission voted to approve Max's plans on a 5-0 vote. Opponents left dejectedly and waited impatiently outside, ready to give full throat to their discontent before heading to the detention center to post bail for their more vocal comrades.

Sarah Penrose from the *Custer Bugle* got some quotes to play up the conflict angle she was seeking.

"This is going to be a disaster for wildlife in this area," said Marhji Crockett-Delino, president of the Custer Area Resource Council.

Regis O'Malley, spokesman for the Alliance of Environmental Organizations, told Penrose that "the commission's green-lighting UkrCX's operations will be the death knell for untold numbers of species of flora and fauna in the tri-state area."

Afterward, Sam and Daniels joined Max for a nightcap at his home. "Good job, men," Max said, hoisting a glass. He was joined by Daniels; Sam had waved off a drink—even a soft one. "That's a major portion of what we're trying to do; that leaves the building code variances on our downtown headquarters."

"And the multi-family housing," Sam reminded Max.

"That won't be an issue," Max assured him. "I've been through this before. It's impossible right now to define the word 'family.' Accordingly, a 'family' is whatever we say it is. We'll just tell the city council and the county commission that we're seeking an increase in residential density— they'll approve it, because they don't want to go down the same path as Jackson and Cody."

Sam and Daniels knew that both Jackson and Cody had seen the expansion of their towns with the building of large tracts of expensive single-family homes demanding services complicated by shrinking availability of housing for workers. The result had been gentrification as service workers flocked to leave the ever-increasing cost of housing, and then traffic congestion as those same workers tried to commute in from lower cost, outlying areas to do the jobs the homeowners needed done. "I think you're right," Daniels opined. He looked at the glass and licked his lips. Quality stuff.

"Agreed," Sam said. It would all happen. "Be careful, Max. A lot of people were there in opposition. Any one of them could prove to be dangerous."

Max recalled the corruption and bent noses he'd seen in Ukraine, then New Jersey. Comparatively speaking, this was lightweight stuff. "I'm not worried about it."

Sam could see doubt on Max's face. "I remind you, all it takes is one."

"You cannot possibly know how impervious I am to threats at this point in my life," Max said, then looked at Daniels and raised his glass. "Another?"

14

After Daniels had staggered off with Sam's assistance, Lana had knocked and entered. "Daddy, I wish you would take it easy on that stuff," she said. Max was somehow looking both slightly jaundiced and flushed at the same time. "You know I worry," she added.

"Yes, you do," Max said. He looked at her and remembered her mother. So tall, so beautiful. And such a nag.

"Mike said you aren't happy," Lana ventured. "I don't understand; it's all coming together. Dad, be realistic. Looking at the number of tasks and the complexity, the weather, and the slow pace of people around here—your deadlines are simply not realistic."

Max was not surprised by her chutzpah. "Thank you, my dear, for your opinion. I'll give it the respect and weight it deserves."

"Don't patronize me! I deserve better," she said. "You won't let me as a woman run the company, but you promised me you would give Mike a fair opportunity. That's what I expect—"

"Or what?"

"Well, I don't know. But you ride him mercilessly—no one could meet your expectations."

"We're about to find out."

"You wouldn't!"

"I damned sure will!" Max barked. "How do you know I haven't already changed the succession plan?" He looked to an uneasy Laika, who had gotten to her feet. "Sit down, girl," he ordered, and watched as Laika folded her legs and sat next to his chair.

"To give it to whom?"

"Alex."

He was bluffing. He must have spoken with Shapiro by now. "Oh, for Christ's sake—he's just a boy," she said.

"What do you suggest?" he asked, knowing full well what her response would be.

She knew he knew. "Me," she said quickly. "Daddy, I can—"

"No," Max said. "I will not."

"Just because I'm a woman—right?"

Max looked at his daughter the way one might look at a misbehaving child. "Exactly," he said. "Business—especially business like this—is no place for a woman."

"Dad, that's such crap! This is the twenty-first century. Women are leading businesses all over the world. Women are running cities, states, even countries!"

"And how's that working out?"

"What? Are you serious? Are you really going to blame women for the world going to hell in a handbasket?"

"Lana, you should be living a life of luxury. When are you and that husband of yours going to have children? Your babies would be beautiful—not due to him, of course. I'd love to be a grandfather."

While Max spoke, Lana stood, red-faced. "I simply cannot believe that you are my father," she said, hands on her hips. "My mother . . . how could she get mixed up with the likes of you?"

Max looked at Lana with no expression. "Because, just like every other woman, she calculated the possibilities. She decided what was best for her at the time." After the door slammed behind her, he leaned over and scratched behind the big dog's ears.

∾

Later, Lana traced a finger from the hollow of Alex's neck down over his muscular but hairless chest to his navel. "That was nice," she said. It wasn't really, but he was learning. You really could never tell. He looked like Adonis, but . . . oh well.

"It was," Alex agreed. "I—I was honestly having trouble focusing. I'm so excited about maybe taking over the company, you know?"

"I understand," she said. "But there are things to be done."

"I mean, in a few weeks—days maybe—I could be the head of UkrCX," he continued.

"Only if Mike is out of the way. Have you done what you told me you could do?"

"Yes," he said. "It looks like a chemistry lab in my room." When she didn't react, he continued. "What if Mike succeeds?"

"It won't matter," she assured him.

"Because I'm ready, right?" Alex asked eagerly. He placed a hand on her breast.

Removing his hand, she sighed heavily. "Alex," she began, "just listen to me and do what I tell you, and everything will be fine."

"And I'll get the company, right?"

"Everything will be fine," she repeated.

"This is so exciting," he said. "I mean, the plan, us being in this together—"

She pressed her fingers to his lips to quiet him. "Come here," she instructed.

15

Max inspected himself in the full-length mirror in the walk-in closet and shook his head disapprovingly. It wasn't so much the gray in his hair, the age in his eyes, or even the lines on his face—hell, he could probably fix most of that. Rather, it was the general shrinking and sagging. As a pilot in the Soviet and the Ukrainian Air Forces, he and his fellow aviators had kept themselves in generally tip-top condition (the "general" exception being copious amounts of vodka and the occasional black market American cigarette). But as time and life had gone by, and as his increasing success brought commensurately increasing responsibilities, staying fit had become a lesser priority. Turning sideways, he looked at his sagging belly and sunken chest, then clenched a fist and tightened a bicep. He sucked in his stomach and held his breath, then let it out. Aw, hell.

Today marked his sixty-fifth birthday, and he had invited his family, friends, and as many of the local VIPs as he could get to come to the party he was throwing to celebrate the occasion. He expected the mayor, the city council, the county commissioners, and local businessmen to be there—they'd better, given the money he was bringing to this town. A little respect would be nice. He was having a local barbeque joint cater the affair, and he'd had his private pilot bring in a case of fine champagne and a couple of pounds of caviar. The menu would be a ridiculous fusion, of course: pulled pork, brisket, and caviar. What the hell. He was sixty-five and staring down a death sentence. He'd eat whatever he wanted.

He selected the items chosen by his California tailor: dark jeans and a snap-button shirt. He debated adding a bolo tie but decided against it, figuring he'd look like he was trying too hard. He was using a shoehorn to don a boot when the sharp pain in his abdomen struck. Sitting back in the chair in the walk-in closet, he took several deep breaths. When that didn't work, he stood and paced, hoping movement would help. When it didn't, he drank from a bottle of water beside his bed. He swallowed as much as he could, then raced to the master bath and vomited blood. "Holy crap!" he said aloud, wiping his mouth with the back of his hand.

Paulie knocked on the outer door. "It's me, boss."

"Come in, Paulie," Max instructed. He smiled inadvertently when Paulie entered. Good old, faithful Paulie. He'd been by his side for a long time now. He should do something for him. "Paulie, do you need anything?"

Paulie was confused. The boss didn't ask him many questions. "What do you mean?"

"I mean just what I said," Max said. "Is there anything you need? Clothes, books, electronics . . . I don't know—a car?"

"I dunno . . . maybe," Paulie said uncertainly. "What's going on, boss?"

"Nothing. Just wondering if I can help you out. Can't a guy offer to help out his man without getting the third degree?" Max growled, then—seeing Paulie recoil in the face of his anger—he softened. "Sorry, Paulie. Not sure why I'm so sensitive," he said, knowing exactly why he was so sensitive. "You've been good to me. I just want to pay you back—"

"You've paid me plenty."

"Well, just before . . ." Max began, but went silent.

"I'm listening, boss," Paulie said when the silence became uncomfortable.

"Well, you know, something could happen. We're all one day at a time —right?" Max faked a smile through the shooting pain in his guts.

Paulie saw the grimace. "Boss, you okay? You want me to call the doctor?"

"No!" Max barked. Realizing he had been louder and more vehement than he intended, he again apologized. "I'm sorry, Paulie. Maybe a little nervous about the party. Gotta give a speech, you know?" Before Paulie could comment, there was another knock on the door. "Come in," Max said, and upon seeing Alex, continued with a strength he didn't feel. "What do you want?"

"Just checking in," Alex said. "The caterers are here, the bartenders are setting up, the band is outside. . . looks like things are coming along," he concluded, watching Max closely. "You okay, Max?"

"Yeah, why?"

"I don't know. You don't look good," Alex said, shaking his head doubtfully. "You look a little pale. Like maybe yellowish or something."

Max had done so much for the boy—it was infuriating to find out he was stealing him blind. To think that just a few weeks ago he was seriously considering giving him the company to run. "I'm fine. Maybe just a little tired. It happens. Help me with these boots, would you, son?"

"Of course." Alex grabbed the shoehorn. When he succeeded in getting Max in his boots, Paulie helped him to his feet.

"Ready to go, boss?" Paulie asked.

"I think so," Max said, then hesitated. "Paulie, give us a minute, huh?" After Paulie had departed, Max looked squarely at Alex. "It's becoming clear that Mike cannot handle this company. If you weren't stealing from me, I'd probably have left it to you."

Alex lost color. "Max, that isn't true. I—"

"I treated you like a son, and this is how you repay me? By stealing me blind?" Max asked. "Igor is rolling over in his grave."

"Max, I didn't—"

"Stop," Max said. "I just wanted you to know that I know. Now, go and get Paulie. And just know things will never be the same."

❧

The party was in full swing by the time Max, Paulie, and a still-reeling Alex joined. Paulie escorted Max to a chair in a corner of the sitting room just off the main living area. "You want me to get you a drink, boss?"

"Make it a double," Max said, looking into the bigger room and returning waves from some of the notable guests. He glanced over the crowd, making a mental note of who had shown, and who had failed to appear. The county's elected attorney was there—Rebecca Nice, if he recalled correctly—along with at least one of her assistants, Cathy something. He'd met her at the commissioners meeting. Nice-looking, that one. And tall! If he was thirty years younger . . . Press Daniels and Sam Johnstone were also in attendance.

Paulie brought his drink and Max took a long pull, then removed his notes from his breast pocket. Across the way, he could see Lana and Mike in a corner, speaking earnestly. Well, Lana was speaking—it looked as if Mike was listening intently to an ass-chewing.

In fact, that was exactly what was going on.

"You need to sober up," Lana seethed, sickened by the booze emanating from her husband. "Then you need to gut up. Get out there and mingle. Max has given you this final opportunity—don't blow it."

"It's no opportunity—it's a set-up," Mike snarled. "He has set me up so he can say I failed so he can install Alex in the position."

"Mike, shh—"

"Don't try and say any different!" he insisted loudly, oblivious to the stares of others.

Lana smiled as heads turned toward the commotion. "Then you need to figure out a way to get around him and make a success of this before you get bent over," she hissed in his ear.

"How about I put a bullet in his ass? That'd be a lot simpler, and a lot quicker." It came out "hish ash" and "shimpler."

"Mike, don't say that!"

"I only say what I mean," Mike slurred. "I'm gonna shoot that bastard."

With a broad, false smile, Lana put a hand on his shoulder and turned him toward an adjoining room and away from several of the guests, including one of the assistant county attorneys, who had clearly overheard, and a tall man she was speaking with. As Mike stumbled beside her, Lana rolled her eyes for all to see and made an empty-handed motion as if she was drinking.

∽

Sam and Daniels made their way through the crowd, Daniels introducing Sam to seemingly everyone. "Is there anyone around here you don't know?" Sam asked, chuckling as he swirled the remaining ice in a glass that had held diet cola.

"Not many," Daniels admitted. "And trust me: that can be good *or* bad."

Sam smiled. The pressing of flesh had never been his style, but Daniels had insisted, and if it was important to Daniels, it was important to him. Making his way to the edge of the room, Sam tried to take up a position against the wall. He was feeling some tightness in his chest, beginning to break a sweat, and was taking deep breaths and repeating a mantra suggested by Bob Martinez when he sensed movement to his right. As he turned to face what he thought might be a threat, he saw an outstretched hand and slapped it away.

"Ouch!"

It was Cathy Schmidt.

"I—I'm sorry," Sam stammered. "I thought . . . I . . . sorry," was all he could say.

"It's fine, Sam," she said apologetically. "I didn't mean to surprise you." Gesturing to the tall man next to her, she said, "I only wanted to introduce Grant Lee. He is an attorney in our office now."

Noticing Lee and Cathy were standing close together, he extended a hand in greeting. Lee looked at it and then away. "I haven't shaken hands since the pandemic started," he said. He was taller than Sam and looked over the crowd with practiced disinterest.

"Somehow, I'm not surprised," Sam said, drawing a sharp look from Cathy. He bit off a further rebuke and turned to walk away, but Cathy's voice stopped him. "Grant is from Custer. He's been gone for some time but has returned."

"I think I remember you," Daniels said, clearly hoping for a response. When Lee said nothing, Daniels turned his back and walked off, ears red.

Cathy saw what was happening and tried to fill the void. "Grant will prosecute felonies," she said. When Sam didn't respond, she continued. "He's been in Cheyenne for a time."

"My understanding is that there have been some issues obtaining convictions in major cases," Lee said. "I think that is about to change." He looked steadily at Sam, expecting a response.

Sam looked from Cathy to Lee and was sure they were together. He'd overestimated Cathy's judgment, perhaps. "Really?" Sam asked. "I guess I don't keep score."

When Sam turned and walked off, Lee smirked to Cathy. "They told me he was a tough guy."

She watched as Sam made his way through the crowd. "He's been very successful."

"I heard he's an alcoholic and a drug addict, PTSD, the whole gamut. Claims to be a hero. Just for your information, none of that matters to me. He steps in the ring with me, he's going down, just like everyone else has. These people have never seen anyone like me."

"I've never heard him claim to be a hero—quite the opposite, in fact. But my God, he lost a leg!" Cathy exclaimed.

"Doesn't make him a hero," Lee opined. "In fact, it could be the case that had he done a better job, he'da been fine."

Cathy looked hard at Lee. He was serious. "I'm gonna get a drink," she said.

~

Under Lana's watchful eye, Mike walked carefully to the center of the main room. "Ladies and gentlemen, can I have your attention?" he began. "Ladies and gentlemen?" he repeated, until the noise in the room had lessened. "Thank you. I want to begin by thanking each of you for attending this celebration of the birth of one of the greatest men I know. . . my father-in-law, Maxim Kovalenko." Mike looked to Lana, who beamed at Max as the crowd broke out in a round of polite applause.

"Mr. Mayor, members of the city council, commissioners, and friends and family, we appreciate you all being here tonight to celebrate Dad's 65th birthday!" he said, and led another round of applause. "Now, before I turn it over to Max, I just want to thank all of you for your hard work and assistance as we make the changes necessary to bring to fruition Max's vision." The crowd murmured its agreement. "Now, without further ado, the man of the hour, Max Kovalenko!"

Max waved off the applause and watched appreciatively as members of the staff rolled out a huge birthday cake. He got Lana to help him blow out the candles and then raised his hands to get everyone's attention. "I just want to say a couple of things to you, the people of Custer," he began. "First, thank you all for being here tonight. It means a lot. As I surveyed this wonderful nation looking for somewhere to bring my business, I had in mind the kind of community I was looking for. One that was comprised of hard-working, industrious people, eager to go into partnership with my firm in pursuit of one thing—a better life for us all. Wyoming was a natural fit, and after visiting several communities in this great state, it was obvious to me that Custer and its people had the right stuff. You're led by a fine mayor and city council; as we saw recently, your commissioners are open to new ideas; and your business community is accepting of open and fair competition." He looked around the room as the crowd gave itself an approving round of applause. "Now, despite what you may have read in that newspaper of yours, I want you all to know that we are here for the long term. That's my commitment to you. Now, how about you give yourselves a round of applause, considering your foresight and openness to new ideas?"

Max looked around the crowd for his children as the locals again enthusiastically saluted themselves. "Now," he continued. "I'd like to do some introductions. You all know me, but I think it is important for you to put faces to names. We've had some threats, so the local folks might as well know who they are threatening—don't you think?"

The joke fell flat. In the ensuing silence, several coughs were heard. Undaunted, Max continued. "I'd like to introduce my oldest daughter, Lana Kovalenko-Brown, and her husband, Mike Brown. Mike runs the company . . . for now," he said, gesturing to a smiling Lana and a stone-faced Mike.

Max looked over the crowd. "My beautiful baby daughter Stacy is here somewhere," he continued, his eyes bright. "Where are you, honey?"

"I'm here, Daddy," Stacy said from the back of the crowd. "Here I am." She made her way through the crowd and hugged her father, then stood close by his side.

"My son Danny should be here somewhere, as well," Max said uncertainly. He looked around the crowd. Not seeing Danny, he quickly looked to Alex. "And last, but certainly not least, my godson, Alex." Alex stepped forward and tried to hug Max, who brushed him off stiffly.

"This is my family," Max said. "And along with the two hundred or so employees who will soon be arriving, we are determined to put Custer on the map. We believe that everything will soon be in place to make Custer the cryptocurrency capital of America!" Max looked on approvingly as the crowd murmured in excitement. "Join me if you will in a toast," he said, raising a glass with a shaky hand. "To Custer, to UkrCX, and to success!"

"To success!" rang throughout the room. Sam took a quick swig of his now-refreshed cola, intrigued by the scene up front. Like all successful trial lawyers, he was an expert at reading people. Stacy and Max drank enthusiastically, Lana was guarded and watching her husband, Mike and Alex were downcast but trying to fake it. A younger man—Danny perhaps?—had joined them and drank deeply of what appeared to be a double vodka or gin.

Next to Sam, Daniels toasted and drank. "I think these folks will be good for the community," he said hopefully. Sam nodded in acknowledgement, his attention on Cathy.

"I'm not necessarily buying this," Lee whispered to Cathy, whose eyes met Sam's own. "I think there's something going on we don't know about."

"What do you mean?" Cathy asked.

"Why here?" Lee asked. "I mean, I know what he said, but seems to me that if Wyoming is the answer, he'd be better off down on the I-80 corridor somewhere. They've got more infrastructure, a location nearer to Denver or Salt Lake City—you know?"

"I guess." She shrugged. "But I'm inclined to take him at his word. I've got to believe he knows his business."

While Lee and Cathy were speaking, Lana had followed a furious Mike into a corner. "It didn't mean anything," she said. "I'm sure it was just a slip of the tongue, dear."

"Lana!" Mike exclaimed. "He's getting ready to run me and replace me with Alex."

"Then fight!" she said. "Alex is young. He doesn't know—"

"A damned thing," Mike finished for her. "The guy has never worked;

he's never had to decide anything with money on the line. He only follows Max around and kisses his ass. I'm not sure how or when that became enough." Mike finished his drink. "I'm going to get another—you ready?"

"Slow down!" Lana snapped. "You've had too many already."

"Yeah, well, maybe I'll get drunk and tell that crusty sonuvabitch what I think."

"I don't think that would be a good idea."

As Stacy and Danny approached, Mike gestured to Max's three children. "Look at you, afraid of one old man." While Lana, Danny, and Stacy exchanged looks of anger and embarrassment, Mike continued. "The old man owns you; you'll do whatever he says in order to stay in the running for a piece of the action when he kicks off."

Stacy's eyes were red and watery. "Mike—" she began.

"Don't try and act like it isn't true, Stacy. He owns you. He owns us all. I, for one, am tired of it, and I'm about ready to do something about it."

"Mike, stop," Lana scolded. "You're being dramatic."

"You'll think so when I put a bullet in him."

"Oh, for God's sake, go get your drink," Lana said.

"We'd all be better off," Mike insisted, ignoring her. "You all know he's going to change his will one of these days and leave everything to the fair-haired boy. And we are going to be left out."

"Go," Lana said, pointing to the bar. When Mike had left, she turned to her siblings. "Don't listen to him. He's under a lot of pressure. Max has been pestering him about progress on the various projects here—and he started on the single malt even earlier than usual."

"He's right, you know. Dad's gonna screw us over—I know he is," Danny said. "He won't hardly even talk to me."

"That's because you're wasted every time he sees you," Lana explained. "Get yourself together, Danny. Fake it around him, for Christ's sake. Take on a project or two and show him you are up to doing something besides getting high."

"Can he do that?" Stacy asked. "Cut us out?"

"I suppose he could," Lana allowed. "It's his money. But why would he? Right now, Mike is running the firm, and you and I are in good standing with him. He's got no reason to."

"But he could," Stacy observed. "And he and Alex—"

"Alex may not be as golden as he once was," Lana offered.

"Lana, you're fooling yourself," Danny said. "Clearly, he is positioning Alex to take over."

"That's not going to happen," Lana assured him.

"Why not?"

"Because if something were to happen to Mike, I'm the next most qualified person to take over," Lana said.

Danny snorted. "You?"

"Yes," Lana said tightly. "Me."

"You're a woman, Sis. Dad's old school. He doesn't think women have any business running . . . business," Danny said. He put down his glass and pointed at Max, who was entertaining VIPs across the room. "I know this. I'm not getting shut out. I'm a member of this family and I deserve a full share of whatever he's got, just for putting up with his bullying. If I don't get it—"

"Go join Mike at the bar, Danny," Lana said. "The two of you can piss on each other's feet. We don't want to hear it, do we?" she asked Stacy.

"Daddy just thinks I'm pretty," Stacy said, fiddling with an olive in the bottom of her glass. "I don't think he knows what I'm capable of. No one does."

~

Twenty minutes later, Sam was making his way to the front door when Lana put a hand on his arm. "Mr. Johnstone? Do you have a minute?"

"Call me Sam. I suppose I do."

"For a client, I mean."

"You want to talk business here?"

"Bill me."

She wasn't the client, but what the hell. "Sure. Let's step over here so we can have a little privacy."

"Attorney-client privilege?"

He pointed at his ear. "Too much automatic weapons fire in my prior life." When they had found a suitable corner, Sam looked at her expectantly. "What's up?"

"I'm just looking for an update."

Sam looked over her shoulder at Max, who was in an earnest conversation with the mayor, and at Mike, who was pouring himself three fingers. Sam remembered those not-so-long-ago days. Open bar . . . lots of women. . . He focused on Lana. "I don't mean to be rude or anything, but you're not the client."

"I'm Mike's wife!"

"I know that."

"Look," Lana said. "I just want to get a feel with where you are—how things are coming along, you know?"

"I understand, but—"

"Sam, Mike is too drunk to do business tonight. But if you insist, I'll bring him over and we can prop him up against the wall and you can tell him the same thing then. Max is pressuring Mike and we need an update."

Sam considered his options. Technically, he shouldn't be talking to anyone other than Max or Mike, but if he didn't tell her now, he'd surely get a phone call later. "Depends on the issue," Sam began. He then laid out the status of the various ongoing projects. "All in all, I think we are making pretty good progress," he concluded.

Lana had focused intently on him throughout his recitation, her blue eyes narrowing from time to time. "What do you need from me? I mean, what can we do to speed things along?"

"I'm not sure," Sam mused. "It's all going to get done, but it will take some time."

"What's the long pole in the tent?"

"The headquarters. It took a lot of work to get downtown re-zoned, and now he comes along and wants a variance. But if he is good on his offer to kick in some cash to help with the schools and services, we'll get it done, Press thinks. Same with the two hundred housing units. Now, I've already let the neighbors know that Max intends to stand on his rights on the property crossing issue—although that might be a good bargaining chip."

"What do you mean?"

"I mean if he was willing to give on that issue, it might give the politicians a little breathing room with the locals on the housing and downtown deals."

"Dad doesn't negotiate."

"I see that." Sam was watching Max. He was now in an obviously heated conversation with Alex, who put a finger in Max's chest, whereupon Paulie appeared and grabbed Alex's hand. "What's going on with your father?" Sam asked Lana, nodding toward Max.

"He hasn't been himself," she said. "At first, I was attributing it to the stress of this move and the relocation of business and all that, but now—oh my gosh!" She rushed to help while Sam followed.

∿

Across the room, Max and Alex had their heads close together. "It's not true," Alex said.

"Bullshit," Max said. "I knew something was up with my accounts. I spoke with Abe Shapiro's kid. He confirmed it."

"There must be a mistake!"

"The only mistake was made by you. Now get out of my face," Max said. He was bent at the waist, coughing. "And here I had changed my succession plan in order to give you the entire company," he lied. "I have given it all to you, but now it is going back to Mike. You're done here."

"You can't do this!" Alex said loudly.

"I can. And what I am going to do is talk with my lawyer to ensure that not only do you take nothing from my estate, but that you pay me back every red cent you stole. Now, go pack your stuff before I have Paulie throw your ass out."

Alex looked at Max for a long moment. "You are going to regret this, old man." He stepped forward and poked a finger into Max's chest. "We're not done here."

Paulie appeared out of nowhere and grabbed Alex's hand. As nearby partygoers watched, he squeezed hard, bringing Alex almost to his knees. "Mr. Alex, go away," Paulie said firmly. Only when Alex nodded acquiescence did Paulie release his grip. "Go."

Max was about to fall when Lana rushed up and took her father by the arm. "Dad, what's going on?"

"It's—It's nothing," he said.

"Let's get him a chair," Lana directed. Several people rushed into the next room and appeared simultaneously with chairs. Lana pointed to a large lounge chair. "There," she said. "Let's get him in that one."

A small crowd including Sam and Daniels gathered in concern. Sam noted that while Lana dealt with Max the rest of the family stood back some distance, watching.

"Our problems might resolve themselves," Mike said under his breath to Danny and Stacy.

"Mike! Don't say that!" Stacy said.

"Why not? You know you feel the same way." He took a sip from his glass and crunched ice. "Maybe it's time for some new thinking."

"Or just sell it off and use the money to live on," Danny said.

Mike looked dolefully at Danny. "I figured that's what you'd think."

"Stop it! Both of you! Daddy's sick," Stacy sobbed.

"Can I help?" Sam offered, having made his way through the crowd. He'd seen the life drain out of people, and he didn't like Max's color. "Has someone called the doctor?"

"I don't need a doctor," Max said through a clenched jaw. "Must be something I ate. Paulie, can you help me upstairs?"

"I'll help, too," Lana said.

"No, dear. I need you to stay here and keep the company entertained," Max said. "I might be back down later." Daniels had followed Sam, and he and Sam exchanged a look of doubt.

When Max had been helped from the room, the crowd noise resumed. Lana joined Mike at the bar. "Mike, just stay calm," she cooed. "Dad is ... unwell."

Next to Mike and Lana sat Lee and Cathy, who couldn't help but overhear.

"The sooner we get rid of that old bastard, the better off we will all be," Mike said. "I swear if I find out he is changing the succession plan I'll shoot the sunovabitch."

"Another round?" Lee asked Cathy. He actually smiled.

16

Several days later, Max sat at the end of the table, picking at his food while the staff busied themselves pouring wine and serving dessert. He was feeling a little better today, so he indicated he needed a refill.

"Dad, are you sure?" Lana asked. "You've been doing so well. With your stomach—"

Max looked at her sharply. "Lana, dear, I think I'm perfectly capable of deciding for myself whether to have another glass of wine."

"You should listen to her, Dad." It was Danny, and it came out "lishen."

The boy was sloshed—as always. If it wasn't that damned cocaine, it was the booze. "You're one to talk," Max replied tersely.

"I'm not sick," Danny said.

"Then what the hell is your excuse?"

"For what?"

"For everything!" Max pounded the table with his fist, forcing the family members to steady their wine glasses. "For being a loser! For being a son of whom I am ashamed!"

"Daddy, please don't get angry," Stacy pleaded. "It can't be good for you."

Max smiled at Stacy. Beautiful, empty-headed Stacy. "Vacuous" was the

American word, maybe. "Stacy, dear, your brother is a waste of good DNA," he said, taking joy in Danny's discomfort. He looked at Mike, who observed quietly, no doubt hoping Max's guns would not get turned on him. Alex studied the table in front of him. Only Lana met his gaze. Behind him, he knew, Paulie would be watching everyone carefully.

"Maybe what I needed was a chance," Danny said. "Instead, you put Mike in charge—how's that working out for you?" he sneered.

"Screw you," Mike muttered. "Drunk bastard."

Lana put a hand on her husband's arm. "Danny, I think you've had about enough," she said. "Why not call it a night?" she added sweetly.

"He's had every chance to make a go of this," Danny insisted. "Meanwhile, I'm his own son and I get nothing!" He looked around the room. "And I think we all know who will get the next shot—Alex, the fair-haired boy, waiting in the wings for his shot to run the company that should rightfully be ours!"

"Danny, I—" Alex began.

"You gold-digging bastard! Kissing Dad's ass, hoping for your chance. See? This is why I've been saying that when Dad . . . passes, we should just sell the company and split the assets before Mike runs everything into the ground!"

Stacy looked like she was going to burst into tears. "Danny, stop it!"

Max watched Alex closely. "I want nothing of the sort," Alex said. "I just want what's best for your father, after all he's done for me."

Alex looked at Lana for support, Max noted. She didn't disappoint. "Danny, Alex is Dad's godson—he is a member of this family. Please, just go somewhere and cool off." Mike was looking at Lana—her failure to defend him hadn't gone unnoticed.

"Danny, I don't know where your mother went wrong," Max said. "Go somewhere and sleep it off." He and the others watched while Danny stood unsteadily and then left. Stacy followed, presumably to console her brother.

Mike then stood. "I don't have to listen to this," he said. "I'll see you all in the morning." He slammed the door behind him as he left.

Max looked at Lana and Alex. "Anyone else want to take a shot at the old man?" He grinned briefly, then sobered. Now was as good a time as any. "Paulie, will you leave us? I'll have you join me here in a minute." When Paulie had closed the door, Max looked at Alex and Lana in turn. "Normally, I don't get involved in my children's sex lives, but in this case, I'm going to make an exception. I—"

"What—what are you talking about?" Lana began.

"Oh Lana, please do not ever think I am stupid," Max counseled as he shook his head sadly. "I know the two of you are having an affair—I've known since almost the moment it began. I will not have the two of you screwing in my house. It is not good for family; it is not good for business. These things never end well. So, do what you need to do—"

Lana had gone pale. She'd thought they'd been discreet. "Dad, you are mistaken," she interjected uncertainly.

"Lana, stop. I know what I'm seeing, and I'm telling you that it must end," Max said. "I'm old, but I'm not stupid." Again, Max lied in an effort to inflict pain. "I've changed my succession plan to give Alex control, but with this betrayal I cannot in good conscience allow that. I'm going to return succession to Mike. Lana, infidelity is above all things reflective of a person's judgment and ability to live up to their word. Should this affair continue, I will assure you there will be no place for either of you not only in UkrCX or any other company I run, but in any estate I leave behind." Max shook his head sadly. "Lana, I am disappointed in you. Alex was like a son to me. Now, both of you, please leave me, and ask Paulie to rejoin me."

∾

Outside the room, after Paulie had returned to check on Max, Lana and Alex spoke quickly in harsh whispers. "Sonuvabitch! How did he find out?" Alex asked.

"It's his house. I'm sure he has spies everywhere," she said. "This is a disaster. We're going to lose everything."

"Except us."

"Us?"

"Lana . . . I can't . . . I don't want to be without you," Alex offered. "I'm willing to forego any shot, any job—"

He was too young, too immature. She should have seen it coming. "Oh, shut up, Alex." Damn it! She should have stayed well away. "Don't say stuff like that," she hissed. "Go. Now." When he hesitated, she pointed. "We'll talk later, but we need to act now!" Oh, Lord—what had she been thinking?

17

Custer County Sheriff's Department Investigator Thiago "Ted" Garcia had parked his unmarked car and was standing in a dirt lot, trying to determine which of the half dozen or so run-down mobile homes he had been called to. The neighborhood was five miles from town at the end of a dirt road, and was locally referred to as "Felony Flats," because its rural location was such that men and women convicted of sex crimes could reside here, away from schools, day care facilities, recreation centers, and other places children might gather without violating the terms and conditions of parole or probation. Despite the late hour and drifting snow, about half the front doors were open, and he could see children peeking through the windows and adults scurrying about—probably attempting to cache drugs. He had been called at the request of EMS, who had been called by rookie deputy Brooke Schmidt.

Emergency Medical Technician Mary Stewart approached Garcia while he donned gloves and booties. "Evening, Ted," she said.

"Hi, Mary. What do we have?"

"Overdose—I'm thinking fentanyl," she said, turning to lead him into a particularly ramshackle structure.

"Is he alive?"

"Yeah. Schmidt gave him a shot of naloxone, which brought him back," she said. "We've got him up and alert now."

Garcia entered the trailer and was immediately assaulted by the smell of cat urine. Dirty diapers, dog feces, and empty food containers littered the floor. The victim and soon-to-be suspect was sitting on the couch, with Schmidt standing close by. Garcia indicated with a motion of his head that he wanted to talk with Schmidt alone. She followed him to a corner where they could speak without fear of being overhead, except by the microphones they were wearing. That was fine, as far as Garcia was concerned—what he didn't want was the defendant hearing him yet.

"Good job," he said to Schmidt. "You okay?"

"I'm fine," she said. "First time I've had to do that."

"You saved his life."

She snorted and indicated the surroundings. "Why?"

"I understand," Garcia said. "Think of it this way: maybe today is the day."

"For what?"

"Maybe today is the day he will decide to change."

"Maybe," she said. "I feel so sorry for that little boy."

"I know," Garcia said. "What happened?"

"I was patrolling Highway 27, and dispatch called. Said the child's grandmother had been at work while the child was home alone with his uncle, a guy named Kyle White. Not sure why, but apparently she had been using FaceTime to check on the child throughout the night—"

"Why wasn't the kid in bed?"

Schmidt made a face. "Who knows? In any event, at some point the kid said, 'Kyle is blue.'"

"Sounds like fentanyl."

"Yeah. So the grandmother—her name is Misty Layton—had the little boy put the phone by the dude and she could see he was blue and called it in."

"What's she do?"

"I think she works at a convenience store in town," she said. "According to Layton, her son is a heroin addict."

"Okay, I think I got it," Garcia said. "What's his name again?"

"Kyle White."

"Let's go see him," Garcia said, and led Schmidt over to White, who was sitting on the couch, drinking water under the watchful eye of a couple of EMS technicians. "Mr. White, I'd like to talk with you for a minute."

"About what?" White asked. He was sitting and appeared to be of average height, but only about 120 pounds. His brown hair was long and cut in a mullet. Tattoos covered one side of his neck and he had a small tattoo in the shape of a star at his right temple. Long hairs—you couldn't really call it a mustache—adorned his upper lip. He donned and removed his flat-brimmed baseball cap repeatedly.

"About what happened tonight," Garcia said.

"I—I don't know. I wasn't feeling well. I think I passed out."

Garcia turned to Schmidt. "What is it about me that makes guys like this think I'm stupid?" When Schmidt merely shrugged, he turned his attention back to White. "You overdosed on fentanyl. You know it; we know it; now you know we know it. This deputy saved your life." Garcia watched closely as White took his hat off and put it back on. "Is there any more fentanyl in the house?"

"I dunno what you're talking about. I worked like twelve hours yesterday. I'm tired."

"You're what? Not even thirty? And you're tired after a twelve-hour day? Bullshit. I'd like to look around and make sure there aren't any drugs here —nothing that could hurt the kid, you know?" Garcia said. "You don't mind if we search the place, do you?"

White sat and thought, calculating his response. "Yeah, I do," he said at last. Indicating the hallway, he said, "I gotta piss."

"Not until we check to make sure there are no drugs here," Garcia said. "That's your nephew, right?"

White nodded. "I'm babysitting on top of working."

"And it looks like you've done a fine job. Kyle, I'm gonna get a warrant. You're just gonna have to pinch it off until I can get that bathroom searched," Garcia said. He looked to Stewart. When she nodded, Garcia turned his attention back to White. "Stand up."

"Why?"

"Because Deputy Schmidt here is going to arrest you for use of a controlled substance," he explained. "Read him his rights, Schmidt."

"I told you, man—I'm just tired!" White wailed.

"Life's a bitch," Garcia said over his shoulder as he walked toward the front door, where a couple of additional deputies waited. "Okay, secure the place."

~

Circuit court judge Melissa Downs had been appointed a couple of years earlier, following the suicide of her predecessor in the wake of revelations regarding philandering and drinking that had arisen during a murder trial. She'd been practicing civil litigation in Cheyenne when her husband of ten years got a seven-year-itch and decided one day marriage "wasn't for him." In a fit of pique, she applied for the judge job and—to her unending surprise—had been appointed to the bench by the governor. She'd moved herself and her now eleven-year-old daughter to Custer to start anew, and for the most part was enjoying the job and the community. She was dozing on a loveseat in her upstairs bedroom when the phone rang and managed to pick it up on the third ring.

"Evening, ma'am. It's Ted Garcia. I've got a warrant I need you to look at. We had a guy overdose tonight in front of a four-year-old. I've got officers on site."

Downs sat up straight and pulled her pajama top closed with one hand. "Thank you, Deputy. Send it," she directed, and swung her feet to the floor. He would be sending the warrant via email. She kept her laptop downstairs on the advice of a more experienced judge who had advised her to do so. "As painful as it is," he had said, "you've got to make yourself get out of bed. Otherwise, you'll sign anything." She opened the door to her daughter's room and heard her breathing softly. Fortunately, her daughter was a heavy sleeper, because as the only circuit court judge in the county, Downs was always on call, and received calls two or three nights per week on average.

Making her way down the steps to the small kitchen where she kept her laptop, Downs heard the audible tone of an arriving email. "Good," she said to herself. "Let's get this over with." She read the affidavit of probable cause and the warrant, signed the warrant electronically, then sent them back to Garcia. Then she drank a large glass of water and made her way back upstairs to see if she could go back to sleep.

Despite the advances in technology, there were still vestiges of the nineteenth century in Wyoming law, among them the requirement for a paper copy of the search warrant to be served on the defendant. Garcia heard the tone on his phone and went to his car. He keyboarded in a password and opened the document, then forwarded it to the desk sergeant, who would hand it off to a deputy who would race to Garcia's location with a hard copy.

While he waited, Garcia moved to the leeward side of the trailer and smoked—the department frowned on smoking in its cars. In the adjacent trailer, he could hear a couple arguing. In her opinion he drank too much; he opined it was because she was a nag. Same old, same old. When a car with two operable headlights came up the drive at a high rate of speed, Garcia stamped out his smoke, left the sheltered space, and stepped into the driving snow. He waved and the deputy pulled up to him, window already down. "Here you go," he said.

"Thanks," Garcia said, taking the copies. He tucked them in his jacket to protect them as he walked to Schmidt's car and served White with a copy of the warrant.

"You won't find anything," White assured him.

"We'll see," Garcia said, then headed to the trailer. Inside, he stomped his feet at the door and nodded to the deputies. "Do it," he instructed. "Be careful, now. Don't reach into any spaces without looking first," he cautioned, not wanting his officers to get jabbed by an unprotected needle. More than one officer had needed emergency treatment after poking himself.

Garcia sat on a rickety chair at a table in the dining area and looked at his phone while the search got underway. He was reading box scores from the night's late season baseball games when a small, frail woman of about forty appeared at the front door. "Hello?" she said.

"Come in," Garcia instructed. "Are you Misty Layton?"

"I—I am," she said. She pushed a lock of pink hair back from her face to reveal red-rimmed eyes. "Where's my grandson?"

"He's safe," Garcia assured her. "We sent him home with the agent from the Department of Family Services. I think they will get him checked out, and then find a home for him to stay in tonight."

"I want my grandson!" she shrieked, startling Garcia. "And where's my dog?"

Garcia had seen the dog crap on the floor, but no dog. "I haven't seen him. What kind of dog is it?"

"He is a French Bulldog. My ex bought him for me. He is worth two thousand dollars."

Garcia nodded. A two-thousand-dollar pooch in a five-hundred-dollar residence. "We're conducting a search right now. When—"

"What are you looking for?"

"Illegal drugs, paraphernalia."

"It's in a package in the ceiling of my son's bedroom."

"Which is his?"

"Down the hall, to the left," she said. "There's also some in that safe in his room," she added. "I want you out of my house. I want my grandson home. I want things back to normal," she concluded, wiping her nose with the back of her hand.

Garcia choked down a comment regarding her definition of normal and looked at her closely. "Where do you work?" he asked.

"Down at the all-night convenience store on Teton." Teton Avenue was the main east-west route through Custer. "I'm the assistant manager and night auditor."

"I thought you looked familiar. So, you were working tonight and Mr. White . . . he's your son?"

"Yes." She shrugged. "He just got outta the pen and needed a place to stay, and I needed someone to watch Ari."

"Ari?"

"Aristotle. My grandson," she explained.

"Where's the mother?"

"In jail."

"Who's the father?"

"Hell if I know," she said. Seeing Garcia's look, she explained. "My daughter was going through a rough patch, okay? There—there were a couple of guys. Kyle went off to prison, my daughter got sent to jail, and I was left with Ari. When Kyle got paroled, he asked if he could hang out until he got back on his feet, so I said, 'Okay, but you gotta watch Ari while I work.'"

"And he's been doing that?"

"Well, kinda. I mean, sometimes I get home and Ari hasn't had a bath or been fed. That's why I was doing the videoconference with him."

"He's four years old and he can videoconference?"

"Oh, yeah," she said, beaming with pride. "Sometimes he will call me and tell me to bring him ice cream."

Garcia smiled despite himself. "But tonight was different?"

"Well, kinda. It was slow so I was trying to tell Ari to go to bed, but he was wound up. I kept trying to get Kyle to put him down but Kyle was . . . different, you know? And then Ari called me and said, 'Kyle's tired and blue,' so I told him to show me, and he put the phone next to Kyle's face and . . . well, I couldn't leave work, so I called you guys."

The lives these people led. "Okay, well, anything like this ever happen before?"

"You mean has he ever overdosed? Oh, yeah. It happens from time to time." She shrugged as if it was as natural as the sun coming up.

"You leave your grandson with an addict?"

Misty's eyes turned to slits and her face reddened. "What else am I supposed to do? I can't afford daycare, my own mom tossed me, my dad is nowhere to be found, and my brother's in jail. His mom's in jail and we don't know who the father is. I gotta work to put food on the table. You people judge me, but you don't have any ideas—do you?"

"What was Kyle in for?"

"Some bullshit involving child porn—he says someone hacked his computer."

"Jesus Christ! You're leaving your grandson with a child molester?"

"Well, I got no real choice now—do I?"

Garcia was about to reply when Schmidt emerged from the back bedroom. "Boss, you wanna take a look?"

Garcia followed her back to the bedroom and saw needles, guns, cash, and foil packages in the safe. On the bed a number of plastic containers from Colorado marijuana dispensaries were laid out in neat rows. Deputies were photographing the scene. "Okay," Garcia said. "Finish the pictures, then bag it. I want fingerprints, too."

"For the dispensary stuff?" Schmidt asked. "What good does that do?"

"Never know," Garcia said. He walked back to where Misty was waiting. "Misty, looks like you're gonna have to come with us. Schmidt here is going to read you your rights."

"Wait, what? What am I being charged with?" Misty was on her feet.

"Possession and endangering a child, as an initial matter," he said. "I'll think about it driving back. Might be some more charges coming your way."

"Wait! I—I can give you some information! I know where Kyle is getting his stuff! I can give you that!"

"We'll talk tomorrow," Garcia said with a nod toward Schmidt. "Get her on out of here." He could hear Misty's protestations as she was taken outside.

"I can't go to jail! I'll lose my job! My grandson! Where is my grandson?"

Garcia shook his head sadly as he toed a filthy teddy bear with a damp boot. "Okay, lock it up, and tape it up," he directed.

18

Nothing could match the adrenaline rush provided by the engine thrust from an Su-24 Fencer, but that was a long time ago, and a close second was mounting a half-ton quarter horse and riding overland. Bred for working cattle, trained from the start by professionals, and selected by trusted associates, Max's stock was comprised of big, strong, well-behaved animals. He was cognizant that behind his back friends and family belittled him for "playing cowboy," but he had learned to ride competently and—as with all other aspects of his life—cared little for others' opinions. Thus, just after dawn on a mid-October morning, Max, Paulie, Alex, and Mike set out for a half day's ride around the ranch.

Paulie hated riding horses. The big animals, to his way of thinking, were dumb, temperamental, and, well, scary. His trepidation was not lessened by the presence of Laika. Paulie was certain the dog made the horses uneasy. But riding had become part of the job, so when the boss said, "Mount up!" he did exactly that.

Neither Alex nor Mike enjoyed riding, but they did grimly what they had to do to keep Max happy. Moreover, at this point, the competition between them was open and fierce; because neither suspected the other was on the outs with Max, neither was willing to allow Max to spend too much time unaccompanied by the other. They'd sullenly dressed and saddled their animals, slid their rifles into their scabbards, and mounted their horses in silence. Just before they departed, Lana had appeared and handed both of them bottles of water. "Have fun," she'd said to Mike. "Good luck today," she'd said to Alex.

In a spitting snow, the four men departed in silence from what would one day be the new ranch headquarters and rode a couple of miles up a dry creek bed, then over a series of small hills to an overlook that afforded Max a view of much of his land. While the others remained mounted, he dismounted and walked around the hilltop, glassing the horizon with a pair of binoculars. Mike stifled a chuckle when Max bent over, snapped off a piece of dead grass, and placed it in his mouth. "God, I love this place, boys," Max said, looking up at the three men.

"I know you do, sir," Paulie said. "But look at the weather. I don't have to be a cowboy to know a storm is headed this way. You heard what they said on that weather channel."

"Max, I think Paulie's right," Mike said. "I'm thinking we ought to head on back."

Max ignored the younger men. "No other people around for miles, and except for you three, there's no one flapping their lips. No internet, no wireless—by God, it's like being alive again! Just think: that American General Custer this area was named after might have scouted for Indians from right here!"

"Could be," Alex agreed. The old man was going batty.

Max resumed glassing the property while the others held their mounts steady, silently praying Max would come to his senses and direct their return to the ranch headquarters before the weather turned. Suddenly, Max extended an arm in a northerly direction. "Look!"

"What is it?" Mike asked.

"The rat bastards are crossing my land! Mike, I thought I told you to keep those people out?"

"Max, our lawyer—Sam—he spoke with their leader just the other day," Mike said. "He said he told them permission to cross had been withdrawn."

"Damn it, man. This is one more thing you have failed to get done."

Mike sat red-faced on his mount, knowing that Alex was likely smirking next to him. Paulie used his own binoculars to scan, and soon saw the trespassers. Maybe a dozen riders, perhaps half a mile in the distance, near the boundary of Max's property and the school section the group was intending to access. "There's a bunch of them."

"I'll tell Sam later," Mike offered. "Maybe he can get an injunction or—"

"No," Max said. "We need to stop them. Now. They need to know I am not going to put up with this."

"How we gonna do that?" Mike asked. "By the time we get down there they will be off your property."

"Not if we get going," Max said. "We are going to ride down there and tell them to get off my land."

"Max," Mike protested. "Look how many there are. What are we gonna do if they refuse?"

"They won't," Max assured him. "Let's go!" When no one moved, he shook his head in disgust. "Oh, hell," he said, and spurred his horse forward. Paulie started to object, but before Max had ridden twenty yards, he pulled his horse to a stop and then leaned forward to the point where Mike feared Max's chest would be pierced by the saddle horn.

"Max, what's wrong?" Mike asked, riding up beside him.

"Just—just a little pain in my chest," Max assured him. "Might be dehydrated," he added.

Quickly, Paulie uncapped a water bottle he had earlier affixed to his own saddle. "Drink this, Max," he urged his boss.

As Max drank deeply, the others watched closely. When Max appeared as if he might tumble from the saddle, Mike had seen enough and dismounted. "Here. Let me get you down before you fall. Paulie, can you give me a hand?"

Max didn't argue, and Paulie assisted Mike in removing him from his mount and setting him gently on the ground. Laika lurked uneasily nearby, watching Paulie and emitting a low growl that ceased only when Paulie stepped clear of Max. Mike handed Max the reins to his horse. "Why don't you have a seat over there?" he suggested, pointing to an enormous ponderosa pine stump. "I'll join you."

"The hell you will," Max said, before breaking into a coughing fit. When he got his breath back, he pointed at the intruders. "Do—do what I told you. All of you. Get them off my land."

"Max, we—"

"I'll be fine," Max insisted. "Better, if I know my property is not being trespassed. I'll be fine. Laika will keep me safe," he added, patting the dog, who had quickly settled on the ground next to him.

Mike was observing Max closely. He didn't like his color and didn't feel right doing anything except maybe riding to somewhere he could get a signal to call 9-1-1. He made eye contact with Alex, who shrugged helplessly. He certainly wasn't going to do or say anything to anger Max.

Paulie tried one last time to dissuade Max. "Are you sure?"

"Go," Max directed, then coughed and spit.

"We'll be right back," Mike said, dropping his bedroll to Max. He turned his horse into the wind, stole a look backward, and saw Max drawing the blanket from the bedroll around himself and Laika. He put the spurs to the big animal, and with Paulie and Alex in his wake, he began to ride toward the trespassers. After cresting a small knoll, where Max's line of sight was interrupted, he pulled his horse to a stop and addressed Alex. "I don't think this is very smart."

"I agree," Alex said. He was looking alternately back toward Max's location and ahead to the trespassers. "I think he needs help. How about I see if I can get service and ask one of the hands to bring a utility vehicle up here to get Max?"

"That works," Mike agreed. "Let's link back up right here." He spurred his horse toward the trespassers, who were now almost off Max's land. They had seen Mike and Paulie approaching and turned their horses to face them. Mike felt his pulse quicken as he and Paulie rode up moments later.

"Folks, this is private property," he began. "I'm gonna have to ask you to leave. You are trespassing."

"Well now, that's your opinion—is it?" The speaker was a large man Mike recognized as Casey Sprague. "We gotta right," he added, indicating his companions.

"Well, I'm not so sure," Mike said. "Our lawyer spoke with some of you about not trespassing here."

"And I think I made clear to Sam that we've been crossing the property for decades. We got adversarial possession, or some such legal mumbo jumbo."

Mike was more afraid of taking a bad result back to Max than he was of these men, but as they had spoken, a semi-circle had formed around him and Paulie. "Well . . . again, that's not how Max sees it," he said, and swallowed hard.

Sprague laughed. "Well too damned bad," he said derisively. "'Cause we don't give a damn. We was here long before he ever heard of Wyoming." As he said that, he nodded almost imperceptibly to a couple of his riders, who quickly rode off to the south. He nodded again, and two more rode off, this time to the east.

Mike was now faced with only four riders but had no idea where the others were. Nor did he know Alex's whereabouts. And he needed to get back to Max, whatever the ass-chewing he would take. "Well, I've warned you," he said lamely.

"Oh, for sure," Sprague sneered.

Mike and Paulie backed their horses away, with Paulie making sure to keep eyes on Sprague, then rode back to retrieve Max, looking for Alex along the way. When Mike heard what he thought was a gunshot, he glanced at Paulie, who was looking in the direction where they'd left Max. "Did you hear that?"

Paulie shook his head. "I can't hear anything," he said.

The snow had picked up, and as Mike rode, he mentally rehearsed what he would say to Max, who would be nothing less than furious. The wind was howling, blowing little specks of snow into his eyes. As he topped the final ridge to where he thought they'd left Max, he saw Max's horse cantering down the dry creek bed, unmounted. The old man had somehow lost control of the reins!

"Can you round him up?" Mike asked Paulie, who nodded, then turned his horse to follow Max's mount.

Mike resumed his ride toward Max's location. He wiped snow from his eyes and rode on, dreading the upcoming conversation with Max. As he topped the hill he saw the stump, but he didn't see Max. He rode up quickly, then circled the stump, assuming Max had moved to the leeward side. He looked at his watch—they'd been gone about half an hour. Max was afoot—where could he have gone? Mike quickly dismounted and scanned the ground, looking for footprints. He was no outdoorsman, but it didn't take a genius to know the blowing snow had already obscured the direction of Max's travel.

"Max!" he yelled as loudly as he could into the wind, startling his ride. He patted the horse's withers to calm it and then yelled again, cocking an ear into the wind, hoping to hear a response. Thinking a better vantage point might solve his problem, he mounted and rode two hundred yards to the west, stopping near a tree-covered ridgeline. He could see no sign of Max or the others. Could the shot have been Max, alerting him to his location? Mike drew his rifle from the snow-crusted scabbard and fired a single shot into the air, then listened for a shot in response.

He had read somewhere that when searching for people, rescue teams gridded off areas, or if they didn't have enough manpower, they would search in ever-widening circles. He rode back down to the stump and began to walk the big horse in a clockwise circle. When he was back on the face of the timbered ridge, it occurred to him that he could be missing something from horseback, so he tied the horse off on an aspen and continued on foot. He had made a complete circle on foot when he came upon Paulie's and Max's horses, tied next to his own.

"Paulie?" he yelled.

"I'm here," Paulie said, stepping out from behind a stand of trees and zipping up. "What's going on? Why are you walking?"

"I can't find Max!" Mike yelled into the wind. "I fired to alert him."

"Is that what I heard?" Paulie asked. "He can't have gotten far in this snow."

"I don't know," Mike said. "Why would he have left in the first place?" The protection of the stump was as good as anything. He gave Paulie the plan, then pulled his collar up, yanked down on his hat, and restarted his search. Paulie did the same, farther from the stump in the opposite direction. When they met again after their round, Mike looked around him. The snow stuck to one side of the animals while he pondered. "We can't stay out here," he said to Paulie at last. "We gotta get back and get help!"

"Maybe Alex found him and took him down—or maybe he has help on the way already," Paulie suggested.

"I hope so," Mike said. If anything happened to Max, Lana would never forgive him. "We need to get back before they are looking for us, too." Twenty minutes later, as darkness settled in, the two men rode into a large indoor riding arena near the ranch's main headquarters. "Have you seen Max?" Mike asked one of the hands as he hopped off the horse.

"Not since he rode off with you," the old man replied, looking at the empty scabbard. He generally racked the rifles. "What's wrong?"

"How about Alex?" Mike asked.

"He was with y'all, right?"

"Right," Mike said. He and Paulie exchanged a look. This was getting worse by the minute.

They handed the man the reins to all three horses. "Where's your rifle?" the old man yelled at Mike's back as the men sprinted for the small farmhouse that had served as the ranch headquarters since the 1930s. Bursting into the tiny living room, Mike looked around breathlessly until he saw Lana in a corner, reading a book.

Seeing Mike's look of alarm, Lana asked, "What's wrong?"

"Where is Max?"

"I thought he went riding with you. I can't believe you guys were out there—"

"Have you seen Alex?" Mike asked.

"No, wasn't he with you?" Lana asked, standing. "Mike, what's going on?"

"Max saw some trespassers and wanted to confront them, but he got sick so he sent us after them. Alex went to get reception so he could call for help. Paulie and I met with the trespassers, then returned to where we left Max, but couldn't find him," Mike said. "We thought maybe Alex had brought Max out."

"You lost my father?" she asked Paulie. "Your only job is to look after him!"

Mike stepped in to defend Paulie. "Now we don't know that yet."

"Oh my God!" Lana exclaimed. She grabbed the front of Mike's shirt. "You've got to find him! Where did you see him last?"

"Up the hill, by a huge ponderosa stump."

"Maybe he just rode back," she said.

"No, he didn't," Mike said. "We—we saw his horse. We brought it back."

She turned her back on her husband. "So he's up there without his horse? Oh my God!"

"Paulie and I searched the area for about a quarter mile in every direction and he wasn't there," Mike explained. "We came back hoping he might have walked back—"

"Or come back with Alex," Paulie added.

"I'm calling the cops," she said. "An old man is lost on foot in this weather?" She walked off by herself, stabbing at the numbers on her phone as she did so.

Mike moved to her and put his hands on her shoulders. "I'm sure he'll be okay, dear," he said. "Probably just took cover somewhere to get out of the storm."

"This is my father!" she exclaimed, looking to Paulie and Mike. "Get out there and find him!" When neither man moved, she exploded. "Now! Get your asses out there and keep looking!"

"We could try a side-by-side," Mike suggested as they jogged back toward the arena.

"It will just get stuck," Paulie said.

While Paulie and Mike were talking, Alex approached, perspiring heavily despite the cold. "What's going on?"

"Where have you been?" Paulie asked. Without waiting for an answer, he continued. "You don't have Max?"

"No," Alex said. "I did what we talked about—rode to the top of the hill and tried to get service, but I couldn't get a signal. I finally gave up. Rode back to the stump, but everyone was gone, so I came back down."

"We never saw you," Mike said doubtfully.

"Christ, the weather was so bad I couldn't see a thing," Alex said. "I heard a gunshot and followed the sound but—"

"I think I heard that," Mike said. "I heard a shot, so I fired in the air hoping to draw Max's attention. We walked the area where we left him, but we couldn't see anything. It was getting dark, and the snow was blinding."

While Paulie and Alex exchanged their version of events, Mike tried to comfort Lana. "I'm so sorry," he said, and hugged her. "Alex is back—he hasn't seen your dad."

She was looking out the window and did not respond to the embrace. "I cannot believe that you lost my dad."

"Honey, I—I'm sorry. It was just a weird chain of events. I'm sure he'll be fine. He was a pilot. He must have had some training about how to survive —the Russians did that, too, right?"

"My father is not a Russian, Mike," Lana said. "How many times have I told you that?"

Mike looked at her blankly. "Are the cops on the way? Maybe they could put up a helicopter?"

"The sheriff's folks are on their way. They said it would be maybe twenty minutes or so. Apparently, the detective is on a call across town."

"Honey, we'll find him," Mike said, again putting a tentative arm around his wife's shoulders.

"We better," she said. "Or you and Paulie are dead men."

19

Garcia had been on duty for twenty-four hours as the result of his response to yesterday's overdose. Surprisingly, his follow-up with Misty Layton resulted in some solid information regarding the source of fentanyl coming into town, and he had chased down some leads and spent some time on the phone with Special Agent Polson from DCI, who had confirmed much of what she had told him: that a man named Trent Gustafson might well be responsible. Garcia was tired and hungry and looking forward to an early dinner when his phone rang. "Detective Garcia, this is dispatch."

"Whatcha got?"

"We've got a 10-65 west of town." She gave the rural route. "It's the old Barber and Detloff homesteads that the new billionaire bought."

A 10-65 was cop-talk for a missing person. "I'll be there in ten minutes. Who is the missing person?"

"A sixty-five-year-old man named Maxim Kovalenko. Last seen riding a horse up in the hills east of town. According to the report, he was riding a fence line. There's been some sort of dispute with some neighboring property owners."

"Okay," Garcia said. "I'm on it."

As promised, exactly ten minutes later he pulled up the paved, quarter-mile private drive to the old farmhouse. Garcia hadn't met any of the

Kovalenko family, but like everyone else in Custer, he knew that the old man had bought the Barber and Detloff places and was in the process of making his ranch headquarters out of them. Garcia was surprised to see that he'd been beaten to the scene by Sheriff Neal Walsh.

"Garcia, good to see you—where've you been?" Walsh asked. As a general matter, Garcia liked Walsh, who had been a deputy for years before his election and—unlike a lot of elected officials—he had an idea.

"Been talking with that Layton gal—her son OD'd last night and I'm squeezing her. I think we might have a line on who is bringing all the fentanyl into town."

"Good, good," the sheriff said. "But set that aside until we can find old man Kovalenko, okay? I need you and every swinging Richard you got on this one."

"Why the urgency?" Garcia asked, genuinely interested. Most missing persons cases ended up being much ado about nothing.

"Because he's the only billionaire we've got missing right now, okay?" Walsh said. "I don't need this hitting the paper. Let's just get this done before we get the press coming to town."

"Okay, boss. Let me see what's going on." Garcia made his way into the house. "Who called it in?"

"I did," replied a tall blonde woman. "I'm his daughter."

"Your name?"

"Lana Kovalenko . . . Brown. That's my husband over there." She pointed at Mike, who was sitting on a spare stool in the corner of the small living room. "Mike Brown."

Garcia nodded his understanding. "Who was the last to see him?"

"Well, I think my husband. He and my dad's chief of security, Pavlo Reznikov—we call him Paulie—and my dad's godson Alex Melnyk were riding a fence line up on the hill. Apparently, Dad saw some trespassers and asked Mike, Paulie, and Alex to run them off because he wasn't feeling well. Mike and Paulie confronted the trespassers, but there were too many to do anything about them, so they rode back and couldn't find Dad."

"Why were they out in this mess?" Garcia asked, exchanging a look with Walsh.

"Dad was kind of a wannabe cowboy," she said. "And he was overly protective of his property. If you," she said, indicating Walsh, "had done what he asked, perhaps he wouldn't have felt compelled to go out."

"Ma'am," Walsh began, "as I told your dad's people, there was not a lot we could do. It's a civil matter. My understanding is that your dad hired Sam Johnstone to look into that."

Lana stared coldly at the sheriff while the others looked on uncomfortably. "Perhaps I should speak with your husband," Garcia suggested to get his boss off the hook.

Lana trailed behind Garcia as he approached Mike.

"Mr. Brown?" When Mike nodded, he continued. "My name is Ted Garcia. I'm an investigator with the sheriff's office. I understand that Mr. Kovalenko is missing, and I'm told you were the last person to see him."

"It's true," Mike said. "Me and Paulie."

"What happened?"

Mike provided his description of events. "We were riding and Max saw some trespassers. He wanted to confront them, but he got sick, so we started after them. Well, we were worried about Max, so we decided Alex would find somewhere he could get a signal and send for you guys."

That made sense. "Okay," Garcia said, making notes. "Then what?"

"Well, Paulie and I met up with the trespassers. We spoke with them, but there was a bunch of them, and they refused to leave. Nothing we could do, so we rode back to check on Max. On the way, we saw his horse. I sent Paulie after it. When I got back to where we'd left Max, he was gone. We searched but couldn't find him. The weather was getting bad, so we came down here, hoping he and Laika either walked back or maybe Alex had brought him back."

Garcia looked up from making notes. "Who is Laika?"

"His dog," Paulie replied. "He took her everywhere."

"Was Mr. Kovalenko in good enough shape to walk back?"

"Not really," Mike said as Paulie shook his head.

Garcia made a note. "Then what?"

"We searched, but we couldn't find him. I didn't know what else to do." Mike looked out of the corner of his eye at his wife. "It was snowing hard, and I felt like we had to leave and get back."

Garcia watched Mike carefully. Being rash or stupid wasn't a crime; neither was giving up too soon. "Okay, thanks."

"Are you going to go find him?" Lana asked.

Garcia took a deep breath. He'd anticipated this. "It's dark and the weather's bad," he said. "We're going to have to wait until morning, or at least until this storm passes over."

"But my father is out there all alone!" Lana said.

"Detective, he is seriously injured, and you're going to wait?" Mike asked.

Garcia looked at Mike for a long time before replying. "Why do you think that?"

"What?" Mike asked.

"That he is injured?"

Mike twice opened and closed his mouth without speaking. At last Lana spoke up. "Because isn't it obvious? If he wasn't hurt, he'd be back!"

"Well, not necessarily," Garcia said. "Lots of things could have happened. Maybe he got lost. He wasn't feeling well; might've holed up somewhere, sick." He eyed each member of Max's family in turn. "I understand this is hard on everyone, but—"

"Oh, for Christ's sake," Mike said with disgust. "We'll go find him ourselves."

"I wish you wouldn't," Garcia said. "By stumbling around in the dark you risk messing up any sort of trail or sign of where he might be."

Seeing continued doubt on the family's faces, Walsh interjected. "And know this: if *you* get lost or go missing, we're not going to risk our people's lives to find *you*, either. One rescue at a time."

Lana's dissatisfaction was undisguised. "Let's go," she said to Mike.

Garcia watched as the family went into the kitchen. "Thanks, boss," Garcia said when they were alone. He then stepped outside onto the small deck of the old farmhouse and shouted his instructions to his people into the wind while Walsh observed from afar.

"What are you thinking?" Walsh asked when Garcia had dismissed the team.

"No idea," Garcia said. "Most of these cases turn out okay, but I'm concerned. It's freaking cold outside and he's older."

Walsh was about to have Garcia define "older" for him when he heard a scream. The two men rushed into the kitchen and saw Lana, who had taken a knee and was petting a large dog while Paulie, Alex, and Mike looked on.

"It's blood!" she said. "Her muzzle is covered in blood."

"Is—is it Dad's?" Mike asked.

Garcia and Walsh exchanged a look. "Ma'am, I'm going to ask you to step away from the dog for a minute," Garcia said. "I'm gonna get a tech here to take a sample, then you can get the dog cleaned up, okay?"

Lana stood, turned, and put her face into her husband's shoulder as he wrapped her in his arms. Suddenly, she pushed him away and began hitting him with her fists. "You killed my father!" she screamed over and over again until she collapsed. As Mike sank to his knees with her, Alex and Paulie stood by awkwardly.

Garcia gave the go-ahead to the crime scene technicians he had called, who calmly gathered the dog and began to take samples. "Why don't the four of you wait in the other room?" he asked. Later, when the technicians had completed their tasks and all evidence had been marked, Garcia returned Laika to Lana and updated Walsh, who looked at his watch. "Still a few hours to daylight. Might want to see if you can get some rest."

◆

The family had stayed the night in the little farmhouse, where quarters were tight and tempers were short. The staff had been called and they had done their best, but breakfast was meager by the family's standards.

"I just can't get over the fact you left him," Lana said to Mike. Paulie stood by quietly, eating a piece of toast. Except when invited to do so by Max, he generally did not take meals with the family. He was "the help," and they made sure he knew it when Max wasn't around.

"Lana, what could I do?" Mike asked.

"You could have told him no to begin with."

"Oh, Lana—you know that's not realistic," Mike said. "No one tells Max no."

"But he would be alive!" Lana said sharply. She bent and scratched behind Laika's ears, then straightened and walked to the kitchen counter, reached past Paulie for a bottle, and added a healthy dose of rum to her coffee. She drank from the cup, swallowed, and made a face. "If he's gone—"

"Let's not go there," Mike cautioned.

"We need to start thinking about possible contingencies," she countered.

"What's to think about?" Mike asked. "I'm the CEO; I'm named in the succession plan. Things will continue as they are. For now."

Lana and Alex exchanged a quick look before Alex began to speak. "I think we all need to—"

"Shut up, Alex!" Mike and Lana said in unison.

Paulie tossed a corner of his toast to Laika, rubbed crumbs off his hands, and left the room.

"He's done when Max is gone," Lana said, indicating Paulie. "Whenever that is."

Mike shook his head slowly. "It sounds like you've been doing some planning," he said as he stalked off.

When they were alone, Lana moved quickly to Alex and picked a nit from his expensive wool shirt. "Did you get everything taken care of?" she asked.

Before he could respond, Garcia entered the small kitchen. "Knock, knock," he said belatedly.

Lana stepped away from Alex, wondering how long the nosy cop had been listening. "Can we help you? Why aren't you out looking for my father?"

"Soon," Garcia said, pointing to his watch. "First light here shortly. I'd like to talk with Mr. Reznikov."

"Paulie just left," Alex replied. "Probably somewhere with Mike."

"Okay, thank you." Garcia started to leave, then turned back to face Lana. "I want you to know we're going to do everything we can to find your father."

～

After finding Paulie in the riding arena, Garcia unfolded a map on a small table used to work on tack. "Mr. Reznikov, we're here," he said, indicating a spot on the map with an index finger. "Now, where do you think you were when you left Mr. Kovalenko?"

Paulie looked blankly at Garcia, then at the page, then back at Garcia.

"Can you read a map?" Garcia asked, eyeing Mike in the background.

"Not—not really," Paulie admitted. "Call me Paulie."

Christ. "Okay, well . . . how long did it take you four to ride from here up to wherever you were when you stopped—do you remember?"

Paulie looked around. Garcia noticed that as Mike approached, Paulie became increasingly uncomfortable. "Ummmm, not sure?"

Garcia was insistent. "Was it an hour? Thirty minutes?"

Paulie stared helplessly at Garcia while Mike watched. "Well, do you know how long it took you to get back?" When Paulie shrugged, an exasperated Garcia asked about the location itself. "What did the terrain look like? Were you on a hill?"

"Yes," Paulie answered, finally. "We were on a hill and in the distance we could see the, uh, 'trespassers' is what Max called them."

"Where's the disputed property line?" Garcia asked Mike.

"It's right here." Mike stepped forward and indicated a spot on the map with a well-manicured nail.

Lana and Alex had arrived and were now leaning over the map as well. "He's right," Lana said. "So if they could see them trespassing—"

"Then they must have been in this area," Garcia concluded, pointing. A quick examination revealed elevation lines, which in turn gave him a pretty good idea where Max was when the men had left him. "We'll start there." Where Max was now was a different question. "So, all of you knew where you were going, right?"

"Max did," Paulie said uncertainly. "I just rode along. Don't know about them," he added, indicating Mike and Alex.

"Did you know?" Garcia asked Mike.

"Kind of," Mike said. "I knew he wanted to check on his land, and probably to see if the trespassers were up there. I had an idea."

"Same," Alex said in response to Garcia's stare. "We all just rode along."

Interesting. "That's my bird," Garcia said when he heard the approaching helicopter.

"Can I go?" Lana asked. "I want to help find my father."

"No civilians." Garcia shook his head. "Lawyers say it's a liability issue."

Mike's face reddened. "For Christ's sake, man—we don't need your money."

"Rules are rules," Garcia said. He rolled the map and stuck it in his vest, glad for the rule. "I'll keep you posted."

He hurried to the aircraft, thinking that—given the blood on the dog—this was going to end badly.

20

As the Bell 407 lifted off, Garcia felt his stomach flutter. The last flight he'd taken in a helicopter had been almost fifteen years prior, in a UH-60 Black-hawk piloted by a couple of warrant officers across Paktika Province in southeastern Afghanistan. Then, small arms tracers appeared in the night sky as hapless Afghan gunners attempted to bring the craft down. It had been unsettling, but he was young and hard at the time and confident bullets were unlikely to bring the chopper down. This morning, the threat was less exotic but probably more dangerous: high wind and blowing snow. As the little chopper flew treetop level from the ranch headquarters over property owned by Max, Garcia got on the microphone. "Get it up!" he commanded.

The pilot looked at him questioningly.

"Up! Up!" Garcia commanded, demonstrating with a thumb. He needed some elevation to give him a wider field of view. You'd think a search and rescue pilot would know that. After getting the craft to 750 feet, the pilot looked to Garcia for confirmation. Garcia nodded, then made a circle with an index finger, directing the pilot to fly in a pattern so he could look for Max, tracks in the snow, or any other indication of the man. According to the family, Max had been a fighter pilot in Russia or somewhere. Garcia therefore assumed he'd had some sort of survival, evasion, and escape training, and he was looking for the standard notification techniques—smoke, markers, stamped-down snow, and the like. On the other hand, the missing billionaire was sixty-five years old, outside in bad weather, and not in the best of health.

And bleeding.

Try as he might, he had failed to convince the family to allow law enforcement to handle the search, and from this elevation, he could see side-by-sides, including one with Mike and Paulie, and horses with riders fanning out from the ranch headquarters. The fear, of course, was that the amateur searchers would miss what they were looking for and obscure clues to Max's whereabouts in the process. The good news was that they were departing from the southwest corner of the ranch, and it would take some time for them to get to the northern boundary, where Max was last seen. Pointing to a spot on a map, Garcia directed the pilot to the northern area, some miles from where they were. On the way, he tried to ignore the area's beauty and remain focused on the search for signs of life, but the mixed conifer forest and open meadow landscape were hard to ignore.

The pilot gave a thumbs-up when his GPS indicated they were over the spot Garcia had indicated on the map during their pre-flight reconnaissance, and Garcia again gave the sign to circle slowly. "Take it down to five hundred feet; that oughta be about right," he instructed.

The pilot complied, and they began the painstaking process of searching for a man—one who might well be injured and hiding from the elements—among twenty thousand acres of forest.

∼

For the better part of an hour, Garcia and the pilot had been circling Max's last known location, flying a pattern of ever-widening circles. Garcia was about to give up when he saw movement on the ground near the base of a tall rock ledge. "There!" he said, pointing to the ground where two men stood waving their arms.

The pilot looked quickly, then nodded to Garcia. "Got it."

"Can you set 'er down?"

"I think I saw a spot a little south of there—let me circle back and we'll take a look."

A few minutes later they were on the ground a quarter mile south of where they saw the men waving. "I'll keep you posted," Garcia assured the pilot. He looked at his phone—no service. "If you would, let dispatch know we are on the ground and may have something." The pilot was on his radio as Garcia stepped off. He could just see the trees atop the cliff of which the ledge was a part. It was uphill, the terrain was rough, and the snow was just deep enough to make hiking tough, so Garcia was breathing heavily as he approached the men, whom he recognized as Mike Brown and Paulie Reznikov. He could see they were near an opening in the cliff atop the approximately four-foot ledge. They stood straighter as they saw him, and waved him on in. As he drew closer, he knew.

"It's Max," Mike said. "There was nothing we could do."

Garcia looked at Paulie, who looked quickly to the ground. "Is it him?" Garcia asked. Paulie only nodded. "How'd you find him?"

"Mike found him," Paulie said. "We were walking up the hill, and Mike said, 'I think there might be an opening in that hillside,' and he checked. There he was."

"That right?" Garcia asked, watching Mike closely.

"Uh, yeah," Mike agreed. "That's about it."

"How'd you know to look here?" Garcia asked. He'd observed the men's tracking leading directly to this spot.

"I—I just felt like this was a possibility," Mike said.

Garcia nodded. "Okay, let me see what's going on. I'm going to ask both of you to stay outside." He entered the depression in the hillside. From the entrance, Paulie could see Garcia moving about from time to time around Max's body. After a few minutes, Garcia exited the cave. "Okay. Well, he's obviously dead . . . Paulie? Can I ask you to do me a favor?"

Paulie looked to Mike, who nodded his permission. "Sure."

"No service here. I'm gonna write a note. Can you follow my tracks down to my pilot?" Garcia asked. "We're going to have to get a team of crime scene technicians up here."

"Okay," Paulie said.

Garcia took out his phone and a small notebook, scribbled some numbers, then tore out the page. "We'll stay here with the body, er, Max. Hurry, please," he urged Paulie, who took off at a fast walk. "When he gets back, why don't the two of you head on back to the ranch?" Garcia suggested to Mike after Paulie left. "I'll get someone to give you a ride down. I think it's best you be there with your family."

"I'm okay here with Dad," Mike said.

Garcia looked at him for a long time before saying anything else. "You touch anything?"

"I suppose I did, yeah. I mean, I saw . . . the body . . . and I knew . . . I grabbed onto him and then rolled him over. Then I hugged him, kinda. I mean, wouldn't you?"

"I'm pretty sure I would, yeah," Garcia agreed. He made a note. "Did Paulie touch anything?"

Mike furrowed his brow in apparent thought. "I don't think so, no. He kind of stood around with his hands in his pockets. He was upset, too. I mean, he . . . spent a lot of time with Max. What am I gonna tell Lana?"

Garcia ignored the question. "Let me ask you a question," he began. "Did you give any thought to *not* doing what Max told you to do?"

Mike actually laughed. "Oh, hell no. I've tried that in the normal course of events. 'Boss, let's do this,' or 'How about we try that?' No way. He said go, we went."

Garcia considered what Mike said. "Forgive me, but you guys left an ailing sixty-five-year-old man somewhere by himself in bad weather."

"I know, I know," Mike said, appearing suitably chagrined. "We shoulda known better."

"Okay," Garcia said. "Whatever happened, happened, I guess. But you didn't see Paulie touch Max?"

"I did not."

"Just so you know, when my techs get here, we're going to need your clothes."

"Why?"

"Just want to confirm some stuff," Garcia said. Might as well let him have it. "We'll want to look for traces of gunpowder."

"Gunpowder?"

"Sure."

"But why?"

"Well, it's pretty clear to me that your father was shot—probably with a high-powered rifle."

"Why do you think that?"

Garcia was watching Mike closely. His quick check of the body had revealed an entry wound lateral to the belly button. No evidence of an exit wound, but he hadn't been able to check thoroughly yet. As soon as he got a tech here, they could verify that. "Because he was gut-shot—like right here." Garcia indicated the spot on himself and watched Mike's reaction as he looked away. "Max had to have been shot somewhere else, and somehow —walked, dragged, or whatever—got himself here where I think he most likely died. Hardly any blood here."

He looked at his watch. He needed to get out and look for blood trails. He was making notes when he heard the chopper lift off, and he watched as it moved south, nose down and low over the snow. "He's off to pick up my techs. Shoulda called in the grid, so we oughta be getting some help here soon."

"You think it might've been an accident?" Mike asked.

"What kind?"

"Like maybe he tripped and fell?"

"Unlikely," Garcia said. "I mean, there's no weapon here. How far are we from where you left Max?"

"I think we left him at a spot that way," Mike said, pointing west.

Garcia made notes and mapped out a plan while he waited. There were a few obscured footprints around the body. A couple of them appeared to belong to a dog—probably Laika. Others would surely match Mike, Paulie, and himself. Beyond that, it would be interesting. There was evidence that Max had bled some, but not a lot. There was a smear on the inside of his coat near where the entry wound was covered by Max's shirt that would probably correspond with the blood on Laika's nose—not unlikely that the dog had nosed around to see what was going on.

Garcia wanted Mike's clothing examined, and he needed to be able to look around. He needed to talk with the men and have them take him to the exact spot where they had left Max. He might be able to re-create the scene if he could figure out where Max was when he was shot. Max had almost certainly been shot from a distance, and it was evident it hadn't happened here. Max was older and in poor health; it didn't seem like he'd get too far with a bullet in him, so where? The snow, people's tracks— Garcia had little to go on. He needed to get started, but right now he needed to stay put. If he left, some smart-ass defense lawyer would make a big deal of that. He fretted and paced until he heard a group of side-by-sides arriving and his helicopter returning.

When the additional deputies and crime scene techs were assembled, he briefed everyone and left Corporal Levi O'Neil in charge. He was a good man and would keep the scene as organized as possible. Dr. Laws, the county's contracted medical examiner, would arrive soon. When the doctor was done, O'Neil would oversee the removal of the body, the proper recording and cataloging of everything on scene, and the entire team's eventual withdrawal. The GPS on Garcia's phone had the current location about halfway between the ranch headquarters and the area where Mike had indicated the dispute over the property was occurring.

Garcia next commandeered one of the department's side-by-sides and drove to a location he believed was on a straight line between Max's body and the disputed property line. He stopped in a saddle between two higher hills and was able to look down a long draw. In the distance, he could see a fence line—probably marking the area in dispute. The men had said they could see trespassers from a distance; given the surrounding terrain, they must have been about where Garcia was now. He slowly turned in a circle until he saw what he was looking for: a large dead tree.

He spent thirty minutes searching on foot in vain for any indication that anyone had been in this spot. As the snowfall began to increase, he searched in all four cardinal directions for signs of blood, or cartridges, or anything else to indicate a crime scene. All he found was a spray bottle filled with clear liquid half covered with fresh snow halfway up the slope. He made a note to have the techs gather it up, and then looked around him. If Max was near that tree at the time he was shot, the shooter could have been up to several hundred yards away. He got back in the side-by-side and drove down to the contested property. Here, he could see tracks left by several horses, but they were covered with snow now, leaving barely discernible impressions in the ground. In an hour, they would be fully covered. At last, he decided he'd seen enough. There was no way to tell from which direction the shot had come. He'd have to wait for Dr. Laws' report, as well as that of Robert Mitchell, the county's firearms and ballistics expert. It was time to talk with Paulie.

21

At the station an hour later, Garcia was pouring coffee. Paulie took his black, which was good, as the small kitchen the detectives used was out of creamer and sugar yet again. Garcia filled his cup as well and made his way down the hall to the interview room, where Paulie was waiting. They'd made small talk on the ride to town; Paulie seemed like a decent-enough guy, although not terribly bright.

"Here you go," Garcia said, placing the coffee in front of Paulie. "It's not very good, but it's hot and it has caffeine."

"I'll take it." Paulie sipped carefully. "Hot."

"Right," Garcia said. He started a small tape recorder. "You don't mind if I record this, do you?"

"No." Paulie studied Garcia closely.

"So, let's start here—you're Max's head of security, right?"

"Right."

"How long had you been working for Max?"

"In this country?"

"Well, altogether, I guess."

"I was part of his flight crew in Ukraine," Paulie said. "He was an officer and a pilot, so we didn't talk much, but I think he appreciated my work. At some point he left for the States and a while later I got a call from him, asking me if I'd like to come here and work for him. I said of course."

"Then what?"

"Well, I got here, and I started out in New Jersey, doing odd jobs—you know? When we got to California, I started doing more stuff—driving him, then delivering packages. Then he sent me to a course in LA. Kind of like basic training all over again. I got my concealed carry and then he gave me the title of head of security."

"Why did he need that?"

"Well, he said that he was getting threats from some of his former business partners—he gave me pictures of them to carry and everything. Plus, the kind of money he was dealing with, and the fact that he had a lot of women around . . . Some of them were married. Well, you know how it is."

Not really. "So you came out here to Wyoming with him?"

"I actually came out before him—with Mike," Paulie corrected. "Max charged Mike with finding a new location. Max had narrowed it down to Wyoming or Montana, but he favored Wyoming—taxes, you know? Then, when Wyoming passed the new cryptocurrency banking laws, Max decided on Wyoming and we visited several places. Max came out and settled on Custer because of the infrastructure—the power plant, railroad lines, and an airport. Plus, that college president's house was for sale, and Max really fell in love with the ranch property."

"So everyone moved out here?"

"Over the past few months, yeah."

"And as the head of security, how did you feel about it?"

Paulie sipped carefully. "Well, at first I thought things would be better," he said. "Max had made a lot of enemies in California."

"What kind?"

"All kinds. Former partners, competitors, union bosses . . . He just kind of got sideways with everyone because he refused to play their game—he's not corrupt."

"What do you mean?"

"Max is a lot of things, but he doesn't believe in payoffs, no 'greasing the palms' of union bosses or any of that. Oh, he'll cut your throat, but he'll look you in the eye when he is doing it. Lotta guys in California didn't like that."

"Anyway, you all moved out here."

"Right. And for a while it was a lot better—Max was an unknown quantity, you know? But he began to make enemies."

"Who?"

"Well, the Green Wyoming Council was opposed to Max moving his operations here at all. And when he announced he'd bought the coal plant to power his Bitcoin mining they went ballistic."

Garcia nodded. He'd heard of the angry confrontations by protestors at city council and county commission meetings. "Any threats?"

"Oh, yeah—but sort of general, you know? Like, 'You people are ruining the environment—get out of here before it's too late.' That kind of thing."

"You took it seriously?"

"Of course—that's my job," Paulie assured Garcia. "We saw faces and had names of people who were against us. We started doing some things differently—took different routes to places, installed all kinds of security cameras, and Max even had the family doing some shooting."

"Who?"

"The men," Paulie said. "He's old fashioned—or *was*. He wouldn't allow the women to shoot."

Garcia was surprised. Except for Paulie, perhaps, this didn't seem like much of a gun crowd. "How'd that go?"

Paulie looked at Garcia questioningly. "The shooting?" When Garcia nodded, he answered, "Pretty well. Alex is actually very good—you wouldn't think so by looking at him. Mike, not so much."

"You?"

Paulie returned Garcia's pointed stare. "I hit what I shoot at."

Garcia made a note. "So you tightened security up—then what?"

"Things were okay until recently, I'd say." Paulie drained the last of the coffee. "When Max told those people they couldn't cross his property, they got pissed. That's when we started to see confrontations with our workers in town, and we started getting a lot of written threats."

"Did you keep them?"

"Max did."

"Why him? You were the head of security."

"He said he wanted 'em." Paulie looked at Garcia for a long moment, something clearly on his mind. "I mean, I honestly think he kind of took pride in people threatening him, you know?"

"Tell me."

"You know, he would pull the letters out and count 'em. I was like, 'Boss, this isn't funny. Don't take this lightly,' and he'd say, 'Better to take a bullet 'cause I was doing things my way than to run away and eventually die of some crappy disease.'"

"One way to look at it," Garcia acknowledged. "You know where those letters are now?"

"In his desk drawer," Paulie said. "I've seen him get them out and put them back."

"I'm gonna want to see them."

"Talk to Lana."

"Fine," Garcia said. Time to clean up some details. "Let's talk about you and Max, Alex and Mike going 'up the mountain,' as you refer to it."

"Okay."

"So Max wanted to go and check on his land, and he wanted you to go with him."

"He didn't ask. It's just part of my job."

"What about Mike and Alex?"

"If one was going, the other would as well."

"I understand," Garcia said. A kind of pseudo-sibling rivalry between the two wouldn't be unusual. "You didn't want to go, I take it—why not?"

"Bunch of reasons. Weather was getting crappy. I don't like horses. I don't like to ride, and I especially don't like to ride when Max has his dog with him. That damned dog makes the horses skittish."

"I could see that," Garcia said. "So what happened?"

"So, we rode up the mountain and we got to a place near that big stump —did you find it?"

"I think so." Garcia was thinking they must've been about where they were earlier today.

"Yeah, so Max wasn't feeling very good and we probably would've come back, but then he seen them trespassers, so he set us on 'em."

"By yourselves?"

"He actually started to go, but then he got sick and insisted *we* go. Wouldn't take no for an answer. The last I seen him he was sitting at the base of that big stump, holding the reins to his horse. Anyway, me and Mike and Alex started off, but Alex thought maybe he should ride somewhere to get a signal for help, so he went off and me and Mike rode down and talked to them guys—well, really, just the Sprague guy."

"Right. What happened?"

"Well, there was six or eight of them—not a lot we could do, so we gave 'em a warning and then rode back to where we'd left Max."

"By the stump."

"Right."

"Together?"

"Well, kinda."

"What do you mean?"

"Well, we were riding back together, and then we saw Max's horse wandering down toward where we'd just been, dragging its reins. Mike told me to gather him up, so I rode after that horse until I could get ahold of him."

"How long did that take?"

"Oh, it took a while," Paulie said. "The sonuvabitch was spooked, and he's a little wild, anyway. I'm not so good with horses, so . . . a while."

"So, you got the horse rounded up—"

"And then I rode back up and found Mike."

"What was he doing?"

"Walking in circles."

"Why?"

"Well, he said he couldn't find Max, and he said he'd read somewhere that if someone is lost to search in ever-larger circles."

"Okay," Garcia said doubtfully. "What did you do?"

"Mike had me walk in a circle the other direction until it started to get so snowy we couldn't see much. We got to thinking Alex had found Max and got him back."

"So you never saw Alex again?"

"Not until we got back."

"Was he back when you got back?"

Paulie sat in his chair, thinking. "I don't know. I just know we saw him later."

"What happened when you got back?"

"Well, we run into a couple of the hands. Asked them if they had seen Max, you know? They had not, so we left the animals with them and ran to the ranch headquarters. We saw Lana, and she asked us about Max, and . . . well, she went kinda crazy when she found out we'd left Max alone. She called you guys."

"Okay," Garcia said. Time to change subjects. "As head of security, who do you think might want to do Max harm?"

Paulie smiled wryly. "Like I said, get in line, man."

Garcia returned the grin. "Let's narrow it down a little. Is there anyone you've been particularly worried about? Anyone who—"

"Sprague. He's really pissed about not bein' allowed to cross Max's land —I think he's a hunting guide or something. He was kind of the leader yesterday. Looking for a fight, you know?"

Garcia sat back and thought about it. He'd known Sprague for years. The guy was rumored to be in all kinds of stuff, but Garcia had always felt like the guy spreading the rumors was Sprague himself—trying to be a badass. "You want another cup?" he asked. When Paulie declined, Garcia reached for the cup. "I'll take that," he said. Always good to have a guy's fingerprints handy. "Anyone else?"

"Guy named Aiden. A former partner. He threatened Max a while back. But he lives in California." Paulie looked at Garcia questioningly. "Am I free to go?"

"You bet. But I'd like to ask a few more questions. Might keep you from having to come back."

"Okay," Paulie said doubtfully. "What else?"

"Tell me about the family." When Paulie didn't respond immediately, Garcia pressed him. "C'mon, Paulie, I have eyes. Tell me what's going on."

"Well," Paulie began, clearly hesitant to rat out his employer's family. "None of 'em wanted to move out here, but Max insisted, so the stuff that wasn't good really started to hit the fan then."

"What kind of stuff?"

"Well, mostly around Mike. See, Mike is the—whattayacallit? Protégé? And so Max had been giving him the chance to run the company. But Mike wasn't doing stuff the way Max wanted, and they were getting sideways. Mike had ideas about doing stuff different. Different investments, methods, you know? Lana is Mike's wife, of course, so she was pissed at Mike for maybe blowing this opportunity. But she was also pissed at Max for being so hard on Mike."

"What about Alex?"

"Max always looked at him as kind of a son," Paulie said. He stopped talking but felt compelled to continue when Garcia just stared at him. "Just recently, Max soured on him, too," Paulie concluded, filling the silence.

Garcia was looking at his notebook. "I understand there are two other children?"

"Yeah, Stacy and Danny—but they aren't around much. Stacy is an actress." Paulie smiled. "Wants to be, really. Danny . . . Danny is a drug addict and a drunk. Lives off an allowance."

"That couldn't have made Max happy," Garcia observed.

"It didn't," Paulie agreed. "Max despised him. Thought he was weak. Blamed his mother. But Stacy was his favorite—she could do no wrong in Max's eyes."

"How'd they feel about him?"

"Max was a difficult man. Very demanding. But you don't come to a new country and become rich by not working hard—right? He just felt like his kids took it for granted, and I think the kids didn't think he understood them or whatever—you know?"

"What about wives or girlfriends?"

"Max had plenty of both." Paulie flashed a wolfish grin. "But not since we got out here. He hasn't been feeling too good and pretty much stuck to himself." He watched as Garcia thumbed through the small notebook and then closed it. "Can I go now?"

"Sure, but one more question. I'm thinking this was either an accident —some hunter shot him—or that it was someone who had something against Max."

"Makes sense."

"Let's assume for the sake of the argument it wasn't an accident."

"Okay," Paulie said, uncertain where this was going.

"Where would you start?"

Paulie sat back, clearly thinking. "You mean around here?"

"I mean anywhere."

"Oh, I'd start with Aiden or some of them cryptocurrency fellas that Max . . . took their money or whatever. They lost millions. Some of them guys are wrapped up with the mob."

"The mob?"

"Yeah. Russians. They weren't happy when Max outsmarted them. By the time we left California I was running an entire team of security there. Max let 'em go when we got everything transferred out here, though. Felt like we'd know if those guys showed up."

"Seen anyone like that around here?" Garcia asked.

"No," Paulie admitted.

Time now to find out what was really happening. "What about family?" Garcia asked.

"What do you mean?"

I think you know what I mean," Garcia said. "Who would you start with if you were me?"

"I'm not going there," Paulie said. "I gotta work with these people."

"Someone killed your boss—the guy who brought you over, the guy who changed your life."

"Yeah, well. . ." Paulie shook his head.

Garcia watched for a long minute, hoping the big man would change his mind. When it became clear he would not, he decided to save it for another day. "Okay, Paulie. I value loyalty, too. Let me have someone get you back, okay?"

22

The single-wide trailer was up a draw on the corner of two intersecting fence lines. Garcia had done a quick search of the property records and discovered that Sprague had been gifted five acres by one Eleanor Sprague —presumably a family member—some ten years back. As he approached the home, Garcia was amazed at the amount of trash and other material littering the yard: broken-down 1970s muscle cars, at least two boat shells, several scrapped lawn tractors, assorted animal drinking troughs, several large wooden spools used to hold commercial-grade wire and cable, dozens of kitchen appliances, and the frame for a clearly homemade gazebo roof. Chickens and goats foraged among the structures, rusting vehicles, and equipment in search of something to eat. One goat lay on its side, chewing its cud contentedly and enjoying the autumn sun's warmth from the expansive hood of a 1972 Buick Electra 225.

Garcia knocked a couple of times before a pre-teen girl appeared at the door. "Is your daddy home?" he asked.

"Daddy's dead," the young girl said. "Casey's here, though."

"Like to talk with him, if possible," Garcia said, and waited outside for a few minutes while the girl retrieved Sprague. Garcia saw the dingy curtains pulled back and then released; seconds later, Sprague appeared in the doorway.

"What do you want?" he asked.

Garcia could smell the odor of cheap beer from six feet away. "Want to talk a little bit," he replied.

"What about?"

"About what happened a couple of days ago to Mr. Kovalenko."

"Don't know nothin' about it," Sprague said. "Nothin' to do with it."

"You talked with his men a little bit before Max disappeared, right?"

"Well, I think so, yeah. Ain't sure when he disappeared," Sprague said. "He comes in here from wherever and starts throwin' money around and the next thing I know I can't access that school section? Kiss my ass, man! I told him that, I told his lawyer that, I told his men that, and I'm telling you that!"

Garcia decided to push a little. "Word I got was you threatened him."

"I did," Sprague said. "I told him I'd shoot his ass if he got me trespassed off'n my hunting property. That's public land. I make a good livin' guiding out-of-staters for deer and elk up there for years. Then here all of a sudden, this boy from California shows up and I can't cross his land to guide no more? I don't think so. I tol' him that was bullshit, then I told his boys that again coupla days ago."

"And then he got shot."

"He did? Well, I don't know nothin' about that, but I can't say I'm sorry, neither," Sprague said. "My wife and I were gonna lose ever'thing if he got his way. But it weren't me. Somebody did me a favor, though. I owe him big-time."

"Any idea who it was?"

"Don't know nothin'—I just told you that." It came out "juss tol"—he was smashed.

"Anything else you can tell me?"

Sprague thought about it for a minute. By the looks of him, it was doubtful he could remember what he'd eaten for breakfast. "Nope. Don't remember nothin' what seems important."

∼

Early the next morning Garcia was in his office, looking at a topographic map he had downloaded from the United States Geological Survey that depicted Max's property and the surrounding land in detail. He could smell the coffee brewing as he estimated the distance between where Max's body was found and where he was last seen alive at half a mile. Because everyone agreed Max wasn't feeling well when they left him, Garcia presumed Max was shot where he'd been seen last.

Distance was an issue. Given modern rifle technology and optics, a hunter could take down an elk—or a man—at a distance of more than a thousand yards. After some study, Garcia felt he had narrowed things down to a few possible locations. Interestingly, while it was *possible* the fatal shot was fired from somewhere else, Garcia's terrain analysis indicated the best bet involved someone shooting Max from a location on his own property. As he sat back and looked at the locations he had plotted, he decided the shooter's probable location would be in one of three goose egg-shaped areas he delineated with a marker.

The first set of possible positions was along the northern boundary of Max's property, likely accessed from the properties owned by Sprague or the other adjoining landowners with whom Max had been disputing access. The second set of likely shooting spots was almost directly north of the ranch headquarters, generally on a line between the headquarters and Max's last known location. These spots were easily accessed and afforded quick egress—the only problem was that no one had seen anyone leave or return on those routes. The third set of shooting positions was grouped along a ridgeline located to the north of Max's property, but well west of the first set. These positions would have a shooter located in the timbered ridgeline shooting downward toward Max. Access to the area could be obtained easily from the ranch headquarters. Alternatively, a shooter could get there from the northern disputed access by walking around the ridge and approaching from the west.

The determination of the shooter's location could narrow the list of potential suspects. If the shot came from the first set of positions, he decided, he would begin by looking at Sprague and his supporters. If the shot came from the vicinity of the second set of positions, he would assume whoever fired it came via ranch headquarters. If the shot was fired from the timbered ridgeline, the identification of a suspect would be more trouble-some, as the shooter could have accessed the location from either direction.

Garcia poured himself a cup of coffee and walked to his desk. In the many interviews he and his team had conducted—now numbering more than a dozen—most believed the shooting was probably the work of a hunter. Max's property was in the middle of one of the prime "draw" areas for elk hunters in the entire state; people paid five-figure fees for guided hunts onto private lands to bag a bull elk, and there would be dozens of hunters in the area on public land at any one time guiding themselves. The locals' disparagement of the newcomers and out-of-staters was fact-based, of course, but the reality was accidental shootings were surprisingly rare. It was much more likely that Max was shot by someone he knew.

Like a family member.

23

Dr. Ronald B. Laws, M.D. was Custer County's contracted medical examiner. An internal medicine practitioner by trade, he contracted with "Doc" Fish, the county's elected coroner, to do the work of M.E. on a part-time basis. Garcia watched as the doctor looked over Max Kovalenko's body while his assistant got things prepared.

"The body is that of an un-embalmed, white male of average build," Laws began. He had a voice-activated microphone attached to his lab coat so he could record his findings as he made them. He stood looking at Max's corpse for a minute, then observed, "I don't like his color, even for a dead man. Something is going on here."

Using a tape, the doctor and the assistant measured Max's corpse. "Body length is seventy inches," he dictated as the assistant provided him a printout from the automated examination table Max was on. "Estimated weight is one hundred fifty pounds," Laws said, and handed the paper back to his assistant.

"The overall appearance is consistent with the stated age of sixty-five years," he continued. "The deceased is dressed in a pair of blue jeans, brown belt, flannel button-down shirt, a heavy vest, and gray wool stockings. He is wearing what the local sporting goods store would call full-length, 'base layer' top and bottoms. Present in the pocket of the jeans is a small pocketknife and several coins of various denominations. The wallet was removed earlier. Livor mortis is present frontally and rigor mortis is marked in all joints. The hair is gray."

Richards retrieved scissors and carefully cut away the clothing, handing each piece to the assistant, who placed it in a plastic bag, noting the date and time. Max's body was then covered with a thin white sheet.

"According to law enforcement, the body was located and secured not more than about fourteen hours after his disappearance, and possibly less. The body was discovered—" Laws looked at Garcia.

"Twenty-four hours ago," Garcia replied, looking at his watch. "Had some trouble getting everyone on scene, as you know."

Laws nodded in acknowledgement. "Post-mortem decomposition, therefore, is underway, albeit somewhat delayed due to the ambient temperatures outside," he continued. "The head is normal, the pupils round and equal; the irises are blue. The nose, ears, jaw, chest, abdomen, and extremities are normal." He handled Max's body with sure, competent hands. "There are several scars on his knees, indicating multiple surgeries. The body is notable for a lack of tattoos," he concluded.

Garcia helped the assistant position Max's body in a semi-reclining position so that Laws could place a plastic, block-shaped object underneath the body, near the upper spine. "Okay, let him down," Laws commanded. Garcia and the assistant complied, and the result was Max's chest protruding upward and his arms falling to the sides. Laws leaned in close to inspect a wound on the dead man's abdomen.

After photographs, swabs, and skin samples were taken, Laws began probing and measuring. "This appears to be a single gunshot wound. The entrance is present in the upper right abdomen, approximately level with the belly button and almost three inches to the right of the midline," he noted. "The wound measures 5/16 inches vertically by 3/16 horizontally. No grains of powder are apparent. The skin is negative for an abrasion ring."

"Does that mean what I think it does?" Garcia asked.

"If you think it means the deceased was likely shot at some distance, it does," Laws explained without bothering to look Garcia's way. As he removed various organs, he commented on their size, weight, and apparent condition. "Here we are," Laws commented, extracting a fragment from

Max's body and dropping it in a vial held by his assistant. "And here's another," he said, and looked to Garcia. "This is why there's no exit wound. The bullet was a frangible type."

Garcia sighed. A frangible bullet was one designed to break apart upon contact with a solid object, making a match between a bullet and gun difficult if not impossible.

"Any way to tell what caliber?"

"*I* can't. You'll have to talk with ballistics. Detective, unless toxicology tells me something different, I think we'll find this man died from blood loss following a gunshot wound to the abdomen. The bullet disintegrated upon contact, resulting in hemorrhage and death."

Garcia was making notes. "Doctor, as you no doubt observed, it didn't appear that Max was shot where we found him."

"I agree; had he been shot there we should have observed a large amount of blood. This wound bled heavily."

"So, with this wound, could he have walked any distance?"

"He might have, yes. I would suspect it took him a while to die. It would have been extraordinarily painful, though."

"So, if you know—how long from the time he was shot until he bled out?"

"Well, that depends. I would think that any sort of physical activity would have hastened the bleeding, of course," Laws said. He bit his lip, thinking. "I guess I would say death occurred perhaps twenty to thirty minutes after he sustained the wound. But that's just an estimate based on the location and size of the wound, and the apparent loss of blood. Preliminary, you understand?"

"I do."

"Don't hold me to that."

"Got it."

"One other thing."

"Yeah, Doc?"

"Look at this." Laws pointed at something he had removed from Max. "This is the pancreas."

Garcia looked and quickly averted his gaze. "And?"

"I'll know more when I get the results back, but I suspect your victim here was a dead man walking."

"What do you mean?"

"I mean it appears he had terminal cancer. Pancreatic," Laws said. "It's amazing he was as active as he was."

"But the bullet killed him?"

"Yes, and we know the bullet was fired from some distance. Not a suicide. Manner of death is homicide. I can tell you that based on the entrance wound the defendant was shot from a downward angle."

"Like he was on his knees?"

"No, more like he was shot by someone who was at an elevation above his own."

"Like on a hill?" Garcia asked hopefully.

"Yes."

Garcia was thinking about the timbered ridgeline. "Okay, that might help. A lot."

"Really?" Laws shook his head, started an electric saw, and pulled the sheet from Max's face. "Now, if you'll excuse me, I have some things to finish up."

∽

Several days later, Garcia was in the office of Robert Mitchell, the department's expert on firearms. Mitchell was slowly and deliberately examining under a microscope the remnants of the bullet that Laws had recovered from Max's body. Garcia sat quietly chewing gum, awaiting Mitchell's insight.

"Frangible," he said.

"That's what Doc Laws said, too."

"Yeah. Most bullets are made of very hard materials, so when they hit something—say, a human body—they penetrate. Frangible bullets, like this one, well, they tend to penetrate, but not as far. That's why they usually do not present an exit wound."

"Same stopping power?"

"It's debatable," Mitchell said. "They have their place. Like, if I was an air marshal or something, I might want to use a frangible round. That way if I had to use my weapon, there'd be less risk that my round might go through the target and then the plane, putting everyone at risk. They are good in cities, too, because they don't ricochet."

"Right. Anything preliminary?"

"I think it is a .270 Winchester."

"Crap," Garcia said. He'd hoped for something less commonplace; the .270 Win was perhaps the most popular rifle caliber in the United States, let alone in a hunting area like Custer. Aficionados of the .270 Win believed it was good for anything from white-tailed deer to bears. Probably one-third to half of the gun owners in Custer County had one. Add that to the fact that the bullet was frangible, and you had the recipe for failure to match. "What makes you think that?"

"The largest piece—it's from the base of the bullet itself, I think. I've got just enough that I think the arc could be calculated. Again, I'm thinking .270 Win, but can't be sure."

"Common round."

"Real common," Mitchell acknowledged. "You got anything to compare it to?"

"No. Are we out of luck?"

"If you could get me a cartridge and remnants from the bullet, I could do a test that might help. I'd fire a round into a metal backstop positioned over a tub of water. The bullet is frangible, so it would break into pieces. You collect the pieces and then begin a comparison—not only shapes and sizes, but chemical composition as well. I might be able to compare what you got here with a sample round from a box of ammo using a mass spectrometer and maybe we'd have something."

"But we need a cartridge?" Garcia clarified.

"That would certainly help."

"Can you tell anything about the distance?"

"No. What did Doc Laws say?"

"No evidence of gunshot residue, stippling, etc."

"You thinking maybe a hunter?"

"Maybe," Garcia said. "But I hope not. Not sure there is any crime statistically less likely to be solved than accidental death by unknown hunter."

"Yeah, tough one."

24

Rebecca Nice had been the elected county attorney for Custer County for almost a decade. Some days, she wondered why in the world she had sought the job. This morning, she had convened a meeting with Garcia, Punch Polson, Grant Lee, and Cathy Schmidt to get an update on the results of the investigation, as well as to begin to build a group consensus on where things were headed. Sitting at the head of the table, she looked at the other four and was thankful for their qualifications and professionalism. Punch, Garcia, and Cathy were known quantities, and she had done her homework before bringing Lee on, and felt he was going to be a strong addition to the team, especially as a trial attorney.

Garcia was explaining his investigation to this point, talking theories, when Punch chimed in. "Elk hunting is like a religion around here," he offered. "And with the number of out-of-state hunters we've seen following the break in the pandemic, it could be your guy got nailed by some rookie with a case of elk fever."

"That's what I'm afraid of," Garcia replied.

"Why?" Rebecca asked.

"Because those cases are almost impossible to solve," Punch said. "You usually have a shooter with no criminal record, who bought his ammo out of state, for a rifle he inherited from his father. The guy probably doesn't have a record so no prints or DNA on file, and it's a long-distance shot so no gunshot residue or stuff like that. The guy gets scared, and—since we don't know who he was in the first place—no one misses him when he leaves town. Just cancels his hotel room and hits the road. There are a lot of these cases that go unsolved."

"Christ, don't tell me that," Rebecca groused. "Why not a family member—or a pro?"

"I think if it was a pro the shot woulda been better," Garcia said. "Since I spoke with Doc Laws, I've been doing some map reconnaissance. There's a timbered ridgeline to the west of the location where Max's head of security left him when he went to confront the trespassers. The doc thinks Max was shot from a slightly elevated angle. The ridgeline would fit the bill as the spot from which the shot was fired. It's only about one hundred thirty meters from the crest of the hill to where Max was, so—"

"He was kind of in the open, right?" she interrupted.

"Well, yeah," Garcia said. "If he was shot where Paulie left him, he was near an old ponderosa stump."

"So, how did anyone mistake him for an elk in the open at one hundred thirty meters?"

Garcia shrugged. "Kind of what I'm thinking. On the other hand, people do stupid stuff all the time."

"But like you said, a pro wouldn't have gut-shot him," Punch observed.

"Maybe on purpose?" Cathy offered. "Make it look like an amateur?"

"But an intentional non-fatal shot would risk him not dying—or even seeing something," Lee said. He was shaking his head, clearly not enamored with that theory.

Garcia was nodding along with Lee. "Right. That's why I'm thinking either a hunter shot him by mistake, or someone with a grudge against him did it."

"From what I hear that's gonna be a long line of suspects," Punch said.

"I know," Garcia admitted.

"What about family?" Cathy asked.

"The family is in disarray," Garcia said. "Sounds like lots of motives there." He explained his discussion with Paulie, the threats that had been made, and his efforts to narrow down the list of suspects. He continued with a review of his discussion with the medical examiner and Mitchell. "He can't be sure, but he thinks we are looking for a .270 Winchester. It'd be better if he had a cartridge, of course."

"So how is the search going?" Lee asked.

"On it," Garcia said, "but it's tough because of the snow. Supposed to warm up here in the next day or so."

Lee looked hard at Garcia. "It's been more than a week."

"I'm peddling as fast as I can," Garcia said. "I don't have a lot—just looking at possibilities. It's like a needle in a haystack. We've got limited manpower."

"Oh, for Christ's sake!" Lee burst out. "Are you kidding me? Let's get some folks in there and get serious. Bring the family in for questioning—every one of them! We'll keep them all here—"

"No," Rebecca said. Her voice was soft, but it stopped Lee cold. "That's not how we do business around here."

"But they could be hiding evidence!" Lee insisted.

"Of what?" she asked.

"Frangible bullets," Lee said, satisfied with himself. He sat back.

Rebecca looked to Garcia. "Frangible bullets are not uncommon around here," he explained. "I would think anyone with a common caliber weapon will have some. What we need is an expended cartridge and a rifle."

"Yeah, right," Punch said sourly.

"What's the issue?" Lee asked.

"Everyone has a .270 Win," Punch replied. "And because of the local weather, a lot of practice and target shooting is done indoors, and frangibles are used so they don't ricochet. They are a lot safer. So, frangible bullets from a .270 Win . . . well, that's not gonna narrow things down much."

"Which is why we need to lean on the family and get a warrant," Lee said.

"I haven't told them what we think," Garcia added, hoping to stem any criticism. "I think we have some time."

"Maybe not," Garcia said. "But Mitchell has a plan, if we could get a cartridge."

Lee stood and began to pace. "I think we start with the assumption that it was a family member. I'm not buying the accident theory. I didn't just fall off the shit-wagon."

Garcia looked around the room and took a deep breath before replying. "Neither did I. We always work from the inside out. I'm starting from the assumption it was a family member, especially given where we think he was."

Lee nodded his approval, which irritated both Punch and Garcia to no end. Rebecca sensed the growing divide and stepped in. "We're going to do a press conference in the morning," she said. "I've spoken with the sheriff, and even though we are thinking someone from the family, the press conference is going to hint at a theory that it was a hunter."

"What about Sprague and his people?" Cathy asked. "Are you looking at them?"

"We are," Garcia explained. "But as far as I am able to tell, Sprague and his group all have alibis—each other."

"Could be a conspiracy," Cathy ventured.

Lee snorted derisively. "A conspiracy of those mouth-breathers?"

Cathy blushed and Rebecca again intervened. "I'm going to leave the investigation to the professionals—whatever they think the possibilities are," she added, looking sharply at Lee, who was oblivious.

"All I know is that this office, and this department, needs a win," Lee said, opening the blinds, peering out, then closing them. "It seems to me that we've been getting our asses kicked by a bunch of small-town douchebags. I came here to change that." In the stunned silence that followed, he seemed to realize his words had hurt everyone in the room. "I mean, I'm here to help... of course."

"Of course," Punch said as he stood and left the room.

Garcia looked at his watch. "I've got another meeting," he said, following Punch out the door.

Rebecca waited until the door had fully closed behind the men before saying anything. Looking to Lee, she enunciated each word clearly. "I'd appreciate it if you'd keep your opinions to yourself. I don't need you coming in here and creating a rift between my office and law enforcement."

"I'm just saying—"

"Grant, I'm talking—why are you interrupting me?" she asked. When he appeared suitably chagrined, she continued, "To date, you've talked a lot, but haven't shown me or anyone else anything. Understand that very soon—very soon—I'm going to expect to see more than talk. I hope you are up to it."

As they walked the hallway to their offices, Lee looked to Cathy. "People can't handle the truth. Results count. I get results."

25

The next morning at precisely ten a.m., Walsh and Garcia stood on either side of a podium with several microphones. Homicides were relatively rare in Wyoming, and one involving a billionaire was sure to draw attention. To the sheriff's immediate left were Rebecca and Lee. Garcia was flanked by the immediate Kovalenko family. Behind them were extended family and members of law enforcement.

The sheriff began by introducing Nice, Garcia, as well as Lana and the rest of the Kovalenko family. He then gave a brief statement, concluding with a plea for anyone with information to get ahold of law enforcement immediately. "We need your help. If this was an accident, contact us. We only want the truth and to do the right thing for this grieving family. Deputy Garcia will take any questions."

Sarah Penrose from the *Custer Bugle* was given the honor of asking the first question. "Do you have any suspects?"

Garcia cleared his throat, his heart pounding. He had never done this before, and it showed. "We, uh, do not. We are in the early stages of the investigation and cannot be sure at this point that a crime occurred. We are still seeking information and—"

"But the medical examiner said it was homicide," another reporter said.

"Homicide is a term meaning death by the hand of another," Rebecca replied after Garcia looked to her. "It does not mean the same thing as murder."

"We continue to investigate this as both an accident and as a crime," Walsh explained. "We will not eliminate any possibility until we have reason to do so."

"What if it was a hunter?"

"Then we would ask that person to come forward and take responsibility," Garcia responded quickly. "We just want to get the facts so that we might provide them to the family."

"So you are looking at the possibility that it was *not* an accident?" The questioner was an out-of-town reporter that neither Rebecca nor Walsh recognized.

"We're looking at everything," Garcia began. "But we think—"

"It's fair to say we are looking at all possibilities," Walsh interrupted, fearing Garcia was about to disclose sensitive information. "As information comes in, we will develop and follow up on leads and begin to refine our theories."

And on it went for another ten minutes, with the press asking increasingly pointed questions of law enforcement. Finally, Penrose said, "I have a question for the family."

Lana stepped forward. "Yes?"

"What do you say to the person who shot your father?"

"We say that we just want to know what happened, and that we are withholding judgment until we find out," she said. "But rest assured, we *will* find out. Ours is a family with many resources, and we will use them all to help determine the identity of the shooter and—if necessary—to bring that individual to justice."

Other members of the press chimed in quickly. "Did your father have any enemies?" "Do you have any suspects?"

Mike stepped forward and was about to answer when he felt Lana's hand on his sleeve, tugging him back into line. He smiled wanly and resumed his place.

"Thank you. Thank you all," Walsh said. "We'll keep you updated. Please route any questions through our press office."

~

Down the street, Sam turned off the small television in his office when the press conference finished. "Wow," he said to Cassie.

"Oh my gosh," Cassie replied. "We're gonna be on the front page everywhere. Your client was famous!"

"He was."

"I'd never heard of him before he moved out here, of course."

Sam smiled. "I suppose you and I just don't move in the right circles."

"I do not," she admitted. "You know what? We read and hear all about these folks from California getting rich, but then they don't like it where they are so they move out here—and bring their values and votes with them!"

"Cassie," Sam scolded softly. "People are looking for the same things everyone wants, like good schools, good roads, and a safe place to raise their kids."

"Well, they had that there, too, before they all went crazy," Cassie said. "I was talking to a realtor friend last week. He told me the Friday before that he closed seven deals—seven!"

"That's a good thing," Sam said. "If you're not growing as a community, you are dying."

"But he said that four of the deals were buyers from California—three of them paid cash, and every one of them paid more than the asking price," she said. "On a couple of the places the appraisal didn't cover, but they didn't care. They are driving prices to the point where us local folks can't afford to buy a place."

"On the other hand," Sam countered, "local sellers are realizing a windfall and will spread that around town."

"I dunno what that means, but I know they're bringing crime and violence with them."

"Cassie, be careful now. You're starting to sound like what those folks from the coasts think we are."

"Well, I'm right, aren't I?" she challenged him.

"I think there's some truth there, yeah. But there are good people everywhere, and there are bad people everywhere," Sam countered. "And besides—among the newcomers in the past few years was a certain broken-down lawyer, right?"

"Sam Johnstone! You know I ain't talking about you, now."

"I know, Cassie. I'm just sayin'.'"

She smiled in understanding. "So, who you think done it?"

"Shot Max?" Sam asked, and when she nodded, he kicked his feet up on his desk. "I don't begin to know. What are you thinking?"

"Well," she said. "At first, I was sure it was Casey Sprague or one a them boys. But then I heard that Max had made all kinds of enemies in the Russian mob. Word is that there's been all kinds of guys showing up over at the Longbranch what looked like this." She moved the tip of her nose to the side with two fingers. When Sam laughed aloud, she continued. "I'm serious! Besides, Casey's first cousin is a friend of mine, and she told me that when Max got shot, Casey was with a bunch of his buddies up in that school section."

"Casey and his buddies would never lie, right?"

"Don't be sarcastic. I'm just tellin' you what I heard."

"Okay. But I'll just say that if the Russian mob was involved, I doubt they'd show their faces—or their broken noses—around here first."

"And if it ain't either one, then what?"

"Then either family, someone hired by the family, or a hunter," Sam said. "Or maybe someone we don't even know about."

"That's a lot of suspects."

"It is," Sam agreed. "I don't envy whoever is heading up this investigation."

"It's Ted Garcia. You know he used to date my cousin, right?"

"Uh, no. Didn't know that."

"You bet he did. A real nice fella."

Sam's phone rang. When Cassie made no move to answer it, he smiled. "I'll get it," he said.

"Good. I've got stuff to do," she said. Holding the door, she mouthed, "Open or closed?"

Sam recognized the number. It was Daniels. "Closed," he said to Cassie. Then, "Press, what's happening?"

"You watching this?"

"I was, yeah—it's over, right?"

"Fortunately," Daniels groused. "By the way, I got to thinking about something. Max passing away here means his estate is going to have to be probated here."

"Well, yeah, but he won't have a probate, will he? I've got to believe he had trusts out the backside. Probably trusts full of trusts."

"Something always falls through the crack and needs to be picked up," Daniels advised Sam. "You need to pick this up. The fee is capped by statute, but given his holdings it will likely be a boatload of money."

"Okay." Sam thought about Marci. Daniels hadn't updated him for almost a week. "How—how is Marci doing?"

"Not so well," Daniels said. "Lots of pain. Test after test after damned test. At some point, don't you think one of these doctors would just say, 'Let's try this?' I mean, what the hell? What's it gonna do—kill her? She can't take much more! I tell you what . . . I—I'm sorry, Sam. I get worked up."

"It's okay, Press—sorry I brought it up. You know, I'm here if you need anything. I don't care if it is just to vent or whatever."

"Thanks, Sam. You've already done more than enough—I'll try not to piss on your foot anymore. Just one thing, though?"

"Anything."

"Next time you talk to someone from Max's family, will you bring up the subject of trust administration and probate?"

"Of course."

"Sam, Marci needs that treatment and I'm gonna get it for her. Eighteen thousand bucks for an hour's treatment—can you believe that?"

∽

Several hours later, Daniels gently shook Marci's shoulder. "Sweetheart, it's time for your pills."

"I don't think so, dear."

He watched her as she labored to breathe. "Come on, Marci. You've got to take your medicine. The doctor said it will make you better."

Marci rolled over and looked at her husband. She smiled briefly, then went sober. "No, he didn't. I was there—remember?"

"Well, it can't hurt," Daniels said lamely.

"Sit me up."

"What?"

"Sit me up," she ordered. When Daniels had piled enough pillows behind her, she was more upright but still somewhat slumped. He administered a pill to her and then sat down next to her, lest she topple over. "What are we doing?" she asked.

"What do you mean?" He knew exactly what she meant.

"What are we *doing*?" she said again, reaching for his hand. "This. This is all . . . for nothing."

He looked away so she wouldn't see the tears forming. "No, that isn't true. We're just kind of at a plateau right now, medically speaking."

She smiled at her husband. He was such a good man. She'd known that from the start, of course. But until she got sick, she hadn't known just how attentive, how kind he could be. Perhaps if their only child . . . well, no use thinking about that. "You and I both know how this will end, dear."

He shook his head vigorously. "But it doesn't have to be now, does it?"

She smiled wanly. "I'm tired, Preston. I'm tired of being sick. I'm a burden on—"

"No, you are not! I won't have you say that! I won't have you think that! You mean everything to me; you always have. You're the most important thing in my life. You have been, for almost fifty years. I—I know I haven't always shown it. I haven't been as kind or appreciative as I should have been. I haven't been the husband you deserved, but—"

He braved a look and saw he was talking to himself. Her chin had dropped to her chest, and she was asleep, the byproduct of the increasingly powerful painkillers she was taking. He picked her up gently so as not to wake her—she couldn't weigh one hundred pounds now—and laid her flat on the bed, then covered her with a blanket, turned off the television, and stood watching the rise and fall of the blankets. When he heard her snoring softly, he closed the door behind him.

Later, he washed down one of her painkillers with three fingers of a single malt scotch he'd found under the kitchen sink—she must have tried to hide it from him when she was still healthy. On the couch he alternately dozed and awoke to nightmares while a succession of black-and-white movies played on a cable channel. At two a.m., he poured himself another drink, checked on Marci, and scrawled a note to talk with her oncologist about a promising treatment advertised on television involving figs and anise developed by some doctor in Greece. At three a.m., an improbably perky woman asked if he or someone he knew suffered from a litany of conditions. Apparently, a call to her law office would fix things with "compensation." He'd done some personal injury work as a lawyer, and he contemplated for a moment the cost versus the return on investment of those commercials. At four a.m. he awakened, eyes crusted shut as the result of his tears. He rubbed them almost raw in frustration, then walked quietly to Marci's door, opened it a crack, and peered in. When he couldn't see her breathing, he panicked and walked into her room.

She stirred. "Press, is that you? What time is it?"

"Yes, it's me," he said. "Just some trouble sleeping. Checking on you, dear. It's a little after four; go back to sleep and get your rest." He kissed her quickly on the cheek—before she could crane her neck to see him, lest she see the tears. "You have an appointment later. I'll get you up in plenty of time."

26

Sam was working on a motion to suppress for a client who had gotten himself arrested for driving under the influence. Apparently, his client had fallen asleep in the drive-thru line of a fast-food restaurant just after nine p.m. The workers had called the cops, who had pulled his client over after he had awakened on his own and gotten his order. The arresting officer had failed to develop probable cause beyond Sam's client having fallen asleep and smelling like a brewery. A prominent local businessman, he was attempting to play the victim and had apparently watched too many television shows where people walked for minor indiscretions on the part of law enforcement.

"This could really hurt my career," he explained.

"I'll do the best I can," Sam assured the man. "But maybe you should have thought that through before you got drunk and went for a burger. Law enforcement had the right to pull you over—if only to ensure you were okay to drive."

"Yeah, but to pull me out of the car and make me take field sobriety tests? That was embarrassing! Those bastards can't do that, can they?"

"Maybe. Give me a chance to look at the video and we'll talk again. In the meantime, I suggest you get a substance abuse evaluation, and if your counselor says you have an issue, start doing whatever he or she recommends. It always looks good to a judge when the defendant is working things out on his own."

"I don't have a problem," his client had insisted. "I'm a respected member of the community, not some gutter-dwelling drunk."

Sam took a deep breath and released it before responding. "Lots of people who are otherwise respectable have issues with booze and drugs," he advised.

"I don't. I'm not a loser. If I had a problem, I'd be able to deal with it without someone telling me how to handle my life. It's just a matter of having the balls to deal with it."

Sam felt the anger well up, and clenched—then unclenched—his fists. Nothing to gain by waxing this pencil-neck. He hadn't really cared for him at all, and this was sealing that particular deal. "Fine. But let me tell you what Judge Downs is going to tell you: there are only two reasons people don't follow the law. One is they cannot—perhaps they have a mental illness or issue, or an addiction to booze or drugs."

"I don't," his client had assured him.

"Then you will fall into the other half of her equation, and that is you are simply a criminal—someone who chooses to violate the law."

The client thought through the ramifications. "What kind of theory is that?"

"I'm just telling you how she looks at things. You be you. But be aware of what's out there."

The client had left in a huff, and Sam was looking at his motion, thinking it was going to be an uphill battle, when Cassie buzzed him. "Sam, it's Ms. Kovalenko-Brown."

He looked at his watch. He had time. "Bring her back." He tidied up while Cassie brought Lana back. "Come in," he said when Lana appeared in the door. She took the seat indicated. To his surprise, she was alone.

"Good morning," Sam began. "I'd ask how the funeral went, but . . . well, they all suck."

"It wasn't actually half-bad," Lana said. "A lot of Dad's friends came by to pay their final respects, and fortunately, a lot of the people with whom he had disagreements stayed away. So, all in all, not bad."

"Closure," Sam said.

"Yeah, that's what they say," she replied perfunctorily. "Sam, I wanted to talk with you. As I understand it, because Dad died here in Wyoming, this is the place to administer his estate."

"If one is necessary," Sam agreed, thinking back to his discussion with Press.

"Dad's California attorneys said I am the named successor trustee and executrix—whatever all that means. So, how do we start?"

"Have your California attorneys get me the originals of all documents and I'll file them with the court along with a petition to have you named personal representative—that's the twenty-first-century term for an executrix." He smiled. "And just so you know, Press Daniels is going to take the lead on this stuff. He's done a million estates as a judge. You'll be in good hands."

"And you'll continue to work the other stuff?"

"Assuming you want to continue, yes." He looked at her expectantly.

"Oh, yes," she assured him. "We're going to continue. The economics are such that it wouldn't make sense not to."

"Okay, we can handle it," Sam assured her. He watched Lana closely, waiting for the other shoe to drop.

"What have you heard about the investigation into my dad's shooting?" she asked at last.

"Not much," Sam said. "But then, there's no real reason for anyone to consult with me. My secretary keeps me up on rumor central. Beyond that, I'm not in the mix."

"Who do you think did it?"

"I've no idea," Sam said truthfully. "Hunter? An enemy of your father's?"

"Could be," Lana said. "I think the cops are looking a little closer to home." When Sam didn't react, she continued. "Garcia, especially. I'm thinking he thinks it is one of us."

Sam sat back in his chair and stared at his wall. "Most murders are committed by people who know the victim well. It would make sense."

"I'll be honest, Sam. If he starts looking for motives, it could be any of us. My father was an extremely difficult man."

"Probably best you keep that kind of thought to yourself," he advised, again making eye contact.

"You're my lawyer, right?"

"I'm UkrCX's lawyer, and I am your lawyer in terms of helping you administer your dad's estate," Sam explained. "But anything outside those parameters is outside our agreement and I could be forced to cough up whatever we talk about."

"Okay, well, just so you know, if someone in this family gets arrested, I'm calling you. I've done my homework," she said. "Sounds like you've won several big cases. You obviously know the community."

"Well," Sam said, "let's just take it one step at a time and see what happens."

"Be ready. You hear it's a family member, know that I'll be on my way to see you."

"Got it."

27

Garcia was back on the Sprague property, this time with a warrant. He was looking for a rifle—a .270 Winchester, as well as some frangible cartridges. He'd brought two uniformed officers with him this time; nonetheless, he had butterflies as he knocked on the door of the dilapidated little trailer. The trash and litter remained, as did the muscle cars and boat shells. Garcia sensed the number of chickens and goats was somewhat less than it had been the last time he'd been here. He pounded repeatedly on the door before the same pre-teen girl finally opened it.

"What do you want?" she snarled.

Lovely child. "I have a search warrant. Is Casey here?"

"Yeah, but he's sleeping."

"It's two o'clock in the afternoon. Why don't you go wake him up?"

"'Cause he'll be pissed," she said. "He's always pissed when he gets woke up."

"Fine," Garcia said, opening the screen door. "I'll do it myself. Where's his room?" When she didn't answer, he asked again. "Where does he sleep?" When she still didn't answer, he looked at one of the deputies. "Take her downtown. Interference with an officer."

"Gawd!" the girl said, trying to wrench her arm from the deputy's grasp. "Let go!"

"One more chance," Garcia said, indicating that the deputy should wait just a minute. Message sent.

"There." The girl pointed. "Last door on the right. And I hope he chews your ass."

Garcia entered the room cautiously, then, seeing a sleeping Sprague, grabbed his foot and twisted it roughly. "Casey Sprague! We have a search warrant!"

"What? Who?" Sprague said, sitting up in his filthy bed. Seeing Garcia, he got angry. "What the hell are you doing?"

"I've got a search warrant here, Mr. Sprague." Garcia handed Sprague a copy of the same. "I've got my officers looking already, but you could make this a lot easier if you'd help us."

"Kiss my ass," Sprague said.

"Fine. We'll just look until we find it. I'm telling you, though, some of my guys, well, they're just not good at remembering where they got stuff from, you know? Results in a lot of complaints from homeowners that their stuff got disturbed but not put back."

Sprague was watching Garcia, calculating. "What are you looking for?"

"A .270 Winchester."

"Won't find one here." Sprague laughed. "That's a woman's gun. And as you can see, ain't no women around here, except my sister's kid, and she don't shoot."

"Why not?"

"Too dumb. Ain't got the sense God gave a horse."

"Well, we're going to look around in any event," Garcia said.

"Knock yourself out. You ain't gonna find nothin'."

And in fact, Garcia and his men didn't find any .270 Wins or ammunition. But they found other items of interest. One of the uniformed deputies appeared in the doorway and beckoned Garcia. "Detective, you want to come back and look at this?"

Garcia followed him down the hallway with Sprague in tow. On the bed was a "rig"—a loaded hypodermic needle prepared to inject liquid, likely methamphetamine, into a user's veins. "That's not good," Garcia said to Sprague.

"Hey, I don't know anything about that!" Sprague said. "Must be my old lady's."

"Yeah, well, you got what I think is meth in the house, and a kid in the house. That's called endangering children—it's a felony. Plus, I think that is a felony amount of meth there. You gonna allow me to search for drugs?"

"Hell, no!"

"Fine," Garcia said. "Deputy, please escort Mr. Sprague here outside. He can wait in your car while I get a warrant." He looked at Sprague. "Shouldn't take more than an hour or so to get the warrant."

"You sonuvabitch! You planted that!"

"Yeah, you're right. I got out of bed this morning and asked myself, 'How can I screw over Casey Sprague?' So I found a loaded rig and planted it in your house," Garcia said. "Because I've got nothing else to do," he finished sarcastically.

"See? He's admitted it! Did you hear him?" Sprague said to the other officers. "Is it on video?"

"Get him out of here," Garcia directed. He got on the phone and dictated the probable cause for a search warrant for drugs to a junior officer back at headquarters. "I'll be there in a minute," he concluded. When he left the property to complete the warrant, Sprague was in the back of an officer's car, gesticulating wildly and yelling at the top of his lungs. He might be a lot of things, Garcia thought, but he was not likely a killer. But this would give him a reason to squeeze Sprague about his source.

28

Sam and Daniels had convened a meeting of Max's family to do a reading of the trust's provisions for distribution of the estate. Generally, Sam eschewed this kind of production, opting instead for one-on-one meetings with beneficiaries. But in this case, he thought it best to meet with everyone at once to get things out in the open. At his conference table were Sam, Daniels, Lana, Mike, Danny, Stacy, and Alex. Paulie had taken a chair but, as usual, pulled it to a wall.

"Should *he* even be here?" Danny asked, indicating Paulie. "I mean, no offense, but he is not part of the family."

"Danny!" Lana scolded. "If that was the standard, then Alex wouldn't be invited, either."

"I'm okay with that," Danny said.

Sam had heard enough. "Perhaps it will make things easier if I tell you up front that all of you are provided for," he said. Looking around the table, he saw a mixture of resignation and understanding. "Shall we get started?" Seeing no objection, he passed around copies of the relevant portions of the trust. He directed everyone's attention to a particular annex, then to a page thereof. "As you can see," he began, "Max provided for everyone here. He named Lana as the successor trustee—she will be in charge of making sure Max's wishes were followed. We work for her, in essence," Sam explained, indicating himself and Daniels and looking to each person to ensure understanding.

"He left everyone here something," Sam again emphasized. "The majority of the estate's holdings are to be sold and divided equally between Lana, Danny, and Stacy. In addition, he left each of you a cash gift. Note, however, that Max left the entirety of UkrCX and its related holding companies to Mike. Max's stated intent—"

"What? That can't be right!" Alex said, looking to Lana.

Sam looked placidly at Alex. "I can assure you it is."

Alex's ears were red. "He said that he had changed his will or whatever!"

"As far as I know he had not," Sam said. "I asked the lawyers from California for the originals."

Danny's eyes were watering. "But he isn't family either!" he said, pointing to Mike. "Could Dad do that?"

"He's my husband!" Lana said.

"It's not right!" Danny insisted.

"It's legal—that's what matters for the sake of this distribution," Sam said levelly. He looked at Alex and Danny as he spoke. "We presume the trustor had a reason for his actions."

"He did for a while," Danny said. "But Mike was failing, and Dad was going to change his trust—we all knew that. Mike knew that, too, so he killed him! He said he would do it, and he did!"

"Danny, stop it!" Lana commanded. Next to her, Mike tried to suppress a sardonic smile while side-eyeing a red-faced Danny.

"Why?" Danny asked. "The old man is dead and buried. I just want what's mine and I'm out of here."

"I think *what's yours* is the money he left you," Lana said. "That's it."

"Oh, no. That's not it," Danny assured her. "I'm in this for the long haul."

Lana stared hard at her brother before looking to Sam. "Please continue."

"Well." Sam focused his attention on Mike. "The bequest of all shares of UkrCX and the other companies means that you have total control of those entities."

Danny fumed. "Such bullshit."

"Well, I think it is what Daddy wanted," Stacy said. She looked at her siblings for affirmation—they all thought she was just the pretty one. Danny looked away.

Mike looked to Lana, who smiled in agreement. "I think you are right," she said to Stacy. "In any event, there is nothing we can do about it now."

Sam explained the remainder of the trust's provisions. When he was done, he asked for questions.

"Dad told us he was going to change his trust," Lana said. "So, the fact that he didn't—"

"Lana, what are you saying? Why are you asking this?" Mike asked.

"I'm simply trying to find out if his intent—even though he didn't act on it—means anything," she said to Mike. She then turned her attention to Sam. "Does it?"

"It does not," Sam said. "The law recognizes only those aspects of intent which are acted upon."

"What if he couldn't act because Mike killed him?" Danny asked.

"Oh, Danny!" Stacy said. "Stop!"

"That would certainly merit consideration," Sam said carefully.

"It's tearing us apart," Stacy said. "Lana, that isn't fair. It would be fairer to leave each of us kids one-third."

Lana looked to Sam.

"It doesn't have to be fair," Sam explained. "Just lawful."

Alex stood. He'd been watching quietly. "Max told me that he had already made changes and that I would take over the company and control the day-to-day operations," he said at last. "I intend to hold him to that."

Sam nodded his understanding. "Well, you can certainly challenge the distribution of the estate, but there is a challenge provision."

"What's that mean?" Alex asked uncertainly.

"It means that anyone who challenges the estate is to be given one dollar as their portion of the distribution."

Alex's eyes bulged. "Jesus! Could he do that?"

"Yes," Sam advised. "It's perfectly legal. In fact, it is common."

"You're not even family," Mike said dismissively to Alex. Then, perhaps realizing what he had said, added, "Or even married into it."

"Max told me that didn't matter," Alex said. "He told me I was replacing you."

"That's such bullshit." Mike stood. "You greedy little—"

"Stop it," Lana commanded. "Both of you."

Mike looked quickly at his wife, who was watching Alex.

Danny stood. "I'm going to see a lawyer."

"So am I," Alex said, and immediately left.

"You have the right," Sam advised when he saw everyone look his way. "Might be best. But make sure you inform your lawyer of the challenge provision. They file, it's in effect should you be unsuccessful."

"I agree," Daniels said.

Danny stormed out, followed by Stacy. Sam looked at the remaining parties. "I have another meeting," he lied. "Anything else?" When no one spoke up, he stood. "Thank you all for being here. We will begin processing the paperwork to file with the court. Lana, we will contact you for signatures when we are ready."

"Fine," she said. "We are at a critical point if we are going to see my father's dreams fulfilled." She left, and her husband followed. Paulie remained.

"Something I can help you with?" Sam asked.

Paulie stood, clearly conflicted.

"We can keep secrets," Sam assured him.

29

From almost the moment he'd been called in, Garcia had doubted this was an accident. It was nothing he could put a finger on or give words to—just the sneaking suspicion of an experienced investigator on a crime scene. The terrain walk had convinced him the shot most likely came from the west or south, making a family member the likely shooter. The money at stake added to his conviction; since time immemorial, money and sex—or both—had been the primary motives for murder. As he mounted the stairs to the mansion, he thought about his next steps. He wanted to pull each family member aside and see what he could find out, to again hear their theories, to see how they reacted to a little pressure. The door was opened by Stacy, who stammered, "Hello, uh . . . "

"I'm Ted Garcia from the sheriff's office."

"I'm sorry. I recognized your face. I've just been a little distracted lately."

"That's fine," he said. His understanding was that Stacy and Danny had returned to California before the shooting occurred. "I'm glad you answered the door. I'm here to talk with Lana, Mike, and Alex. Can you get one of them for me?"

Stacy left him in the library. Moments later, Lana walked in the room. "Ms. Brown, do you have a minute?"

"For what?"

"To get your recollection of the night your father disappeared, what happened the next day, who might have wanted to harm him—stuff like that."

She eyed him head to toe. "I'm not sure what I can tell you now that you don't already know, but shall we sit?"

"Sounds good." When they were seated, Garcia began. "So, I want to begin by talking about any enemies your father might have had."

"Most of them were merely people with whom he'd had business dealings. My father worked by the letter of the law, but if the law allowed him to do something, he did it. That resulted in a lot of hurt feelings."

"Anyone so hurt they would want to put a bullet in him?"

"Maybe," she said. "He cost a lot of people a lot of money."

"Any names for me?" he asked. She gave him several names and last known locations. All were Californians, except for a couple of former associates from New Jersey. He'd gotten the same names from Paulie, but took them down, along with what little contact information she had, then put away his notebook. "Anyone closer have a motive?"

"What do you mean?"

"Let's start with people closer . . . geographically."

"Well, Casey Sprague and that crowd. They threatened Dad right in front of Paulie and Mike. And you've probably been to some of the city council and county commission meetings. They made no secret that they wanted him gone."

"Right. I'm following up some leads toward that end."

"Good," Lana said. "I want this over. I know it is going to be tough identifying the gun and all that, but I think if you start there you'll be on the right track."

Garcia took his pen and notebook back out and made a point of scribbling. "How do you know that?"

"What?"

"That it's going to be tough identifying the gun?"

She looked at him blankly. "Well, I'm assuming if it was easy, you'd already have it done—am I right?"

"Potentially," he allowed. He felt his pulse quicken and went through the motions of making a note while composing his thoughts. "Let me ask you this—what about someone closer? Someone related to Max? I'm told there were some hard feelings about how the estate was divided—especially the shares of UkrCX."

"Who told you that?"

Garcia didn't answer. "Mike got it all, right?"

"Well, yes, but that was expected. He runs the company. That trust was made some time ago."

And perhaps she wanted to see it stay that way. "I understand that. Now, I've been told that Max was thinking about making some changes."

She snorted. "I don't know who told you that, but as far as I know my husband has been the guy all along. I mean, I know Alex says Dad had promised the company to him and all that, but don't believe it. He's a child." When Garcia raised his eyebrows, she continued. "Look, a lot of this was just Dad being Dad. Keep the pressure on Mike, and string Alex along, you know?"

"Did Alex understand that?"

"That he was being toyed with? I doubt it."

"So Alex could have thought the estate had been changed, and that he would be put in charge if something happened to Max?"

"Well, that's what he says Dad said, but it didn't happen—did it?"

"What about *you*?"

"What *about* me?"

"Did you think your husband would keep control?"

"Of course," Lana said. "He was doing the heavy lifting of running the company every day—and under Dad's watchful eye, I might add. He deserved it."

Garcia sat back and stared hard at Lana, trying to make her look away. When she wouldn't break eye contact, he asked his question. "Did *you* know Max had threatened to transfer control to Alex?"

"Not until Alex said so at the lawyer's office," she said. "Look, if you are thinking Mike did anything to . . . to—"

"Protect his interests?"

"Then you are wrong. Mike would never do anything like that!"

"How about Alex? He might have thought—"

"He's a child."

"A lot of young people do terrible things," Garcia said. Time to needle her a bit. "Just so I understand . . . *you* knew about Max threatening to change his will?"

"Trust."

"Whatever."

"Not until after he was shot," she insisted.

Garcia nodded, even though he didn't believe her. "Tell me where you were when your father disappeared."

"Seriously?" she asked. When Garcia merely stared at her, she smirked. "I have no idea, because I don't know when he was shot, do I?"

Good answer. "Did Mike ever threaten your father?"

"Well, yes—but only out of anger, you know? Just like anyone else who is under stress and pressure might."

"But you can't say where Mike was around the time of the shooting?"

"On the mountain, right? Ask him."

"I will." Garcia needed to ask his next question. "How about Alex?"

"What about him?"

She wasn't being straight about something. "Do you know where he was just prior to your father's disappearance and shooting?"

"I thought he was up on the mountain with Mike and my dad and Paulie. Are you saying he wasn't?" She lit a cigarette, inhaled, and blew smoke into the air. She looked at him like she might a cockroach. "You disgust me, coming around here, snooping around my family, trying to dig up dirt."

He was under her skin now. "I'm simply trying to find out who shot your father—why do you find that offensive?"

"Because no one in this family would do that!" she said. "You are off track, Detective."

"Perhaps." He decided to tweak her. "You'll agree that if Mike lost control of the company, *you* would lose a lot of money and influence as well —right?"

She exhaled smoke and stood. "We're done here."

"One last thing," Garcia began. "You seem . . . stable, compared to the other members of your family, but your father—"

"Wasn't going to leave the company to me—that's right," she said, bending to stub out the butt. "Which means I had no motive."

Except for the spousal benefit of Mike keeping control, of course. Then again, if what he thought he'd seen and heard between her and Alex . . . "Okay, thank you," Garcia said, standing. "Well, I guess I do have one thing. Where is your husband?"

"I'm not sure. Probably down at the office," she said. "Somebody's got to keep the company going."

"Just trying to clear some things up." Garcia nodded to her. "I'll see myself out." When he closed the door behind himself, he lingered, and heard her on the phone. Brown would be well-prepared by the time he got downtown.

~

Garcia was on the phone in his unmarked sedan moments later when Alex approached the home. He jumped out of the vehicle and intercepted Alex. "Mr. Melnyk, do you have a minute?" Garcia asked.

Alex was uncertain how to react. He looked at the car, then at Garcia, and then to the house. Garcia followed Alex's eyes and saw Lana standing in the window, watching them. "You want to go somewhere more private?" Garcia asked.

"No. We can talk here . . . I guess."

"I'm just cleaning up loose ends about last week. My condolences."

"Uhh, thanks," Alex said, glancing toward the window.

Garcia positioned himself between Alex and the window. "You and Max were close, I hear."

"Well, yeah. He was my godfather. He took me in."

"I'm told he had big plans for you."

"Not as big as I thought," Alex snapped, then quickly recovered. "Sorry," he added.

"Well, things happen," Garcia said. "I heard Max had told you that you were gonna be the man."

"He did," Alex said. "But apparently, he lied. So, what do you want?"

Motive, for sure, assuming he didn't know Max had lied to him. "I'm trying to figure out who was where when Max got shot. Where were you?"

"I was . . . well . . . I went up the mountain with Max and Paulie and Mike." Alex then explained the same chain of events as Mike and Paulie. "So, anyway, we left him and went to confront the trespassers, just like he told us. I thought it might be wise to see if I could get a signal and call for help, so I rode around, but I couldn't get one."

"Where did you ride to?"

"Oh, I don't know—just all around, you know? I remember being on kind of a timbered hillside. I thought for sure I'd get a signal there. But I didn't," he said. "So I came back to where we'd left Max."

"Could you see Max from that hillside?"

"If he'da been there, yeah."

"How long were you gone?"

"I dunno . . . twenty, thirty minutes, maybe?"

"And then you rode back without getting help?"

"Well, I wasn't helping just riding around, was I?" Alex asked, trying to peer around Garcia. "I was worried."

Right on cue. "Why?"

"Well, because I'd been gone awhile and . . . well, the gunshot, I guess."

Garcia was very still. His eyes narrowed. "Gunshot?"

"Yeah," Alex said. "I heard a gunshot. I didn't know where it came from —the wind was howling—but I got kind of worried. When I got back, Mike said *he* had heard a shot, then *he* fired into the air in order to try to alert Max, or to orient him to where Mike was, or whatever."

Garcia was watching Alex closely, trying to figure out why this hadn't come up before. "So you heard a gunshot. Then what?"

"Well, then . . . I didn't know what to do, you know?" Alex said. "So . . . I went back to the ranch, and I met up with Mike and Paulie—they were already back. Lana showed up. She called you, I think."

Garcia was thinking about three goose eggs he had drawn. "Why didn't you tell me about Mike shooting the gun earlier?"

Alex looked everywhere but at Garcia. Finally, he took a deep breath. "Look, I don't know what to believe, okay?" When Garcia didn't respond, he looked at the house. Garcia followed his eyes and saw the shadow. Lana, no doubt. "Look, I mean. . . I don't believe any of it, but Mike . . . he'd made threats, you know?"

"What kind of threats?"

"Like, you know. . . threats. Like . . .he said that he'd 'put a bullet in his head,' or something like that. 'Shoot his ass'—I can't remember."

"Can you try?"

"I mean, that was it, you know? He was drunk and angry because Max was on his ass. I think he was afraid."

"That Max was going to replace him with you?"

"Well, yeah. I mean, that's what Max said," Alex admitted. "But I'm not saying he shot him. I mean, Max was . . . hard. He was controlling. Frustrating. I mean, everyone was mad at him at some point, you know?"

"You ever threaten him?"

"Maybe, but just talking shit—you know?"

Time to change subjects. "Right, so when you got back to the ranch, Mike and Paulie were looking for Max?"

"No, I think they'd already figured out he wasn't there—from the hands, I guess."

"Did you see Lana?"

"Yeah. She was yelling at Mike for leaving her dad out there all alone."

Garcia had a thought. "Where are the guns?"

"I suppose in the gun rack in the tack room. The hands put our stuff away. Listen, Detective Garcia . . . I'm not trying to get Mike in trouble, you know?"

"I know," Garcia said. "You're just trying to do the right thing—right?"

"Yeah."

Garcia started to turn, then stopped. "Your gun—"

"Yeah?"

"What kind of rifle is it?" Garcia asked.

".270 Winchester."

"All right," Garcia said, getting that same old warm and fuzzy feeling he always got when things were coming together. "You don't know what kind of rifle Mike Brown shoots, do you?"

"It's the same. Max bought two identical weapons."

Garcia smirked. "Seriously?"

"Yeah. So, uh, Detective, you're not going to tell Mike I said anything about him, are you?"

"No, not right now."

"Because you know, I'm not saying he did anything—you know what I mean?"

"I do. No sweat."

30

Mike was making phone calls and feeling more than a little irritable this afternoon. He might have been out from under Max's shadow now, but between redneck townspeople, city councilmen who were afraid of their own shadow, and contractors putting the squeeze on him for "change orders" while citing the supposed increased costs of goods and labor, he was beginning to wonder if this building would ever be finished. His own damned lawyer, Sam Johnstone, had just left, having come in to ask him to "tone it down" a bit. He was chewing an antacid when the phone on his desk rang. "Yes, Leslie?"

"There's a policeman here to see you. A Detective Garcia."

Christ. Just what he needed. "Okay, send him back. But tell him I've only got a few minutes. And I want you to interrupt me at a quarter till —got me?"

"Yes, Mr. Brown." Moments later Leslie knocked at the door, opened it, and introduced Garcia.

"We've met," Mike said. When Leslie was gone, he indicated the chair across the desk from his own. "Have a seat. I've only got a few minutes. How can I help?"

"That'll work. I've only got a few questions." Garcia stared hard at

Brown until he broke eye contact and looked away. "I've been visiting with members of your family about your father-in-law's shooting."

"Why? We've been through all of this. We left him to confront the trespassers. Came back and he was gone. I looked for him but couldn't find him. Figured maybe he walked out, or maybe Alex picked him up. Went back to the ranch, and he wasn't there. Lana called you. That's all I know."

"Okay, well, I want to clear up a couple of things."

"What's that?"

"Alex went for help?"

"Oh, yeah." Mike nodded. "Max didn't look good. We didn't want him conking out on us."

"And you sent Paulie after Max's horse?"

Mike's eyes narrowed. "I did. What are you getting at?"

"So you were alone for a while," Garcia said without answering the question or asking one of his own. Mike was sophisticated enough not to respond to a non-question, so the two men stared at each other until Garcia spoke up. "How come you didn't tell me about firing a shot in the air?"

That got Mike's attention, and he went very still. "Didn't think it was important."

"You didn't think a gunshot was important in the context of your father-in-law dying of a gunshot wound?"

"I thought I heard a shot. I figured maybe Max was trying to alert us to his location."

"Hear anything in response?"

"No."

"Where were you when you fired?"

"Why?"

Garcia didn't respond. "Do you remember where you were?"

"Yes," Mike said. "There's a, uh, kind of a tree-lined ridge to the west of the saddle where we left Max. We were riding back when I thought I heard a shot. Then I was searching and I'm not sure when, but I got the idea to fire that signal round."

"Did you police up your brass?"

"Meaning what?"

"Did you pick up the cartridge after you fired?" Garcia asked, hoping the answer was no. He might have a round to recover for comparison's sake.

"Of course not. I wasn't worried about littering."

"Thanks," Garcia said. Things might be turning his way. "Speaking of things you didn't tell me," he began, then noticed that Mike was leaning forward in his chair. "You seem to know what I'm going to say."

"Look, I shoulda told you I threatened him, but it was just talk," Mike said. "It was frustration—you know? I mean, no one could meet his expectations and he was always threatening to fire me and cut me out. Danny and Alex threatened him, too."

"So, you and Paulie came off the mountain and then what?"

"Spoke with the hands," Mike said. "No one had seen him. Then we found Lana and—we already told you all of this."

"Just tying up some loose ends, okay?"

"Okay, but I've got a meeting here in a minute."

"I'll try not to take up too much of your time trying to figure out who killed your father-in-law and benefactor."

"I'm sorry, it's just . . . well, it's tough."

"What happened to your rifle?"

"What do you mean?"

"When you got back?"

"I suppose the hands took it and racked it with the others. Why?"

"I'd like to take a look at it."

"Why?" Mike asked, and then realization dawned. "Wait! You're not thinking I—"

"I'm just trying to clear everything up," Garcia said. "Might be the quickest way to show you didn't have anything to do with it."

"I don't know—maybe I should talk with Sam."

"Maybe," Garcia allowed. "But tell him I already got a warrant."

"What?" Mike stood. "You've been pimping me for information while—"

Garcia made a show of looking at his watch. "Yeah, my people will be serving it here momentarily if they haven't already. In fact, I probably ought to be getting to the ranch right about now."

Mike walked to his door and opened it. "Maybe I should go too so I can watch your men!"

"It's your property, but I'm going to keep you out of the way, and I warn you I will not have any interference."

"I have a right!"

"You will if charges are brought, certainly," Garcia said pointedly. "Anything you want me to know in the meantime?"

"I'm done talking with you," Mike said, pointing out the door. "You think I shot Max!"

He had that right. "I'm not convinced of that, but I will admit I'm intrigued. You didn't tell me about shooting a gun, and you failed to mention threatening Max. Now you say the threats were empty, but you don't want to let me examine the weapons or otherwise help me exonerate you. You understand why I might find all that intriguing, right?" When Mike didn't respond, Garcia zeroed in. "When did you find out your father-in-law was thinking about changing his trust to give Alex control of UkrCX?"

"What are you talking about?"

"Was it before or after he got shot?"

That rocked him. "I'm not saying anything else without my lawyer present," Mike said.

It was before. Garcia was sure of that. The question was, did Lana know and help him somehow? He stood. "Fine," he said. "For now. Don't leave town, okay? My department has a limited budget and I'd hate to have to waste any money flying out to California or wherever to bring you back for questioning."

"Get out."

Garcia did so, thinking he needed to get some men back on that hillside as soon as possible. He stopped at the station to do some paperwork on another case he was working, then headed to the ranch. From his car, he called Deputy Springs to tell her he was on his way and to see how the search was going.

"We got a problem, Ted," she said. She was going to be good someday, Garcia felt, but was a little green.

"What's that?"

"We've got a .270 Win, but the hands here tell me there were usually two. I found a guy who racked this one. He said Alex gave it to him the same night Max disappeared."

"Mike didn't give them one?"

"No."

"Okay, well, take custody of the one they have," Garcia said. He had a thought. "Did the same guy take Mike's stuff when he got back that night—the gun, I mean?"

"Yeah, but he said there was no gun in Mike's scabbard. He said Mike and Paulie came back and went running into the house, and he asked Mike about his rifle but never got an answer."

Convenient. "Get ahold of that guy—I'm gonna want to talk with him. Locate any .270 ammo?"

"Couple of boxes, several cartridges in each box."

"Did you give them a receipt?"

"Yup."

"Who'd you give the receipt to?"

"Gal named Lana Kovalenko-Brown."

She was way ahead of Garcia—literally. "Right on. She's the power behind the throne, I think."

"Oh, there's no doubt about that," Springs said. "She knew we were coming, by the way."

Good to know—husband and wife still talking, apparently. "Well, thanks, Springs."

"See you tomorrow, boss."

~

Garcia was in his car, eating a sandwich, drinking coffee, and watching a known drug dealer enter the home of a known drug user. He wasn't doing anything more than monitoring what was going on—he wasn't interested in these two. He was interested in the source. "Sooner or later," he said aloud. He was considering calling it a day and heading back to the office to do paperwork when he got a call from dispatch.

"Garcia."

"Cale Pleasance says he has something for you."

"Right. Tell him to hang on," Garcia said. "Be right there." Cale Pleasance was the department's fingerprint expert. He'd had the rifle for a couple of days. Garcia was hoping that between Pleasance and Bob Mitchell—the department's ballistics/toolmark expert—he'd be able to tie the weapon to one of the family members.

Ten minutes later, Garcia walked into Pleasance's office. "Whattaya got?"

"Good afternoon to you, too."

"C'mon, Cale, I don't have time for that crap. I'm up to my ass in alligators."

"Prints belong to one Aleksander Melnyk—know him?"

"I do," Garcia said. "Are you sure?"

"I'm as good at my job as you are at yours."

"Where is the gun now?"

"Mitchell has it."

"Thanks, Cale." Garcia walked quickly to Mitchell's office. The deputy sheriff had received extra training in toolmark examination and ballistics. For a small department like Custer's, the cost for a full-time employee to perform those tasks would be prohibitive. Using state resources only would be too slow, so the department compromised, and sent Mitchell to Virginia for training. While he could generally handle the job, he knew his limits.

"Ted, I think this is the right caliber," Mitchell said. "But I really need a cycled round."

"I know, I know. I'll keep looking."

"They tell me there's another gun missing. Be best to have both."

"No kidding."

"Want some good news?"

"Please."

"I'll do a chemical comparison between what was found in the deceased's body and the composition of a bullet you got using that search warrant. That will tell us whether the manufacturer was the same, and maybe whether the cartridge came from the same lot."

"Narrows it down some," Garcia mused.

"Depending on the manufacturer and how much ammunition they produce annually—"

"I hear you," Garcia said. Back to the bad news. He'd had about enough of that for one day.

"Get me a cycled cartridge and I can augment the chemistry with tool-mark analysis," Mitchell said. "Look here." He gestured to the eyepiece on what looked like a fancy microscope. "See that?"

"Yeah."

"That's a toolmark from the rim of the base of a .270 Win cartridge that's been cycled through the rifle you got. Assuming you could find me a .270 Win cartridge, I could compare them and tell you whether this was the gun."

"That's not conclusive, though—right?" Garcia was aware that a number of courts had ruled toolmark evidence more art than science, and insufficient to obtain a conviction. Maybe he needed to re-think everything.

"Not in and of itself, no," Mitchell admitted. "But get me that, and with the chemical composition I can narrow things down to where you can certainly narrow your field of suspects. Up to you to take it from there. Cale says you got prints. Where you at on DNA?"

"They swabbed. God knows when we'll hear back. I've had two guys with metal detectors searching for the other gun," Garcia said. "And I'm bringing in a dog from the Bureau of Alcohol, Tobacco and Firearms that is supposed to be able to sniff out a single cartridge if it was fired recently."

"Amazing—but in that country?"

"Exactly." Any good defense attorney would know hunters had been traipsing around and pulling triggers in that area for more than a hundred years.

"But *if* you find me a cartridge, and *if* I observe toolmarks that match those on this cycled round, or on one from any other rifle, then *maybe* I can neck things down for you. Then you add prints and DNA and—"

"Don't get my hopes up."

31

Lana rolled out of bed, walked to the window, and opened the shades. The sun was still up, and the wind was blowing snow sideways. "Jesus, this place is a hellhole," she groused. "How anyone could live here is beyond me."

"People are where they are," Alex said. He had stacked pillows behind himself and was propped up with his fingers interlocked behind his head.

"That's deep," Lana said. Deep thinker, this one. "Cover yourself," she ordered, and flipped the threadbare blankets over Alex's waist. "I'm gonna take a quick shower—assuming something doesn't crawl out of the shower head and bite me. Christ, this place is a dump."

"I couldn't find another room," Alex said. "Most of 'em have been rented by the week by construction crews building on your dad's empire. So what's next? When can we be together?"

Why were all men such idiots? "Assuming you didn't screw anything up, it shouldn't be long now. If that dumb cop does his job, he should find the rifle soon."

"And the bullet!"

She sighed heavily. "Cartridge," she corrected. "The bullet is in Max."

"Oh, yeah. Right." Alex looked at his stomach, admiring the taut muscles. "But the important thing is we'll be together, right? We're gonna go somewhere warm and live it up. Just the two of us?"

When she didn't answer, he looked up as the bathroom door closed behind her. She must not have heard him.

∽

Garcia was back in his unmarked car, watching the drug house, when he got another call. He looked at the greasy cheeseburger he had just unwrapped, then reluctantly re-wrapped it and answered, "Garcia."

"Ted, this is Levi O'Neil."

"Tell me something good."

"You aren't going to believe this."

Garcia sighed. "Try me."

"We found the gun and—"

"No shit!" Garcia put the cheeseburger back in the bag and wiped his hands on his pantlegs. "Good work!"

"Even better, we found a cartridge."

"Where?"

"Up there on that hillside to the west where you thought we might find something. The rifle was just sitting there right next to a tree amongst some deadfall. The cartridge was out in the open, but the snow had covered it."

Garcia felt his pulse quicken. "Caliber?"

".270 Winchester!"

"Tell me they haven't messed with it."

"No, it's still in place."

Garcia was thrilled by the news. This wasn't *Columbo*; in real life, criminals made dumb mistakes all the time. "Okay, get the crime scene techs up there. You go with them and handle the evidence. No mistakes on this one, Levi!"

"Right."

Garcia hung up and called Walsh to report the developments.

"Sounds good," Walsh said. "I'll let Rebecca know."

"I don't know that it will match," Garcia cautioned. "I mean . . . I can't believe we're getting this lucky. It's almost as if—"

"Don't overthink it, Ted. It's another brick in the wall," Walsh said. "I'm sure she's gonna want to meet. Be here early tomorrow and we'll go see her together."

"You sure?"

"I'm not sure of anything."

Garcia smiled. "Got it. I'll be there."

∼

The next morning, Walsh and Garcia walked to Rebecca's office. On the way, Garcia told Walsh that Pleasance had matched the prints on the gun and cartridge to Mike Brown.

"Good morning, gentlemen," Rebecca began, indicating chairs across her expansive desk. "You remember Grant Lee?"

Nods were exchanged. "Rebecca says there have been some developments?" Lee asked.

"Ted, why don't you bring counsel up to speed?" Walsh suggested.

Garcia explained in detail the investigation's findings, up to the team with the metal detectors discovering the rifle and cartridge. "So that's where we are right now," he concluded.

Lee leaned forward in his chair. "So, you've got a guy—Mike Brown—with a billion-dollar motive, who made threats, who perhaps created an opportunity, who shoots a gun of the same caliber. He came back from the ride with his gun missing, and now you've got a gun and cartridge found near the location from which you think the shot may have been fired. The same guy admits to firing a weapon, but says it was a warning shot?"

"Well, now we've got prints on a rifle and cartridge found right about where we believe the shooter was," Garcia said. Seeing Rebecca's doubtful expression, he added, "I'll admit it's thin."

"Like onion skin," Rebecca snorted.

"I've convicted with less," an unamused Lee said quickly. "The toolmark expert is where?"

"Here. He's a deputy in the department. This is a side job. He's working on it," Garcia said.

Hearing the supposed "expert" was a part-timer, Lee rolled his eyes. "How long?"

"Well, he's already done a chemical composition of some bullets found with the rifles, and he's cycled rounds through the guns we took into evidence in preparation for us finding a cartridge. Not long. Days, maybe?"

"And the DNA?"

"It usually takes weeks to—"

"I'll get someone on that," Lee said.

Rebecca shook her head. "Wyoming state lab is way behind, Grant. Even with expedited cases, we're seeing it take several weeks—"

"I've got contacts," Lee interrupted. "I can make this happen." He looked to Garcia. "Get your paper straight and line up someone to transport the evidence south. I'll get us a date and time for delivery."

Rebecca couldn't hide her surprise.

Lee sat back smugly. "And get your affidavit drafted," he said to Garcia. "I'll start working on the warrant. I think this is more than enough."

"Slow down, now," Rebecca said. "We need to be certain. A guy like Mike Brown is going to hire first-class defense counsel. We need to ensure every possible 'I' is dotted, and every 'T' is crossed."

"I'll see to that," Lee said. "I understand there have been some issues in the past—"

"Those issues included counsel jumping the gun," Rebecca said. "I am the county attorney. Do not file charges until and unless I approve it —understand?"

"Understood," Lee said.

The room was quiet until Walsh slapped his thighs and stood. "Ted, let's go get some evidence."

Garcia was up quickly. Moments later, as they crossed the street to the sheriff's office, he said, "He's gonna file, isn't he?"

"He is," Walsh agreed. "You'd best be ready. What are you working on today?"

"I want to talk with Paulie again."

"The big guy?"

"Yeah." Twenty minutes later, Garcia pulled into the driveway of the Kovalenko manse. Announcing himself, he followed the housekeeper until he saw Paulie speaking with Lana. When he and Paulie made eye contact, he indicated with his head that he wanted Paulie to join him. Alone. When he did, Garcia asked without preamble, "How come you never mentioned a gunshot?"

Paulie looked surprised. He looked toward the room where Lana had remained. Garcia prodded him. "Not a hard question. Tell me about the gunshot."

"I—I thought I heard a gunshot."

"When?"

"When I was up on the mountain."

"I know that, but *when*?" Garcia pressed. "When you were looking for him, when you were coming down—when?"

Paulie looked up as if he was trying to remember. "I—I don't know, exactly. Me and Mike were coming back, and we couldn't find Max and—no, wait! It was when I went to get Max's horse. We was heading back to where we'd left Max and we saw his horse going by. Mike said, 'Can you gather him up?' So I followed the thing until I could get ahold of its reins. Then I brought him back to where Mike was."

"Okay," Garcia said. "So when did you hear the shot?"

"I can't be too sure."

"Well, was it before or after you got ahold of Max's horse?"

"It was before."

"How do you know?"

"Well, 'cause now that I think about it, I wasn't chasin' that horse too long before I heard the shot, but it took me a while after that to get ahold of him."

"And what happened after that?" Garcia asked.

"Well, after I got the horse, I rode back to where we'd left Max," Paulie said.

"And what happened then?"

"Mike was walking in a big circle to try to find Max or a trail or something—I already told you all of this."

"Did he tell you about the gunshot?"

"Yeah," Paulie said. "Told me he shot into the air to try to alert Max."

"Did you believe him?"

"Of course!"

"Then what?"

"Then just what we told you. We looked for Max until Mike said we had to come down."

"Really." Garcia looked hard at Paulie. "You and I have spoken, right? Paulie, your boss got shot, and you didn't think Mike firing his gun was important?"

"No. He said he fired it to alert Max."

Garcia would have to determine at some point whether Paulie was stupid or complicit.

32

Sam was in his office early, working on a complaint for civil trespass against Casey Sprague and other locals. Despite Sam's requests, and despite having sent a formal cease and desist letter to Sprague and others, the use of the access had continued and he was forced to use the courts to stop it. He hoped that after getting served with the lawsuit, Sprague would hire an attorney. At that point, perhaps they could have a productive conversation. Sam was irritable and anxious and struggling to get words on paper when Cassie knocked on his door. "Yes?" he asked tightly.

"Did you hear? Max's son-in-law got arrested last night and charged with his murder. Do you think you'll get the case?"

"I doubt it," Sam replied. "I think they'll probably hire a name firm. Besides, I represent UkrCX and Max's estate—probably a conflict of interest."

"Good. I don't like them people."

"I know," Sam remarked. "You've made that clear." He sipped coffee from a cup adorned with a picture of a cutthroat trout, then handed her the draft complaint. "Can you clean this up for me? And I dictated a couple of letters, as well."

"My, haven't we been busy?" Cassie mocked.

"We have, and the hope is that our legal secretary will soon be busy as well."

She was about to reply when the front door chimed. "You're just lucky I have to answer the door."

"I am," he said. "Otherwise, I'd have to do it myself."

He heard Cassie greeting a woman and then approaching his door. "No walk-ins," he said, anticipating her request. In his experience, the kind of clients who walked in to see him without an appointment usually lacked impulse control and were in a bad position as the result of decisions they had made. More trouble than they were worth.

"It's Ms. Kovalenko-Brown," Cassie explained.

"I'll see her."

"I figured as much." When Cassie had retrieved Lana and she was seated in his office, Sam instructed Cassie to close the door behind her. Lana's perfume was both strong and distinctive. Her eyes were red-rimmed and puffy. "You look tired," he said without thinking.

"Thanks. Anything else about my appearance you wish to remark on?"

Sam felt his ears redden. "I'm sorry. I just meant that . . . How can I help you?"

"Mike got arrested for my dad's murder."

"So I heard."

"How'd you hear already?"

"It's a small town. Sometimes good old-fashioned person-to-person gossip beats social media to the punch."

She smiled, showing her perfect teeth. The smile was brief. "I want you to represent Mike. He didn't do it."

"I think you'll need to find another guy," Sam said. "I have a conflict of interest. You folks hired me to represent UkrCX, and I'm representing the trust as well. It would be a conflict for me to represent the trust, and then to represent one of the beneficiaries of that trust who is accused of killing the trustor."

"What if I hired you myself? In a private capacity?" She looked at him levelly, expecting an immediate answer. When Sam didn't respond, she continued, "He's my husband."

"I'd have to think that through," Sam said. Daniels had agreed to do most of the trust work, anyway. Now that Max was dead, a trustee would oversee UkrCX's ongoing projects. But Lana *was* the successor trustee, so it was a distinction without a real difference. "What does the family say?"

She shrugged. "I haven't asked them. I mean, what can they say? It's my money."

"Well, yeah, but again, there is at least the appearance of a conflict of interest."

"I don't think any of them will object," she said. "They know Mike didn't do it."

"And how do they know that?"

"Because they know what I know."

Sam's curiosity was piqued. "And what is that?"

"That he doesn't have the balls to shoot anyone."

The vehemence of her reply made Sam recoil slightly. "Well," he said. "There are a lot of people sitting behind bars for life who no one ever thought capable—"

"Sam, my husband is a squish. No way he shot Max. For one thing, he'd be afraid of what would happen if he missed."

"Why would he think about that?"

"Because that's the kind of glass-half-empty, wait-for-the-other-shoe-to-drop lightweight he is. Mike didn't kill Max, and he didn't conspire with anyone to have it done, either. That's not how he does business."

Sam had watched her closely while she spoke. The conflict could probably be waived, of course, but something was bothering him. "I don't know, Lana. I guess I'm surprised you want to pay someone to defend the guy accused of killing your father—even if it is your husband."

"Because he didn't do it. I mean, I *know* it," she emphasized, pointing to her heart. "You said you think you have a conflict, right?"

"Right."

"Conflicts can be waived, right?"

Sam was surprised at her insight. "Well, generally, yes."

"Then I'll sign whatever you need, and I'll write you a check right now."

Sam sat back in his chair. It wasn't quite that easy. "I hear you. But I might have an ethical problem here."

She looked at him for a long moment. "Got a piece of paper?"

He pushed a yellow legal pad in front of her and she wrote a number on it. "That cover it?" she asked.

Sam spun the paper around and looked at it. It was an obscene amount of money for one case. "Well, yeah—if I take the case."

"I'm going to write a check and give it to that secretary of yours to deposit into your trust account as a retainer. If you decide not to take the case, you can refund it, okay?" She knew full well that would be difficult. "Think about it, will you?"

"I will," Sam promised. "I'll have an answer for you later this afternoon."

After Lana left, Sam picked up the phone and called Daniels. He got Julie, Marci's new home care assistant, who said Daniels was just finishing up Marci's breakfast. "He is such a good man," she said.

Sam agreed, thinking he didn't have it in him to show such kindness to another human being. When Daniels came on the line, Sam explained Lana's visit, the retainer, and his thoughts regarding the possible conflict of interest.

"Are you nuts?" Daniels asked. "You can't walk away from that kind of money!"

"You think the conflict can be waived?"

"You bet. I'll handle the corporate stuff and the estate," Daniels said. "I'll wall you off." In the legal world, a "wall" was an imaginary construct, and referred to a situation where one or more lawyers were cut off from certain information by others in the same firm. It was a glorified pinky swear.

"Can you do that?"

"What do you mean? Sam, I was practicing law when you were riding your first bike!"

Sam gave it a second. "I mean with . . . Marci."

Daniels realized he'd been short. "Sorry, Sam. It was kind of a long night, but Julie's been a lot of help, I'll tell you that. I'll be good as new as soon as I get her fully on board."

"What about doctors' appointments and all that?"

"Well, one good thing about corporate and estate work is that you can take it with you," Daniels said. "I spend a lot of time on these trips in airports or otherwise sitting around with my thumb up my keister. Might be good to have something to do while I wait."

Daniels' impatience as a judge had been legendary; Sam couldn't help but smile at the thought of him trying to sit patiently. "Are you sure?"

"I'm sure. And I'm gonna have some time. Me and Marci are going to Tijuana next week for a new treatment. The initial trials seem promising."

Sam's heart sank. Daniels was a man of great intellect, and yet here he was hoping against hope for a miracle. "Okay . . . Press, if you need anything, you know all you've got to do is ask, right?"

"Right," Daniels said.

33

Sam had asked for the meeting with Lee for a couple of reasons. First, he wanted to see if he could get a feel for the strength of the state's case before formally agreeing to represent Mike. Second, he wanted to feel out Lee. Litigation—especially criminal litigation—was largely a one-on-one exercise, and it could be trying if the opposing counsel was a jerk. Looking around Lee's office, Sam was struck by the paucity of personal items displayed. The requisite law school diploma and permission to practice in the courts of the state were displayed as required; beyond that, there was nothing to indicate what Lee was all about.

Lee indicated a chair in which he wanted Sam to sit. Sam complied.

"I only have a few minutes before I have to appear in court," Lee said, skipping the small talk. "What can I do for you?"

Sam was surprised by what appeared to be a blatant lie. Downs was out of town this week, and he had just seen Bridger at the bank, and he said he was on his way to an early lunch. Sam wondered if Lee was confused or if he was playing a mind game.

"I wanted to hear what you have against Mike Brown," Sam said.

"Have you made an entry of appearance?" Lee asked.

"No, but I am considering it," Sam said. "Rather strongly, to tell you the truth, although I wanted to get a feel for the case before committing. Right now, all I have is a potential client."

Lee shook his head. "In the absence of an entry of appearance I am not going to provide any information. It's a rule."

Sam was quickly getting irritated. "What rule?" he asked. "It's certainly not in the rules of procedure, and this office has given me exactly this kind of information previously."

"*My* rule," Lee said. "I can't help or be accountable for anything that happened before I got here."

"Should I talk to Rebecca?"

"You could, but I've already informed her of my plans should this occasion arise, and she okayed my proposed course of action."

"I'm just trying to understand what you've got, so I can advise my client's benefactor accordingly," Sam said. "Might save us all a lot of work," he added hopefully.

"No dice," Lee said. "Without an entry of appearance, I can't help you." Sam took the measure of the man. He was tall and lanky. His hands were steady, and he made eye contact readily as he leaned forward over his desk. "I'll tell you this: I filed the charges and I see little difficulty proving your client's guilt beyond a reasonable doubt."

Sam was exasperated. "I don't know where you practiced before, but you realize, of course, that if I do an entry of appearance and ask these same questions, you're going to have to give me everything that you've got. Wyoming is a discovery state, no surprises."

"That's true, counselor—but by rule I'm not required to give you squat until and unless I have a request for discovery, which will come only after —and *if*—you make an entry of appearance."

Sam had made his decision. Lee was making anything else impossible. "There's no *if*; you'll have my entry and my demand concurrently—later today, in fact. Get your documents ready." Sam stood and was watching Lee for a reaction when Cathy appeared in the door.

"Hi, Sam, how are you?" she said.

"I'm well." Sam smiled. "How are you?"

"Doing well. What's up?"

Sam looked at Lee. "I am trying to pimp Grant here for information."

She grinned tightly, then sobered. "How is that going for you?"

"Not particularly well. Grant here seems determined to hide the ball until the last minute."

"I am sitting right here," Lee said.

"Ah, I forgot." Sam winked at Cathy. Seeing her eyes twinkle, he asked, "Cathy, you want to get a beer?"

"Not tonight," Lee said. "She has other plans."

"Maybe let her answer, huh?" Sam said.

Cathy looked at Sam and then Lee. This could be a career-making decision. "He's right, Sam. We're supposed to look at the case tonight."

She sounded almost apologetic. "Well, your loss," Sam said.

"My intent is to show and tell her how she can best assist me," Lee said.

"Sounds like a blast," Sam said. "You sure?" He looked at Cathy. Then a thought occurred to him. "Wait, why is *she* assisting *you*?"

"I'm first chair," Lee said.

Sam looked at Lee quizzically. "Why? I know she has tried murder cases. How many have you tried?"

"I think you have everything that you need or have a right to know at this point, Mr. Johnstone," Lee said, standing. Sam took it as his signal to leave. Accordingly, he stubbornly remained in the office. Juvenile, of course —but by the reddening of Lee's ears, he could see it was effective.

"I think it is time for you to leave," Lee said. "We have work to do."

"Really, and here I thought we were just getting to know each other," Sam said. His eyes met Cathy's and he saw the silent signal. "Okay," he said. "I'll send Cassie to file my docs momentarily. Don't be late with your responses now," he cautioned Lee. Then he turned to Cathy. "I'll see you later—and tell Kayla to keep jacking them up, okay?"

"It always amazes me," Lee said, shaking his head sadly after Sam left. "People volunteer for the military, then get deployed. They lose a leg or whatever, and people say they are a hero. But if they just decide to go to the store and lose a leg in an accident, they are just a dude without a leg."

"Do you not see a difference of circumstance there?"

"Not really. A decision was made, and consequences resulted—just like his decision to take this case."

34

Hours later, having inspected herself in the mirror, Cathy made an honest appraisal: not all that bad, she had finally decided. She tried to keep herself in shape, but with Kayla, increasing job responsibilities, and—frankly—a lack of motivation, it was challenging. Adding to her frustration was that her favorite exercise—running—was becoming increasingly problematic. It seemed the more she ran, the more she ended up with some sort of injury. Her doctor attributed it to decades on the hardwood basketball courts she'd played on around the country. He suggested swimming, but she'd never been particularly good at it, and had no real interest in learning. So, relying on a careful diet and limited exercise, she tried to maintain a good weight, at least.

She had selected a dress that she wore to work on occasion—nothing too fancy. Grant had indicated that this would be a working dinner. But it was dinner, so why not look nice? Besides, he was an attractive man, and it had been a while since she'd been out to eat anywhere other than fast food with Kayla. Her mom had stopped by and scooped up Kayla to get her to practice and then take her for pizza. The plan was for Cathy to call when she was home and her mother would bring Kayla home, or, if it was too late, she would simply stay with Grandma.

"Oh, Mom," Cathy had said. "That isn't going to happen."

"You never know, dear. You're an attractive woman. I hear he's an attractive man. No reason it wouldn't."

"It's work, Mom."

"Sure it is," her mother had said. "That's why he's asked you to dinner. Don't be naïve, dear."

They met at the restaurant an hour later; she was glad to see he was on time and already seated at a table in the corner. Good sign. "What'll you have?" Lee asked.

"I'm going to have a glass of wine, I think. Merlot."

"Really? I'm just going to have a soft drink. This is a working dinner."

See, Mom? "I think I'll be okay with a glass of wine under my belt," she assured him.

When the drinks arrived, they silently toasted and looked over the menus. She ordered a filet with a salad and oven-roasted vegetables, although she would have preferred a loaded potato. He ordered baked chicken and a mixed salad with so many "hold thes" that what he ended up with was a bowl of greens covered in vinaigrette dressing. They made awkward small talk while awaiting their meals. He was several years older than she was, had attended his final year of high school in Custer, and then went off to college back east before returning to practice law in Colorado and then Cheyenne. He practiced primarily as a civil litigator but was drawn to prosecuting after having been appointed a special prosecutor for a case against a prominent southern Wyoming politician. "I don't know," he said. "I just felt like at that moment I realized I'd missed my calling. Like maybe prosecuting criminals was my life's work."

"Really, that's all it took?" She smiled, but it wasn't returned.

"Somebody has to ensure that bad people do not take over our communities," he said earnestly.

"I agree," she said. "But bear in mind, at least around here, most defendants are addicts or alcoholics. They are not bad people."

He ignored her. "In too many places across the country, the inmates are literally running the asylum. My intent is to bring law and order to this community."

Cathy sipped carefully from her glass and tried to show no emotion. Good Lord. Like any other convert, a zealot. "I've heard that."

"It's true. We cannot let criminals dictate how the rest of us will live. Across this country, prosecutors have chosen to overlook crime. The result, of course, is more crime. You agree, don't you?"

He was finally asking her opinion. "Absolutely. Failing to prosecute is a miscarriage of justice. But I would argue our best course is to employ the least restrictive measures possible to ensure the safety of the community and see to it the defendant is afforded every opportunity to change. That's especially true for addicted offenders."

"Fantasy," he said, then—seeing her wipe viciously at her mouth with her napkin—he softened somewhat. "What I meant to say was that so many of these approaches have utterly failed. I just think we need to focus more on the victims and a little less on the defendants. Don't you agree?"

She agreed, of course. But. "I think that after having my opinion called fantasy, I'll keep my thoughts to myself."

"I'm sorry, I get passionate about these things—"

"Who doesn't?"

"And I was just trying to explain—"

"Yeah, I got that."

"What I believed."

"That was crystal clear," she said, and finished her wine. Thankfully, the waiter appeared with their meals. "I'll have another glass of merlot," she said to him.

"Are you sure?" Lee asked.

Oh, hell yes. "I am."

"We've got things to discuss."

"It's two glasses of wine. After all, I'd be presumptively capable of driving—true?"

"Well, I suppose. It depends on how much you weigh."

My God. "Bring the wine," she instructed the waiter, who had been standing by uncertainly. She cut into her steak and was pleased to see it had been grilled to medium-rare perfection, just as her father had taught her to order it. She cut a small bite and was savoring the flavor of a locally sourced bovine when Grant interrupted her reverie.

"How can you eat something like that?" he asked, indicating her steak. "It's a bloody mess."

"One bite at a time," she said. She swallowed and then tried not to gulp red wine. "I take it you don't imbibe?"

"Oh, I do, but I like mine fully cooked," he said, and watched silently while Cathy cut a larger piece, forked it, and put it in her mouth. "Anyway, I wanted to talk with you tonight about the upcoming trial."

"Which one?"

"The Mike Brown trial. The only one that matters!"

"There will be lots of trials between now and then."

"I know," he said. "But this one will be high visibility. This will show that we are equal to the task."

"Really," she said.

Perhaps sensing that she was again offended by the remark, he again tried to backtrack. "Look, I'm not saying the office wasn't up to the task before—"

"Oh, I think you are," she said. The wine was good. Going to her head a little, perhaps.

"Well, results count, right? And the conviction rate on murders hasn't been great."

"Maybe because the people charged weren't guilty?" she posited. "And maybe you have forgotten that Lucy was convicted of two murders the second time around? *We* did that." She pointed to herself. "So perhaps justice was done? I think you were alluding earlier to the purpose of our lives being justice?"

"Look, I'm just saying that we need to get this one right. We need to get by Johnstone."

"Sam? He's just an attorney doing his job—pretty darn well, as a matter of fact."

"I hear he's a drunk."

"You mentioned that before. I think for a while there he was coping as best he could," she said. "But I understand he's on the wagon."

"Is he going to treatment?"

"I don't know. None of my business—or yours."

"But it *is* our business. He is opposing counsel."

"This is not a competition between attorneys," she said. "We're advocates—not opponents in a ring. Remember? I think that is somewhere in the rules of professional conduct. Perhaps page one." That last part was gratuitous, and she regretted it. Some.

"I remember. But I know that in the real world, attorneys must deal with each other's courtroom presence as well as with the facts and the law. Anything less than that understanding is naïve."

"Well, what you'll find with Sam is that he is a good lawyer and a straight shooter."

"You like him."

Maybe. "I admire him. There's a difference." Oof. The wine was going to her head.

"Some people find him intimidating."

"Why wouldn't they? He's a war hero, a survivor, and he's dedicated his life to helping people in need. And he wins. That's kind of the total package."

"Well, I don't," Lee said, forking what looked like a dandelion leaf—hell, it might have been one for all she knew. "Whatever he did in a war we didn't need means nothing to me. And as far as his courtroom heroics go, every defense attorney sees him or herself as some sort of white knight, standing athwart the law defending the oppressed. The reality is that most are misfits trying to stick it to the man."

"Wow," she said. She was watching him closely now. "This is personal for you."

"I'm here to win. To see justice done."

"And you see winning and justice as synonymous."

"I do. I don't bring charges unless I'm convinced the guy did it. Once we've crossed that threshold, I'm going to do whatever it takes to see the defendant convicted."

"Isn't that the jury's job? What if you're wrong?"

"Juries do what I tell them." He drank from his cola, put the glass down, and fixed his eyes on her. "Let me ask you a question. Are you up for this?"

"What?"

"Trying this case with me? And against Johnstone."

"Of course. You'll recall I've actually tried cases against him. You're just talking about it. I'm just not seeing it as the life-or-death struggle you are," she said, finishing the wine. That was enough. "Our job is to present the facts to the jury and allow them to make their decision."

"Jurors need to be guided. If we don't guide them, Johnstone will."

"He will—within the law."

Lee looked hard at her for a moment. "I'm concerned that your view of Johnstone will color your actions in preparation for this case."

"Back at you," she said.

"I think I need to have a talk with Rebecca."

"Do it."

He tried lamely to initiate a little small talk while they awaited their checks, but she wasn't having any of it. When they'd paid their tabs, they walked to their cars. "See you in the morning," he said.

She didn't answer. Instead, she looked at her watch and decided that if she hurried, she might be able to share some ice cream with Kayla.

35

The Custer County jail had been on site for almost a century. Walking down the windowless corridors, Sam was reminded of his time on military installations—tiled floors, painted cinderblock walls, few windows, and long hallways. The weather had changed again and his leg was bothering him some today, but accompanied by Tom, one of Custer's longtime jailers, Sam arrived at the assigned interview room at last.

"You know the drill," Tom said, indicating Sam should assume the position by raising his arms. He handed over his briefcase and watched while Tom performed a perfunctory search. When he was done, Sam held out his hands for the even more perfunctory pass with a metal detector. Their eyes met when the wand buzzed as Tom passed it over Sam's left leg. "You, uh, got anything that could hurt anyone?"

"Not unless I decide to take it off and beat you over the head with it," Sam said. When Tom laughed, he added, "How've you been?"

"Been fine. You know, we're busy what with all these outsiders coming to town. Jail population's up ten percent."

"Job security," Sam replied.

"True enough." Tom started to open the door, then hesitated and looked at Sam. "Can I ask you a question?"

"Sure."

"You hear anything from Paul?"

Paul Norquist had offered Sam a job in Custer when he was at his lowest. They'd been partners until Sam—against Paul's wishes—had called Paul's son Ronnie to the stand in the Davonte Blair murder case, whereupon Ronnie proceeded to confess to the killing. The partnership—and more importantly, the friendship—had dissolved almost immediately afterward. "No, I haven't."

"Paul took it hard," Tom continued. "I hear he moved to Rawlins to be closer to the prison—Ronnie's there, you know. My sources tell me Paul's been drinking and Jeannie left him."

"Oh my gosh," Sam said. "I'm sorry."

"None of your doin', of course," Tom said. "But I gotta tell you I never did believe that story of Ronnie's. I just didn't see him as a killer—know what I mean?"

"I do," Sam said truthfully. He looked pointedly at his watch. "Tom, I've got another appointment here soon."

"I hear you," Tom said, opening the door. "I'll be out here. Knock when you're ready."

Sam entered and placed his briefcase on the small metal table in the center of the room. Mike had been issued the regulation orange jumpsuit. His hands were cuffed together, and he was chained to the far side of the table, the links running from the cuffs through a C-shaped weld on top of the table. A pane of plexiglass separated the two ends of the table. "Forgive me if I don't get up," Mike said.

Sam had heard the same lame joke at least a dozen times.

Looking back to ensure Tom had closed the door, Sam began. "Mike, Lana has hired me to represent you. I wanted to meet briefly with you tonight to go over some things."

"Okay," Mike said. He was wringing his hands in the cuffs.

"Careful," Sam said. "Those things can chafe you."

Mike nodded. "When do I get out?"

"We're going to have a hearing in the next day or so. The judge might set bond. I don't know. That would be the soonest."

"What do you mean *might* set bond?"

"You are charged with murder," Sam reminded Mike. "Because that carries a life sentence—or worse—Judge Downs doesn't have to set a bond."

"Or worse?"

"Well, technically, the state could seek the death penalty."

"Christ! What kind of hillbilly justice is that?" Mike asked.

"The situation is the same most everywhere," Sam replied. "Before we get too wrapped around the axle about that, let's talk about what happened after you got arrested." Sam's habit was to first talk with defendants about what happened after their arrest. That allowed him to begin with an unvarnished view of what the state's evidence likely was, rather than the defendant's view of the facts. He'd get that later.

"Did you say anything to them while all this was going on?" Sam asked when Mike had finished his recitation.

"Of course. I told Garcia he was making a mistake. Told him I didn't shoot Max. I had no reason to," Mike said. "And I told him I was gonna sue their asses off when this was over."

"Did you talk about what had happened at all?" Sam asked. This was a key question. Too many defendants locked their attorney into a story early on.

"Told 'em I didn't do it. Told 'em I wanted a lawyer. Garcia read me my rights and said he had probable cause to believe that I was the guy who killed Max."

"What evidence did he say he had?" Sam asked.

"He said he had the weapon with my prints and DNA on it. He said he found it next to a tree near where he suspected the shots had been fired from."

"What else?"

"He said the bullet in Max's body came from my rifle. He said he had a cartridge that matched my rifle found near the rifle; said he found it where he expected to find it. He said he had motive—"

"What was that?"

"Well, he somehow knew that Max had been threatening to change his will or whatever."

"Any idea who told him that?"

"Probably Alex."

Sam agreed. "Anything else?"

"And the threats."

"Threats?"

"Well, I got drunk a couple of times and threatened to kill Max. To shoot him, really," Mike said. "But that was just talk—know what I mean?"

Threats were never good. "I do," Sam said. Maybe he could get them suppressed. "Who did you threaten Max in front of?"

"Well, like Lana."

"No problem. Wives can't testify against husbands."

"And I don't know who all heard me at the party."

That would need checking. He remembered Lana scolding Mike at the birthday party. "What else?"

"That's all I can remember."

"Other than the inventory, did you make any statements or sign anything?" Sam was watching Mike closely.

"No."

"Did they take any blood samples, cut any of your hair, clip your nails, or test you for drugs or alcohol?" Sam asked.

"Took my fingerprints and ran a swab around in my mouth—DNA, maybe?"

That was standard operating procedure. "Mike, I'm going to have to go do some paperwork and prepare for what I think will be tomorrow's hearing, to try to get you out. I'll see you tomorrow, okay?"

"Okay, Sam."

Sam knocked on the window, and Tom retrieved him and walked him out. "Have a nice night, Sam," the old guard said.

"Thanks, Tom. You, too—and hello to the missus." As he walked the quarter mile back to his office, he reflected on what Mike had told him, which wasn't much. After tomorrow's initial appearance, he would meet with Mike again and get his version of events.

36

As expected, Mike's initial appearance the next day had drawn a full house. In Custer, where murders had historically occurred about once every other year, this kind of hearing would naturally draw interest. Given the victim was cryptocurrency billionaire Max Kovalenko, and given the accused was his son-in-law, Downs correctly anticipated the crowd size and had the sheriff double the usual court security. She had ordered there be no cameras in her courtroom, as well, but had set aside a few seats for media coverage.

"I think it's in the best interest of justice that cameras be allowed in the courtroom," Lee had opined brazenly during their informal pre-hearing meeting in her chambers.

"Thank you, Mr. Lee. Is there any other opinion about matters totally within my discretion you wish to offer?" Downs asked icily.

"No, ma'am. I just thought—"

"Thank you. Will there be anything else, gentlemen?" When neither Sam nor Lee responded, she continued. "Keep it clean. I've got another hearing in forty-five minutes and I want court security to have some time to clear the courtroom. Be brief, be bright, be gone," she concluded, and it seemed to Sam she was staring hard at Lee as she spoke.

Moments later, when all were seated and she had taken the bench, she called the case. "The first matter before the court is State of Wyoming versus Michael Brown," she began. As a circuit court judge, Downs didn't have the jurisdiction to take a plea to a murder charge. Instead, the purpose of the hearing was to ensure the defendant understood his rights, the charge, and the possible penalty should he plead or be found guilty. She would, if necessary, arrange for attorney representation. "Mr. Brown, would you please step to the podium?"

His feet constrained by steel shackles, Mike rose and shuffled to the podium, where he was met by Sam.

"Your Honor, Sam Johnstone, appearing for the defendant."

"Welcome, Mr. Johnstone. Have you been retained by Mr. Brown for all proceedings?" When Sam acknowledged that he had been retained by the family, she continued. "Mr. Brown, you are here pursuant to a warrant alleging you are guilty of one count of murder in the first degree. Mr. Brown, the statute reads as follows: 'Whoever purposely and with premeditated malice, or in the perpetration of, or attempt to perpetrate, any sexual assault, any sexual abuse of a minor, arson, robbery, burglary, escape, resisting arrest, kidnapping, or abuse of a child under the age of sixteen years, kills any human being, is guilty of murder in the first degree'—do you understand that?"

Mike looked to Sam. "What the hell?"

Sam smiled at his client. "Just say, 'Yes, ma'am,'" he instructed through gritted teeth. "We'll talk about it later."

Mike looked to Downs. "Yes, ma'am."

"The statute goes on to say," Downs read, "'a person convicted of murder in the first degree shall be punished by death, life imprisonment without parole, or life imprisonment according to law.' Mr. Brown, do you understand that?"

An audible murmur had emanated from the crowd at the mention of a possible death penalty. Mike stood quietly, then turned to Sam. "Are you kidding me?"

Sam looked at Downs. "Your Honor, might I have a moment?"

"Of course," she said. Sam was obviously having some difficulty with his client—a situation not unusual for attorneys with rich clients. Money brought with it a need to control.

Sam spoke earnestly with Mike. "Just acknowledge you understand. That's the possible penalty. It's on the books. Nothing we can do about it right now."

"This is ridiculous."

"We'll talk later. Right now, just tell her you understand."

While Sam struggled to get his client under control, at the prosecution's table a few feet away, Lee leaned over to a stolid Cathy. "Just wait until his client hears my bond request," he said under his breath.

When Sam and Mike had concluded their brief conference, Mike looked at Downs. "I understand, Judge," he said.

"Thank you, Mr. Brown," Downs said, shuffling through papers on her desk. The most important issue was whether to allow the defendant to remain out of jail on bond pending trial, and if so, under what terms and conditions. Her strong inclination was to keep him in jail. "Does the State have a recommendation for bond?"

Lee rose and took two quick steps to the podium. His opportunity to make a first impression had arrived, and he was well-rehearsed. He looked around the courtroom quickly, then focused on Downs, exulting in the media presence. "Your Honor, as the court knows, Mr. Brown has been charged with first-degree murder, one of—if not *the*—most serious crimes on the books. A new member of our community, one who had the potential to bring promise to the lives of so many, has been murdered. Mr. Brown has no prior record worth mentioning, but as the apparent heir to the Kovalenko fortune he is possessed of almost limitless funds, and as a man facing the possible imposition of the death penalty, he poses a flight risk just as anyone would. For these reasons, we would ask that the court allow no bond and order him held until trial."

Downs had expected nothing less from the new prosecutor. No bond was a perfectly reasonable request given a crime of this magnitude. She looked to Sam. "Mr. Johnstone, does the defendant care to respond?"

"Yes, Your Honor," Sam replied, gathering materials and stepping to the podium. "As the court well knows, my client is presumed innocent until proven otherwise. Mr. Brown vehemently denies these charges and looks forward to the opportunity to defend himself. He is married—in fact, his family is funding his defense. His wife—the daughter of the victim—sits mere feet away from me, fully supportive of him and hoping the court will release her husband subject to conditions sufficient to keep the community safe. He has no record and therefore no missed court hearings. He has retained counsel. Because my client presents no threat to the community, I'd ask the court to set a reasonable bond, and would add we expect strict terms, including house arrest and electronic monitoring. Thank you," Sam concluded. It was the best he could do, and he sat, fully expecting Downs to hold Mike without bond.

Downs was preparing to announce her ruling denying bond when Lee stood to get her attention. "Mr. Lee, what is it, sir?"

"The State would like to make an additional argument, Your Honor."

It was highly unusual and, frankly, unnecessary. Downs was convinced Brown could post virtually any bond. Therefore, the best choice was no bond. "What would you like me to know?" she asked tightly.

"Judge," Lee began, "I recognize that I'm new to practicing in this jurisdiction and in this state. But everywhere else I've been, where a defendant had committed a crime of this magnitude—"

"An *alleged* crime," Sam interjected.

Downs extended her arm with the palm down, indicating Sam should sit. "Mr. Johnstone, please let him finish."

"As I was saying," Lee said, pointedly side-eyeing Sam. "In other jurisdictions, bond would be summarily denied. All I can offer is that in my experience—"

She had heard enough. "Thank you, Mr. Lee," Downs said. "You'll agree with me that it is *this court's* opinion that matters, I am sure?" she asked, and before he could respond, she continued. "Having heard and considered the arguments of counsel, this court is going to set bond in the amount of ten million dollars cash." She then outlined the terms and conditions that Brown would have to operate and live under, to include house arrest and the turning over of his passport to the court.

"I'm getting out?" Mike asked Sam. He seemed as surprised as anyone.

"Assuming your family has enough money," Sam acknowledged. "But I want you to contact me as soon as you get out. We need to talk."

"Okay," Mike said. "I didn't do this," he assured Sam.

After Mike was led from the courtroom for transport back to the jail, the public rose and left as well, eager to discuss the events they had just witnessed. Sam remained behind. He was surprised—only the rare judge would allow a man charged with the murder of a family member out on bond pending trial. Lee picked up his papers and, with Cathy in tow, left the courtroom without saying a word. Sam allowed a few minutes to pass and then picked up his materials and left, fully prepared for what he knew awaited.

⁓

Outside the courtroom, the press was ready with cameras and microphones. "Mr. Johnstone, were you surprised by the judge's decision?"

"No, the judge made the right call," Sam said. "The court's job is to ensure that the defendant will appear for trial, and that the public's safety is assured. My client poses no risk to the community and looks forward to his day in court."

"Mr. Lee has told us the evidence is substantial and that he is confident your client will be convicted," Sarah Penrose said. "Are you considering a plea agreement yet?"

"I've only just been retained," Sam replied. "Mr. Lee owes me a look at whatever evidence he has—both favorable and unfavorable to the State. Once I see that, I will discuss options with Mr. Brown. Until then, Mr. Brown would ask that you recall that he is to be presumed innocent of all charges, and that you respect his privacy. He denies any involvement in his father-in-law's murder, and looks forward to answering these charges," he concluded.

37

The next morning, both Mike and Lana showed up for Mike's meeting with Sam. As they entered Sam's office, he put up a hand. "Just a minute," he said.

"What?" Mike asked.

"It has to be just you and me," Sam explained. "Otherwise, anything we say could be deemed outside the normal attorney-client privilege." That was debatable; she was his wife, and it was almost impossible to have a wife testify against her husband. But he wasn't in the mood to do the research, and he wanted Mike's unvarnished thoughts.

"She's my wife," Mike said.

"I'm paying the bill," Lana pointed out. "Technically, I'm the client —right?"

"Technically, yes," Sam allowed. "Look, I don't want to spend a whole lot of time debating this. If there are three people in a room, I don't know that we have attorney-client privilege."

Mike and Lana exchanged a look. Mike shrugged.

Lana stood. "This is crap," she said as she left.

When the door closed behind her, Sam looked to Mike. "Now, how are you doing?" He eyed Mike carefully. It was mid-February, and Mike's preliminary hearing would be next week. He was a poor dresser—Sam kept expecting to see him pull a dryer cloth out of a sleeve. He would have to talk with Lana about that before next week's hearing.

"I'm charged with killing my father-in-law, a man I loved and respected. How the hell do you think I'm doing?" Mike asked. "What kind of question is that?"

"Feel any better?" Sam asked, and when a chastened Mike looked to the floor, he continued. "Let's get something straight: I'm not one of the hired help whom you can yell at. You want to yell at somebody, get a dog, because I'm not going to put up with it. I've got other cases, other clients, and even if I didn't, I'm not the kind of guy to put up with some rich guy's bullshit."

"Oh, there it is!" Mike exclaimed. "Like everyone else in this town, you're jealous of my money!"

"You're a client," Sam said. "No more, no less. You'll get my best effort. No guarantees, no special treatment. If that doesn't work, tell me now."

Mike turned and looked steadily at Sam. "I've been doing some reading about you," he said. "You've got problems."

"I do," Sam admitted.

"You're a drunk."

"In recovery."

"PTSD."

"Being treated."

"Lotsa fights."

"Can't deny it."

"Don't always listen to your clients."

"That's fair."

"I think I might be more comfortable with another attorney. From what I was looking at, there's a bunch of good attorneys over in Jackson. How far away is that?"

"There are some good ones," Sam agreed. "Not far—maybe four hundred miles."

"Four hundred miles?" Mike repeated, aghast.

Sam looked at an obviously torn Mike for several seconds. "What are you going to do?" he asked. "I don't want to waste my time if you're gonna go find another lawyer."

"I didn't do it."

"I understand—"

"I didn't *do* it!" Mike shouted.

"Stop yelling!" Sam commanded. "You've got a preliminary hearing in about a week—what do you want to do?"

"I don't know."

"It's my responsibility as a lawyer to provide you with the best defense possible, but I can't do that if you are going to fight me," Sam explained. "Look, why don't we do this: we'll waive a speedy preliminary hearing, tell the judge that you are looking for another attorney, and ask to continue next week's prelim—that'll give you time to find someone else. When you get your new guy, I'll withdraw."

"You'd do that?"

"What?"

"Walk away from this kind of money?" Mike asked. "I know my wife paid you a wad."

"She put a large sum on retainer, I'll say that. You can have it back."

Mike looked Sam up and down. "You *are* different."

Sam smiled despite himself and motioned for Mike to sit down. "Look, we are wasting time. I need to know what happened."

"I don't know. I wasn't there, and I didn't shoot him."

Sam took a deep breath. "Let's start with what you do know. What do you remember about that day?"

For the next hour, Sam alternately listened and asked questions until he felt he had a good handle on Mike's version of events. From what he already knew of the State's evidence, the location of the cartridge and rifle, the prints, the DNA, the motive, and the threats were damning. Time to have what Sam liked to call his "come to Jesus" speech with clients—time for a reality check.

"Mike, a jury is comprised of twelve imperfect human beings—imperfect individually, and imperfect as a group. I'm your lawyer, and I've tried some cases, but based on what you are telling me I can't sit here today and tell you or promise you—let alone guarantee you—that the jury in your case will not find you guilty. So, we need to look at all possible defenses. To that end, given your father-in-law's overbearing nature and the pressure you've been under, I want you to agree to be evaluated by a psychiatrist to see if you are fit to stand trial now, and if you were legally sane at the time of the killing. We can get a doctor from wherever—"

"No."

"Mike, I'm your lawyer; as of now, even if you won't agree, I can ask the judge to order you to undergo an examination. I don't want to do that. What I want is for you to sign a consent form so that I can ask for an examination."

"What happens if you are successful?"

"The judge stays all proceedings while you see a doc from the Wyoming State Hospital."

"Then what?"

"Well, it depends. If he says you aren't fit—"

"He won't; I'm fine. I am not crazy. I wasn't there when Max was killed. What are the other options?"

"Very limited. Either self-defense—which doesn't fit what we know—or what I call the S-O-D-D-I defense."

"SODDI?"

"Some other dude did it."

"That's it! That's what we gotta go with, because that's what happened, Sam."

"You told me you threatened him," Sam offered.

"I did." Mike looked at the floor, seemingly discouraged. "But it was all just like bluffing—trying to act tough. Max was a bully. And honestly, he'd kind of gotten behind with respect to business. I mean, in the cyber currency world, stuff happens fast, and Max wasn't keeping up. I wanted to try some different things, and he was stuck in the old ways. It was . . . complicated."

"You threatened to shoot him; someone did shoot him. I've seen the affidavit of probable cause supporting the warrant. The prosecutor says they found that gun and a cycled cartridge that matches the gun with your prints and DNA right where you said you were at the time he got shot."

"Sam—"

"Just a minute," Sam said. "They say that Max had told others he was going to change his estate plan and write you out of it."

"Sam—"

"They say that after the four of you rode off, Alex went to get a signal, and then you sent Paulie away, meaning you were the only one with Max at one point."

"It's all just—how do you say it? Circumstantial!"

"Lots of folks in jail for less," Sam observed.

That seemed to stun Mike, who sat quietly. "I need to talk with Lana," he said at last.

"Fine," Sam said. "Talk with Lana, but you and I are going to have to move forward until and unless you replace me."

"I understand."

"Okay, one last thing. I want to go over the bond conditions with you." Sam proceeded to explain all the conditions Mike would have to live by prior to trial.

"It's like I'm guilty already!" Mike protested when Sam had finished his review.

"I hear you," Sam said. "But that judge has a responsibility to keep the community safe, and she's outlined steps and ordered you to follow them. You'll regret it if you don't listen and pay attention."

$\sim$

Several weeks before trial, Sam asked Mike to meet with him to discuss some evidentiary matters. It was after hours, and Sam noticed immediately that Mike had been drinking. "How did you get here?" he asked.

"I drove."

"Mike, that's not smart," Sam counseled. "You get pulled over for DUI and the judge will revoke your bond."

"I couldn't find Paulie," Mike explained. "He hasn't been around much."

"Then call me, for crying out loud!" Sam scolded. When Mike looked down as if sufficiently remorseful, he continued. "I got something here. The State says that near the rifle and the cartridge they found one of those clear spray bottles—can you tell me what that's about?"

"Maybe. Coulda been one of them—I don't know anything about the rifle. I told you already, I didn't leave the rifle there, and I don't know nothing about some spray bottle. Lana gave me and Alex some water bottles before we left."

While Mike had stuck to his story from the start, Sam was having trouble believing him. "You said you fired a shot from there. A cartridge matching one fired from that gun was located right there. The rifle was right there. It has your DNA on it. You sure you didn't set it down?"

"Maybe it fell out of my whatchacallit?"

The idea that someone would be so careless as to lose a rifle was inconceivable to Sam—he'd seen a company commander in the 101st Airborne Division relieved of command when one of the men under him had lost a pistol. "Scabbard?" Sam asked. "And landed barrel up next to a tree? Mike, everything you tell me seems . . . lame."

"I meant the bottle."

"Explain the rifle to me."

Mike looked down at his feet, then leaned forward in his chair with his elbows on his knees and cupped his chin in his hand. "Sam, I don't know."

"Okay, we'll look into it," Sam said. There were three possibilities. First, his client could very well be lying and might have placed the rifle there after shooting Max. That was clearly what the State thought. Second, the rifle did—as Mike was speculating—fall out of his scabbard and land barrel-up next to a tree. A jury would find that unreasonable. Third, someone else put the rifle there. But when and how? And who?

⁓

Standing on a hill on Max's property, Sam felt the sunshine on his neck. The northeasterly breeze was in his face and the sun was in his eyes. He looked downhill perhaps one hundred thirty meters to the large ponderosa stump where Max had apparently been seen last. Turning to face uphill, he observed the small aspen stand where the rifle had been found. He paced the distance to the stand—twelve meters. The cartridge had been located approximately five meters from the aspen stand.

Sam's interviews with the family had not been particularly revealing. Everyone agreed that Max had been extraordinarily hard on Mike, that Mike had made threats but didn't have what it took to carry them out. Stacy and Danny had been in California at the time of Max's interference, so they could add nothing regarding the events of that day. Lana agreed that the four men had left, Mike and Paulie returned first, without Max, and Alex came down the mountain moments later. Alex reported hearing a shot but had no idea from what direction it might have come. In sum, while Sam had some doubts about his client's story, he had a bigger problem: if you're going to claim some other dude did it, you needed another dude—and he didn't have one.

Worse, Mike's threats had apparently been overheard by several people, and as the witness and exhibit lists began to come in, it was becoming clear that in the weeks before Max's death, an increasingly embittered and panicked Mike had threatened him both loudly and frequently.

As Sam walked the hillside, admiring the azure sky and cumulus clouds and anticipating the summer ahead, he realized he was humming an old Clint Black tune. It had been years since he'd found himself humming. Part of sobriety, he was learning, was having fun again. He glanced at his watch and saw that it was well past time to get back to his office—Cassie was probably pacing away right now, hands on her sizable hips, awaiting his signature on something. He smiled to himself and began the walk back to his truck when his phone rang loudly in the still mountain air. He stopped, pulled the phone from a pocket, and stared at it. Four bars. He replaced it without answering, took a last look at the aspen stand just yards away, and began making his way carefully down the still-muddy hillside toward the truck.

He had another dude—but when and how?

38

Days later, Sam made his way through the crowd and found a seat at the bar of the Longbranch Saloon. He had ordered a cheeseburger to go and planned to wait until it was ready. He held up a hand to summon Gino. "Club soda," he said when Gino made his way over and was wiping down the spot in front of Sam.

"Sounds good," Gino said. "I heard you were on the wagon. That's a good thing." He dispensed the bubbly water into a glass full of ice, dropped in a slice of lemon, and placed the glass on the bar in front of Sam. "On the house."

Sam took the soda water and swiveled on his barstool to look around. The place was full tonight, with people gathered at tables drinking, shooting pool, and playing shuffleboard. He liked the music, and lamented the fact he'd never learned to two-step, and now with the leg, well, it probably wouldn't happen.

"Sam! Good to see you!"

It was Cathy. She looked good. "Good to be seen," he said, toasting her with his water glass. "Got the night off?"

"Yup. Mom said she'd watch Kayla so I'm out with a couple of friends."

"Very cool."

"Yeah. It's been a while. How about you?"

"Me? Oh, I just thought I'd take a break. Just waiting on my burger."

"How's it going?" she asked, leaning in close to him so he could hear her. She smelled nice.

"Fine, fine," he said. "You?"

"Me? Did you hear? I'm off the case. Grant decided you and I were too close," she said. "He felt like I might be . . . that I might find it hard to try the case against you."

"That's bullshit," Sam said. "We tried a murder case a while back. You threatened to thump my melon, as I recall."

"Yeah, well, let me quote Grant the Great: 'That was then, Cathy.' Can you believe that?" she asked with an exaggerated wave of her arms. "It's like you can't know someone and still try and kick their ass!" She was slurring badly, and he could smell the tequila.

"You got a ride home, right?"

"It's kind of you to offer."

"That's not what I meant," he said quickly. "Just trying to ensure you aren't driving."

"Then you're the only defense attorney I know takin' money out of his own pocket." She signaled to Gino. "One more."

"Maybe, but you've got a lot to lose."

The stool next to Sam had been vacated and she sat on it unsteadily. "Maybe. But my job prospects seem to be dwindling by the day."

"Rebecca didn't back you?"

"Nope." Cathy raised the shot Gino had poured. "Bottoms up." She swallowed and made a face, then leaned into Sam. "I think she's doin' him."

"Who?"

"I think," she began, putting a hand on Sam's shoulder and pulling him up close. "I think they are sleeping together. Grant and Becky."

Sam was surprised. He'd figured Rebecca for better judgment. He wasn't one for gossip but couldn't help himself. "You sure?"

"Oh, yeah," she said with an exaggerated wink. "Trust me. And she just appointed him chief deputy."

"Over you?"

"Over all of us—doesn't that suck?"

"I don't even know what to say." Sam reached up and removed her hand from his shoulder, then turned to see if he could find Gino, who had disappeared. In the mirror he saw their reflection. Two lonely people. Not good. "Where are your girls?" he asked Cathy.

She pointed to a pair of women sitting at a nearby table. "The one with the cowboy hat, and the one wearing the running shoes. Those are my girls."

"Good," Sam said. "I think you should join them. I'm headed home."

"Could you give me a ride?" Her hand was on his knee.

She was drunk. And she was a friend. "No. To tell you the truth, I walked," he lied.

"I'll give *you* a ride," she said.

Sam was beginning to panic a bit when her friend in the cowboy hat came over. "Cathy! Listen! It's our song!" she yelled, and grabbed Cathy's hands. She dragged her over to a corner near their table, where Cathy quickly forgot about Sam and joined an impromptu all-woman dance party.

Gino appeared and looked at Sam meaningfully while handing over the paper bag containing his dinner.

"We square?" Sam asked, dropping a twenty-dollar bill on the bar.

"Soda's on the house," Gino said, handing the bill back to Sam. "You paid by card for the food."

"Right." Sam set the bill back on the bar. "If it'll ease your conscience, pour a round for Cathy and the girls on me."

Later, with the echo of the music in his head, he drank water and brushed his teeth before calling it a night. As he drifted off, he noted he could still smell Cathy's perfume.

And the tequila.

39

Sam was awakened by his answering service; Mike had been calling repeatedly. "We told him you don't take client calls on the weekend, but he was insistent," the worker said.

"I understand, and I appreciate it," Sam assured her. He made a pot of coffee and then punched in Mike's number. "What's going on?" he asked.

"It's Lana. She's taken over the company," Mike said. "Besides that . . . well, she's been cold, if you know what I'm saying. She says that because I've been charged with killing Max she can assume management of the firm as an overseer. Says your partner said it was okay."

It would not be unusual—most close corporations had provisions for misbehaving shareholders, including those charged with a crime. Daniels would stick to the books. "That's just a temporary situation," Sam said. "I'm sure that—"

"I don't understand, Sam. It's like she's changed. We haven't slept together in weeks."

That was not unusual, either. Sam had seen innumerable relationship problems develop while cases were pending. People needed to survive. The stress and uncertainty of pre-trial caused some people to seek out safer alternatives—"safer" being someone other than the accused. "Look, I'm sure she is just doing what she thinks or is being advised is best for the company."

"Can you look into it?" Mike pleaded.

"No," Sam said. "That was part of the deal. Press is advising Lana, and I'm advising you. If Press said to do it, it must be righteous. What did she say?"

"That because I am under suspicion, she was going to defer distribution of the estate—sound right?"

"Possibly," Sam said. "There may well be a clause in the estate authorizing a delay or deferral of distribution when there are criminal charges involving one or more beneficiaries."

"You've got to fix this; she has no idea how to run the company."

"Don't you have vice presidents? Surely there is someone who isn't family she could appoint?"

"Sounds like she is going to try to run things herself," Mike said. "She did say she will put me on a retainer as an adviser."

It was something, at least. A lot of former business owners were retained as advisers until the new owner got on his or her feet. If it became an issue, he could highlight his client's retention and continued involvement. "Okay, what else?"

"What do you mean?"

"I mean is there anything else you want me to know?"

"Not right now," Mike said. "I—I just want this to be over."

Sam had intended to call Lana the next day anyway, because his many attempts to interview Paulie had been rebuffed. "I hear you. Look, it's going to take a while, just like I told you it would. Where is Lana right now?"

"I have no idea."

~

She picked up on the second ring. "Hi, Sam," she said. "What can I do for you?"

Sam could tell she was in a moving vehicle and could hear her quieting someone in the background. "A couple of things. First, can you get Paulie to answer my call?" he asked. "I've been trying to get him to come in so I can ask him some questions."

"Of course," she said. "When do you want to see him?"

"As soon as possible. I'll be in the office tomorrow morning," Sam said. "It's important," he added unnecessarily.

"I understand," she said. "I'll get him—stop it!" she giggled, then muffled the phone. A moment later, she was back on the line. "Are you still there?"

"I am." Sam considered his options for a moment, then asked, "Is Mike there?"

"Oh, uh, yes," she said. "But he just stepped out. I'll have him call you. Are you calling because Mike called you? Because I just did what Press advised."

"He advised you to dump your husband in the middle of a murder trial?"

"He said I could," she said. "And Mike needs to be focused on the trial, don't you think?"

"Of course," Sam allowed. "But the optics aren't good. It's going to look like his own wife gave up on him."

"Well, the truth is, on the advice of counsel I am acting to protect UkrCX."

Sam poked at the buttons on his phone, then placed it on his desk. This was a problem. Moments later, Daniels called. Lana worked fast. "Press, what the hell?" Sam asked without preamble. "I know we got a wall, but this is not good."

There was a delay before Daniels answered. "I apologize for not giving you a heads-up. I'm down here in Tijuana. Things aren't going well." He then embarked on a two-minute summary of the events surrounding Marci's treatment—every one of which was bad. "Anyway, I'll be back late tomorrow night and can catch you up, okay?"

"Press, I—I'm sorry."

"The doctors down here think we're going to start to see some improvement any day now," Daniels added hopefully.

"Okay, well . . . Look, if you need anything, let me know."

"Will do. See you Tuesday. I'll explain to you how this all went down. I tried to talk Lana out of it, but . . ."

After they hung up, Sam considered what he'd heard. Lana said she acted on advice of counsel, but Daniels was indicating she acted against his advice. Even given Daniels' ongoing distractions, Sam believed him. Most likely, then, she was undermining the defense for her husband—the defense she was paying for.

~

Daniels touched the broth with the tip of a trembling index finger. It was still too hot, so he dropped a couple of ice cubes into it before positioning the bowl on the small tray he used to ferry Marci's meals back and forth. The round trip to Mexico had taken a lot out of him and he was unsteady as he carried the tray into her room. He spilled some.

"Damn it!"

"What is it, dear?" Marci asked. She was facing the window, her back to him. He had raised the blinds when she lay down for a short after-dinner nap. "I like to look at the stars," she'd said. Indeed, she always had. He remembered walking with her on a snowy night on their college campus decades ago. He'd invited her out to "look at the stars," a lame ruse to get her away from some rather protective sorority sisters.

"It's nothing," he said. "Spilled a little soup. Don't want to upset you."

He heard her laugh, then cough. "You've always been so clumsy, haven't you?"

"I have," he said as he carefully counted her pills. That Mexican doctor had said her dosage was extremely high to begin with; anything beyond that could be fatal. "I'm getting your pills ready, darling. How about you try and sit up and have some broth? I brought you some juice, as well."

"Would you pour a little whiskey in it?" she joked.

He laughed softly. The truth was, they didn't have any whiskey in the house—he'd drank the last pint yesterday. Had she known that . . . "C'mon, love. Sit up and have some."

With his help, she sat up and had some broth. When he tried to help, she brushed his hand away—she still had some pride, which he took as a positive sign. He helped her change into a dry blouse and brought her a warm washcloth. She asked him to bring her makeup—another good sign —and after she'd applied it as best she could, he lifted her into a wheel-chair and pushed her into the living room so they could watch a movie together. While he got her IV reconnected, she looked around the room. "You're doing a pretty good job," she commented.

"I'm a big boy," he said, and moved her IV so she could see the television.

"Oh, I know *that*," she said. "I'm just surprised—for more than forty years I cleaned up after you, and now I find out you're not helpless after all," she teased.

He kissed her forehead, fiddled with the controller until he found a 1950s musical she favored. "How about that?" he asked.

"Perfect," she said, and pulled a small blanket up over her frail shoulders.

"I'll be right back," he said, and walked to the kitchen. He carefully measured out a small bowl of ice cream to share. "I got us a little ice cream," he said upon his return. "It's chocolate." When she didn't respond, he started to rush to her until—seeing her shallow breathing—he slowed and sat in the chair next to hers.

He watched her for a time before carrying her to bed, then returning to the living room to savor the ice cream. The tears gave it a salty aftertaste.

40

Sam was at his desk, looking out a dirty window at the melting late March snow and thinking that he should get ahold of his landlord to have that taken care of when Cassie buzzed him. The past few months had gone quickly. Mike had waived a preliminary hearing in circuit court and the case had been transferred ("bound over," in court parlance) to district court. He and Sam had thereafter made an initial appearance in front of Bridger, who had accepted Mike's not-guilty plea, continued bond, and set the matter for trial. Despite his initial threats to replace Sam with other counsel, for whatever reason Mike had kept him on, and as the weeks passed, the two men had begun to see eye to eye as Sam prepared for trial.

"Sam, it's Russ Johnson from Cheyenne," Cassie said.

"Send him through." Sam had been expecting this call. Weeks earlier, having continued to wonder about the bottle—and over Lee's objection—Sam had obtained the court's permission to test the liquid in the spray bottle found near the rifle and cartridge. Lee had argued that because no prints or DNA were located on the outside of the bottle, its contents were not relevant. It was a lame argument, and Sam had prevailed.

"Sam?" Johnson asked.

"It's me," Sam replied. "Tell me something good."

"Well, I'm not sure this is good news for you. Your client's DNA is in that liquid."

"Aw crap. I was hoping the bottle belonged to someone else. You didn't prepare any kind of report, did you?" If one had been prepared, the rules required him to disclose it to the prosecution.

"Not yet. I was waiting for your guidance."

"Well, I think we'll pass. Send me your invoice and we'll call it good."

"There is one thing, though."

"What is it?" Sam asked, looking at his watch. Johnson had proved to be a valuable resource over the years, but he was long-winded. Sam had another client in just a few minutes. "Can you give me the short version?"

"Well, I can tell you this: the concentration of your client's DNA in that liquid was many, many times what might be expected if he'da been drinking and backwashing or whatever."

Sam sat up in his chair. "What are you telling me?"

"Well, first, let me explain," Johnson said, and commenced a lecture on DNA and the extraction thereof from liquids. Sam was looking at his desk when Johnson began to sum up. "So I'm thinking this isn't what it appears to be."

"You're saying there's too much DNA in the sample?"

"Way too much."

"What are you getting at?" Sam asked impatiently.

"I think the liquid in that bottle is what's called a *cultivated* sample. I think someone got a sample of DNA and then cultivated it. Here's how that could happen, and here's how you'd use it." He then explained the process. "It's called 'erase and replace,'" he concluded. "You can look it up on the internet. There are commercial products you can buy."

"Who *does* that?"

"People who are afraid of being traced; people who are maybe somewhere they shouldn't be, like with someone else's wife; even the tinfoil hat brigade."

"So, you spray—"

"A cleaner on the surface of whatever, then you spray the DNA on whatever you want to hide your tracks on. Now usually, we'd see several people's

DNA on an item to try to confuse law enforcement. But in this case, we just got the one guy's."

"So, you're saying—"

"Only your guy's DNA is on that rifle, right?"

"Right."

"And you'll remember from our prior cases that's kind of unlikely given touch DNA—right?"

"Yeah."

"I'd usually expect to see someone else's DNA on something like a rifle, but here we've got only your client's DNA in the liquid, and a correspondingly high concentration of your client's DNA on the rifle."

Sam saw it now. "My client's being framed?"

"I'm not going there; I'm just saying that this is strange," Johnson said. "Very strange."

"Russ, you're going to get a subpoena to testify—do your homework. And let's do this: prepare your report, but here's what I want." Sam then carefully prescribed how he wanted the report prepared. If Cathy was the prosecutor, he very likely would have called her, told her what he had discovered, and awaited a possible dismissal or an offer on a lesser charge. But with Lee running the show, he had no such hope. He would disclose what he had found—an unusually high concentration of his client's DNA in the liquid and on the rifle—and that was it. Now, he just needed to get his client on board.

∽

As soon as he hung up with Johnson, Sam put in a call to Mike. "We need to talk."

"Sam, it's after five. I—"

"Now," Sam said. "I insist. And it's just us."

An hour later, he had finished a summation of what Johnson had told him.

"So you are saying someone faked the DNA?" Mike rubbed a hand over his face.

"I am."

"Who?"

"Well, it wasn't Max," Sam said. "That leaves Paulie or Alex."

Mike sat back in his chair and said nothing. At last, he stood and walked to Sam's window. "I don't think Paulie would do that," he said. "I don't think he could." He turned to Sam. "It had to have been Alex. The little shit has been after my job forever!"

"Right," Sam said.

"So, what do we do?" Mike asked. "Do we have him arrested?"

Sam looked at Mike for a long time, trying to discern whether his ignorance was real or feigned. "Who?"

"Alex!"

He seemed sincere. "What about Lana?" Sam asked. Mike acted truly surprised. "She gave Alex bottles of water before you left, right?"

"She gave *me* water, too!"

"Mike, you said she's been aloof. You said she's removed you from your position. And think of it this way: if she thought Max was going to remove you—"

"You think she framed me!"

"I'm saying it's possible," Sam said.

"I don't believe it! She wouldn't do this!"

Mike was in denial. Not surprising. "I understand," Sam said. "I—"

"No, you don't! You can't! She didn't . . . she wouldn't!"

He wasn't going to get anywhere with this tonight. "Maybe not," Sam said. "But the deal is this. We have evidence that indicates *someone* tried to frame you. And if Lana gave that bottle to Alex, well—"

"I'm not going to listen to this," Mike said.

Sam let him go. He couldn't blame him.

~

Long after Mike left, Sam sat drinking green tea, eating gumdrops, and weighing the implications—legal and otherwise—of having one client framing another. When the phone rang, he punched wildly at the buttons.

"Press, what are you doing?"

"I was taking a walk. It's been a long day."

"Tell me about it," Sam said, before realizing how that sounded. "I'm sorry. What I'm facing is obviously—"

"No sweat. How's it going?"

Sam could hear Daniels breathing. He must have been walking outside. "Oh, fine."

"I saw the lights on. Just checking in. Anything I should know about?"

Oh, hell yes. But he couldn't tell him. "No, not really," Sam lied.

"Got it," Daniels said. He was about to hang up when Sam asked about Marci. "She's okay. Sleeping a lot. We go back to Mexico again next week."

"Press, do you think that's a good idea?"

Daniels took a deep breath and let it go. "Sam, I'll decide what's in the best interests of Marci, if you don't mind."

Sam was chagrined. "I know. I'm just afraid—"

"Don't be," Daniels said. "It's in God's hands. And mine."

Sam looked at his phone when Daniels disconnected. Odd.

41

On April 1 at precisely nine a.m., the dull buzz of conversation died when Bridger appeared and made his way to the bench. He ordered all to be seated and looked over the packed courtroom. "Good morning, ladies and gentlemen," he began.

"Good morning," was the polite but unenthusiastic response.

"My name is Walton Bridger, and I am a district court judge here in the 12th Judicial District of Wyoming." Scanning the panel of potential jurors, he continued, "Most of you don't look happy to be here—and that's too bad, because you are about to fulfill one of the most important civic duties that you are asked to perform as a citizen, and that is to serve on a jury. You may recall from your high school civics courses that very few countries entrust their citizens with this kind of responsibility, and I'm proud to say that I believe Wyoming citizens make some of the best jurors in the country."

Bridger then gave a short history of jury duty in Wyoming before moving on. "Now, I want to stress up front that what you are about to do is not for your entertainment. In the real world, trials are not like on television. They are not like the novels you have read or movies that you might have seen. As an initial matter, the judge is much better looking." Bridger smiled while everyone in the courtroom laughed nervously. Because

Bridger used the same line that Judge Daniels had, Sam had Mike prepared, and he and Mike laughed along as well. Turning serious, Bridger intoned, "Instead, your job as jurors will be to search for truth—a truth with consequences, one that directly affects the lives and liberty of those who are involved.

"If you are selected for this jury, you will be expected to pay close attention to what's going on in this courtroom. In just a few seconds the clerk is going to call the names of twelve of you to be seated in the jury box. If your name is called, please come forward." Bridger indicated the jury box with a wave of his hand. "The bailiff will direct you to your seat. Madam Clerk, would you seat a jury, please?"

After twelve potential jurors were called and seated, Bridger continued. "The case that has been called for trial is the State of Wyoming versus Michael Brown. The defendant in this case is present and seated at the counsel table to the court's left next to his attorney, Mr. Johnstone."

Mike made eye contact with each potential juror and smiled, just as Sam had instructed. Sam too flashed a winning smile as Bridger continued. "Seated at the other table is Chief Deputy County and Prosecuting Attorney Grant Lee, who is lead counsel in this matter. Also present is Rebecca Nice, who is the elected county attorney. They are the lawyers for the State of Wyoming; the burden of proof in this case rests with them."

Lee smiled and nodded upon the introduction. Rebecca nodded, recognizing her constituents. "Mr. Brown has been charged with one count of first-degree murder in the death of one Maxim Kovalenko, which is alleged to have occurred here in Custer County on or about last October 17," Bridger said. "Mr. Brown pleaded not guilty, and as you look at him right now you should understand you are looking at an innocent man, and he'll remain so until and unless you decide otherwise."

While Bridger spoke, Sam scanned the face of each potential juror carefully and arranged pages of notes in the order in which each had been called. Several days prior, the clerk of court had provided each side with questionnaires completed by the potential jurors. Sam, with some assistance from Daniels and Cassie, had spent time reviewing each questionnaire and gathering background on the jurors, mostly through social media accounts. Daniels' and Cassie's familiarity with the community was invaluable; together they were able to advise Sam on the suitability of all but a very few of the potential jurors. The initial slate was randomly drawn; Sam was satisfied, for the most part.

"Ladies and gentlemen, we will now proceed to select a jury through a process called voir dire—which means 'to tell the truth.' The purpose is to select a fair jury. Mr. Lee will first ask questions of you as a group; he may follow up with questions to you individually. When he has finished with his questions, Mr. Johnstone may ask questions as well. Mr. Lee, please proceed."

Lee stepped to the podium and for the next hour asked questions of the jurors relating to their knowledge of the case, the players, the process, and their predisposition toward conviction and/or acquittal. He inquired of the jurors regarding their schedules, state of mind, and willingness to partici-pate. For the most part, his questions were proper, but he had a bizarre habit of interjecting bits about himself in his questions: "As an experienced trial attorney, I've seen jurors who . . ." or "During the many cases I've tried . . ."

Sam sat quietly, observing and taking notes, but it finally got on his nerves and he stood. Lee, seeing Sam stand, stopped mid-sentence. Bridger, who had been taking notes, looked up. "Mr. Johnstone?"

"Your Honor, may we approach?"

When Sam and Lee had gathered in front of the judge's bench, a red-faced Lee spoke first. "Judge, I don't like being interrupted during voir dire."

Bridger looked to Sam. "Mr. Johnstone?"

"Judge, Mr. Lee's tactic of throwing his experiences into every question is a blatant attempt to ingratiate himself with the jury."

"It is rather odd," Bridger agreed. "I'm not sure it is out of bounds, however."

"There is nothing barring it in the rules," Lee said.

"True," Bridger agreed. "But for the sake of timeliness, how about you just ask your questions without prefacing them with your life experience? Gentlemen, please return to your places. I'd like to have a jury by mid-afternoon."

Lee thereafter curtailed his questions, and when he was finished, Bridger looked to Sam.

"Does the defense care to inquire of the panel?"

"Yes, Your Honor," Sam said, standing and buttoning his jacket. "Ladies and gentlemen, because Mr. Lee did a fine job of asking questions, I'm only going to ask you a few more. They will be simple and straightforward, for all Mike Brown wants is a jury of fair-minded people. So, here we go. First, is there anyone here who believes my client is guilty because he is rich and from out of town?" Sam watched as most of the jurors grinned and then shook their heads. "So, can we all agree to judge my client not by the size of his wallet or the fact that he is from California, but instead by applying the evidence to the law Judge Bridger will instruct you on later?" Again, each juror grinned and nodded.

"Okay," Sam said, looking at each juror in turn. "Let me ask you this. If you were my client, would you be comfortable having yourself as a juror?" Sam smiled and allowed his eyes to meet the eyes of each juror. "In other words, do you see yourself as an open and fair-minded person?" Some of the jurors shifted in their chairs, some smiled slightly, but all met his stare and eventually nodded their assent.

"Well," Sam continued, moving to the side of the podium and gesturing with one hand. "How about this: there has been a lot—a *lot*—of newspaper and television coverage of this case. Max Kovalenko was one of the richest men in the country, it seems. Lots of talking heads out there on court television shows flapping their lips. Has anyone heard or seen anything so far that would make it hard for you to judge my client just as fairly as you would the other side?"

All jurors were still shaking their heads when Sam asked the next question. "Knowing what you know about my client and his family, can everyone here set aside their knowledge of his wealth and judge this case on its facts?"

Seeing nothing but head shakes, he continued, "So no one here has a problem with rich people that would keep you from judging this case on its merits?" Again, the air was still. "This family moved into town and made some changes. My client was at the forefront of that effort. Can we agree that rich out-of-towners are not automatically bad?"

Again, Sam met each pair of eyes with his own. While Sam was generally satisfied with the random selection of jurors, he harbored doubts about
a young male juror in the front row, and a couple of older men in the back.
They looked at his client with disgust. On the other hand, there were two
female jurors who were looking at Sam with a degree of attraction.

Having set the baseline, Sam inquired of the prospective jurors for
more than an hour. Some were excused for cause and new ones summoned
to fill their place, whereupon Lee and Sam asked questions of them as well.
As the process wound down, Sam asked two final questions. "Is there
anything that any of you would prefer to discuss in private?" he asked.
"Raise your hand if you'd like to meet with us in private."

No hands were raised, so Sam continued, "Is there anything we haven't
asked you that you think we should know?" Seeing no hands, and nothing
but blank stares or head shakes, he finished up. "Ladies and gentlemen,
thank you for your patience." Turning to Bridger, he said, "Defense passes
the panel for cause, sir."

"Thank you, counsel," Bridger said. "Ladies and gentlemen, we have a
sufficient number of jurors from which to select the jury to hear this case. I
am going to release you here momentarily so that we might select that jury
in your absence. We'll do this as quickly as possible, but it sometimes takes
some time," Bridger said, smiling at his word play. "Do not leave the courthouse and follow the directions of the bailiff. Bailiff?"

Following the jury panel's departure, the parties selected the jury and
the alternates. Sam struck the young man in the front row. Surprisingly, Lee
struck both men who had been seated in the back row that Sam had
concerns about, and both of the women who had made eyes at Sam
remained.

When the jury that would hear the case had been reconvened and
sworn, Bridger looked pointedly at the clock. "Well, ladies and gentlemen,
you are the jury which will hear this matter. It's been a long day, so we will
go ahead and take our evening recess and hear opening arguments and get
started in the morning. First, I'm going to read you an instruction regarding
your conduct during daily and evening recesses. Please listen closely."

Bridger proceeded to read an instruction warning the jurors against following news accounts, discussing the case, or performing their own investigation. When he concluded, he looked to the jury for acknowledgement. "The bailiff will tell you where you need to be and when you need to be there." He stood, and everyone followed suit. "Thank you for your attention. Bailiff, you may escort the jury."

42

Twelve hours later, Sam rolled over and looked at the alarm clock next to his bed. It was 3:10 a.m. on Tuesday morning. In the red glow of the ancient clock he found his prosthetic leg and slowly, deliberately attached it. He stretched and moved to ensure it was properly affixed, then swung his legs down to the floor, donned a pair of slippers, and stood in the dark. He felt for and found the pistol he kept in a holster on the bedpost. Removing it, he began a slow patrol of his townhouse. He'd performed this drill a hundred times over the course of the past couple of years. Sometimes it was the wind, sometimes an animal, sometimes a dream, sometimes nothing at all. Once—during Davonte Blair's trial—it was in fact someone surveilling him.

At last, satisfied that he was not being stalked or surveilled, Sam sat at his kitchen table and pulled out a small book given to him by a treatment provider. The book was arranged by date and contained passages and prayers to help the alcoholic cope with the stresses of life one day at a time. It had been a couple of weeks since Sam had done the reading he had promised himself he would do daily, so he sat quietly and read until he was current.

～

Hours later, when all were assembled, Bridger looked to Lee. "Mr. Lee, does the State wish to make an opening statement?"

"We do, Your Honor." Lee was already on his feet and took a yellow legal pad and bottle of water to the podium with him. "May it please the court," he said to Bridger. Nodding to Sam, he continued the customary introduction. "Counsel."

"Counsel," Sam replied.

"Ladies and gentlemen, I want to begin by again thanking you for your service," Lee said. "This, in my experience, is an unusual case. Unusual in that in matters such as this, where the evidence is overwhelming, a plea agreement can usually be reached. But here—"

It was dangerous to interrupt opposing counsel—jurors wanted to get to the heart of the matter—but Sam had heard more than enough and was on his feet.

"Please approach," Bridger instructed.

When the men were together, Bridger looked to Sam and nodded. "Your Honor, he's vouching for the truth of the evidence that will be presented. That's improper on its face. Further, he's commenting on efforts to settle without telling the jurors he never even made an offer. This is totally misleading."

Bridger looked to Lee, who shrugged. "I'm just giving the jury the benefit of my view of the case, Judge. My experience—"

"How long have you been practicing law?" Bridger interrupted.

"I'm not sure that's relevant," Lee replied.

"I asked you a question," Bridger said. "How long?"

"Five years."

"Mr. Lee, spare the jury the war stories garnered from five years of practice, and no discussion of plea bargain efforts," Bridger instructed. "Counsel, return to your places."

A red-faced Lee and a satisfied Sam took their places, whereupon Lee tried to pick up where he'd left off. "Ladies and gentlemen, we are going to prove to you what happened. We are going to prove to you where it happened. We will prove to you when it happened. We are going to prove to you who committed the crime. And together, those facts will prove the elements of the offense."

He looked at each member of the jury. "What we're *not* going to prove to you, because we are not required to do so, is the motive for the crime. We don't have to prove it. Oh, we will provide some evidence from which you can probably derive the motive, but don't forget—we don't have to prove the motive. Now, I am sure defense counsel will go heavily into motive, arguing that his client had no motive to do this or to do that," Lee said, pointing at Sam. Pre-emptively arguing against the defense's case was a time-honored tradition among prosecutors. "But just remember, it doesn't matter—what matters is whether at the date, time, and place stated, Mike Brown intentionally killed Max Kovalenko. The who, what, when, where, and how matter—there is no *why* in the elements required to be proven."

Lee was speaking faster now, caught up in the moment. "Now, you should know that during this trial I'm going to introduce you to Max Kovalenko, the victim. You will hear that Max was a remarkable man. An immigrant from the Ukraine, he rose from having whatever change he had in his pockets when he arrived to being a billionaire. This man led an extraordinary life, and the evidence is going to show that he was going to build upon that life right here in Custer, Wyoming."

Walking to the prosecution table, Lee placed his hand on Garcia's shoulder. The detective recoiled slightly at Lee's touch—he had clearly not been told that was going to happen. "This is a big, complicated case, and I will begin by talking about the investigation itself," Lee continued. "Max Kovalenko disappeared on October 17. An investigation was undertaken shortly thereafter. It was led by Investigator Ted Garcia, who will tell you his initial task was to see if Max Kovalenko could be found alive. Well, on the 18th he was located, but it was obvious that he had been shot. No gun was near him—it was obvious he didn't shoot himself, so Detective Garcia here opened his investigation. You'll hear from him. You'll hear from experts, specialists, and other witnesses who are very, very well qualified and who have no reason to testify to anything except the truth."

It was objectionable; Sam's eyes met Bridger's, but Sam let it go. He had a plan.

Lee was oblivious. "You will hear the steps each of these experts took to ensure that their examination, processing, and testing of the evidence was done with exactitude. You will hear Investigator Garcia talk about missing persons investigations, gunshot investigations, and how the thought process goes when an investigation is underway. You will hear his reports on each of the people he felt it necessary to interview. You will see how—through the process of elimination—he began to question the activities of the defendant. You'll learn he did not undertake this investigation with the thought that Mike Brown shot Max. In fact, you'll hear him testify that he felt at the outset that the most likely explanation was one of a hunter accidentally shooting Max. But you will hear as he testifies how he began to change his thinking as the evidence came in. You will hear from ballistics experts that the weapon used was a very specific weapon, and that it used a very specific ammunition. Finally," Lee said, pointing at Mike, "you will hear from the specialists who will show you the remains of the bullet that killed Max, and the weapon that was used to fire that bullet. You'll learn that weapon had Mike Brown's fingerprints and DNA on it—and only Mike Brown's."

Lee scanned the jury and saw what he expected: acknowledgement. DNA was powerful in the minds of jurors. Sam was observing and saw the same thing. He made a note as Lee continued. "Finally, you will hear Detective Garcia's testimony that Mr. Brown, and only Mr. Brown, could have fired the fatal shot."

Lee extended a hand in Sam's direction. "Mr. Johnstone, of course, will try and throw you off the scent," he said dismissively. "Like a lot of successful businessmen, Max had enemies—a lot of them. His competitors, some of his providers, even some members of his family didn't particularly care for him. But the evidence will show that only one person had the means and opportunity to kill him, and that person was Mike Brown. And again—even though we don't have to prove motive—you'll hear witnesses say that Mr. Brown was extremely upset at the deceased, because he thought the deceased was about to replace him," Lee said. "And finally, you will hear that shortly before the shooting, Mike Brown threatened to shoot Max Kovalenko. He made that threat publicly, he did it earnestly, and he did it intentionally."

When he was satisfied that every juror had snuck a peek at Mike, Lee concluded. "You, as jurors, are triers of fact. You don't decide what the law is —the judge does that—but you decide the facts of the case. And the facts in this case aren't just going to point to who did it. We're also going to show you why no one else could have done it. In other words, we'll show you positive evidence about who did it and negative evidence that necessarily excludes others. You will hear the facts, and at the end of the case you will apply the law that the judge gives you in the search for truth. When you have done so, I have no doubt in my mind that you will conclude—just as Detective Garcia has—that Mike Brown intentionally and with malice aforethought shot and killed Max Kovalenko. When you have done that, we will ask—and I expect you to return—a verdict of guilty. Thank you, Your Honor."

Bridger nodded at Lee, then directed his attention toward Sam. "Mr. Johnstone, does the defense care to make an opening at this time?"

Sam rose. "We do, sir."

He made his way to the podium, took a long drink of water, and made eye contact with each of the jurors before he began talking. His intent was to speak briefly and forcefully to the idea of the State's inability to prove his client's guilt. Studies had shown that jurors rarely remembered anything beyond the tone of the attorneys during their opening statements. Lee had been certain and forceful. Sam wanted to use that against him later. Therefore, he would be quiet, professional, but just as certain of his position. The strategy was to poke holes in the State's story, not to reveal his own yet.

"Good morning, ladies and gentlemen. As I listened to Mr. Lee speak for the last hour or so, I was struck by the firmness and the certainty with which he promised you evidence in this matter. I was struck because I have seen the exhibits and I know who the witnesses are and what they will testify to knowing or believing. You see, in Wyoming, there are no surprises in a trial. The defendant has the right to see the evidence of his supposed guilt. I have. And despite all that, I find myself nowhere near as certain as Mr. Lee with respect to Mr. Brown's guilt. In fact, I think there are some glaring and gaping holes in the evidence. I was surprised to find out that Mr. Brown was charged, and I've been surprised since then that Mr. Lee has not made an offer to settle or seen to it that these charges were dropped." Sam looked at Lee. "In my experience, cases this weak are generally not brought to trial," he added. It was probably objectionable, but—as Sam anticipated—Lee didn't take the bait.

Sure that each juror had snuck a glance at Lee, Sam continued. "The State's witnesses are, of course, under the control of the government. Most of them are employed by the government. The State frequently lists more witnesses than it intends to call as a tactic designed to confuse the defense. He might call them; he might not. So as of now, all I can do is to give you what we used to call a SWAG—a serious, wild-ass guess—as to how he will try this case. This is my only opportunity to give you our theory of the case, and to tell you some of what we think took place. It's also my opportunity to call your attention to certain things so that you will be looking for them, and when you see and hear them, you'll realize they may have significance and you will be alerted to them."

"Now, you will be happy to know that in this case we will probably stipulate to virtually all the evidence that Mr. Lee will seek to have introduced, okay?" Sam saw a couple of jurors' eyebrows raise in surprise. "It's true, and I hope you appreciate that. I'm telling you right now we will do that because we agree with a lot of what he will say. Remember, I've seen the evidence. The witnesses saw what they saw; the evidence is generally what they say it is. So, instead of quibbling about unimportant things, we want you paying attention to the areas where we disagree with the prosecution. And let me tell you what we think is important. We think the motive is important. People do things for a reason. We think dates and times are important. Listen to the dates and times when events are said to have occurred. We think state of mind is important. Listen to evidence regarding state of mind of the State's witnesses. And make no mistake, we will challenge the State's witnesses, but I want to make one thing clear: whatever testimony is given, whatever evidence is introduced, we are not trying the police and we are not trying the prosecution."

Sam moved from one side of the podium to the other, forcing the jurors to follow him with their eyes if they were paying attention. In this way, he could begin to discern which jurors were actively listening, and which might have already made up their minds. "We think what is not said is important. Listen actively, remembering the State must prove beyond a reasonable doubt that my client is the *only* person who could have done this. As they testify, ask yourself after hearing each witness's testimony whether that testimony tends to show that *only* my client could have done this."

Sam moved back to where he started. "Remember I said I was surprised? I believe that after hearing and viewing the testimony and evidence in this matter, you too will come away surprised. Not surprised at the violence involved. Not even surprised that Max Kovalenko was shot. Rather, you'll come away surprised that my client was charged, let alone tried. Mr. Lee will ask you to connect dots that do not connect. Remember, you do not have to do so, and it is your duty not to do so if it is unreasonable."

Sam paused for effect, and to gather his breath. "Mr. Lee and I do agree on one thing, though: your job is to listen to the evidence and apply the law given to you by Judge Bridger. I happen to believe that after the evidence is viewed and the testimony heard, you will do your duty and quickly and unambiguously acquit him of all charges. Thank you."

Mike nodded in acknowledgment as Sam took his chair, exhausted despite the brief opening.

When Sam was seated, Bridger ordered Lee to proceed. "Your Honor, the State calls Thiago Garcia," he said. After Garcia was sworn and seated, Lee began the direct examination. "Please state your name for the court," he directed.

"Thiago Garcia—but everyone calls me Ted."

"Mr. Garcia, are you employed?"

"Yes."

"What do you do?"

"I am an investigator with the sheriff's office," he said. Lee then had Garcia answer questions tending to show he was a qualified investigator capable of conducting a thorough, professional investigation.

"Were you on duty on or about October 17?"

"Yes."

"And on that date, were you called to a location in rural Custer County?"

Sam watched Garcia closely. He had testified before, Sam knew, but due to the rural nature of the sheriff's jurisdiction and the lesser number of serious crimes, he didn't have the experience on the stand that the Custer

Police Department's detectives did. Nevertheless, Lee was right to call Garcia first. He would give the jury the story of what happened, setting the scene for all witnesses to follow. Wyoming juries generally liked cops; cross-examination would have to be undertaken carefully.

"What was your understanding of why you'd been called?"

"As I understood it, it was a 10-65—a missing persons complaint."

"Did you know at the time who was missing?"

"Objection. Vague," Sam said.

Bridger sustained the objection. It was penny-ante but proper: the question didn't specify what the time was and Lee had yet to establish foundation showing anyone was missing. Lee looked at Sam and all but rolled his eyes. "Let me ask the question again. At the time you were called to the residence, did you know that the missing person would ultimately be the deceased, Maxim Kovalenko?"

It was still improper and now it was leading, but because the question would sound acceptable to a juror, Sam let it go, lest he be seen by the jury to be interfering.

"No. I only knew it was an elderly man."

Sam smiled as many in the audience—more than 65 years of age themselves—groaned. Lee was oblivious. "And what happened next?"

"I met first with the reporting party, Lana Kovalenko-Brown."

"Brown?" Lee asked, acting surprised. "Any relation to the accused?"

"She's his wife," Garcia said.

Lee waited for the whispering to die down. "Any relation to the deceased?"

"His oldest daughter."

Again, Lee allowed the whispering to stop before he asked his next question. "What did you learn?"

"She told me that her father had gone horseback riding on his property with her husband, his head of security, and a young man named Aleksander Melnyk—they call him Alex—and had yet to return."

"She was concerned?"

"Yes. It was cold out, and he was, well . . . mature."

Sam smiled along with everybody else at Garcia's obvious attempt to again avoid calling Max old. "What did you do next?" Lee asked.

"I talked with some of the other family members."

"And what, if anything, did you learn from them?"

"Their accounts corroborated what Ms. Brown had told me."

"What did you do after that?"

"Well, I was talking with members of the family and trying to dissuade them from conducting a search on their own due to the dangerous conditions outside. About that time, a dog came into the area and appeared to have blood on it. I found this concerning, of course, and when Ms. Brown told me that the dog had accompanied her father, I had an officer take a blood sample from the dog. At that point, I was very concerned, but after consulting with Sheriff Walsh, and due to the weather conditions, I made the decision to delay a search until the weather cleared and it got light."

"The search began when?"

"On the 18th day of October, just after seven o'clock in the morning."

"Between the time that you made a decision to delay the search until the search commenced, what did you do?"

"I coordinated the next day's search and spoke with the family."

"Did you discover anything of particular interest during your interviews with the other family members?"

"Not really," Garcia said. "Everyone's story seemed to support Mr. Kovalenko's having gone missing. My hope was that he would find a safe place to take shelter. The information I had was that as a young man he had been a fighter pilot. Because most pilots have training in survival skills, I was hopeful that he would use those skills to get through the night so that we would find him alive."

"Let's move to the next morning. What happened then?"

"Well, I had asked everyone to allow law enforcement to conduct the search, but family members and volunteers got involved."

"Why was that a problem?" Lee asked.

"Ultimately it was not, but I feared they would put tracks in the snow and otherwise disturb the land on Max's property. I was afraid this would make it difficult to track Max."

"It wasn't a problem, then?"

"No, we got there first."

"How?"

"Initially, I was in a helicopter, searching by air."

"And at some point, was the victim's body located?"

It was minor, but at this point no evidence on the record showed Max was a victim. "Objection," Sam stated.

"Sustained," Bridger replied.

This time Lee did roll his eyes. "Did you at some point find a body you later determined belonged to Max Kovalenko?"

"*I* didn't," Garcia replied. "I was in a helicopter above the area where Max was found. I was signaled by two men on the ground."

Lee ignored the clarification. "What did you do when you were signaled?"

"I ordered my pilot to land the helicopter, which he did some distance from the men's location. I then hiked up the hill to where I estimated the men to be. I made contact there with the defendant and Pavlo Reznikov. They call him Paulie. He is—er, was—Max's head of security."

"The defendant located the body, you say?"

"He did," Garcia said. "Went almost directly to it."

Lee looked at the jury, ensuring they had time to process Garcia's answer.

"And when you questioned them, what did you conclude?"

"They were with a body they identified as Maxim Kovalenko."

"What did you do then?"

"I checked to ensure that the decedent was in fact dead, and then I sent Paulie back to the helicopter to alert the remainder of the law enforcement team."

"Why did you do that?"

"Because there was no reception up there. I couldn't get a signal."

"And while Paulie was gone, did you talk with the defendant?"

"I did."

"What did he tell you?"

"The same thing he had told me the evening prior—that he had been riding with Max when they observed trespassers along the north boundary of the property. It was a significant ride to the location of the trespassers, and Max did not feel well. Nevertheless, he wanted the trespassers run off. He sent Mike, Paulie, and Alex to confront them. According to Mike, they left Max next to a ponderosa stump. He was with his horse and dog. The plan was apparently to confront the trespassers, and then to come back and get Max."

"Can you describe the defendant's demeanor after he had located the decedent and was speaking with you?"

"Calm," Garcia said.

Sam made a note as Lee followed up. "Did they come back and get Max? Is that what happened?"

"No," Garcia said. "According to the defendant, Alex went to see if he could get a signal to call for help. The defendant and Paulie confronted the trespassers, who refused to leave. The defendant decided to return and pick up Max. On the way back, he and Paulie observed Max's horse by itself, heading north without Max. The defendant told Paulie to retrieve the horse and continued on to the location where Max had been."

Lee watched the jury to ensure they understood that Mike had possibly been alone with Max. "So the defendant got back. What then?" he asked.

"Well, according to him, Max was not there, so he began searching the immediate area for him. He didn't find him, so he began searching a broader area for him."

"Did he find Max?"

"Not that day."

Lee nodded. "What did the defendant tell you happened next?"

"Paulie returned with Max's horse, and the two of them continued the search until it began to get too dark to see anything."

Sam had a thought and made a note. He would need to talk with Mike about who was where.

"Then what?" Lee was getting impatient, as was the jury.

"The defendant decided to return to the ranch headquarters, as he was hoping Alex had somehow found Max and taken him down the mountain."

"Is that what actually happened?"

"No. According to the defendant, they all met up at the ranch headquarters and discovered that Max was missing. That's when we got called."

"What was your first impression of the decedent?" Lee asked.

"Deceased," Garcia said.

Lee shot Garcia a withering glance but faked a smile while everyone in the courtroom laughed nervously. "Let's try that again. Did you have a theory immediately upon seeing the deceased?"

"Not right away," Garcia said. "The only thing I felt fairly certain about initially was that he didn't shoot himself."

"Why?" Lee asked.

"Objection," Sam said, standing. "Outside his area of expertise."

Bridger looked to Lee. "I'm not asking him as an expert," Lee said. "I'm just asking him in his role as an experienced investigator."

Sam was fine with that explanation—it would enable him to pick apart Garcia's testimony later. "Withdrawn," he said.

"No gun on scene," Garcia replied. "And I'm no expert, but I felt like the body had been moved."

"Why?"

"No blood."

Lee had an annoying habit of nodding as if in understanding of a crucial point in response to Garcia's answers to even the most mundane questions. "So almost immediately an investigation was undertaken?"

"Yeah. Doc Laws got there soon after, and he and the crime scene techs looked things over."

"Then what?"

"Then I supervised removal of the body and started interviewing people."

"Who?"

"I started with the family."

"Why?"

"Because I wanted to see if they knew of anyone who might want to shoot him, and because it seemed like they were the last to see him alive."

"What did you learn?"

"I think it is fair to say he had a lot of enemies."

"Did you speak with any of them?"

"I spoke with all of them—at least, the ones I got names for."

"And what did you learn?"

"They all had alibis—most of them were still in California."

"And the rest?"

"Accounted for," Garcia said, then added, "We spent a lot of taxpayer money chasing down people out of state."

"Did you interview a man named Casey Sprague?"

"Yes. His name came up several times."

"Why?"

"Dispute over access to a school section. Apparently, he'd been doing that for years and he felt like he had a right," Garcia explained. "He was gonna lose a lot of money if he couldn't cross Max's land."

"What did you learn?"

"He'd been close to the scene, but he had seven or eight guys saying he was with them at what I determined to be the relevant time."

"How did you determine that?"

"Well, assuming that what the other horseback riders told me about when they'd left Max was true, and knowing what time we found him, I asked people about Casey Sprague's whereabouts between those times. He had a solid alibi."

Lee then led Garcia through a long list of questions designed to show a thorough and comprehensive investigation.

"So at some point you settled on Mr. Brown as a suspect and arrested him?"

"I did."

"Will you point him out to the jury?"

"He's sitting right there in a dark suit with a white shirt and blue tie," Garcia said, pointing as requested. "The man beside Mr. Johnstone."

"Now, how many interviews of the defendant did you undertake personally?" Lee asked.

"Two or three, I guess."

"Did you read him his rights?"

"Not before I arrested him, no."

"Why not?"

"Because I was just interviewing him."

"He knew that?"

"Yes."

"And he spoke to you anyway?"

"He did. He never refused."

"In any event, you made the decision to arrest."

Garcia sat for a long time, recalling Lee's pressure to arrest Mike. He thought about his answer.

"True?" Lee pressed.

"Yes," Garcia said at last.

"Why?"

"Well, it was a variety of things."

"Such as?"

"Well, as a threshold matter, he had a strong motive."

"What was that?"

"He told me his father-in-law was going to change his will or whatever and not leave the company to him. He had a financial motive."

"What else?"

"He owned—or at least had access to—the gun used to kill Max. He admitted to having fired the gun as—"

"Excuse me?" Lee asked, feigning surprise.

"The defendant told me he shot the gun."

"Did you believe him?"

"I had no reason not to—he said he fired the gun to try to alert Max to his whereabouts."

"Did you believe that?"

"It's a technique," Garcia said noncommittally.

"Do you believe he fired a weapon on that mountain?"

"I did after I got the results from the ballistics guy, toolmark examiner, and the DNA, yeah."

"Why?"

"Because I found a rifle with his DNA on it right about where he said he was when he fired. I found an expended cartridge that I was later told was cycled by that rifle nearby with his prints on it."

"Interesting," Lee said.

Sam was about to object when Garcia continued, unprompted, "And the bullet that killed the deceased came from the defendant's gun."

Lee studied Garcia. He might as well ask the question—or Sam would. "How do you know it was the defendant's weapon?"

"Well, I should say it came from the one with his DNA on it."

Sam thought about objecting. The entire line of questioning was arguably improper. But it would all come in later, in any event. He let it go, figuring he would challenge each aspect later.

"And what else?"

"He—Mr. Brown—couldn't account for his whereabouts at the time of the shooting, except to put himself near the exact spot where we later found the rifle and the expended cartridge."

"What else?"

"Well, there were the threats."

"Threats?" Lee repeated, acting surprised.

"Yes. The information I gathered indicated that the defendant had threatened to shoot Mr. Kovalenko on multiple occasions."

Lee watched as the majority of jurors turned to look at Mike. To his credit, Mike sat quietly, taking notes and showing no emotion—just as Sam had instructed him. Sam had attempted to get the threat suppressed prior to trial but was overruled by Bridger. Sam's recourse would be to place them in context.

Lee then had Garcia testify to his team's efforts in recovering the body, taking blood and other samples, and the processing of the scene as well as evidence—including the rifles. He took Garcia chronologically through the effort to locate the suspected location from which Max was shot, and the discovery of the expended cartridge and rifle. Finally, he had Garcia discuss the linkage between the remains of the bullet recovered from Max's body, the expended cartridge, the rifle, the DNA, the fingerprints, and his ultimate decision to arrest, all focused on why Mike had been identified as the shooter. Sam was somewhat surprised that Lee didn't have Garcia discuss the bottle found nearby. Toward the end, Lee asked Garcia to sum up. "And after this extensive investigation, what did you conclude?"

"Mr. Brown was the only person I could find who had motive, means, opportunity, no alibi, and whose activities fit the forensic evidence."

Lee consulted with Rebecca briefly, then—after almost five hours of testimony—looked to Bridger. "No more questions, Your Honor." He sat. "Tender the witness."

Bridger nodded, and looked at Sam. "Mr. Johnstone, I anticipate a rather lengthy cross-examination?"

"Yes, sir," Sam said, standing.

"Then I'm going to find that this is a good time for the evening recess," he said, anticipating Sam's objection. Defense attorneys generally hated having a key prosecution witness's testimony stand overnight, but Sam surprised him.

"Thank you, Judge," Sam said. He watched the jurors closely as they departed for the evening, knowing most were sure of his client's guilt.

43

Sam spent a fitful night preparing for Garcia's cross-examination. He arrived at the courthouse early Wednesday morning and walked down the hallway only to discover Mike holding court with the press. He was coffee-powered and jittery, and now this. He got Mike's attention and had him follow while he obtained a key from Bridger's judicial assistant to a room off the courtroom reserved for counsel to meet with clients. Mike took a seat while Sam told Lana to wait in the hallway.

"What's going on?" Mike asked when they were alone.

"Why are you talking to the press without me there?" Sam asked. "I specifically told you not to do that."

"I can talk to whomever I want," Mike began. "I am paying you to defend me, not to be my boss."

"I am your attorney. You are charged with murder. I can handle what I hear in court. What I can't deal with is what you say to the media that the jurors are bound to hear."

"But the jurors aren't supposed to be reading or listening to—"

"Oh, grow up, man," Sam interrupted. "They won't follow the judge's instructions any better than you do mine. It's farcical."

"What do you want me to do?"

"Refer them to me."

"So you can get your face on TV, right?"

Sam took a deep breath. "No, so that I can keep you from saying something that puts your neck in a noose."

"I didn't do it."

"Yeah, you've told me that."

"You don't believe me."

"Mike, if I'm going to defend you, I need you to do what I tell you. I'm not going into court with a client who is undermining my efforts. Now, I'm going to have a talk with your wife here in a minute. Maybe you'll listen to her."

"Look," Mike said. "I was just telling them I'm not guilty."

"That's not the point. The point is that you need to follow my instructions. Got me?" He stepped back from Mike and searched for signs of a commitment. "Mike, just help me do my job. Just trust me." He looked at his watch. "Let's go," he said, and walked with Mike through a throng of media and spectators. At the courtroom doors, Mike stopped to give Lana a hug while Sam and Alex stood by. Sam entered the courtroom having inhaled a whiff of Lana's perfume—from Alex.

∽

Moments later, when all were seated and Bridger had ordered him to do so, Sam began his cross-examination. "Good morning, Investigator Garcia." Garcia's testimony had been extremely effective, and Sam wanted to hit him hard and fast. In his experience, the best strategy in that case was to start and finish with strong, material points showing weakness in the State's case. But since Garcia was relatively inexperienced, he decided to begin with what was really a meaningless point, but one he thought might shake the young investigator.

"Investigator Garcia, you testified my client was 'calm' when you first met him—isn't that true?"

"I said he looked that way," Garcia allowed cautiously.

"And how did he look?"

"Well, I mean, he was . . . well, quiet and composed," Garcia began. "A lot of times I see people and they are running around and yelling and . . . none of that."

Sam studied Garcia while watching the jurors using his peripheral vision. When several had looked to Garcia, Sam followed up. "How does my client look right now?"

Lee was on his feet. "Objection. Relevance."

"Overruled," Bridger said quickly. "You may answer," he said to Garcia.

"Well, he's sitting there and—"

"Is he running about, yelling, sweating?"

"No."

"In fact, you'd never observed my client in a stressful situation before that morning on the mountain, right?"

"Right."

"You really have no idea what his normal affect is, do you?"

"I don't."

"So, my client—who is literally on trial for his life—is here right now, again exactly as he was when you described him as calm, true?"

"Well, I guess."

"Do you think he's calm as he sits here and fights for his life?"

Lee was up again—and rightfully so. "Objection. The question calls for speculation."

It certainly did—and that was exactly the point. Sam looked to the jury members. They understood. Then he looked to Garcia—he understood, as well. "I'll withdraw the question, Judge," Sam said.

"Detective Garcia, you never did figure out where the decedent was when he was shot, did you?" Sam asked. Now that he had Garcia off balance, he planned to hit the high points early.

"We did not," Garcia admitted.

"That bother you?"

"Of course."

"The case would be stronger with that evidence—true?"

"True," Garcia said. He looked at Lee.

"If I heard you correctly, you said my client threatened the decedent—is that true?"

"Yes."

"During the course of your investigation, did you discover whether anyone else had issued threats against Max Kovalenko?"

"I did."

"Who?"

Garcia shifted uncomfortably in his seat and looked to Lee. "A lot of people," he finally said.

"How many?"

"Your Honor, I'm going to object. The witness cannot possible know—"

"I'll settle for how many he interviewed or came to know about," Sam interrupted.

"Gentlemen! Communicate with the court only, please," Bridger snapped. "The objection is overruled. You may answer."

"Dozens."

"Dozens of people made threats against the deceased?"

"Yes."

"Let's move on. Did you have any other suspects in this murder?" Sam asked, now switching subjects rapidly.

"Not really," Garcia admitted. "I interviewed a lot of people, but—"

"Why not?"

"Well, I began with the premise that everyone could have done it. Then I eliminated folks by checking alibis, their story, looking at the evidence, and eventually I arrested the person the evidence fit."

This was how Punch Polson did business, Sam recalled. "The evidence —such as it is—in this case is all pretty circumstantial, is it not?" he asked. He was looking at the jurors.

"That's not uncommon," Garcia replied.

"Do you know the difference between direct evidence and indirect evidence?"

"I do," Garcia said. He looked at the jury and back at Sam.

"Direct evidence is testimony from actual knowledge—like a witness who sees or smells something. Is that right?"

"Yes."

"And circumstantial evidence is proof by way of evidence from which the finder of fact can infer facts—like maybe footprints in snow proved someone walked there. True?"

"Yes," Garcia said warily. Sam suspected he could see the next question coming.

"Detective Garcia, do you have *any* direct evidence of my client's guilt?"

Garcia sat quietly, rubbing one hand on another. He looked at Lee and then back to Sam. "The DNA?"

"Are you asking me," Sam said, "or telling me?"

"I'm telling."

"Let's talk about that," Sam said. "Regarding the DNA, you—"

"Objection, Your Honor. He's not an expert," Lee said.

Bridger looked to Sam expectantly. "Please approach," Bridger said. He had warned the attorneys before the trial that he would not tolerate so-called talking objections or responses. In other words, no argument in front of the jury. When the men had assembled in front of his bench, he looked to Sam.

"Judge, Mr. Lee asked what evidence the witness relied upon to arrest my client. One factor was DNA. The witness just told me the DNA was direct evidence. I'm merely going to question him as to his understanding of DNA."

Lee started to speak but was stopped by Bridger's hand. "Overruled," Bridger said.

"Your Honor—" Lee began, but was again stopped cold by Bridger.

"I've made my decision, counsel. Return to your places."

When everyone was back in place, Sam looked at Garcia. "Let me ask it this way: the DNA you are referring to—there was more than just my client's DNA on that rifle. True?"

"No."

"No?" Sam pretended to be surprised. "No? Is that unusual?"

"Objection," Lee said, standing. "He's not—"

"I'm just asking him in his role as an experienced investigator," Sam replied, parroting Lee's earlier response.

"Overruled."

"I'm not sure," Garcia said.

"And you don't know when that DNA—"

"Judge, I'm going to object again—"

"Overruled," Bridger said. "Please continue."

Sam nodded and did so. "You don't know when or how that DNA got on that rifle, do you?"

"No."

"Because your own expert doesn't know, does she?" Sam concluded. The question was improper. He expected and got an objection from Lee and expected the judge to sustain the objection. He did. Sam would bring it all up again later, when the time was right. But the seed was planted.

"Any other direct evidence?" Sam asked Garcia.

"I—I'm not sure," Garcia said. "I don't know."

"Okay, so fair to say that the only direct evidence—what *you* refer to as direct evidence, I should say—of my client's guilt is some DNA that your expert can't say when or how it got on the weapon?"

"Objection," Lee said. "Compound. Complex. Calls for hearsay, and the witness is not qualified—"

"Sustained," Bridger said quickly.

Sam was looking at the jurors, several of whom were scowling in Lee's direction. They wanted to hear Garcia's answers. He redirected his attention to Garcia. "Will you agree that almost all of the evidence against my client is entirely circumstantial?"

"I think so—but there's a lot of it," Garcia said.

Sam smiled. "Well, let's take a look, then, at *all* of the evidence, shall we?"

"Sure."

"Let's start with your assertion that my client had a motive. I think you said he was afraid he was going to be written out of the will—is that right?"

"That's what he told me."

"To your knowledge, was he in the will when Max got killed?"

"Well, yeah."

"Max hadn't changed his will?"

"Not yet."

"Not yet? How do you know he was going to?"

"The defendant told me that," Garcia said. "And others."

"So, you discerned a motive from something the defendant said the deceased said?" Sam asked. Again, he looked to the jury.

"Uh—"

"Let's move on," Sam said. "You mentioned bullet identification?"

"Yes."

"Are you talking toolmarks?"

"Yes. That and . . . other stuff."

"You are aware, are you not, that many courts have disallowed toolmark identification as a valid science?"

"Objection," Lee said. "He's not an expert."

"Overruled," Bridger intoned. "You can answer to the extent you know."

"I—I know they aren't proof in and among themselves, but in combination with . . . other proof."

"Like DNA?"

"Well . . . yeah."

Sam looked to the jury. They got it. "Fair to say you spoke with both the county attorney and the sheriff shortly before you arrested my client?"

"Yes, but I always—"

"Fair to say they wanted an immediate arrest?"

"Well, of course," Garcia said, looking at Lee. "But I made the choice to arrest your client, Mr. Johnstone."

"Did you have the evidence you wanted?"

"Of course not. I never do," Garcia said.

"In this case, though, you'd have preferred to wait, right?" Sam was guessing, but the worst he could get was a denial.

"I made the decision to arrest, counselor."

Not responsive, but Sam let it go. "So, toolmarks, DNA, and unknown location for the victim and the shooter, rumors about changed wills . . . Let me see what else . . . Oh, sending others to help. That was part of it —right?"

"Yes."

"My client sent Paulie to get Max's horse—true?"

"That's what they told me."

"Did you find that suspicious?"

"Well, sort of. He was alone with the decedent as a result."

"But isn't it true that he sent Paulie after a horse that got loose? How might he have known that Max was alone?"

"Objection, calls for speculation," Lee said.

"It does indeed," Sam said aloud, drawing a dark stare from Bridger. "Withdrawn," he said before he was counseled by the judge.

"And Alex went to get a signal to call for help—true?"

"That's what they told me."

"Who?"

"The defendant and Alex."

"So my client's stories on that subject match those of your other interviewees?"

"Yeah."

"You found my client's rifle right near the location where you found the extracted cartridge—right?"

"Yes."

"In the open?"

"Well, kind of. Right next to a tree in some brush."

"Did it appear to have been hidden?"

"No."

Sam was thinking about something Mike had said. "How many murder investigations have you done where the murder weapon was left out in the open, awaiting somebody's efforts to find it?"

"None," Garcia admitted. "But maybe he panicked."

Sam looked at Alex and Lana when he asked his next question. Lana met his glance. "Where was Alex when he was trying to get a signal?"

"I'm not sure, exactly."

"Did you ask him?"

"Yes, but he wasn't real sure."

"In your affidavit of probable cause, you mentioned he rode to a wooded hillside to try to get a signal—didn't you?"

"I did."

"Was that the same wooded hillside where you found the rifle and cartridge?"

"It could be."

"Could you get a signal from where the rifle was ultimately found?" Garcia looked briefly at Lee and then back at Sam. He either knew that one could and hadn't thought—or was told—it wasn't important, or he didn't know. "Did you understand the question?" Sam pressed. If the jurors were listening, they now could conclude there were at least two people in the area where the rifle was found.

Lee could see it coming. "Your Honor, I'm going to object as to relevance—"

"Overruled," Bridger said. "Answer the question," he instructed Garcia.

"I don't know."

The jurors were rapt. Sam sought to plant another seed. "Paulie helped Mike search for Max—true?"

"That's what they told me."

"And that search was conducted in almost the exact area where the rifle was eventually found—true?"

"That's what I think based on what they told me, yeah."

"So we know there were at least two, and perhaps as many as three guys milling around in the same area where the rifle was eventually located on the day of Max's disappearance—true?"

"Yes," Garcia admitted.

"But you settled on my client—true?"

"Yes—it was *his* rifle." Garcia looked to the jury as if it was a simple deduction.

Sam smiled. Perfect. For the next half an hour, he worked the edges of Garcia's testimony, highlighting minor inconsistencies and forcing him to acknowledge differences between conclusive evidence and results achieved. At last, he walked to the table, poured himself a cup of water, and drank enough to wet his throat. "It's true, isn't it, that—aside from the possibility of DNA—every bit of evidence you have is purely circumstantial, is it not?"

Garcia was tired and edgy. He rubbed at his chin and looked at Sam steadily. "I think we have the evidence to prove Mr. Brown's guilt," he said. "But that's why we're here. To have the jury decide, isn't it?"

"Indeed." Sam returned to the defendant's table and tried to squat next to Mike. He'd been on his feet for a while, and his good leg was killing him. "Anything else?"

"Not that I can think of," Mike said.

"No more questions, Your Honor," Sam said. He had a theory of defense in front of the jury now, one he could flesh out later.

Bridger nodded. "Mr. Lee, any re-direct?"

"Yes, Judge," Lee said, and proceeded to ask questions designed to undo the damage caused by Sam's cross-examination. When he was done, Bridger called the lunch break.

～

Sam spent the lunch recess in his office, trying to discern why Lee hadn't mentioned the bottle. It had Mike's DNA in it and would certainly augment efforts to put his client at the location where the rifle and cartridge were found. On the other hand, Sam's theory—and Lee had to see it coming—was going to be that it was part of an effort to frame his client. Was Lee trying to keep others—Lana, for one—out of the picture? Or was Sam missing something? On a whim, he called Daniels and explained the issue.

"I think he probably forgot," Daniels opined. "Remember, as the prosecutor he's got to make the case. He's got a million things to think about. A defense attorney is a back-seat driver, a Monday morning quarterback. All you have to do as defense counsel is to create enough doubt for one juror to justify a not-guilty vote. Lot more pressure on those guys. He just missed it, is my bet."

"Okay, thanks. That makes me feel better," Sam said. "How's Marci?"

"Not good," Daniels responded quickly. "Julie's giving her some medicine right now, but . . . you just try your case, we'll talk later."

"Thanks, Press. I'm sorry," Sam said, gathering his materials for court.

～

The State's first witness after lunch was Dr. Laws, the medical examiner. Sam pulled a file from the banker's box he had filled with files and quickly reviewed his notes. He didn't expect much to come of this testimony. Having gotten through Dr. Laws' bona fides, Lee began asking the pertinent questions.

"What is the medical examiner?"

"The medical examiner is the physician assigned to the coroner's office. The coroner is an elected position and does not have to be a licensed physician," Laws said. "The medical examiner heads the office in charge of investigating the two major types of death investigations: non-natural deaths—the accidents, suicides, and homicides that take place in a community every day—and sudden, unexpected deaths—deaths where there was not a doctor in attendance who might be in a position to sign a death certificate. We investigate those cases."

"Do you also perform autopsies?"

"I do."

"How many autopsies have you performed?"

"Well over one hundred, I would think."

"Let me take you back to October 18—were you employed as medical examiner on that date?"

"I was."

"Did you perform an autopsy on an individual named Maxim Kovalenko?"

"I did."

"Other than yourself, who was present during that autopsy?"

"I have an assistant who was present. I think Detective Garcia was there as well. The coroner may have stopped in. I'd have to look at my notes."

Lee led the doctor through an extensive recitation of the steps he had taken in conducting the autopsy. "Now based on your training and experience and your findings from the autopsy, do you have an opinion as to the cause of death of Maxim Kovalenko?" Lee asked.

"I do."

"And what is that opinion?"

"I believe the victim died as the result of hemorrhage following a gunshot to the abdomen."

"So he got shot and bled to death?" Lee asked.

"Yes. You could say that."

"Did you visit the crime scene?"

"Yes."

"Did you have the opportunity to observe how the victim's body was positioned in the depression in the hillside?"

"I did."

"And did that help confirm your opinion that this was a homicide?"

"Well, that and other facts. I don't believe the defendant could have inflicted the fatal wound upon himself. There were no powder burns or stippling on the victim. There was no gun present. Death would have resulted in a short time—thirty minutes at the most—from the gunshot. Bleeding was sudden and fairly significant."

"Your Honor, those are the State's questions," Lee said, and sat down.

Bridger was thinking about the morning break. He looked pointedly at his watch and then to Sam. "Mr. Johnstone, how long do you suppose you'll take?"

Sam had cross-examined Dr. Laws on many occasions. He was irascible but competent and would not comment on areas outside of his expertise. Sam had only a couple of points to make—the primary one being the doctor's inability to pinpoint an exact time of death. "Not long, Judge."

"Proceed."

"Yes, Your Honor," Sam said. "Just a few questions. Dr. Laws, as the result of the autopsy, were you able to determine a time of death?"

"Only an approximation."

"Could you give an approximation?"

"Well, he was reported missing at approximately four p.m. on the 17th of October; he was located at about nine a.m. the next day. It's difficult due to the time of year and exposure to the elements, but I'd say late afternoon, early evening the afternoon before he was found," he said. "That would make it the 17th of October between four and seven p.m."

"You testified the bleeding that killed him would have done so in fairly short order—is that fair?"

"Yes. It was a significant injury," Laws said.

"Was he shot where he was found?"

"Based on the lack of blood at that location, I don't believe so."

"So he could have been shot in one location, and died in another?"

"I think that's exactly what happened," Laws said.

"In fact, he could have been shot in one location, traveled to another and died, and been found in a third location—where you examined him?"

"Objection," Lee said. "There's no evidence—"

"Overruled. You may answer, Doctor," Bridger said.

The doctor shrugged. "Could have."

"No more questions, Your Honor," Sam said, having established the

State couldn't say with exactitude when or where Max died. It wasn't critical, but he would play it up at closing. As he walked back to his chair, his eyes rested on Paulie, who looked away. There was something going on there.

"Any redirect?" Daniels asked Lee.

"No, Judge."

"All right, Dr. Laws, you may step down," Bridger said. "Let's take our morning recess."

44

Lee spent the remainder of Wednesday and all of Thursday calling a series of professional fact witnesses who testified to the handling of specimens and evidence. Experts at testifying, they combined to paint a circumstantial picture of the premeditated shooting of Max by Mike. Sam asked a few perfunctory questions, but Lee had done a good job in preparing his witnesses. He was able to get Pleasance to testify there were no prints on either the water bottle or the other rifle, and none except his client's on the murder weapon. While it was probably appearing conclusive to the jurors at this point, Sam would use that same evidence against the State later. No witness faltered, and in the face of Mike's increasing unease, Sam could do little aside from sitting patiently, attempting to portray confidence in the face of the State's mounting evidence.

"Sam, why aren't you going after these witnesses?" Mike asked after the court recessed for the night, his face red and his eyes bulging. Sam had seen these signs in combat zones—his client was in a state of near panic. Lana stood back with her arms folded, making no effort to comfort him.

"Mike, there's not a lot of headway I can make." He placed a hand on Mike's forearm. Sometimes a touch helped. "The evidence is what it is."

"But they are burying me!" Mike protested.

"I know it seems that way," Sam acknowledged. "But I want you to understand something: in this part of the state, juries take the State's burden seriously. They are expecting to see conclusive evidence of your guilt—*CSI*-type scientific evidence, the whole bit. They aren't going to get that, because it doesn't exist. I know it seems as if the evidence is piling up, but I need you to remain calm. Our turn at bat is coming. We'll get a shot with the jury," he assured Mike. "Trust me, and try to get some sleep tonight."

∼

Mike was even less put together than normal on Friday morning, so Sam had him run to the men's room and comb his hair before the jury was called. It was the best he could do. Robert Mitchell was the State's first witness. Because his testimony was critical to the State's case, Sam was certain his would be a long and carefully scripted direct examination. He wasn't disappointed.

"Please state your name for the record."

"Robert Mitchell."

"How and where are you employed?"

"I am employed as a deputy sheriff, with training as a forensic scientist, by the Custer County Sheriff's Department here in Custer."

"How long have you been doing that?"

"Almost fourteen years."

Lee then led Mitchell through a detailed review of his training, education, and experience such that the jury would view him as an expert in the field of toolmark identification. When his witness's qualifications were established, Lee probed further. "What does a toolmark examiner do?"

"Among other things, I examine firearms to see whether they are in mechanically operating condition. Thereafter I test firearms and components—cartridge cases and bullets—from weapons that I know were recovered and compare them with questioned items that have been submitted by law enforcement for testing."

"Have you in the past been qualified as an expert in firearm and toolmark examination?"

Sam was on his feet. "Your Honor, may we approach?" Toolmark identification and examination had in the early 2000s been discounted as an exact science in many courts, which had found toolmarks insufficient in and of themselves to be conclusive in identifying the firearm that had discharged a particular bullet, nor could an expert testify that a cartridge had been cycled by a particular weapon with certainty. During pretrial hearings, Sam had argued this point. Lee had argued that the evidence would be introduced for the limited purpose of buttressing other evidence. Bridger had indicated that he would decide when the time came.

At the bench, Sam began, "Judge, this is exactly what I was talking about. For all the reasons we discussed, this evidence should not be introduced."

"Your Honor," Lee began, but was again stopped short by Bridger's hand.

"Relax, counsel, I'm going to allow it," he said to Lee. "Take your places," he told the attorneys, and looked at the papers on his desk.

"Please note my objection," Sam said unnecessarily before returning to the defense table.

Lee looked at his witness when everyone was back in place. "You have testified previously?"

"More than fifty times," Mitchell said.

"How do you go about comparing known samples with samples you are given to identify?" Lee asked.

"The first thing we do," Mitchell began, warming to his subject, "is to look at the evidence cartridge. That's the one we *know* was fired by the gun in question. We chamber and cycle a cartridge of the same type as the suspect cartridge. Parts of the gun—generally the extractor and ejector—make marks on cartridges as they are fired through the weapon. We then look to see if it shows microscopic marks of value. Basically, if there are no microscopic marks of value on the evidence cartridge, there would be no reason for us to do a comparison. If there are, then we can compare it with a sample cartridge law enforcement provides."

"So, if I understand you right, in this case you took the suspected firearm, chambered a round, cycled it, and found microscopic marks of value?"

"I did," Mitchell said.

"What next?"

"Then I compared the microscopic marks on the cartridge found in the field with the one I cycled in the lab."

"I'm handing you what's been marked as State's exhibit 32," Lee said. "Please take a look at it and let me know when you are ready to proceed."

"I'm prepared," Mitchell said quickly.

"What is that exhibit?" Lee asked.

"This is an illustration showing the comparison between the evidence cartridge I was provided in this case and the suspect cartridge."

"What did your examination indicate?"

"My examination indicated that the cartridges were cycled through the same firearm."

Sam felt Mike stiffen next to him, then lean over in Sam's space. Sam had provided his client with a legal pad to write questions on—client questions during a trial were generally distracting and rarely of value. "Stop him! He's killing us!" Mike whispered.

Sam looked to his client, who was perspiring heavily. "It's okay," he assured Mike. "We'll get a shot here in a minute." He made a mental note to spend some time with his client during the next recess.

Lee had pressed on. "In more simple language, is it fair to say the same rifle fired both the test cartridge and the recovered cartridge?" he asked, attempting to drive the point home.

"In my opinion, yes."

"Did you look at anything else in relation to this case?"

"I did," Mitchell said. "I used an electron microscope to compare fragments of the bullet taken from the decedent's body to a bullet provided me from a case of unfired cartridges retrieved by Detective Garcia."

"And how did you go about doing that?" Lee asked.

"Well, in order to answer that question, I should probably explain a little bit about the bullet used in the killing of Mr. Kovalenko. It is an unusual type of bullet," he added.

Lee encouraged Mitchell to do so, and while Mitchell lectured the jury, Sam alternately watched the jurors and made notes. He might have objected as Mitchell's answer was a lengthy narrative, but the jurors' body language indicated there was no need. He'd lost them, although Mike was fidgeting uncontrollably next to Sam. Finally, Mitchell concluded, "In the end, I determined the two bullets were of the exact same chemical composition."

"Thank you, Mr. Mitchell," Lee said at last. "No more questions, Judge. Your witness," he said to Sam.

Sam was up quickly, intent on getting the jury's attention. Several jurors stirred in anticipation. "Mr. Mitchell, the suspect cartridge—you don't know *how* that was recovered, do you?"

"I don't," Mitchell admitted. "I mean, not really. Garcia told me—"

"But *you* don't know, right?"

"I don't."

"And *you* don't know *where* the suspect cartridge was recovered from, do you?"

"No," Mitchell said, seeing where this was going. "I don't."

"So, all *you* know is that the toolmarks on two cartridges—one of which you have no knowledge regarding how it was sourced—seem to match, right?"

"Right."

"The cartridge you know about could match a cartridge that has nothing to do with this case—true?"

"Well..."

"It is true or is it not?"

"Yes."

"Now, let's turn to the whole idea of cartridges matching based on toolmarks."

"Fine."

"Mr. Mitchell, isn't it true that, since around 2006, it has been generally accepted that the science of toolmark comparisons isn't really a science at all?"

Mitchell was reddening. "A small number of courts have said that, yes," he said to the jury.

"And that's because a number of studies have concluded that toolmark science is really an art at best, right?"

"Well—"

Sam smiled indulgently at Mitchell. "You'll agree with me that it would be a bad idea to put my client in prison solely because of your conclusions, right?"

"Objection," Lee said. "Not his area of expertise."

"Overruled," Bridger said. "I think the question goes to reliability. You may answer."

"Of course," Mitchell said. "My analysis doesn't prove who fired the weapon or when. It just shows—I think—the same gun did."

Better than he could have asked for, Sam thought. "Let me ask you this. In your capacity as a witness here today, the fact that a cartridge is found in one place is no reason to believe that the location where it was found was where it was extracted—is that right?"

When Mitchell didn't respond, Sam continued quickly. "If I found a cartridge here," he said, pointing to the spot on a demonstrative exhibit Garcia had used to show where he'd found the cartridge, "would that mean the shooter was there when he pulled the trigger?"

"Well, in that area, yeah," Mitchell said.

"Really? What if I fired from here, then gathered my cartridges, moved over here, and dropped the cartridge?"

"Why would anyone do that?" Mitchell looked at the jury and smirked.

Sam looked hard at Mitchell. "Did you understand the question?"

"I did."

"Then answer it, please. It's possible, isn't it, to find a cartridge somewhere other than where it was cycled?"

"It is."

Sam then extracted an admission from the witness that because the bullet recovered from Max's body was frangible, it could not be proven to have been fired by Mike's weapon.

"So, to sum up, you don't know where or how the suspect cartridge was sourced; you don't know when or by whom the cartridge was cycled or the bullet was fired; and you don't know with absolute, scientific certainty if the bullet in question—the one alleged to have killed Mr. Kovalenko—was fired by the weapon they are saying belonged to my client, do you?"

Lee was on his feet. "Objection, Your Honor. Question is compound, complex, and—"

"I don't," Mitchell said. "I just know the samples appear to match."

Lee turned to talk to his witness but was stopped by Bridger. "Overruled," he said. "Sounds to me like the witness understood."

Sam pressed on. "Now, Mr. Mitchell, how many cartridges and bullets were manufactured by the ammunition manufacturer on the year the bullet of which you have fragments was manufactured?"

Mitchell shook his head. "I have no idea."

"Did you ask the manufacturer?"

"I did not."

"What is a lot number?"

"It is a number corresponding to a . . . batch of ammunition manufactured."

Close enough. "How many cartridges were manufactured as part of the lot number from which the suspect cartridge came?"

"I don't know," Mitchell admitted.

"Millions?"

"I doubt it."

"Hundreds of thousands? Tens of thousands?" Sam pressed.

"Your Honor," Lee began. "I'm going to object."

"Overruled," Bridger said. "Answer the question."

"No idea," Mitchell admitted.

"So, because you have no idea of the lot size, you have no idea how significant it is that the fragments in the decedent appear to match the type and kind of ammunition found in cartridges similar to the suspect cartridge, do you?"

"Not really."

"How common is the .270 Winchester?"

"Very common," Mitchell said, and Sam noted that two jurors nodded in agreement.

"No more questions," Sam said. He sat and drank water. If the jurors were open-minded, they could now entertain doubts about the time and place of Max's death, the match of the rifle and cartridge used, and even who was involved. He looked over the jury, some of whom were making notes. He then looked at Mike, who was shakily wiping at his forehead with a dingy handkerchief. Lee did some re-direct, and Bridger called a recess.

❦

Sam spent much of the brief recess counseling an openly nervous Mike. "Mike, remember: sometimes they will have momentum, sometimes we will. Just have faith and remain calm." He looked to Lana for assistance, but she just shrugged when Mike put his head in his hands. "I hesitate to say it —I'm not an optimist by nature, but we're actually making some headway."

Back in the courtroom following the break, Bridger—who was pleased with the pace of trial so far—looked to Lee. "Please call the State's next witness."

"Your Honor," Lee said, "the State calls Dr. Katherine Desmond."

Jurors and the audience members watched as Desmond walked confidently to the stand, turned, and raised her hand steadily while the judge administered an oath. All observing knew this was a key witness—if nothing else, television and film had taught them that.

"Please be seated," Lee directed when she had sworn to tell the truth. Sam had cross-examined her as a witness before. She was knowledgeable and tough, but he felt he could make some headway when the time came.

"How are you employed?" Lee asked.

"I am a senior forensic scientist with the Wyoming State Laboratory in Cheyenne," she said.

Lee then asked a series of questions designed to show the jury that Desmond—as the product of her education, credentials, and experience— was an expert in the field of DNA.

"Ms. Desmond, can you give us sort of an overview of the science of DNA?"

"DNA is a chemical found in various cells throughout the human body. It determines our unique individual characteristics," Desmond began. "The majority of human DNA is very similar from person to person, but there is a small percentage that varies a great deal from person to person and makes us unique. It is these regions or areas of the DNA that we use in forensic DNA analysis to generate a person's specific DNA profile."

"So everyone has a specific profile?"

"Just about. Except for identical siblings."

"And I think you said the majority of our DNA is similar but there are areas which are unique—is that right?"

"Yes."

"And without getting into too much detail, when you are doing your analysis, do you look at the similar areas or the unique areas?"

"We look to the unique areas, the polymorphic areas. Those vary greatly from person to person."

"Now, Ms. Desmond, what can you get a DNA profile from? What sort of material?"

"DNA is taken from cells. We can obtain DNA from blood, saliva, semen, or skin cells."

"Skin cells?"

"Yes."

"What is touch DNA?" Lee asked. "If I hear that phrase, what is that?"

"Touch DNA refers to skin cells transferred to an item by having physical contact with it."

"And is it different from other DNA?"

"Well, the source is," Desmond said. "In touch DNA, we are obtaining nucleated cells in skin cells rather than in a fluid as in blood, semen, or saliva."

Sam was watching the jurors closely. They appeared to be paying attention.

"So if I touch an item, my cells will be transferred to it?" Lee asked.

"Possibly," Desmond allowed.

"But not in every case?"

"No. It depends on a number of things, such as the duration of the touch, the type of surface of the item—there are a number of variables."

"Could submersion in water or being covered in snow affect the deposit of skin cells?"

"It could."

"Could it affect the duration skin cells would remain on an item?"

"It could."

Sam was thinking Lee might be aware of the significance of the lack of DNA on the bottle and rifle. "Might it impact the ability to recover DNA?" Lee asked.

"It might."

"I am handing you State's Exhibit 10," Lee said while he did so. "Will you take a look at that for me, please? Can you tell me what that is?"

"It is a sample of cells collected from a rifle."

"Have you handled that before?"

"Yes, I have."

"How do you know that?"

"It has my initials and I dated it right here," Desmond said, pointing to a pen entry.

"And what, if anything, were you asked to do with that?" Lee asked.

"To develop a DNA profile."

"How is that accomplished?"

Desmond then embarked on a lengthy explanation of the process used to make a comparison of DNA samples.

"Were you able to do that in this case?" Lee asked when she finally concluded.

"Yes."

"I am now handing you State's Exhibit 24," Lee said. "Take a look at that and let me know when you are ready to answer some questions."

She looked at the exhibit. "I'm ready."

"What is that?"

"This is a buccal swab—a cheek swabbing identified as coming from Michael Brown," Desmond said.

"What were you asked to do with this item?"

"Compare the DNA profile from the swab with that developed from the cells found on the weapon."

"And when you did that comparison, what did you find?"

"Well, I found that what came from the gun was consistent with that from the buccal swab. The profile from the rifle matched the DNA profile from Michael Brown."

Sam thought Mike was going to come out of his chair. He placed a hand on Mike's thigh. "Calm down," he whispered fiercely.

"I didn't shoot him!" Mike hissed back.

"Very important you have a little faith now. Trust me," he said to Mike, who was turning and shaking his head at Lana.

Lee was watching Mike with a satisfied smile, and Sam knew some of the jurors were observing as well. "No more questions, Judge," Lee said, then turned to Sam. "Your witness, counsel."

～

"Thank you," Sam said. He stood, picked up a pile of papers, and carried them to the podium. Just a few points to make here. "Ms. Desmond, I just have a few questions. Are you familiar with the term secondary transfer?"

"Of course."

"What does that term mean?"

"Basically, it is DNA transferred from one item that is also transferred to another item."

"Let me see if I understand. Let's say I'm sitting in the courtroom here next to Mike, my client. He shows up and shakes my hand, then picks up this pencil," Sam said, brandishing a short pencil. "Is it possible that Mike could have my DNA on his hand?"

"Yes."

"So, my DNA could end up on Mike's hand simply from touching me?"

"Yes, that's touch DNA," she said.

"Continuing with my example," Sam said, pausing for effect. "Is it possible, then, that my DNA could end up on the pencil he picked up?"

Desmond recalled Sam using this same example in a prior case. "As you'll no doubt recall from the last time you cross-examined me, counsel, it is possible, but not probable. But it could happen."

A couple of jurors frowned at the witness. "So my client's DNA could be on a rifle he never touched."

"Or one he did." She smirked.

"But the state of the science isn't such that you could tell the jury whether the transfer of cells was the result of my client touching the rifle, or of someone else touching my client and then the rifle—is it?"

Desmond's smirk was gone. "It is not."

"Moreover, even if the DNA on the rifle is my client's, and even if it is the result of touch DNA, you can't tell us when it was deposited—can you?"

"No," Desmond said. "But—"

"So, you cannot exclude as a possibility that the cells you found on that rifle got there not from my client firing the weapon but in some other way —including secondary transfer?"

"I'd say it was a remote possibility."

"But it could happen?" Sam persisted.

"Objection," Lee said. "Asked and answered."

"Overruled," Bridger said. "Answer the question posed."

"It could happen," Desmond admitted.

"And it is true, is it not, that when you are analyzing a sample and doing your analysis, there is no way to tell *when* the DNA was transferred to the item?"

Desmond looked hard at Sam. "That is generally correct."

Sam decided to take a chance. "Let me ask you this: fair to say that it isn't unusual to find more than one DNA sample on an item you are asked to examine?"

"It's not unusual, no."

"In fact, it is common—isn't it?"

"I'd agree with that."

"So let me ask you this: if I was to tell you that I had reason to believe that a number of people had touched that rifle, would you find it unusual—"

Lee was on his feet. "Objection!"

"She's an expert," Sam said, before Bridger could rule.

"Gentlemen," Bridger barked. "Please approach." When Lee and Sam were before him, Bridger spoke through clenched jaws. "Your personal animus is beginning to show. I won't have it. The question is proper. Overruled. Back to your places, and I will tolerate no more of this."

"You may answer," Bridger said to Desmond when everyone was back in their places.

"I would find it somewhat unusual," she admitted. "But not unheard of."

Probably as good as he would get. "So, it is fair to say that one's DNA can go places one does not—that's true, isn't it?"

"Correct—but rare."

Sam stood staring at Desmond. It was enough. "And it's fair to say that one's DNA does not always appear where one did go—true?"

Desmond's face was red. "True."

Sam watched her for a long time without saying anything. "Mr. Johnstone?" Bridger asked. "Do you have more questions?"

"I do, Judge." He looked again to Desmond. "Are you familiar with the term 'erase and replace' as it refers to DNA?"

Lee was looking around the courtroom but leaned over to whisper with Rebecca when he heard the question. "I am," Desmond eventually answered.

"What does that refer to?"

"Your Honor—" Lee began.

"Please approach," Bridger instructed. When they had assembled, Lee began a vociferous objection, arguing that Sam's questions were beyond the scope of direct and irrelevant. "Mr. Johnstone?" Bridger asked when Lee finally stopped talking.

"Your Honor, this witness had been designated as an expert. I am fully able to inquire as to her base of knowledge. Mr. Lee has chosen to raise the issue on certain items found in connection with the State's investigation. I'm intent on asking her questions in her capacity as an expert about DNA found in another object that was found near the crime scene. It was listed as State's Exhibit 37, as I recall. It's a bottle of water that her lab analyzed. You will recall that my client, in his list of exhibits, listed that one as well. I don't believe it is beyond the scope, as my questions have to do with DNA and the transfer thereof. But I will also remind the court that we reserved the right to call any of the State's witnesses, so if the objection is sustained, I can call her in my client's case-in-chief and likely treat her as a hostile witness."

"Judge—" Lee began.

"Sounds reasonable to me," Bridger mused. "Return to your places. Objection overruled."

When Sam had returned, he faced a more composed Desmond. Lee's objection had given her time to think. "'Erase and replace' refers to getting DNA off of an item and replacing or augmenting one's DNA with others'

DNA." She added, "It's a complex process that in my experience doesn't work particularly well."

Sam asked permission to approach the witness, and when Bridger granted it, he approached Desmond with the bottle and the lab report he had provided to the State. "Please take a look at these two items and let me know when you are ready to answer questions about them," he said. As he walked back to the podium, he stole a glance at Lana and Alex, who were whispering.

"I've not seen them before," Desmond said.

"Take as much time as you need," Sam responded quickly. "I'm sure the judge will grant the jury a recess if need be."

She sat reading for a time, carefully turning pages, anticipating a trap. "I'm ready," she said at last.

Sam led her through a few questions to develop the jury's understanding. "Fair to say that the liquid examined in Exhibit 37 showed the presence of my client's DNA?"

"Oh, yes."

"And I think you said it is possible to remove your own—or someone else's—DNA from an item?"

"Of course."

"And it is possible to substitute DNA?"

"It is."

"Can you tell the jury how that might be done."

"Well, someone could apply a solution with DNA in it to an item."

"By using a spray bottle, perhaps?"

Desmond sat quietly. "Yes, but—"

"Thank you very much, Doctor," Sam said. "No more questions."

Lee was up quickly and led Desmond through a thorough re-direct examination designed to show the difficulty involved in erasing and replacing DNA.

"It's not rocket science, but it's not easy," Desmond concluded.

Bridger nodded in recognition and looked pointedly at his watch. "Ladies and gentlemen, it's been a long day and a long week. I think we will take our weekend recess." He then embarked on a lengthy explanation of actions the jurors were—and were not—to take over the weekend. "We'll see everyone back here at nine o'clock on Monday morning." With that, he released the jury. When they had departed, he looked to Sam and Lee. "Anything further we need to discuss?"

"No, Your Honor," they said in unison. With that, Bridger was gone.

Lee approached. "Got a minute?"

"Sure," Sam said.

"My office," Lee said, then turned and was gone.

Mike looked at Sam. "What's that about?"

"He wants to talk."

"What about?"

"I'll call you here in a few. Don't go far. This won't take long."

45

Lee's office was next to Cathy's in the old courthouse basement, down the hall from Rebecca. He was sitting behind his desk when Sam was escorted in. Sam looked at the piles of paper that had accrued since the last time he'd been here and knew what he was seeing: work unaccomplished due to the murder trial. He had similar piles needing attention in his own office.

"Have a seat, Mr. Johnstone," Lee said. When Sam was seated, Lee wasted no time. "Your guy pleads to murder two and we recommend he does the minimum twenty years."

Sam stood. "I think we're done here."

"Are you kidding me?" Lee asked. "The evidence is circumstantial, but it is overwhelming."

"That's one way to look at it. The other way—and the way I prefer—is that it is circumstantial. And you've got nothing showing first degree," Sam said.

"The jury can infer premeditation from the actions!"

"They can," Sam allowed. "But will they? You are going to have to ask this jury to infer premeditation and pile that on top of a circumstantial fact set? How many times have you seen a jury infer intent in a murder trial?" Sam knew well the answer was zero—because Lee had never tried a murder before. "The best you do is second degree and that's in serious doubt." This was a crap offer, his leg was hurting, and he wanted to go home and get something to eat. "You should never have brought this case."

"Second degree has a top number of *life*," Lee countered. "I'm offering the minimum."

"Not happening. Even if you can get a verdict—which I doubt—we'll bring him and the family in, have him apologize, and everyone will say Mike is a nice guy and that Max rode him hard, and he freaked out in a moment of passion. Bridger will look at the pre-sentence investigation—which will say Mike is a Boy Scout—and he'll get the minimum. Besides, my guy won't do the deal. I think I could get him to plead to manslaughter, though."

As Sam spoke, Lee had been fiddling with a pen on his desk. Abruptly, he dropped it and stood, measuring Sam. "The offer is withdrawn. You had your chance," he said. "I tried. Make sure you tell your client I had one on the table."

∼

Sam ate a quick dinner from a paper bag and then headed to the office to consult with Daniels, as he did every night. Since the pandemic, Wyoming courts had broadcast trials over the internet. When he wasn't taking care of Marci, Daniels listened in and consulted with Sam. Sam began by relating his meeting with Lee.

"Have you called Mike?" Daniels asked, pouring himself a couple of fingers from a stash Sam kept for him. The judge's eyes were red-rimmed, his thinning hair was askew, and his clothing was wrinkled. This was not the same man Sam had known since his arrival in town a few years ago.

"I did; he's on his way. Lee made a point of *withdrawing* the offer, but I want to run it by Mike," Sam said.

"Good plan. Lee will keep the offer out there. He's bullshitting," Daniels surmised. "He'd be a moron to walk away. His case is crap."

"We'll see," Sam mused. "I will say that the State is way, way short of being certain of conviction. They never should have brought this."

"Pure hubris. I spoke with a judge from down south," Daniels said, staring at the tumbler of amber liquid. "In Cheyenne, they call him 'No Plea Lee.'"

Sam smirked. "He couldn't wait to get in the ring."

"I think he pushed Garcia; he should have given him the time to develop some additional evidence," Daniels opined. "On the other hand, I'm not sure what else is out there. By the way, I haven't heard anything from that good-looking deputy prosecutor."

"Cathy? Lee had her taken off the case."

"You kidding? She's good," Daniels observed. "And I wonder where Rebecca has been in all of this? When I was on the bench, she was always front and center, overseeing everything the attorneys did. She's been a ghost in this one."

Sam considered passing on Cathy's gossip, but decided to hold off. "I've thought the same thing," he said, then—hearing the front door chime— went to retrieve Mike. The man smelled of booze and smoke and was red-eyed and wary. When everyone was seated, Sam explained to Mike the offer Lee had made.

"No," Mike said. He pulled out a hankie and wiped his face.

"So, I told him that's what you would say—"

"Good."

"And I'm technically not bound to communicate the offer to you, but I think we should talk about it."

"Well, talk all you want, but that Lee guy can go f—"

"Stop it," Sam interrupted, holding up a hand.

Mike's eyes narrowed and met Sam's for an instant before he turned to look at Daniels, who was staring at his tumbler. "What is this?" he asked quietly, looking from Sam to Daniels and back again.

"What do you mean?" Sam replied.

"You're selling me out," Mike said. "You're gonna see me put in jail for something I didn't do—why?"

Sam leaned forward in his chair. "Whoa. What are you talking about?"

Mike stood. "You and Lee. You got some sort of agreement—"

"No," Sam said. "I can assure you we couldn't agree on the time of day."

"I'll vouch for that," Daniels said, looking up at Mike, who was now pacing. He was clearly unconvinced, so Daniels continued. "Mike, Sam has done a great job to this point. He's poked some major holes in the State's story. They can't show when or where Max was shot, they can't show that the rifle and cartridge match the bullet in Max, and Sam's cross of the DNA expert was outstanding. The jury must have some doubts, and Lee knows that. He's trying to save some face by making an offer. But just understand, while Sam's been killing it in there, juries are unpredictable, and you never know. Why, I've seen—"

"Twenty years!" Mike barked, literally stomping a foot.

"I hear you, son," Daniels said. "But remember, if you are convicted, you could do life. I wouldn't impose it, but Bridger might. He's a political creature."

Sam was watching his client closely—he was perspiring heavily, his hands were shaking, and he was licking his lips constantly. "Mike, Lee has a witness or two left. I feel good about this case, but a plea agreement eliminates risk," Sam said. "If we do a deal, we have certainty."

"Certainty I'm going to prison!" Mike snapped, locking eyes with Sam. "First you tell me my wife is framing me, then you tell me the trial is going well, and now you're telling me I'm going to prison? So let me get this straight: I do the deal and you can say you did your best, but your client took the plea deal. You come away looking like a crafty negotiator; you and Lee can shake hands and tell each other 'Good job!' and I'm off to prison for twenty freaking years!"

"I've heard enough." Sam stood. "I'll see you Monday."

"You need to get ready for trial," Mike said.

Sam took a deep breath and exhaled. "*We*," he said. "It's *our* trial." He pointed to Mike with an index finger, then to himself with a thumb.

"Sure," Mike said.

Sam escorted him out and locked the door behind him. "See you Monday," he said, but got no reply. When he got back to his office, he noticed Daniels had refilled his glass.

"I'm not surprised," Daniels said. "Don't blame him. And for the record, I think you've got a pretty good shot. Wyoming juries want to see proof before they ring someone up—especially in this part of the state."

"I'll be honest," Sam said. "I'm surprised at how bad the State's case is. But I keep waiting for the other shoe to drop."

"That's because you are a glass-half-empty kind of guy, for sure," Daniels said, taking a large pull. "Don't underestimate Lee, but don't over-estimate him either."

~

Later that evening, after rolling around in bed for an hour, Sam gave up and drove to the office. He had just gotten started when his phone rang. It was Lana. "Sam, I'm at the front door."

Christ. "Be right there," Sam said. "It's late," he said after he'd let her in.

"Couldn't sleep."

"Okay," Sam replied. "Coffee? Soda?"

"Got anything stronger?"

"No," he lied, before having second thoughts. "We might have a beer in the fridge in the break area."

"Sounds good," she said. "It's been a long day—and night."

"Be right back," Sam promised, leaving to retrieve the beer. "How can I help you?" he asked when he'd handed her the beer and a glass and sat down.

Eschewing the glass, she chugged half the beer. He couldn't mask his surprise. "That's good," she remarked. When he didn't respond, she continued. "What did he say?"

"I can't tell you that," Sam said. "Ask him."

"I will when I see him." She finished the beer. "Haven't seen him."

Sam looked up sharply. "Excuse me? He left here three hours ago. Where is he?"

"How would I know?"

"Because he is your husband? And he has a curfew on his bond —remember?"

"It's not my job to watch him."

"True, but if he blows off curfew, the judge could forfeit the bond," Sam pointed out. "Cost you some serious money."

She shrugged. "All I want to know is whether he agreed to the deal. Got any more beer?"

He nodded, walked to the kitchen, and got two beers from the refrigerator. He looked at one for a long minute, then put it back. Not yet. She was standing when he got back, looking at his office wall.

"Those the men you lost?" she asked, indicating the five framed photos.

"Yes," he said, handing her the beer.

"I'm sorry." She took a seat in an overstuffed chair. "That must suck. And the way we left—"

"Listen, I've got a lot to do, and—"

"We do need you at the top of your game." She opened the beer and drank the whole thing in a single pull. "Party trick," she said, crushing the can and tossing it in a small wastebasket. "Lee has to know you are kicking his ass. What was the offer?"

He thought about it for a few seconds. Screw it. "Plead to second in return for twenty years," Sam said. "Mike rejected it out of hand, got pissed, and left. Now go find him."

"Thanks, Sam," she said. She rose and sidled up to him, putting a hand on his collar. "Better him than me."

"You?" Sam recoiled and removed her hand from his collar. "Why you?"

She smiled and replaced her hand, then pulled him up close and kissed his cheek as he tried to avoid her. "Good night, Sam," she said. "See you in court."

"What do you mean, *better him than you*?" he said to her back. He stumbled after her to the door, then walked to his office window and watched her drive away.

46

Sam's calls to Mike had gone unreturned all weekend, and he was hollow-eyed and paranoid by Monday. Having fitfully tossed and turned until finally giving up just after three a.m., he woke with the feeling everything was going south. Now, five minutes before the day's session began and still not seeing Mike, he was pacing in front of the large double doors when Lana arrived alone. Sam pulled her aside and whispered in her ear so that the lurking members of the press would not hear. "Where's Mike?"

She shrugged. "He never came home."

"All weekend?" he asked. When she merely nodded, he took her sleeve and pulled her toward a corner. "And you didn't call me?"

"No," she said. "He's a big boy."

"Lana, this is serious! This could blow everything!" Sam seethed, then, seeing the media watching, he forced a smile and said through clenched jaws, "Can you at least call Custer County Memorial and see if he's been admitted?"

"I'll try."

"Thanks," Sam said. It was time to go. Feeling both panicked and self-conscious without his client, he rushed to the defense table and made it just in time to be there when Bridger was announced. Sam stood with the others as the judge mounted the stairs, took the bench, and ordered everyone to be seated. The judge looked around the courtroom quickly, his eyes stopping at the empty spot next to Sam.

"Mr. Johnstone, you are alone."

"Your Honor." Sam stood. "I'm unsure regarding the whereabouts of Mr. Brown at this time."

Bridger looked around the courtroom to quiet the whispering, then sighed. Things had been going so well. He should have known. "Are you telling me that he stepped out for an instant, or is his absence more substantial than that?"

"I spoke with his wife Friday night—she came by my office to see if he was there. And we spoke just moments ago—she hasn't seen him. We are concerned, of course."

Bridger frowned. "I'm assuming you've checked with the hospital?"

As Bridger spoke, Lana entered from the rear of the courtroom. She made eye contact with Sam and shook her head. "We have, Your Honor," Sam said, turning to face the judge. "Fortunately, he has not been admitted."

The whispering had begun anew. "Ladies and gentlemen," Bridger began. "I'll not have that talking amongst yourselves. It is very distracting." He appeared to be lost in thought for a moment, and then beckoned to the attorneys. "Gentlemen, please approach." When they had assembled in front of the bench, Bridger spoke. "This is highly unusual, but not unprecedented. The rules contemplate just such a thing, so here's what I'm going to do. Mr. Johnstone, I'm going to announce a need to take a few minutes so that the court might attend to other matters to give you time to find your man," he said, emphasizing *other matters*. "After that, assuming you have not located him, we will continue without him. Any objection?"

Sam shook his head. It was the best he could expect. "No, sir."

"Mr. Lee?" Bridger asked.

"Your Honor, I object. I believe that Mr. Johnstone and his client—"

Bridger's eyes had narrowed. "Mr. Lee, before you finish that sentence and thereby besmirch Mr. Johnstone's good character, I'm going to warn you that you'd best have solid evidence of any nefarious actions on his part. Not sure how the game is played where you've been, but in my courtroom, if you accuse opposing counsel of misbehavior, you better have your stuff rolled up in tight little balls. Anything short of that and I'm going to be an unhappy man," he concluded expectantly.

"Well, it's just that he must know—"

"Thank you, Mr. Lee. That doesn't sound like it is going to meet spec. Your objection is noted and overruled. Return to your places, gentlemen," Bridger ordered. When Sam and a red-faced Lee were back at their tables, the judge looked pointedly at Sam. "Ladies and gentlemen, a matter of some importance has arisen that is going to require the court's attention for thirty minutes or so. Please be in place at nine-thirty sharp so that we can hear the State's next witness."

Before he had left the bench, people began talking among themselves. From the corner of his eye, Sam could see Sarah Penrose and other media pool members race out of the courtroom to file updates. He motioned for Cassie. "Got any ideas?" he asked her.

"Not really."

"Talk to members of his family—I'll handle Lana," he said. While Cassie made her way to the family, Sam gestured for Lana to meet him outside the courtroom. They found a spare conference room and Sam closed the door. "This isn't good."

"I understand," she said. "I don't know why he would disappear."

Sam was watching her closely. He'd dealt with family members who were worried about loved ones. In contrast, Lana looked like she'd misplaced a set of keys. "Lana, if you know something, you need to be straight with me."

"Sam, I don't know where he is," she said, looking at her expensive watch. "I'm worried sick."

She wasn't even trying. "Tell me he didn't run because he is afraid of being convicted."

"Sam, we haven't spoken in weeks. I don't know where he is."

She had framed him and probably knew where he was now. He decided to try a different approach. "Lana, the State has overlooked something. It's not unlikely that, well . . . it's not unlikely that Mike could be acquitted. I think Lee got greedy and prosecuted before law enforcement was ready," Sam explained, watching her closely, hoping she would see Mike's fleeing as futile. "But if Mike's ass is not in the chair next to me, the jury might well draw a different conclusion." He continued watching her closely for a reaction.

She met his stare with one of her own. "I don't know where he is."

"Lana, your family has resources," Sam said. "I suggest you use them to find him and drag him—if you have to—back to court." He looked at his own watch. "We've got twenty-five minutes." He escorted her back to the family and pulled Cassie aside. "Anything?"

"No," she said, shaking her head. "They all say they've tried, but have no idea where he is."

"I'm not buying it," Sam said. "No way he pulled this on his own, unless . . ."

"He's hurt?" she finished the thought.

"Or worse."

∾

At precisely nine-thirty, Bridger reappeared, took his seat, and called the court to order. Even before the audience had fully settled in, he looked to Sam. "Mr. Johnstone, have you heard from your client?"

"I have not, sir."

"You are, of course, aware that Rule 43 of the Wyoming Rules of Criminal Procedure allows me to continue the trial without him if there is reason to believe he has voluntarily absented himself?" Bridger asked, not for Sam's understanding but for the audience and media present.

"I do."

"You've checked emergency rooms and followed up with the family?"

"Yes, sir."

"Is there a reason I wouldn't find he voluntarily absented himself?"

"Judge, I'm not sure that's the right question," Sam said carefully, knowing he needed to tread lightly. "I think the proper inquiry is whether there is any evidence that makes it apparent my client's absence *is* voluntary."

Lee was on his feet with the rulebook in hand. "Judge, how could the court ever know that?" he asked. "The defendant is not here. He is required to be here."

"It very well could be an emergency," Sam pointed out.

Bridger appeared to have anticipated the discussion and made up his mind. "This trial has moved along nicely and we're just a few hours ahead of schedule. I'm going to send the jury out for an early, lengthy lunch. You can do whatever you need to do to locate your client, Mr. Johnstone. The bottom line is that we are going to reconvene this afternoon at one-thirty, with or without him. Now, one more question: Does the defendant intend to testify?"

"I'm not sure, Judge," Sam said truthfully. "We were going to confer on that this morning."

"All right," Bridger said. "The court will meet with counsel at one o'clock this afternoon to get the jury instructions straight so that we'll be ready to go when the time comes. Bailiff, let's get the jury in here so we can get them out of here," he said, and smiled at the audience's laughter.

～

At the instructions conference hours later, Sam was anxious, distracted, and hamstrung by Mike's absence. Mike had been charged with first degree murder, but because there was only inferential evidence of premeditation, second degree was probably the better charge, as it contained the same elements minus the requirement for proof of premeditation. If Mike testified, Sam could probably get the judge to instruct on manslaughter—voluntary or otherwise, depending on the facts. In either case, a much less serious charge. But absent Mike's testimony, there could be no evidence of a heat of passion on Mike's part, or a reckless activity, and Bridger assured Sam and Lee that absent any testimony from Mike, he would deny Sam's request for those instructions, although he would reserve on the question until the end of trial.

He'd spent the hours pre-conference coordinating a search for his client and trying to contact Daniels, who must have seen similar situations. He'd asked the old judge to look at the jury instructions proffered by Lee, but he'd heard nothing. At last, the conference was finished. "Call the jury," Bridger ordered. When the jury was present and seated, Bridger turned to Lee. "Call the State's next witness."

Lee was on his feet and turned to the audience as he spoke. "The state calls Aleksander Melnyk."

Alex, seated next to Lana, started in apparent surprise, looking first to her and then Lee. When Lee nodded his encouragement, Alex stood and walked self-consciously to the witness box where he was sworn to an oath. He had barely taken his seat when Lee began his questioning.

"Please state your name for the record and spell your last name."

"Aleksander Melnyk. M-E-L-N-Y-K."

Lee then posed a series of questions to obtain Alex's background and basis of knowledge for the questions he was about to ask. "Are you familiar with the defendant, Mr. Brown?"

"I am. He is the son-in-law of my godfather, Max."

"You know him well?"

"I do," Alex said, looking somewhat uncertainly at the empty chair next to Sam.

"And were you able to observe relations between your godfather and Mr. Brown?"

"I was, yeah."

"And how would you describe them?"

"Well, pretty good, I think . . . for the most part."

"Have you ever heard Mr. Brown threaten Mr. Kovalenko?"

Sam was on his feet. "Objection."

"Please approach," Bridger instructed. When Lee and Sam were in front of him, he looked to Sam. "Mr. Johnstone."

"It's hearsay, Judge," Sam began. "Beyond that, even if you find the statement an exception thereto, the potential prejudice far exceeds the probative value."

Bridger looked to Lee, who was ready. "Judge, it's absolutely an exception to the rule against hearsay. And the probative value is significant: Mr. Melnyk's testimony will show that Mr. Brown threatened on multiple occasions to do exactly what he did: shoot the deceased."

Bridger nodded and made a note. The decision was, as an appellate court would say, a matter of judicial discretion. "I'm going to overrule the objection," he said at last. "Please return to your places."

Sam was disappointed but not surprised. As he returned to the empty desk, he looked to Lana, whose gaze was fixed squarely upon Alex.

"Mr. Melnyk, let me ask you again. Did you ever hear Mr. Brown threaten the deceased?"

"Oh, yes," Alex said. He then outlined several events and circumstances where Mike had threatened to shoot Max. "I'm not saying he meant it, of course," Alex said lamely.

Lee effectively probed the circumstances of the threats, extracting the damning testimony bit by bit. Sam renewed his objection, but the best he could do was to create an issue for appeal should Mike be convicted. In combination with his client's absence, Alex's testimony was devastating, and Mike's future was now in peril. Watching the jurors, Sam noted that many of them returned his glance and then fixed their eyes on the empty chair next to him. The holes he had poked in the State's circumstantial case had been repaired to some degree with Lee's efficient direct examination of Alex. Sam was thinking all might well be lost when Lee said, "I want to talk about the day of Max's disappearance." Lee quickly led Alex through the events of the day. "Now, what happened as you rode to confront the supposed trespassers?"

"Well, Mike said we needed to get some help, so I rode to get a signal," Alex said.

"Were you successful?"

"No."

Sam was watching Alex closely. Alex met his eyes briefly and then looked away. He knew. "And when is the next time you saw or heard from Mike?"

"Down at the ranch house, later."

"Did you hear anything while you were trying to get a signal?"

"I heard a gunshot."

Lee looked to the jurors to ensure they understood the implication. "Did you later get an explanation for the gunshot?"

"Yes," Alex said. "Mike told me he had fired a shot to try to alert Max."

"Did you believe him?"

"Well . . . yeah," Alex said. "I mean, that's what he said."

Lee finished with a series of questions designed to hint at the idea that

Mike had taken advantage of a brief opportunity to shoot Max. Having derived from the witness that Mike had both motive and opportunity, Lee looked to Sam with a self-satisfied smile. "No more questions, Judge. Tender the witness."

Sam stood and looked to the jurors, ensuring he had their attention. He then fixed a stare upon Alex. "Mr. Melnyk, if something were to happen to my client—including incarceration or death—who would take over UkrCX?"

"Objection, Judge. Irrelevant, argumentative, beyond the scope of cross—"

"Mr. Lee, I've cautioned you about speaking objections previously. I believe Mr. Johnstone's questions go to bias. Your objection is overruled," Bridger said. "Please continue, sir," he said to Sam.

Alex sat quietly, not sure what to do. "You can answer," Sam said. "If you know."

"I—I guess Lana would," Alex said.

Sam side-eyed the jurors. Two were making notes. "But in fact, it was your understanding at the time of Max's death that you were taking over, wasn't it?"

"Well, yeah."

"You recall our meeting in my office—"

"Yeah, I thought it was me," Alex snapped. "Max told me it would be me."

"You were disappointed it wasn't—true?" Sam asked. In his peripheral vision, he could see an ongoing discussion between Rebecca and Lee.

"Yeah—wouldn't you be?"

"So, I want to be sure I understand. When you were riding up the mountain, you thought that if anything happened to Max, you would get control of the company—true?"

Alex looked to Lana. "Well, kind of. No, not really."

Sam let the answer hang before continuing. "Why not?"

Alex's eyes had never left Lana. Sam wondered if the jury was paying attention to the nonverbal communication between them. He walked away from the podium and asked his next question from behind Mike's empty chair. Alex's eyes never left Lana. "Because right before he died, Max told me the company was going back to Mike."

"Mr. Melnyk, I'm over here," Sam said. He watched as the jury looked to Alex and then to him. "He was going to change his plan back?"

"That's what he said."

Lee was still talking with Rebecca and had missed the objectionable testimony. Sam moved back to the podium. He could see jurors' heads move as they eyed Alex, then Sam.

"So fair to say you had a brief period of time to see to it that Max didn't change his plan—is that it?"

Alex wiped quickly at his brow. "I didn't do anything!"

Sam said nothing, but watched Alex carefully, fully aware the jurors were watching him. The old adage advised never to ask a question without knowing the answer. Sam did a quick calculation and decided to risk it. He walked to the table with the State's exhibits and pulled a photo of the white spray bottle that had been introduced during Garcia's testimony.

"Take a look at this photo, Mr. Melnyk. Let me know when you are ready to answer a question or two." Sam noted Alex's hands shaking as he took the photo. While Alex was looking at the picture, Sam could sense Lee and Rebecca continuing the heated discussion at the prosecution's table, which probably accounted for Lee's failure to object to Sam's line of questioning. Finally, Alex looked to Lana and then made eye contact with Sam. "That's your bottle, isn't it?" Sam asked without preamble.

Alex's eyes widened and then narrowed. "Uh, no, I don't think so."

Sam decided he was all in. "I'm prepared to call witnesses—some of the hands—who will testify that you got two bottles of water from Ms. Kovalenko-Brown before you rode off that day, but that you returned with only one." Pure bluff. It wasn't a question, and there were a million innocent explanations, but only one actual explanation for that bottle being there—and he and Alex knew it.

Alex again looked to Lana. Sam followed his stare and watched Lana as well. She quickly looked away, as if in disinterest. Sam turned and looked again at Alex. "Well?"

Lee was on his feet. "Your Honor, that wasn't a question—"

"Rephrase," Bridger directed.

Sam did so.

"I guess it was mine," Alex said. "I mean, I guess . . . Coulda been."

"Your Honor," Lee began, "I fail to see the relevance of this line of questioning—"

Bridger was clearly irritated with Lee. "Mr. Lee, if that was an objection, it is overruled."

Time to change subjects. "Mr. Melnyk, did you hear Cale Pleasance's testimony that your fingerprints were not on the bottle?"

"See? It wasn't mine!"

"Did you hear him testify there were *no* fingerprints on that bottle?"

"Yeah. That's what I just said."

"Did you wipe your prints off that bottle?"

"What? No!"

Sam measured Alex. His next question was improper, but Alex's answer would either exonerate Mike or remind the jury of Sam's defense in advance. "Mr. Melnyk," Sam continued. "Did you erase and replace my client's DNA on that rifle?"

"Your Honor!" Lee was on his feet.

"What? No! Of course not! Are you nuts?"

"Mr. Melnyk, please just answer the question and be quiet!" Bridger instructed Alex. "Overruled," he said in the direction of Lee.

Sam watched the jurors eye Alex. "Mr. Melnyk, you testified you went to get a signal—is that right?"

"Yes," Alex said warily.

"Do you know that you can get four bars from almost the exact spot where Mr. Lee thinks the shot was fired from?"

It was improper testimony by an attorney and Lee was instantly on his feet, sputtering. Bridger barked at the young attorney. "Mr. Lee! Stop talking! Your objection is sustained!" He then fixed a glare on Sam. "You know better than that, Mr. Johnstone."

"I apologize, Your Honor." The jurors were eyeballing Alex; it was the best Sam could do at this point—he had his *other dude.* What he couldn't explain was how Alex had pulled it off. He would connect—or not—the dots with his witnesses. "No more questions," Sam said. He took his seat at the empty desk and continued to survey the jury. One juror—a thin, frail man in the front row—made eye contact with him and seemed to nod imperceptibly.

"Any redirect?" Bridger asked Lee.

"No, Judge."

"Call your next witness."

"Your Honor, may I have a moment?" Lee asked. When Bridger indicated he could, Lee turned and consulted briefly with Rebecca. After a minute of sometimes animated conversation, Lee stood. "Your Honor, the State rests."

Spectators whispered among themselves but quieted quickly under Bridger's stare. He swiveled in his chair toward the jury. "Ladies and gentlemen, we'll take our afternoon break at this time," he said. "There is a matter the court needs to discuss with counsel that does not require your consideration or your participation." When the jury had departed, he turned his attention to Sam. "You have a motion?" he asked, clearly hoping Sam would answer in the negative.

Sam had made the decision overnight that he would not ask for a judgment of acquittal, which was a motion asking the judge to make a finding that the prosecution had failed to present evidence sufficient for a reasonable jury to find guilt. They were rarely granted, and not infrequently made by defense attorneys anticipating a post-trial allegation of ineffective assistance of counsel or otherwise worried about possible malpractice. Moreover, while Sam was hopeful for an acquittal, Lee had presented plenty of evidence that *could* lead a reasonable jury to find evidence of his client's guilt. "I do not," Sam said.

"Thank you," Bridger said. "Mr. Johnstone, recognizing you are on your own here, is the defense going to present testimony?"

"Yes, Your Honor."

"Okay. We'll reconvene in twenty minutes and begin the defendant's case-in-chief."

~

Sam spent the short recess conferring with Cassie and scanning his phone for responses to his increasingly plaintive texts to Daniels, as well as any communication from Mike. Seeing none, he took his seat in the courtroom next to an empty chair and reviewed the outline for his witness. When he was satisfied, he sat quietly, studying the ceiling fans twenty feet above his head and debating, if Mike showed up, whether he would hug him or slug him.

He stood with the others when Bridger entered and called for the jury. When the jury was present and seated, Bridger looked to Sam. "Please call the defendant's first witness."

"Your Honor, the defense calls Russ Johnson," Sam said. He had deemed Johnson a key witness early on; together they had discussed his testimony multiple times. Sam began by leading Johnson through a thorough review of his background and qualifications before beginning the substantive line of questioning. "Can you tell the jury a little bit about touch DNA?"

"Of course," Johnson said. "Touch-transfer DNA was first discovered by an Australian scientist in 1997. The scientist discovered that tiny bits of DNA would transfer through touch, together with fingerprint markings, allowing for the collection and analysis of DNA from fingerprints. Soon after, scientists discovered the ability to search for touch-transfer DNA from other objects and surfaces. As you might imagine, this had law enforcement applications and pretty soon we saw the prosecution of individuals based on DNA from these objects."

"Are there problems with the technique?" Sam asked.

"Oh, yes," Johnson said, warming to his subject. "While the sensitivity of the testing keeps increasing, making it possible to obtain DNA from smaller and smaller samples, it is kind of a double-edged sword."

"Why?"

"Because the technological ability to use smaller samples means it is not so clear-cut that the person whose DNA is found at the crime scene is actually involved in the crime, or that they were even anywhere near the crime scene to begin with."

"Why is that?"

"Well, it makes sense if you think about it: if we're getting DNA results from just a few cells that somehow sloughed off someone, we have to consider how easy it is for just a few cells to arrive where they were found."

"Well, how easy is it?"

"Well, in study after study it has been shown that DNA transfers not only through primary contact with an item, but secondarily, and maybe even beyond that."

"Meaning?" Sam asked. The jury was following, he observed. They'd heard the State's witness, now they would have to consider Mike's.

Johnson leaned forward eagerly and pushed his glasses up on his nose with a finger. "It is possible that if you touch my hand, and I touch a third person's hand, it is possible—I'm saying *possible*—that someone checking the third person's hand could find not only your DNA, but that of someone else you touched before touching me."

"So," Sam said, "is the science of any use at all?"

"Of course, but we have to be aware of the limitations. We cannot tell you when the DNA was deposited or how. We have to remember the DNA could have been deposited perfectly innocently, or even by someone else," Johnson explained. "And if that isn't complicated enough, the literature says that DNA can be transferred from one area of an item to another area."

Sam walked over to the table where the admitted evidence was and retrieved the rifle that was purportedly Mike's. "So, Mr. Johnson, my question is this: If I were to tell you that this rifle has my client's DNA on it, would you automatically assume my client was the one who handled and fired it?"

"Oh, no. Not necessarily." Johnson shook his head. "I'd say that you have to evaluate all the evidence. DNA is just one part of it—especially touch DNA."

"Speaking of touch DNA, you mentioned that our cells slough off relatively easily. So we can expect that whatever we touch will have our cells on it—can't we?"

"No. We're not real sure why, but we do know that in controlled experiments, sometimes cells transfer, and sometimes they don't."

Sam took a minute to walk to the table to feign getting a drink. What he really wanted was to be able to look at the jury and make certain he had their undivided attention. He picked up the rifle the State had entered into evidence. "So, let me ask you this: Are you saying that someone could touch this rifle and have their DNA *not* appear?"

"Oh, yes."

Sam was watching the jurors. They were still with him. "Did you examine the rifle in question?"

"No, but I examined the State's expert's report."

"And what did she conclude?"

"The DNA on the rifle belonged to your client."

"Do you agree?"

"Oh, yes," Johnson said, and pushed his glasses up again. "There is no doubt."

Sam could see Lee sit back in his chair and spread his hands in a "why are we here?" gesture. "And my client's DNA was the *only* DNA present—is that right?"

"According to the State's experts, yes."

Lee sat back in his chair and crossed his arms, playing to the jurors, indicating this was all a waste of time. "Is that unusual?" Sam asked.

"Normally I would say yes. But in this case, it is not unexpected."

Sam was watching the jury and noticed Lee sitting up straight now. "What do you mean by *in this case*?"

"Well, the concentration of DNA on the rifle is extremely high. Given that density, I'm not surprised there is only one person's DNA on the rifle."

"Let's break that down," Sam said. "How high is the concentration?"

"About fifty times as high as one would expect from a normal touch DNA concentration."

Sam stood silently for a moment, allowing the jury to take it in. He could hear restlessness among the audience behind him, as well. He had everyone's attention. "Did you say fifty, or fifteen?" Sam asked, knowing very well what Johnson had said.

"Fifty."

"And that leads you to believe what?" Sam asked as he moved again to the table holding the exhibits. "Do you have a theory?"

"I do," Johnson said. "I suspect the DNA on the rifle was cultivated."

Lee was sitting rigidly in his chair now. The crowd began to murmur as Sam walked back to his desk and retrieved a copy of the simple report Johnson had prepared. "Your Honor, may I approach the witness?"

"You may," Bridger said.

Sam dropped a copy of the report in front of Lee, then walked to the witness box and handed a copy to Johnson. "Please take a look at what I've marked as Defendant's Exhibit 501." In Bridger's court, it was customary for the State to number exhibits beginning with 1, and for the defendant's exhibits to begin at 501. "Let me know when you are ready to answer questions about it."

"I'm ready," Johnson said immediately.

"What is it?"

"It's a report I prepared containing information on a sample of liquids I received from you. You asked me to identify any DNA in the liquid. I did. I determined the DNA was that of Mr. Brown, your client."

Sam looked to the judge. "Move to admit Exhibit 501," he said.

Lee was in a box. He could fight the admission, which would make the jury wonder all the more what the document was, or he could try to act as if the relevance and importance was minimal. Lee chose option two. "No objection," he said. "Although I don't really understand the relevance."

He would. "Anything of particular interest?" Sam asked.

"Oh, yes. The concentration of the DNA—which is from Mr. Brown alone—is again extremely high."

Sam looked to the jury. They were listening intently. "How high?"

"Well, exactly as high as on the rifle," Johnson replied. "Fifty times what one would expect."

Sam allowed that to sink in before asking his next question. "Is it unusual to see two samples of a person's DNA, taken from two different sources, show the exact same level of concentration?"

"Unusual? No." Johnson pushed at his glasses. "It's unprecedented, to my knowledge. I've literally never heard of such a thing."

Again, Sam let that sink in. "Can you explain how it could happen?"

"I can," Johnson said. "It's called 'erase and replace.' It's a technique used by some to erase their own DNA and replace it with that of another—"

"Objection! Judge, that's pure speculation!" Lee said over the talking going on in the courtroom. "The witness—"

"Mr. Lee," Bridger said, "sit down. The witness is an expert. You'll have a chance to cross-examine momentarily."

"Your Honor, I'd like this entire line of testimony stricken as irrelevant," Lee argued.

Sam was all in. "Mr. Lee consented to the admission of the exhibit. The exhibit notes the source. What's irrelevant are his histrionics."

"Take your seat, Mr. Lee," Bridger said. "Mr. Johnstone, do not argue or interrupt again."

Sam quieted as instructed. Lee was undeterred. "You haven't ruled on my—"

"Overruled. And counsel, I'm growing weary of your constantly disobeying my pre-trial order," Bridger warned.

Lee began to protest but stopped when Rebecca put a hand on his shoulder. She then smiled at the jury, attempting to undo the damage.

Sam led Johnson through a brief explanation of how a person could erase DNA from an item and then replace it with another's DNA. "No more questions," Sam said when Johnson had opined how someone could have framed Mike. "Your witness."

~

"Mr. Lee, cross-examination?" Bridger asked.

Lee was already at the podium looking at the witness. "Very briefly, Judge." He then set about cross-examining the affable and experienced Johnson, who stuck to his three main points. One, it was unusual to find only one person's DNA on a rifle. Two, that the concentration of DNA on the rifle was unusually high. And three, that the concentration level in the liquid in the bottle found near the rifle matched exactly that on the rifle, which led to his belief that the DNA had been placed there.

"But you don't *know* with certainty that the DNA on that rifle was sprayed on by someone using that bottle, do you?"

"Nope," Johnson admitted.

That wasn't good enough for Lee. "Is that a no?" he asked, voice thick with sarcasm.

"In Wyoming English it is," the unflappable Johnson answered, then smiled as the audience tittered.

A red-faced Lee then asked a series of pointed questions designed to show that Johnson had no proof that anyone had framed Mike using the technique. "All I was asked to do was to explain how something I've never seen happen might have happened," Johnson concluded. "Proof is *your* responsibility."

"No more questions, Judge," Lee huffed.

"Re-direct?" Bridger asked. Sam could swear he saw a twinkle in the judge's eye.

"None, Your Honor," Sam said. Turning to survey the audience to see if Mike had come in, he noted that Paulie averted his eyes while Lana studied her manicure. He looked at Cassie, who shrugged. He had no witness to call. "Defense rests," he said simply, and took his seat.

Bridger stared down the whispering and murmurs. "Mr. Lee, any rebuttal evidence?"

Lee took a few moments to confer with Rebecca before standing. "No, Your Honor."

Bridger nodded. As the audience began to realize the trial was almost over, Bridger raised a hand to quiet them before turning his attention to the jury. "Ladies and gentlemen, the evidence in this matter is closed. We're going to take our evening recess. I want to remind you: no discussing the case, no reading about the case online or in the papers, no watching television or listening to the radio or discussing the matter with anyone. Please let the bailiff know if anyone attempts to discuss the matter with you. Finally, do not make up your mind based on anything you have heard to this point. Wait until all the evidence is in, I have instructed you on the law, and you have been retired to the jury's deliberation room to take the matter under consideration."

~

Long after dark, Sam remained in his office refining his closing argument. His back was getting stiff, so he stood and was stretching when he heard the pounding at his door. Walking to it, he touched his left side and felt the .38 special in its holster. Seeing Daniels, he smiled and swung the door open wide.

"Press, come in! Are you okay?"

A disheveled Daniels rushed up to Sam. "You've got to help me! The bastards are killing my wife! I'm gonna—"

"Whoa, Press!" Sam put his hands on the older man's forearms and guided him inside, then shut the door behind them. "Come in. Sit down and have a drink."

Sam poured for Daniels, then sat and listened while the older man poured out his heart. Apparently, Marci was going downhill fast, and Daniels was getting increasingly desperate and—in Sam's mind—irrational over the situation. "Press," he said at last. "When's the last time you got some sleep?"

Daniels eyed Sam closely. "What does that matter?" he asked. "You don't believe me when I tell you what these doctors are doing to my Marci!"

"It's not that," Sam said. It was. "It's just that I'm having a hard time understanding what it is that you want them to do."

Daniels drank from the tumbler, then slammed it viciously on the tabletop and stood. "They got to you! You, of all people!"

"Press! What are you talking about?"

"I'm talking about you being bought off by pharmaceutical companies and hospitals—they are buying everyone! Test, test, test, then do as little as possible to conserve profits . . . It's a crime! I'm sick of it! I'll not let her suffer any more!"

"Press, stop!" Sam tried to grab the older man's arm as he brushed by him. "Let's talk!"

"Nothing to talk about!"

Sam watched his mentor go, and waited before walking to the entrance and locking the door. Returning to his office, he looked at words on paper for half an hour but saw nothing.

47

At nine o'clock on Tuesday morning, the parties reassembled in the courtroom. Sam had spent much of the morning attempting to contact Daniels and coordinating efforts to locate Mike. He could only conclude Mike had lost his nerve and absconded. In his last call to Lana, Sam had begun to threaten her. "If I find out you had anything to do with him taking off—"

"Oh, Sam, stop. I had nothing to do with this."

"For your sake, I hope that's true," he had said before punching off viciously. Now, he was examining the crown molding on the roofline with sand-papered eyes, taking deep breaths, and trying to remind himself that he'd done the best he could. It was all one could do—attorneys who gauged success by the returns of juries had stomach linings that looked like the surface of the moon. Before taking his seat alone at the defense table, he had exchanged perfunctory greetings with a pale, waxen Rebecca. The trial had taken a toll on all of them. He stood alone at the defense table when Bridger entered.

"All right," Bridger began. "We're back on the record, and *for* the record, I do not see the defendant. Mr. Johnstone, any update on your client's whereabouts?"

Sam stood. "None, sir," he said, and took his chair.

Lee was on his feet. "Your Honor, may we approach?"

Bridger took off his reading glasses and sighed heavily. He was beyond faking tolerance for Lee. "Certainly, Mr. Lee."

Sam made his way to the bench, noting that Rebecca had accompanied Lee to the podium. He looked at her for a sign of what was to come, but she quickly looked away.

"Judge," Lee began. "The sheriff's office tells me they think they have recovered the defendant's truck. It's in a remote part of the county—almost seventy miles from here."

Bridger sat quietly. "No sign of the defendant?"

"None," Lee said. "But I'm told they are conducting a full-scale search."

Bridger turned his attention to Sam. "Mr. Johnstone?"

Sam's initial reaction—anger at not being provided the information—had to yield to quick thinking. "If we can keep this information from the jurors, I'd prefer to drive on." Seeing the judge's surprise, he continued. "We've tried this case to conclusion. I'd simply request that—if need be— the jurors be sequestered until their deliberations are complete. I think it is critical they be unaware that my client's vehicle has been located. Similarly, his whereabouts at this point are not important."

"Mr. Lee?"

Lee was looking at Sam quizzically. "I agree, Your Honor," he said simply.

"Fine," a pleasantly surprised Bridger concluded. "Let's get going. The sooner we wrap this up, the sooner we can get the jury under wraps," he said, smiling wryly at his own word play.

∼

The closing arguments by Lee and Sam were forceful and diametrically opposed. Lee, speaking at length, rehashed in detail the voluminous evidence arrayed against Mike and asked the jury to apply its collective common sense and convict him. Sam emphasized the circumstantial nature of the evidence, highlighted gaps and holes in the State's theory, reminded the jurors they took an oath to follow the law, and emphasized that Bridger instructed them to acquit unless the State had proven its case beyond a reasonable doubt.

After concluding, Sam returned to his office expecting a long wait—it was that close, in his mind. Accordingly, when Cassie knocked on his office door just three hours later, Sam nearly jumped out of his chair. "They have a verdict," she said simply.

While perhaps outwardly calm, Sam made the short walk to the court-house with emotions alternating between cautious optimism and an over-whelming sense of doom. He swallowed a handful of antacids in the hallway before making his way through the throng of observers to the defendant's table. A solitary Sam stood as Bridger entered and approached the bench. At the State's table, Rebecca and Lee stood as well. Sam realized he hadn't seen Garcia for days—probably searching for Mike. When Bridger had been seated and the jury returned, he turned to them and asked, "Has the jury reached a verdict?"

"We have, Your Honor," a tall, thin man in the front row of the jury box responded.

"Please give the verdict form to the bailiff," Bridger instructed, and when the bailiff had retrieved it and given it to him, the judge read it to ensure it was properly completed. Satisfied, he handed it to the clerk. "Ladies and gentlemen, upon the reading of the verdict, there will be no demonstrations, remonstrations, celebrations, vocal disapproval, or sound of any sort. Violators will be removed summarily," he concluded, nodding to the security officers arrayed around the courtroom.

"Mr. Johnstone, in the absence of your client, please stand," Bridger ordered. Sam stood, and then Bridger looked to the clerk. "Ms. Marshall, please read the verdict."

Sam's stomach was tight and he held his breath as Violet Marshall, the county's elected clerk of district court, stood and, with shaking hands and a quiver in her voice, read, "As to the charge of murder in the first degree, we the jury find the defendant, Michael Brown, not guilty." Sam closed his eyes and said a brief prayer of thanks. Violet took a deep breath and continued. "As to the charge of murder in the second degree, we the jury find the defendant, Michael Brown, not guilty."

Sam felt the air go out of the room before the audience gasped in shock. He looked to Lee and saw him slumped in his chair, then turned to Lana and observed her covering her mouth with her palm, then joining Paulie, Stacy, and Alex in quickly departing the courtroom. For a fleeting instant Sam thought they had left to contact Mike, but that didn't make any sense. He could only hope if Mike was alive he would soon return.

Bridger thanked the jury, formally acquitted Mike, released the ten-million-dollar bond, and sent everyone on their way. It was over.

Sam quickly collected his materials, and after a quick handshake with Rebecca he left the courtroom, noting Lee in his chair with his head in his hands. Following a brief interview with the assembled media with Lana at his side, he had janitor Jack Fricke let him and Lana out the back door of the courthouse unobserved. When they were alone, Sam studied her closely. "I'm surprised," he said.

"Me, too." Lana exhaled and watched her breath dissipate in the cool evening air. "I was sure—especially after he left—that he was gonna be, well, you know."

"Right," Sam said. "And now you're shit out of luck."

She turned to face him. "Excuse me?"

"Well, he's gonna know that you and Alex set him up, right?"

"Oh, Sam." She eyed him sadly. "He'll never believe that."

"Garcia's gonna figure it out," Sam said. "It's obvious Alex doesn't have the balls to do something like that on his own. He had to have help. He's a *boy*, as you say."

Lana looked at Sam for a long time. "You are my attorney—remember that. Anything and everything I told you, I told you in confidence. You say a word and it'll cost you your license—and a lot more. I've got friends."

"I don't like being threatened."

She smiled. "Think of it as—how do you say it? An *advisory opinion* —maybe?"

"So, Mike—"

"Was about to lose the company," she said. "I couldn't live with that. Something had to be done. Max should have given the company to me. Then none of this would have been necessary."

Sam smiled despite himself. "You knew."

"Of course I did." She laughed. "I had Mike telling me he was gonna lose the company, and Alex telling me he already had."

Sam stood quietly, thinking it through, toeing gravel on the sidewalk. "So you actually had Alex kill your father? And you framed your husband?"

"It was business," she said. "The way I figured it, if Mike had been convicted and was the beneficiary, then—"

"The company would go to you by operation of law."

"Right."

"And if Alex was the beneficiary, then—"

"Well, Mike would be in jail, right? I couldn't be expected to remain married to the man who killed my father, could I? And Alex would owe me a little debt of gratitude."

"But now that Mike has walked—"

"It's a little more complicated, but he'll never believe I had anything to do with him being framed. If he's alive, we'll be fine."

"Is he?"

"I have no idea." Seeing Sam's doubt, she added, "I really don't."

He wasn't so sure and was about to say something when Jack Fricke appeared at the back door. "Sam, Punch Polson is here. He says he wants to talk with the lady."

Lana and Sam exchanged a look. "Be right there," he said. Inside, they walked the hallway to a point near the double doors to the courtroom, where Punch was pacing with his phone to his ear. Seeing them approach, he hung up.

"Mrs. Brown," Punch said. "I'm sorry to have to tell you this, but we've located a note we believe to have been written by your husband."

"Is he all right?" Lana asked, then put a hand over her mouth.

"I'm not in a position to know, but it says that he—" Punch began, then helped Sam catch Lana as she fainted.

"Let's get her in here," Sam said, indicating one of the nearby attorney rooms that he knew featured a couch. "Jack, can you get us some water?"

"On my way," Fricke replied, looking excited.

Sam and Punch got Lana inside and situated on the couch. She opened her eyes soon after, and when Fricke arrived, Sam placed the cup in her trembling hands.

When it seemed safe, Punch sidled up to Sam. "Can we talk?"

"Sure," Sam said. "Lana, we're gonna step out for just a second—are you okay for a minute?"

"Of course, Sam," she said, then placed a hand on his forearm. "Should I call my friends?"

He ignored her and closed the door. "Speak," he said to Punch.

Punch indicated Lana with his head. "She gonna be all right?"

"I think with some acting lessons she might be adequate."

Despite himself, Punch laughed aloud, then sobered. "Well, for what it's worth, looks like a suicide to me," he said. "Left a note and the whole bit. He was thinking he was going down. Said he didn't want his wife to have to live alone with him locked up, blah, blah, blah. We've got a chopper up, dogs—the usual."

"Right," Sam said, looking up and down the hallway.

"You okay?" Punch examined Sam. "What a day, huh? You walk the guy and before he finds out he offs himself." He shook his head. "You need any help with your client?"

"Naw," Sam said. "She'll be fine, thanks." He turned and entered the conference room, closing the door behind himself. "You can sit up now."

"A hand, please," she said, raising a hand to seek his assistance. She appraised him. "Oh, Sam, don't be angry. Mike made his decision."

"And now you and Alex live happily ever after? Is that how it goes?"

"Oh, no," she said. "I've no need for him."

"I'll remind you, Garcia will figure it out," Sam said. "And Alex will crack like an egg."

"Not my problem," she said. "First of all, I'm not as sure as you are that these local cops will figure it out. And if they do, Alex knows I have friends who can reach him, too. A phone call to some of my father's former acquaintances and, well, you know."

Sam's phone was vibrating in his pocket. He'd had it off for court. He pulled it out and looked at it. Daniels. Finally! "I'm gonna have to take this."

"Another client?" She stood and smoothed her dress. "You know you'll never have another like me, Sam."

"God willing." He started to leave and then remembered something.

"You know what the real tragedy in all of this is? I mean, beyond you killing your father and framing your husband?"

Her eyes narrowed and her nostrils flared. "I can't imagine."

"Max was going to die anyway. Pancreatic cancer."

She didn't even blink. "Bye, Sam—and don't forget about my friends."

He stepped into the hallway. Placing a hand over the phone, he looked to Jack, who had been lurking outside the door. "Would you see the lady out?" he asked, then watched Jack and Lana depart, waiting impatiently until the click of her heels on the marble had faded sufficiently. "Press, where the hell have you been?"

"It's Marci, Sam. She's dead," Daniels said. "I need your help."

"On my way."

48

South of Casper, Wyoming, the North Platte River flows through the high Wyoming desert. The snowmelt on both sides of the Colorado and Wyoming state line fills the drainage, and with river flows managed to facilitate irrigation, the result is a predictable, controlled flow facilitating one of America's blue-ribbon fly-fishing rivers. Generally, Sam preferred small streams to rivers, but with spring in Wyoming still weeks away, he had taken advantage of a referral and was on the water, guided by a fellow disabled veteran on this mid-April weekday. The men talked units and times good and bad while in the service of their country while Sam boated fish after fish with his guide's help.

The man knew his water.

At lunch, while the guide did some fishing of his own, Sam stretched in the sun behind a small hill that blocked the omnipresent wind and thought about Daniels. He was considering stopping at the dry cleaners on his way home to retrieve his black suit for Marci's funeral when his phone buzzed, startling him—he hadn't expected service. Removing it from his vest pocket and intending to silence it, he glanced at the screen and saw that he had missed a call from Cassie. It was unlike her to call him on a day off. He debated briefly, then returned the call.

"Did you hear?" she asked breathlessly.

"I doubt it. I've been on the river all day. What's up?"

"Ted Garcia arrested Alex Melnyk for Max's murder."

"Interesting," Sam said. And predictable.

"Right?" she replied. "Well, I just thought that was maybe important enough to interrupt your fishing. Doing any good?"

"Lotsa fish," he assured her.

"Good. Have fun. Be safe."

Sam was thinking about Lana's plan—she would likely be successful in having both Mike and Alex cut out of Max's estate. And with Max having divested Danny of any interest in UkrCX, Lana and Stacy would own the company. It wouldn't be long before the conniving Lana had it all. Days earlier, he had made a call to the state bar association's attorney ethics advisor seeking advice on how to handle what Lana had told him. It was complicated, but given Daniels' situation, the right thing to do was probably get back to town and look over the estate documents. He would probably need to convene a meeting, and there were papers to file with the court. It was going to be a mess.

Two hours later, Sam was heading north out of Casper when his phone rang. It was the Custer County Attorney's Office. Wyoming phone service was intermittent on back roads, so he stopped on the shoulder on high ground to ensure he would maintain service.

"Sam?"

"Cathy," Sam said, genuinely glad it was her. "What's going on?"

"I wanted you to know that Garcia just arrested your client."

"I heard," he said. "But you should know I'm not going to represent Alex."

"Not Alex," she said. "Lana Kovalenko-Brown. Conspiracy and murder in the first degree."

That didn't take long. "Cassie called a couple hours ago and said they had arrested Alex."

"They did, but he apparently squealed like a pig. She's denying everything and has asked for you. You should know they got permission to search the mansion and found a bunch of the materials that Garcia suspects were used to frame Mike in and among Lana's things. She conspired to kill her father—can you believe that?" Sam sat by the road in silence, weighing it all out. "You still there?" she asked.

"I am," he said. "If I were Lee, I'd have the jailers keeping a close eye on Alex or he could have an 'accident.' Lana isn't going to be happy, and she has resources, if you know what I'm saying. You might want to tell him—"

"He's not going to listen to anything I tell him."

"Sorry, I forgot."

"No problem," she said. The service was bad, and there was noise in the background. "Still there?"

"Yeah. Couple of oil tankers just went by," Sam explained. "Hey, just between us, who authorized the search?"

"Oh, uh, let me see," she said. He could hear papers rustling as she quickly perused the affidavit of probable cause supporting the arrest warrant. "It was Anastasia Kovalenko. That's the little sister they call Stacy —right?"

Sam laughed. "That's right." Apparently she wasn't as dumb as everyone thought.

"Yeah, and according to the arresting officer, Stacy said to tell you that if you need her to sign any papers or anything, send them to her in LA. By the way, Garcia is looking for that Paulie guy."

Of course. "Try Ukraine." Ukraine had no extradition treaty with the United States. Someone had given Mike's rifle to Alex—it had to have been him.

"Does any of that make sense to you?"

"It makes perfect sense," he said. "Hey, Cathy. One of these days . . . You, uh, want to get a beer?"

"Sure!" she said. Then, "Sam, what are we waiting for? I'm up for one tonight."

"I mean, I don't want to get you in trouble, but—"

"I gave Rebecca my two weeks' notice today."

No surprise. "I'll be there in a couple of hours. If I'm late, go ahead and start without me." He pulled his hat down, put a compact disc into his old truck's player, and listened to Clint Black all the way to Custer.

49

Saturday afternoon's celebration of Marci Daniels' life had been a dignified affair, with much of Custer attending. Hers was a life of service; for sixty-five years she had worked and volunteered and assisted and dedicated her time and effort to others. The displayed photos and tearfully delivered eulogies together painted the picture of a productive, loving woman whose singular sorrow stemmed from the loss of a child. Luminaries from the legal community statewide had attended to show their respect, and Sam observed with interest those in attendance included Rebecca Nice and Grant Lee, who sat in the back pew but were conspicuously absent as Daniels left the sanctuary, shaking hands with mourners.

The private graveside service had concluded half an hour before. Daniels had called Sam days after their blow-up to apologize; Sam had attributed his rantings to stress. At Daniels' request, Sam was driving today. He and Cathy had spent some time together in the past few days, and she had agreed to accompany him to the funeral. Now, long after most of the family had left, they stood back a respectful distance, shivering as a wet, sleety snow flew into their faces while Daniels and his extended family swapped tales from long ago. At the edge of the graveyard, two police cruisers remained, probably the last vestiges of the escort that had led the party from the church to the graveyard.

When at last Daniels and a sister-in-law parted, he looked to Sam and Cathy. "Are you ready?" he asked, walking to the truck. "Get in the front," he instructed Cathy, who began to protest. "I'll ride back here." He climbed into the back seat of Sam's crew cab. "Thanks for the ride," he said when he was seated. "I sure as hell wasn't gonna ride in a limo and I don't think I'm up to driving."

"Of course," Sam said. "Give me just a second." He reached for his phone.

"What's wrong?" Cathy asked.

"I'm getting text after text and it's bugging the hell out of me. I'll be just a second." He pulled the phone from his pocket and entered the passcode. Recognizing the number, he quickly scanned the first text in the series.

SORRY I LOST FAITH. YOU WERE RIGHT. WE NEED TO TALK.

He dropped his phone into the inside breast pocket of his suit. Skipping out on a trial wasn't a crime. Technically, Bridger could hold Mike in contempt, but that was unlikely.

Cathy watched as Sam drove, and they rode in awkward silence until she couldn't stand it. Probably not her business, but she decided to risk it. "What is it?" she asked.

"Oh, just a client," Sam said, watching Daniels in the mirror. "Nothing that can't wait." They continued in a silence broken only by the rubbing of Sam's in-need-of-replacement wipers on the truck's cracked windshield until he turned in his seat. "Press, you need to stop anywhere on the way?"

"Watch the road," Daniels instructed. "But yeah, maybe the liquor store."

"You got it," Sam said. "I could use a drink myself. Or twelve." They continued on, Sam glancing in the mirror repeatedly along the way. The cops were still behind them.

"You are joking, right?" Daniels asked at last.

Sam could feel Cathy's eyes on him as he drove. "I think so," he said. He gave her a wink, then checked the mirror.

"You two look good up there," Daniels observed.

Sam and Cathy shared a bemused glance as he pulled into the parking lot. "Press, I think maybe I'll just have—"

He was interrupted as the cop cars pulled in on either side of the truck and screeched to a halt. Before anyone could react, there were officers with weapons drawn on either side of the vehicle. "Exit the vehicle! Now! Exit with your hands up!"

"What in the hell?" Sam began as he opened the door. "Do you know who he is?"

"We do, sir," said a uniformed police corporal Sam recognized as Mike Jensen. He turned his attention to Daniels. "Judge, we've got a warrant for your arrest."

Sam and Cathy had gotten out as instructed and were watching with their hands in the air. "For what?" Sam asked. "There must be a mistake! And this is unnecessary—you know that!"

Daniels was shaking his head slowly. "No mistake, Sam. They are going to say I killed Marci. I did, of course."

"Judge Daniels," Jensen began reciting as two officers put the cuffs on Daniels and placed him gently in the back seat of a cruiser. "I'm arresting you on a charge of murder in the first degree of Marci Daniels. You have the right to—"

"Press, don't say anything!" Sam moved toward the judge but stopped when he saw the guns trained upon him.

"Mr. Johnstone, please stop!" a younger officer ordered. "We have our orders."

"I know my rights, dammit!" Daniels protested.

Jensen was reading Daniels' rights verbatim from a wallet-sized card as Daniels was taken away, leaving Sam and Cathy behind as the patrols vanished in the blowing snow.

Sam turned to Cathy, who paled. "Sam, I swear to God I did not know anything about this!" she said in a near panic. "You have to know that!" She closed on him, and they embraced.

He closed his eyes and held her tightly, a mix of fury and concern—but mostly fury—bringing tears to his eyes. He smoothed her wet hair with a hand and held her until he felt her go rigid in his grasp. He turned to see what she was watching over his shoulder. There, in the adjacent parking lot, stood the unmistakable figure of Lee, who snapped a mock salute, then turned and walked away, hands in his pockets, shoulders hunched against the sleet, overcoat flapping in the blustery, omnipresent April wind.

THE TRUTHFUL WITNESS

The line between truth and deception is as thin as a razor's edge...

Determined to enjoy the pace of small-town life, lawyer Sam Johnstone has left his painful past behind and looks forward to taking each new day as it comes. Yet just as he sees peace and tranquility on the horizon, a close friend is charged with murder. Unable to stand quietly by, Sam quickly signs on for the defense.

But how can he defend a client who has already confessed to the crime?

Further complicating matters, an ethically-challenged prosecutor with an axe to grind seems embarked on a personal crusade against Sam.

Now, in a case that seems doomed from the start, Sam must risk his reputation, his livelihood, and more to help a friend in need. But how far is he willing to go to uncover the shocking truth?

Get your copy today at
severnriverbooks.com/series/sam-johnstone-legal-thriller

ABOUT THE AUTHOR

Wall Street Journal bestselling author James Chandler spent his formative years in the western United States. When he wasn't catching fish or footballs, he was roaming centerfield and trying to hit the breaking pitch. After a mediocre college baseball career, he exchanged jersey No. 7 for camouflage issued by the United States Army, which he wore around the globe and with great pride for twenty years. Since law school, he has favored dark suits and a steerhide briefcase. When he isn't working or writing, he'll likely have a fly rod, shotgun or rifle in hand. He and his wife are blessed with two wonderful adult daughters. Misjudged is his first novel.

Sign up for James Chandler's newsletter at
severnriverbooks.com/authors/james-chandler
jameschandler@severnriverbooks.com